The Nightmare Queen

Copyright © [2024] by [C.V. Betzold]

Cover Design by Selkkie Designs – www.selkkiedesigns.com

All rights reserved.

No portion of this book may be reproduced in any form without written permission from the publisher or author, except as permitted by U.S. copyright law.

AUTHOR'S NOTE

Dearly Beloveds,
Thank you so much for stepping into this world with me. I hope that you find a home as I have in Eveera and Rorin. Before you enter into The Realm of Allora, a word of caution. There are multiple themes featured in the book that could be potentially triggering for readers. This is a dark romantasy, and darkness is one thing I have grown over the years to not shy from. We are not all in the same place, and more so than sharing their story, my reader's health is of utmost importance. Please take the time to read through the Content Warnings.

With that...
Welcome Home, Dears.

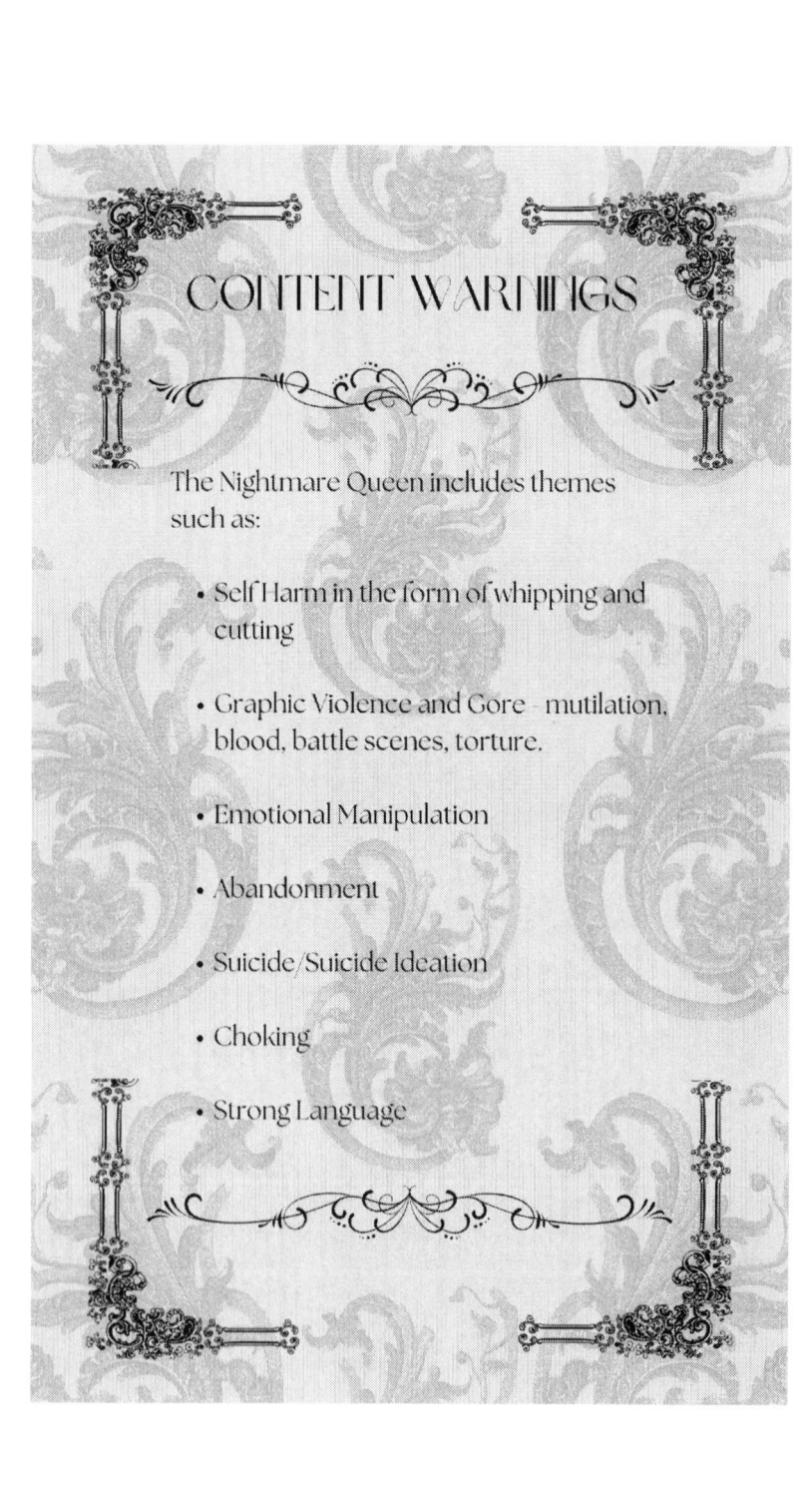

CONTENT WARNINGS

The Nightmare Queen includes themes such as:

- Self Harm in the form of whipping and cutting

- Graphic Violence and Gore – mutilation, blood, battle scenes, torture.

- Emotional Manipulation

- Abandonment

- Suicide/Suicide Ideation

- Choking

- Strong Language

THE WIELDS OF ALLORA

THE EVENDELL KINGDOM

COMMON WIELDS:

GEO MAGES
AQUATIKS
NATURISTS

RARE WIELDS:

ANIMALISTIKS

KINGDOM OF VELLAR

COMMON WIELDS:

HEALER MAGES
DEFLECTIONISTS

RARE WIELDS:

ILLUSIONARIES
BANE

KINGDOM OF OBSIDIAN

COMMON WIELDS:

VOIDS
OBLIVIONARIES
SHADOW MAGES

RARE WIELDS:

SIGHTS
NIGHTMARIST

THE SORREL KINGDOM

COMMON WIELDS:

CHAOTIKS
VOLTAGISTS
SONIC MAGES

RARE WIELDS:

MAGNETIKS

THE WIELDLESS KINGDOMS

KINGDOM OF HADAR

KINGDOM OF SURAM

KINGDOM OF MELLAHT

KINGDOM OF PEVERELL

THE VAST TERRITORIES

ORIKS TERRITORY

SHIFTER TERRITORY

SERPENTES TERRITORY

Kingdom of
Mellant
Kingdom of Hadar
Kingdom of
Peverell
Kingdom of
Vellar
The Evendell
Kingdom
The Sorrel
Kingdom
Sira
Kingdom of
Suram
Sabel
The Obsidian
Kingdom
The Vast

CONTENTS

Dedication	XI
The Prophecy	XII
1. Eveera	1
2. Rorin	11
3. Eveera	44
4. Rorin	49
5. Eveera	54
6. Rorin	67
7. Eveera	76
8. Rorin	86
9. Eveera	92
10. Rorin	100
11. Eveera	105
12. Rorin	118
13. Eveera	135
14. Rorin	149
15. Eveera	172
16. Rorin	180

17.	Rorin	194
18.	Eveera	203
19.	Rorin	219
20.	Eveera	228
21.	Rorin	243
22.	Eveera	255
23.	Rorin	269
24.	Eveera	282
25.	Rorin	293
26.	Eveera	308
27.	Rorin	313
28.	Eveera	324
29.	Eveera	333
30.	Rorin	343
31.	Eveera	348
32.	Rorin	361
33.	Rorin	369
34.	Rorin	374
35.	Rorin	380
36.	The Battle of Vellar	387
	Acknowledgements	391
	About the Author	394

DEDICATION

To those whose fury is fueled by both rage and love.
Burn them all.

THE PROPHECY

*When the light burns out the dark,
the Queen painted in blood and shadows shall rise.
Lying in wait—
The man loyal to no Wield who answers only to peril,
lay waste to all in his path.
Deals made in blood that binds.
A battle of Kings and Queens to tip the scales,
an outcome known only through Sight.
Shadows stolen and shadows returned,
enter in the Age of the King with poison for blood.*

EVEERA

Fourteen Years Earlier

Her blood was everywhere. My mouth, my sinuses, coated over my hands and hair.

I could hear screaming, but her mouth wasn't moving.

Not anymore.

The voice however felt familiar...who is screaming? I think to myself.

My eyes flit around, surveying the destruction. Pooling around me, blood slowly turned from red to black.

I didn't see them rushing in to help, only saw their bodies once they crumpled and clattered to the ground, the blood splattering as they did so.

Their faces blurred together as I moved my gaze upwards to stare into her dimmed eyes a final time. My attention snags on her wrist where a fresh brand has melted into her now lifeless flesh in a shape that looks a lot like the sun.

Nausea churns inside of my stomach. My fingers reaching out to touch her. She's so cold, her hands used to radiate warmth, there is none of that left now. Monotonously I drag myself off the floor my face becoming level *with the carnage they left behind. My feet back me up slowly careful not to trip over any of the other bodies. So many bodies.*

The skin on my heels hit cool, dry, stone as black edges into my vision sweeping me into the darkness.

I can still hear the screaming. So much screaming...

Present Day

The memory startles me awake, my body bolting upright.

My hands feel around the comfortable, soft bedding. *No blood.* I think to myself. It takes a few seconds for my heart to stop racing, but once it's stopped I drag myself out and into my bathroom. The reflection staring back at me is almost as startling as the dream. The circles underneath my eyes are so dark I look bruised, the muscles in my back twinging as I attempt to stretch out my arms. I tilt down my shoulder to look at the cause and find angry red scabbing welts are torn all across my shoulder blades. *I'd forgotten those were there...*

Tenderly I drop my arms down, leaving behind the miserable glass reflection to turn the shower on. I make sure it runs hot, replacing the pain with a different type of discomfort I hope numbs me. I step into the stream once I see steam rising off of the droplets, hissing as I do so.

The dreams have been more frequent lately, the Gods only know why, but it's agitating.

It's just a dream now. I remind myself. But it wasn't once and that knowledge has haunted me ever since, always lingering in the back of my mind, waiting for its moment to resurface and torment me from within until I take extreme measures to forget. The evidence of those measures is plain on my back.

Carefully I wash the dried blood and the remnants of the previous day away, allowing the hot water to purify me. I replace the harsh memory with the endless list of things I avoided yesterday. The council has become more insistent as of late, with my queendom hitting double digits, impressing some bullshit that I need to have a "sense of urgency" when it comes to court matters. No more running around. If it were up to them my routine would be the same drab thing every day - but instead of dressing in my leathers and heading down to spar with my private guard. They'd have me in something more queenly and my hours filled with meetings. And while I don't mind the dresses, meetings make me twitchy.

The water runs cold, pebbling my skin as a shiver takes over. The change in temperature is enough to convince me to step out and towel myself off. It doesn't take me long to finish getting ready, attempting to rub healing salve on the welts is the last step in my routine before hopping into my leathers. I give myself a final once over before snatching my weapons off the nightstands and tearing into the passageways.

I know these tunnels well enough that the walk to our sparring room is quick. My men's voices and the familiar noise of metal clanging against metal reaches my ears before they even come into view. *I guess they didn't feel like waiting for their queen, to start.*

"Ah, the prodigal Queen returns." Axel, my second appointed guard, greets me as I walk in and set my things down.

I scoff at his choice in words.

"Oh, shut up and set up." His crooked grin breaks across his face as he saunters onto the mat and brings up his sword. I mirror his stance waiting for the signal my head of guard, Ezra, gives before lunging at Axel. He blocks my advance, sidestepping to circle around me. His sword swings out at my side forcing me to jump back and cut my sword down quickly to block his blow. *CLANK!* Our swords slam together sending the ring of metal reverberating off the walls.

He spins and in the brief moment he has his back to me, I take a cheap shot, sending the edge of my blade at the back of his knees. My weapon just barely tickles his pant legs as he finishes the turn and faces me.

"Oh, come on, Evie. You can do better than that." He taunts. I duck as he swings his sword over my head. I Wield a small amount of magic at him, pulling him off his feet. His sword clatters loudly to the ground next to him. "HEY!" Axel shouts.

Ezra glares at me from where he stands. "Eveera, no magic during practice spars. Get off the mat." I roll my eyes, my lip jutting out into a pout. Before rotating out off the mat I reach my hand down for Axel to grab. He does, but instead of standing, he pulls me to the ground on top of him. My body thudding into his skinny yet solid frame.

"Asshole." I say at the same time he calls me a cheat. My hands move to his chest, pushing myself off of him, and this time I don't offer my hand. We make our way back to our things against the wall as the remaining three of my men take the center of the mat. The brothers, Maxwell and Orem, against my oldest guard Armond. The brothers move gracefully in sync. They have to be when going against the barbarian that is their opponent.

The three of us not sparring relax against the stone wall, watching the match go down. Well - Axel and I relax, and Ezra...does whatever his equivalent to relaxing would be. Which in my opinion looks uncomfortable.

My men are panting, a flicker of electricity zaps down Max's sword. "MAX! OFF THE MAT." Ezra shouts in his direction. He groans in frustration as he abandons his brother, who now stands facing Armond alone. They're nearly the same height, their hair the same shade of red, if you didn't know it you might mistake Orem for Armond's younger brother not Maxwell's based on solely appearances.

A shadow moves from the corner of my eye causing me to turn my head. Felix, the head of my council stands in the passageway, his finger crooking in my direction. The motion is a direct summons to follow him. Ezra is the only other person who notices Felix, his hand grazing my arm briefly and in an awkward way as I walk past him, leaving the men and my stuff behind.

"Felix." I greet before passing him up. The halls are quiet this morning, spare a few staff members rustling about their early chores. Most of the families who live here haven't woken yet, save for their spousal counterparts that play a part on my council. The doors to the council room come quickly into view where I find each member is already sitting in their usual place upon my entrance. Their faces bear small, polite smiles in my direction that I return in my usual fashion of flopping down into my chair and kicking my feet up. My intent reading loudly and clearly that I'm ready to get this over with before it even starts. Felix takes his place next to me, pulling a piece of parchment from inside his vest and setting it down on my legs.

I look down at it and then back up at him, his eyes are wide giving me an insistent look. "Ugh, you're joking." I mutter before picking up the paper and unfolding it. I glance back up at him from the corner of my eye to see if he's changed his mind and wants to read it for me instead, but his face remains unchanged. Clearing my throat loudly I begin reading the words scrawled in front of me:

"OFFICIAL REQUEST FOR PORTAL ENTRY:

PRINCE RORIN COLLIER OF THE KINGDOM OF VELLAR, HUMBLY REQUESTS ENTRY INTO THE KINGDOM OF OBSIDIAN FOR A ONE ON ONE MEETING WITH ITS QUEEN."

A few gasps echo around me. *Vellar*. My stomach churns at the name of the kingdom nestled against my northern borders. "Felix...didn't you say the gentleman getting cozy in our cells had a strange Wield?" He nods. My finger taps against my chin, scheme and plot brewing in my mind. "I think he and I need to have a little chat." Some of the council members eyes find something suddenly very interesting on the ceiling as my Wield flares from my fingertips, black creeping up to my wrists. I slide my legs down, pushing up from my seat, the paper crinkling underneath my grip. "Am I supposed to do something with this?" I ask Felix.

But it's Lord Frederic who answers, his eyes flicking back and forth nervously. "Well, it's prudent that we, that we, that we…"

Bleeding gods. "Spit it out, Frederic." His chin quivers and Felix finishes for him.

"Your highness, we don't like to decide things for you…" I roll my eyes at that. *Since when?* I want to say, but he continues on. "It would be appropriate to send a response."

I make a noncommittal noise and read over the paper a second time. Everyone's eyes are on me, their stares heavy and their breaths held in anticipation of my reaction.

"Denied." I say flatly. The chair scrapes against the floor behind me as I kick it out of my way the movement of my feet carrying me swiftly out towards the exit. Leaving the lot of them to bicker and argue over my decision.

The hallways of the castle are warmly lit, illuminating a orange glow against the black stone but as I grow closer to the cells even that small glow dissipates. The darkness for some is frightening, for me it's a comfort. Unfortunately for the man cowering in the corner of the cell I now stand in front of, the dark is just the beginning of what I'll subject him too.

Clink, clink, clink. My fingernail taps against the metal bars.

"Hello, dear. You have something I need."

Screams ring out through the Room. My familiar, Vada, watches us closely from the mouth of her cave. *"You're salivating."* I note down our bond.

She gives me an agitated huff but I see right through it, she gets a high off this as much as I do. The screams, the blood, the occasional mutilation. Tonight however, isn't about that, this is more of an extracurricular interrogation. It would have happened sooner or later, but with the missive today from his prince, I felt eager to get a head start.

CRACK!

"Again." I command as I pick out the blood from beneath my finger nails.

CRACK!

"Again." The man's skin is peeled open as each of the tassels lacerate it. One of the tendrils of my Wield is wrapped lazily around his hand so that he doesn't drop the whip. The main focus of my Wield is in his head, manipulating the commands of his brain, bending it to the will of the nightmare. "Again."

CRACK!

"This can all stop if you just tell me why your king sent you and why your prince sent me a sweet little note asking to meet me." His actions still as I temporarily stop the nightmare. I want his full attention for this interrogation.

"Tsk tsk tsk. Percy was it?" I jerk his chin towards me. His shoulders go slack. He's lost a lot of blood but not enough to kill him. His blonde hair has turned pink at the ends from the blood staining it. He can't be more than thirty, handsome enough, that's too bad.

"Percy, Percy, Percy..." My hand lightly slaps either cheek, once for every time I said his name. "See it doesn't add up. You have quite an impressive Wield, *Illusionary*. Poor Felix had no idea you'd followed him home from that big...what are they called?" He whimpers while eyeing the slithering ink on my arms and chest and then the dragon behind me. "T-trade meetings." *Ah, yes. I don't know why we go to those still.*

I crouch down to where he is kneeling, my shoes sticky with his blood, "the way I see it is either, the prince is requesting to visit because they greatly miss a talent such as yours. Or your here on very specific orders not even the prince is aware of. And what a concern that would be, the ruler and his heir keeping secrets from one another. That makes for a dodgy relationship doesn't it? Maybe the king had plans for you to use your oh so special magic to come and spy. Maybe even *harm*. Harming a pretty face like mine would be simply devastating, don't you agree?" He flinches as he feels cool metal prick against his collar bone. His eyes darting everywhere to avoid my gaze, his expressions giving me reason to believe my assumptions could be correct. "You must've been so proud that your King picked you, huh?" The tip of my dagger digs into the bone just a little causing him to squeal like a pig.

I stand up walking over to the table against the stone wall and pick up two vials. One to mute his Wield, boosting the mage shackles he wears and another to replenish his lost blood just enough that he doesn't die on me quite yet. I shove the vials into his shaky hands, while he tries to fight against my grip. "Drink." My Wield steps back into his mind convincing him of much worse horrors if he doesn't drink them. Each of the vials liquids goes down his throat and he swallows thickly. I pace slowly in front of him, "of course if the king and yourself are in on a secret plan to destroy me, that still doesn't answer the small issue of why the prince wants a meeting." Percy's eyes are squeezed shut, his breathing evening out as the liquids do their job. I lean back down into his face, "do you know why your prince...what's his name again?"

"Rorin." He chokes out, bloodshot eyes finally staring back at me.

"Rorin." The name glides off my tongue. "Percy...do you know why Rorin wants to meet me?" He shakes his head vigorously back and forth, holding in his answer. My lips curl up into a smile, "liar." I loosen my Wield just a little that it tickles against his face.

He sucks in a fast sharp breath, "yo-your," he starts.

The small tendril strokes his dirtied tear-stained cheek. "Yes..." I coo.

"a-a-armies." *My armies? Interesting...*I think. I want to ask more, but the vials worked too quickly as his body relaxes and he passes out on me, the exhaustion of our conversation kicking in. My foot lands a kick into his boot, but he remains unconscious. I look up in the direction of the rooms human-sized exit where two of my guards wait, "you can take him back to the cells, boys. I'll finish playing with him later." They enter the room, wary, not wanting to be too close to Vada as they hoist the wounded Vellaran back to his cell.

I call my Wield back into me, my inked serpents settling and moving less on my skin now that my magic isn't agitated. My gaze catches on the little two dimensional creatures that curl around my arms as if they are snuggling into me. The ink is interesting enough, done by some common Mages when I was young to help hold the Wield.

"*Go, little demon. I can feel your exhaustion, and you smell. It's irritating me.*" Vada's voice invades my mind snapping me from my hazy thought, my attention leaving the tattoos and landing on her golden stare.

"*I smell? You're a giant fucking lizard. It's not like your scent is always pleasant.*" I quip. The end of her tail snaps against the stone above my head as she turns from the room leaving me among the mess.

"*Irksome human.*" She grumbles forcing me to hold back my laughter. I dust off the debris that fell down on me while she's disappears back into her hovel. The black of her scales melting completely from view. I take the moment to go through my mental checklist before leaving the Room and the mess behind.

Refuse a prince: Check

Torture: Double check.

Tease Dragon: Triple check.

Fulfilling night all in all, I think.

RORIN

Five Days Earlier

He's a fucking idiot. My fingernails form crescent shapes into my palms as I force my fists tightly closed, both to not punch my father or Wield at him.

"You are not out there. You don't *see*. These tactics they are preventing *nothing*." The words come out through my clenched teeth.

My father's face remains stony. "They will wear them down. You'll see to that."

"SEE TO WHAT?!" The shout leaves before I can stop it. "You've appointed me as a General to farmers, metalworkers, shopowners for gods' sake. Men who have never seen battle. Fuck, *I HAD NEVER SEEN BATTLE! UNTIL YOU PUT ME IN ONE. AND WE. ARE. LOSING.*" My face heats matching the anger I feel. I suck in a breath in an attempts to regain my composure, "men are dying, father. You are sentencing them to an unfair death because you refuse to accept aid. If we just send a request to the Obsids—"

His sharp blue eyes snap up at the name of our neighboring kingdom. "We will not." The tone is final, but I can't find it in me to relent, to listen as I always do regardless of my personal feelings towards his decisions.

I subdue my anger so that my voice is even as I press the issue. "Her army is rumored to be outstanding. Skilled, professional, and massive. All things we need against Baelor."

His hands slam down onto the desk sending papers flying off of it. "Rumored! It's all rumors with their demented queen and her monster infested kingdom. I will not stoop as low to request the aid of a heretic queen who remains to be seen in the public eye herself."

"You did once. For the Battle of Vellar, King Killian sent his aid. They might do it again." A low laugh leaves him as he picks his palms off the desk, rubbing his hands together and clasping them in front of himself. A fake smile is plastered across his cheeks. One I've grown used to, it's the smile he uses to make you feel like he's listened even though he hasn't. A smile meant to placate and remind you who is really in charge here.

"You have a...soft heart, boy." The compliment is backhanded - laced with a threat. "You will not bring this up again. If you can't handle one simple task, then you have proven to be more of a disappointment than I could have imagined. Figure it out, Rorin. This is your problem." With that last word, he returns to his paperwork not bothering with the pieces strewn across the floor as he dismisses me.

It should be his problem, as the king, he'll damn us all at this rate and not even the gods will step up to save us. I turn on my heel breaking my stare from the top of his head and close the door behind me. His guards don't look at me as I depart from them, they keep their stares trained on the wall ahead.

I could return to my room, but my body is too agitated, my magic to anticipatory, waiting for me to use it as it clashes with my emotions and—

"I take it things didn't go well?" Will's voice sounds from behind me. I blink a few times, clearing my blurred vision and find myself sitting in the center of my old instruction room. Bile burns the back of my throat as I look at the worn floors the memories threatening to resurface.

How did I get up here? I ask myself. *I was just in front of his office...*

My eyes turn to where Will's voice came from but he's moved, I tilt my head back around to find him standing above me, his hand outstretched..

"Ahem. I think it's best we head to Bair." His brows draw together but he doesn't question me at the moment instead he grabs my hand and pulls me up.

"Ready?" He asks and when I nod he walks back around me to exit the weathered and tired room. The room has deteriorated from the lack of use over the years. It seems it was created for only one person and when I no longer needed it...well it's turned into nothing but a shell. These walls hold more horrors and secrets than I care to admit.

"It seems smaller." The words come out a whisper, he looks back over his shoulder at me. Shame heats my cheeks and —

SLAM! Dust picks up around us from the force of the door shutting, making my nose twitch. *Why the gods would I come back here?* I ask myself this time as my father's voice pierces my mind. His words as painful as a blade slicing into me. *"Figure it out."*

I'll figure it out alright, you just won't like when I do. I say back to the version of him that lives only in my mind. Now I just hope that what I "figure out" works.

We left for Bair immediately after returning to my room.

It's been three days now.

Three days from the disastrous meeting with my father, three days since I'd had Will send a missive off to Obsidian - an official request for an audience with their queen, and three days since he found me back in that fucking room. My Wield flares at just the thought of it and with all the resolve I have I yank it back down.

I've been pacing the room for an obscene amount of time, wearing holes into my rugs while I wait for the response to come back in from their queen. It took some convincing to have Will send it in the first place and while going against my father's wishes on things isn't new to me...this isn't some petty rule breaking. This could be taken as an act of war should he find out on a day he's in a sour mood.

A few of my soldiers pass below my office window, looking haggard, dirty, and tired. For the past several months Hadar's Guards have gotten closer and more manipulative with their tactics. Our border towns have suffered from the occupation of our small garrisons along each front while my military is suffering from the constant skirmishes. In short, everyone is bloody exhausted.

BANG! My line of thought veers as Will comes busting into my office clutching something in his fist. The look he gives me is wild as he extends it out towards me. I snatch what I now realize is an envelope from him and tear it open. Neither of us are breathing as I unfold the paper that hinges on our plan going smoothly.

"*DENIED.*"

Dammit. I look grimly up at Will. Without even saying a word his brow creases in disappointment. "Do not tell me, what I think that you are about to tell me."

I really wish I didn't have to, I think. "We have to go on foot."

He throws his hands up. "No. No, Rorin. I'm sorry but, no. Your father already told you no. Now I am telling you as your head guard no. N.O."

I laugh, mostly because he thinks he can tell me what to do. He knows it's a battle lost, but he still tries. "We don't have another option Will."

"No other option— do I need to remind you, that if we go against his wishes it's our heads on the chopping block?!" He shrieks.

The paper crinkles underneath my grip as I mull over his words. "It's a risk." I say, a smirk twitching at my lips but he doesn't look amused.

"This isn't funny. This isn't a joke Ror! We already broke one rule by reaching out. They've told us no. Everyone, Rorin, is telling you no. Do you know what that means?" His face has gone beat red, sweat dripping from his brow. I lean back against my desk, waiting for him to tell me what it means anyways. "We should stay and listen to the directives we were given."

My eyes find the ceiling navigating my next words carefully.

"If we do that, we die anyways. At least this way, I'll die knowing I did everything I could to save this fucking kingdom." That reminder hangs over us, dread settling in like a heavy blanket.

The door slams, the noise is jarring and it takes me a second to notice Will has stormed out. We've always disagreed on things - especially my decisions - but lately it feels like things between us have grown more tense. I straighten out the crinkles in the page, looking down at her response a second time.

Denied.

It'll take us the next two days to make preparations to leave. According to rumors we will need to be armed to the teeth if we are going to stand a chance against whatever lives in the outskirts of her territory. The rumors about her are no better, even if we do make it to her doorstep there is still the risk we won't be leaving Obsidian - alive that is. I crush the paper again and cast it into the hearth, watching it light quickly and burn to nothing but ash.

The sound of the dinner bell sends a grumble through my stomach. I can't remember the last time I ate. I toggle with the idea of eating up here in my apartments and staying with the growing stack of papers on my desk, but I figure if I am set on the course for death I might as well enjoy my final few meals with friends.

The walk to the eating hall is brisk, the drab stone walls create a dim environment, a stark contrast to the halls in Valen. Bustling noise and conversation sound around the corner as I come around it. Soldiers are seated at every table, mostly of higher rank, clamoring for the food and ale. A few voices quieted but mostly my appearance seems not to have interrupted their meals. My seat at the head table sits empty between Will and Bennett, my commander. Bennett's face lights up as he sees me walking down the center aisle.

"Buddy!" Bennett shouts, his ale cup tipping the contents into his mouth a dribble escaping down his chin. He swipes at it with the back of his hand before giving me a dopey grin. "Decided to grace us with your presence eh Highness?"

I scoff my eyes flicking to Will who's kept his head down, his eyes drilling holes into his potatoes. Bennett tracks where I look as I take my seat, a frown stealing away his smile. "Don't tell me mom and dad are fighting again?" He groans. *THWACK!* *"Ow!"* Bennett shouts, rubbing the back of his head.

"Thanks." Will grumbles, the only acknowledgment he's willing to give me at the moment. My head bobs at him as I stab the piece of gristly meat in front of me. The three of us sit there quietly for a moment listening to the conversations happening around us.

"So…" Bennett starts, "when are you two leaving?" The question surprises me, I whip my head at Will who's moved on to staring at the liquid in his cup.

I pick at a piece of stale looking bread on my plate, "uhm — a few days. We'll need to get everything prepared." He grunts, shoving a piece of food into his mouth.

"Sure you don't want me to come too? You could probably use another hand." He suggests through garbled words and a full mouth. I bring the cup of ale up to my lips taking a sip and shaking my head. I don't need another one of my friends in direct danger because of me. At least in this case, if he plays ignorant and stays here doing his job, he won't seem disloyal to the crown. Not until we bring back her army that is, but I haven't planned that far ahead yet. We go back to eating quietly, and I go back to listening in on a few of the men around me. Their words are mostly just the same complaints you'd here at any war post - not enough hot water, disputes amongst the ranks, sexual frustration from being away from their partners or spouses. Nothing of interest, though I can't say I disagree with them.

If it were up to me they'd all be at their homes, with their families and jobs, not set to be a part of some makeshift military serving under a resentful prince. A few taps hit my plate bringing my attention back up to Bennett. "Where'd you go just now?" He asks, confusion lining his forehead.

"Nowhere." I say quickly and push my plate away from me. "I should go through some paperwork and start packing. A lot to do before we leave."

"Yeah, alright. You'll let me know though right?" He asks.

"Hm?"

"If you change your mind and need me to come with you." His tone is hopeful. I know staying behind here is less exciting than the possibility of meeting a queen no one has set eyes on outside of her own kingdom. I down the last of my drink, gripping his shoulder in assurance.

"You'll be the first to know." I say. A small smile settles on his face, but his eyes give him away, he knows I am only placating him and that he's needed here. I decided I was okay if he chose to resent me for the decision to leave him behind if it kept him blameless for a little while longer.

The walk back to my apartments was quiet most soldiers having headed back to their own quarters after eating. The door clicked shut with a thud behind me and I take in the spaciousness of it. These rooms are really meant for the King and Queen should they deign to visit their outer towns. But they never do.

The whole post was covered under a thick layer of dust when I first arrived a few years ago. It hadn't been occupied in decades until the issue with Hadar and King Baelor cropped up. At first the problem was mostly with the kingdoms that had no ley line magic. We thought maybe it was a border dispute, that King Baelor had gotten a little hungry for more space to rule, we never imagined that he'd move onto a magic imbued kingdom.

After the occupation of Evendell it was clear Baelor wanted more than just land to own, he wanted control. Of what that much is still unclear - but my father decided he wouldn't allow some tyrant to take Vellar from us. It's probably the only thing we've agreed on. His choice in tactics to shield us against Hadar's Guards however have grown repetitive, consistently failing us and leaving us with the same result. Loss of men and resources, but he won't listen to reason. As long as his borders have not officially been breached he feels we are being successful in our efforts.

His inability to see reason and sense for the depletion in our ranks is how I ended up in the library going through history books upon history books until I found the record of the Battle of Vellar. King Killian of Obsidian allowed us to employ his mercenaries and militia to squander an internal dispute that cost him his life in the end. Some time after that, his wife Ayla, was killed in their home. The circumstances behind her death were not disclosed at any annual meetings of the realm and the only man we saw in their stead was their regent, Felix Grim.

No one knew they had a royal sitting under their noses until ten years ago when the elusive Queen Eveera took up her official role and title. The different courts bombarded him with questions at the next trade meeting, wondering why her parents had proclaimed her dead at birth. Rumors ran wild that she was as monstrous as the beasts that lived out in the woods of Obsidian. Others still don't believe she's alive as she's never shown herself in the public eye before. But, I only have one option left to me now, and that's to hope she is as generous as her father was - despite the tension our kingdoms share.

Sleep didn't find me easily the past two nights. There was however no time to waste and with our things packed, and horses loaded we set out towards Obsidian. I had a conversation with Bennett yesterday morning detailing what his job would be for when we were away and when we came back. We settled on him being the one to let us back in. We'll do our best to keep in touch, and he'll do his best to break the news to the army that Obsids would be joining our ranks.

I look over to Will on top of his horse, his face is scrunched in what seems to be a now permanent frown, "I don't know why I go along with your insubordination." He gripes, shaking his head.

My hand clasps his knee, "because you're subordinate to me. I thought that was obvious."

He rolls his eyes. "The only thing that's obvious, is you're going to get me killed one of these days. And all because you thought you knew better." I don't miss the venom in the last sentence.

I shrug off the bite in his words and muse my thoughts aloud. "I wonder if it's as bad as the rumors claim. The monsters, that is. Suppose it must be if even she barricades herself from whatever they are." Bair is close to the border of Obsidian, almost a full day's ride. We should make it to the edge of Vellar by nightfall. The earlier we left the sooner we could begin our scheme.

Our kingdom grows depressing as we leave the post behind. The crops are almost barren from the high demand, most villages are falling into disrepair thanks to our overbearing presence. Another thing my father refuses to look into - the actual welfare of people without noble blood.

We stay quiet the entirety of our first day, our horses powering through the terrain getting us as close to the border as we can. As the day grows darker and air colder, I start to see the border wall and gates come into view. I had Bennett ride ahead of us yesterday to let us out without any questions. His presence being here early was to help avoid any back and forth from the few groups that patrol here on rotation.

We dismount our horses, making camp next to Bennett's things. "I see you made it here with no issue." He says cheerfully, Will claps his shoulder but still says nothing, he just laid out the mat next to Bennett's and closed his eyes. My friend looks down at him and back up to me, "rough ride?" he whispers.

"Let's just say it would have been much more entertaining had I waited to send you here." He laughs at that while helping me unload the packs on the horses. The darkness of night sweeps quickly over us, and if I closed my eyes tight enough I could pretend we were all kids again, hiding out in a field from our responsibilities. But the anxiety sitting in my chest is a persistent reminder that we are not children and there is no more hiding from our responsibilities.

Bennett's snores take over the camp.

"You ready for tomorrow?" I turn my head towards the voice. Will is staring up at the sky his eyes staying focused on the stars.

"You're talking to me now?" I ask.

He ignores my remark, "my father is a smart man." I want to respond to that and ask what that has to do with anything but he keeps speaking. "He's been serving under your father for his whole rule. I've never doubted my father's loyalties or his concern for Vellar. But you doubt yours."

"You don't have to share the same feelings I do for my father and you don't have to think less of yours just because he works for the crown."

He snorts, his laugh one of disbelief. "We all work for the crown. But now you've made me an enemy to the crown. An enemy to my kingdom and to my father. I'm proud to have this role and serve, but I think being your friend may end up being the biggest mistake of my life." I don't have any words, the sting of what he said burning through me.

"I—"

"I hope you know what you're doing." Will flips back over to face Bennett, ending the conversation.

Great. That talk will making sleeping so much easier, I think.

The wind rustles quietly through the branches above me, the fire burnt out awhile ago and I came to the conclusion awhile ago that sleep was going to continue dancing around me. Every time my eyelids fell heavy enough my brain would start up again. Two many thoughts of the journey, the risks, my father's wrath once he finds out.

My mother protested to me leaving for Bair again. Rambling on about how much pressure my father was under, that I should be more understanding. Neglecting to notice how much of that pressure has actually fallen on her son's shoulders. But if it doesn't have frills, parties, or gossip involved my mother rarely notices anything. Her head is stuck in the clouds of aristocracy with every noble socialite wife's lips secured firmly to her ass.

I would have thought that their ignorance would have sowed more hate amongst the common Vellaran folk, but apparently my golden parents could do no wrong - except for appointing their broken son as general of their armies.

My Wield was seen as taboo, *poisonous mist* instead of healing mist. It was blasphemous, an abomination, a curse. For those not included in my ranks they think that the reason our armies numbers keep falling lower and lower is because of me. They couldn't possibly imagine a king as great as my father, King Eiser, would lead their husbands, fathers, and sons to die a worthless death.

No, the failure of the armies is solely because of it's leader and the curse he bears. My mind whispers to me. Thankfully, the men we've enlisted have sense, and quickly came to discover that I was not the problem. But scared women and children don't listen. They don't care who the blame falls to, just that it falls.

The shadows on the trees are slowly starting to melt away as first daylight breaks through. Having no desire to lay down anymore, I roll up my mat and pack my horse back up. Bennett and Will rise not to shortly after, the smell of food stirring them from their mats. We have a quiet breakfast, quickly eating through it as to not burn too much daylight for the ride into Obsidian.

The ride to the gates it brisk, we camped not to far out from them. Will and I facing opposite Bennett to say our goodbyes. "Last chance." He tries, his dopey grin back on his face. But the worry is there in his eyes.

"I need you here Ben. You're our key to the inside." I say. He trots his horse in between the two of ours reaching over to bring us both in for an awkward hug.

"You two die out there and I'll find you in Helys. I'll bring you back myself just to kill you again for dying without me the first time." The three of us laugh a weak laugh, our hearts all beating faster than normal. When we pull a part I give a final nod to Bennett and then look to Will. He nods at me before turning through the gates, crossing the border into Obsidian first. I look over my shoulder at Bennett before spurring my horse on to catch up with Will.

The rusty metal gates creek shut behind us. *No turning back now,* the voice inside my head croons.

In an instant the air, the energy, the *magic*, shifts drastically. The difference between Vellar and Obsidian has never been more clear. The sudden change makes me nauseated, apparently Will had the same visceral reaction as he heaves the contents of his breakfast off the side of his horse.

Dark, thick, bare woods stand before us. The sky is gray with a thick cloud coverage overhead. The temperature has dropped easily fifteen degrees from where we were even just a few feet ago. Will pulls himself back up, his face a sickly green.

"Yeah. This is off to a great start." He grumbles, taking a long swig of his water and swishing it back and forth to spit.

"Well, we weren't ambushed by monsters so that has to be a good thing." I say under my breath, but he's riding too close not to hear me. He huffs incredulously, the thought crosses my mind on if he'll be able to put this disagreement past us. If he is coming with me out of loyalty or out of spite. At the moment, I'd venture to say both. But the loyalty thing may be wishful thinking.

The deeper we travel into the dark kingdom the more my magic seems to twitch and turn inside of me. We have several more hours of daylight left before we have to decide to make camp. The anticipation of meeting the queen gnaws at my insides. I prepared as much as I could but the history texts say nothing of her. I'd have a better shot learning about her by listening to the servants various gossip claims.

Shadows cast on the ground next to our horses feet from the lack of light streaming through the trees bare branches. It was marveling to me how drastic the terrain changed once we crossed the border. I can't help but wonder if it's just the magic running through the veins of the kingdom or if it has to do with the curse settled over it.

SNAP!

My back straightens, reaching for my knife as we both swivel our heads from side to side, looking for where the noise came from.

SNAP! CRACK! SNAP!

Grabbing at Will's reigns I pull his horse into mine keeping us close together. He sits forward in his seat, his hands gripping the hilt of his sword. "Why did you do that?" He gripes.

"SHH!" I hiss.

SNAP!

"Great, we probably tripped some magical wire and the queen's already sent someone for us." Will squeaks, his voice going up an octave. Bright red beady eyes appear all around us. Their bodies blending into the gray bark of the trees. They pause across the way from us, Will and I's horses step around nervously as they pick up on the strange presence. An inhuman screech emanates from one of them. Their jaw unhinges as the noise pierces our ear drums, their motion like a snake preparing to devour its prey. "Now or never, Will." We kick our horses off into different directions, straight at the beasts. I fling my knife at one quickly unsheathing my sword as soon as the small handle leaves my grip.

SQUEEELCHH! My blade slices through the thick skin, going through the belly and cutting stem to stern with the force. I watch *it* crumple to the ground in a heap but I don't have much time before I move onto skewering the next monster.

With each slice, jab, and cut I pay close attention to the chests I puncture. To my remarkable surprise, I notice the beasts ribs are moving in and out in a *- sort of -* steady rhythm.

It breathes. Relief washes over me, my Wield flickers to life in my palm. I scout the area quickly, looking for Will. It's been years since I have voluntarily called to the Wield and my control on it is unreliable.

Come on, I beckon it. *Will needs you, come on.*

"What a disappointment you turned out to be", *"an omen if there ever was one"*, *SMACK! "stupid boy!"*, *"cleanse, cleanse, cleanse"*, *"you're weak, tainted, broken"*, *"if you want to make me proud..."*

The words all slam around in my mind my vision blackening as I fight for control over the magic. In a huff of frustration I snuff out what mist lingers in my palm, choosing to run for Will and aide him by hand. He's off his horse, fighting too many to his one while on foot. I jump off the back of my landing in a roll. An ungraceful landing, as I scramble to my feet, my horse taking off in the opposite direction of me.

The two of us fight back to back as we take on the remaining creatures. Black sludge coating our blades, clothes, and skin. With each successful kill we narrowly dodge another creature's attempts to swipe at us with their gnarled claws. We find every last shred of strength that we have to end them, their bodies falling into ungraceful piles along the wooded forest floor.

Thunk! The last body goes down in two halves. It's insides a black, goopy, rotted mess.

"Oh gods." Will chokes before turning and vomiting all over the remains. The smell is abhorrent to the point I can't help but gag along with him.

I pat his back before rubbing in slow motions, trying to ease the sickness along. We collapse against the tree, panting. The bodies ooze out a few feet from us, the forest floor littered with the piles of slayed monsters. "What. the. fuck." I breathe out.

We sat against that tree for awhile. By the grace of something our horses made their way back to us. While Will's face returned to it's more natural hue, I made a pile of the torn a part bodies. I put the fire between us. Hoping that maybe the scent of their sludgy blood will help ward off any others from creeping our way. I squint through the flames to get a better look, trying to figure out what exactly they *are.* The adrenaline having worn off I can finally feel true sleep coming for me until Will taps me on my shoulder, forcing my eyes to open. I'm about to ask what he needs when I see his arm out and extended next in front of him, pointing.

I turn my head slowly to see the pile of bodies I made was- *rustling?* An arm that was dismembered and left off to the side moves along the ground until it finds its original owner. "The creatures are piecing themselves back together and reanimating...what. the. fuck?" I breathe out, my hand closing around Will's arm to stand him up with me.

"They don't fucking die?!" He shrieks, drawing his sword again. I'm wracking my brain trying to figure out how I am going to get us out of this, especially when turning around isn't an option.

If we want to have a home to go back to, I need Obsidian.

I drag Will behind me shoving him into the flank of his horse, the two of us scrambling to mount them. We take off at breakneck speed before the monsters can fully put themselves back together.

Thankfully, the ground is more flat, making it easier on the horses to gallop through the forest. "How long do you think we can push the horses?" Will shouts. *I don't know.* I think. I don't want to push them too hard and risk losing our ease of transport through the outer territories.

"Just a few more miles." I shout back. The woods sound with strange yipping noises, and every so often I swear I see pairs of red eyes staring straight at us, unease washing over us.

A few more miles turned into several. We only stopped when we heard the sound of water running. It was daylight again when we saw the river come into view. It's water so clear you can see the stones glittering at the bottom. Will and I both hop off our mounts, guiding them to a slower part of the current. The two steeds greedily lap up at the liquid. Feeling some security under sunlight we set our things down, stripping of our dirtied and bloodied clothes and step into the frigid water.

The stones underneath our feet are smooth. Slick and sleek black stones line the bottom. I reach down to pick one up and look at it under the light. Veins of red shine through it like blood under the surface of skin.

"Obsidian." Will notes.

"What?" I ask, opting not to turn around and see the bare body of my guard.

"The stones, they're Obsidian." *So they are*, I say to myself.

I toss the flat stone in my hand, before skipping it across the water. "Appropriate I suppose. Considering the name of the kingdom we're in." He hums in response. The sound of the water splashing as we wash away the grime taking over the conversation. Suds flow down the current. I've never been more grateful for the foresight to bring soap along with us, even if it only lasts us this one wash, as it scrubs away the black sticky reminder of the creatures we fought only hours ago.

Will and I set the fire up afterwards, shivering under thin blankets, waiting to dry off. Our meal is a measly one of bread and dried jerky. Not much to fill our stomachs but enough to get us through next few hours. "*Ha. Ha-ha-ha.*" Will's laughter cuts through.

"Wh-what are you laughing at?" I sputter. He's gone into a fit. His blanketed arm banded across his stomach as a deep belly laugh roars out of him. "Wh-ha. What is so funny?" I ask again, not being able to help the laugh infecting me as well.

"Ha—" he tries to catch his breath between hiccups. "Ha- it's just so insane. Phew." He says, his hand swiping across his forehead. "This whole plan. This whole day. We weren't inside the border for more than a few what? Hours?"

"Y-yeah, maybe." I laugh.

"Before something tried to kill us? I mean here I was worried about being on your father's list to kill. But...by the looks of it Obsidian will do the job for him." He slips back into his fit and the two of laugh at the absurdity of the hand I've dealt us. He's right though, hate it as I may. We barely scraped by that last fight, and if they reanimate then I'm not sure what we can do.

"A-hem. I'll get you back home Will." I say, he's hobbled over to his pack, digging through it for his mat and some dry clothes.

He shrugs, throwing his shirt over his still damp hair, shaking it out as he does so. I wish I could convince him of that, but I'd have to first convince myself of it. His snores don't take long to drift from him. I maintain first watch as he gets undisturbed rest, it would be wasted on me anyways.

Thankfully, the creatures didn't find us that night. The next however I unfortunately couldn't say the same. We heard them earlier this time, it was a smaller group, but no less vicious. These ones looked more monstrous, their features were practically melting off their skeletons. The noises that left them were animalistic. Screeches and guttural moans emit from their gaping maws.

Will and I cut left and right, spinning around each other. I watch each body that fell for movement in their chest, and sure enough no matter which way I stabbed, sliced, or cleaved, the fucking things kept *moving*.

"I counted twelve bodies." Will states.

I circle around the pile of limbs and torsos, "it won't be long before they reanimate again. But—" My feet stop short at a pair of shoulders with its disfigured head resting a few feet away. My knees bend forcing my body into a crouch.

"What are you..." I lift my hand, silencing him. My eyes squint staring hard at the chest cavity. I wait for the unusual rise and fall of their uncoordinated breathing. *Nothing.*

I jump to my feet, raising my sword to the body to my left, cleaving the head clean off. *THWUMP!*

"What the?!" Will shrieks, but I can't stop myself. I run around the pile finding every intact head and shoulders I can find and hack into them, their sludgy blood splattering across my body and clothes. My feet stumble back, my eyes fixed on the carnage. No chests moving, no bodies reanimating.

My sword clatters to the ground. "The heads. They can't reanimate without their heads." I say between pants.

"How in the bleeding gods did you figure that out?" He says, his shoulders slumping.

"I-the first time, I stared at their chests. I wanted to know if they could breathe. I tried—" a frustrated sigh leaves me as I drop to pick up my sword, wiping the blade clean with the edge of my shirt, "I tried to Wield, I was going to poison them...but, it failed. I couldn't control it and I wasn't going to be responsible for your death. When I noticed the one without it's head lying there, I crouched down to see if it was breathing. It wasn't so..." my hand sweeps out to motion at the pile.

Will's bobbing his head up and down. "So you decided to go manic and hack all their heads off."

"You're welcome." I bite, exhaustion pulling at me.

We guide the horses a few miles further before I couldn't take it anymore. Our bodies were littered with cuts and bruises and my lack of sleep had finally caught up. No wonder her military is considered professional, if this is what they have to deal with. "It's your night to take watch." I say, as I flop onto my mat. *One more day,* I think as I close my eyelids. *One more day, and we'll be in Oriya. One more day and we will be one step closer to surviving Hadar.*

The next day's ride was simple. No unusual sounds, no beady red eyes, or shifty horses. By nightfall we could hear the city before we actually saw it.

Tall spires of cream buildings with dark brown beams came into view. Relief sinking into my shoulders. *People.* As we brought our horses closer we could see the buildings were lit with bright orange flames.

"Well, this is shocking considering what lay just a few feet outside it's borders." Will mutters. I'm inclined to agree. The place had an energy around it that was in direct contrast with both what I expected of Obsidian *and* just experienced out in the outer lands.

I spurred my horse on galloping the rest of the stretch into town. The streets were busy. Vendor carts filled with lively patrons, music from every corner, and not a single person caring to notice us. A tavern comes into view and I pray to whatever god is desperate enough to listen to me that this tavern will have a bed for me to stretch out on. We tie our horses up outside by a water trough, they look in much better shape than Will and I, who drag our dirt and blood covered bodies into the building.

It's packed.

We elbow our way through to two vacant spots at the bar, a surly woman says 'hello' while handing us two mugs filled with a dark drink. I mutter a brief thank you and swivel the stool around to look at the locals. They have darker hair, and mostly darker complexions than the my people, but other than that they don't seem much different. Loud music plays from one side of the room, people dance in the center, while others disappear into alcoves and upstairs. "Can I get ya anything else deary?" The barmaid asks.

"Two beds, if you can." I say, giving her my best smile. Her nose scrunches at me. *I must not look too appealing,* I muse. She slides to keys over to me before disappearing down the counter. Will catches my attention with his gagging. "*Blech!*" He spits his drink back into the mug, coughing and sputtering.

"Lightweight." I snicker which forces him to look up and scowl at me. He then gestures at my untouched mug.

"You try that and tell me you wouldn't sputter and gag too. Go on," he nudges my elbow beckoning me to pick up the mug. I lift it to my lips and sip. I suppress the urge to retch, stopping the drink from coming back up my throat, the burn overwhelming the taste of the alcohol.

"See?" I force the word out of my mouth steadily, but fail to conceal my grimace. Will's face lights up in a smug grin.

"I told you! Call me a lightweight." He whines, mindlessly he grabs the mug and takes an accidental sip and ends up repeating the same, spitting, coughing, and sputtering he did just a minute ago.

A large gentleman with fiery red hair, his face marred with a jagged scar cutting through both brow and cheek, looks us up and down as he tips his own mug back. "You two don't seem like you belong here."

My mouth curves into a whisper of a smile, polite enough, but not exactly warm and welcoming either. "We have important business here."

His brow quirks, "Oh? With who? Know just about everyone here. Maybe I can point you in the right direction."

I shake my head, "I doubt you'd know her personally."

Lifting his cup again, he gulps down the rest of its contents. "Ah. I see." *Thud!* He drops the now empty mug onto the ale logged counter sliding it to the barmaid. The man gets up from his seat swiftly, calling out a farewell to the barmaid and turning towards us. "Well, good luck with your 'important business'." His fingers crook into air quotes on the last sentence before he makes his way to the door where a small shadowy figure stands in the arch of it, waiting for him. He loops his arm around her shoulders but the act looks more parental than it does romantic. The hood on her cloak covers her face concealing any features except for two inhuman gold eyes that bore into me. My Wield flickers underneath my skin the longer I hold her stare, only settling down when he urges her out into the street.

"You alright?" Will asks.

I shake my head and refocus on the present company. "Yes, yeah, of course. Tired is all. We should get some rest before tomorrow." He inclines his head and hands me one of the two keys.

The rooms weren't anything special but it wouldn't have mattered, the bed in the center of the small room was all I wanted next to the bathtub that connected our two rooms to each other.

The warm water almost put me to sleep and I had to drag myself out of it and onto the lumpy mattress. Morning I knew would come to quickly. And I was right. Will claimed to have spent fifteen minutes shaking me awake until I finally came too. I had expected to be the more anxious one when it came to our plan to just show up on her doorstep, but it was Will who couldn't stop fidgeting next to me as we stared up at the imposing castle.

"Do we knock?" He asks. His voice is as twitchy as my Wield, which writhes under my skin in anticipation or maybe that feeling is dread.

CREAKKKKK!

The doors open to reveal a group of guards laughing and spilling out onto the steps. The men nearly colliding with Will and I.

"You." The guard closest to the opening points at me his voice filling with vitriol. I have to squint for a moment until the recognition hits me, *the man from the tavern.* Same red hair, same scar, just this time his hair is pulled up and he wears armor.

He sweeps down the steps quickly drawing his sword. The rest of the men follow suit, caging the two of us in. I put him my hands up in mock surrender. "Me." I say, but his face remains hard. Mistrust and anger taking over. "Based on your clothing today I guess you do know the woman I'm looking for. If you recall, I have business here."

"Not here you don't." He growls, the blade pressing deeper into my shirt.

"Oy!" Someone whistles from inside flagging the redhead over to him, when he doesn't heed the summons, the other soldier trots down the steps to whisper into his ear. He looks unconvinced of whatever the other man is telling him, nevertheless he drops the sword from my stomach and beckons us to follow him.

"Ror, do you really think this was a good idea?" Will whispers to me, trying to not draw the attention of our silent escorts.

"Which part of 'this' are you referring to?" I snip. "Personally, I am going to take it as a good sign that the guards are choosing to escort us instead of killing us on sight." His blue eyes widen.

"Oh great. Is there any part of this plan where we don't end up dead?" He bites back, I shrug my shoulders. "I'm getting tired of you shrugging." He mutters under his breath. I slide a glance towards Will and see a frown forming in his brow. "She is supposedly sadistic. What makes you think someone as prolific as she is, would extend their aid again?"

"You're just now asking these questions?" I droll. He stops mid-walk, turning in towards me. His face searches mine the frustration plain. I look past him at the guards waiting for us, locking eyes again with the redhead. "Apologies gentlemen. Just stopped to admire the view". I say waving my hands around at the high ceilings.

The two closest to us move to open the doors we've stopped in front of. The stone groans as it opens, our group shuffling in. I gape at the massive arches and red hue cast over the black walls and floors from the stained glass ceilings. All except for one spot. Behind her single throne is nothing but an ominous wall of black. Not even the light emanating from the stained glass penetrates it. The entire room looks like it is bleeding. I don't know why I am not surprised to find that there is no queen waiting for us.

"Off to a great start." Will complains.

I roll my eyes at him, trying not to make too much of a scene in front of her soldiers. "Will! Are you going to be angry with me and gripe the entire way? Because I could've left you behind instead of Bennett!" I hiss. His face flashes with hurt before his agitation returns.

"This better work." He snaps under his breath.

It has to, I think. *If my father keeps squandering what little resources we have left, we won't survive another season against Hadar's Guards.*

I toggle back and forth between addressing the armed men and keeping my face forward. Unfortunately, my companion's fidgeting starts to wear on my resolve.

"Excuse me," My voice echoes off the stone drawing their conversation to a close as all eyes turn on me, "but do you know when the Queen plans to join us? We don't have time on our side I am afraid." I try to convey the urgency while also curbing my annoyance. I can be diplomatic, I can be charming, but patience has never been my strong suit. It already has run out with my imp of a father, and I would prefer it not run out with my only chance at saving my kingdom.

The guards all exchange looks with one another, and then the burly one from the tavern laughs. A big, almost disturbing, laugh considering the circumstances and the others are quick to join him. "I'm sorry, but did I say something humorous?" My tone gaining an edge.

"Turn yourself around and wait. Could be a while." Murmurs of agreement rumble through the group. Will, disgruntled by the disrespect shifts, in a slightly defensive stance by stepping ahead of me. It dawns on me then that we never introduced ourselves. We never introduced ourselves and they let us in anyways. *What are they playing at...* an unsettling feeling sinks into the bottom of my stomach as I lean into my friend.

"Will, this is obviously not our court."

He rolls his eyes at me and mumbles "What makes you say that?"

"We never introduced ourselves." I say.

"Hmm?"

My shoulders sag, "I said, we never introduced ourselves. They have no idea who we are and yet they're allowing us to meet their queen."

"Supposedly." He mumbles.

I ignore the remark, "it'll be fine." I whisper, more to myself than anyone else. "I'll just announce myself when she accepts our audience." He doesn't acknowledge what I am saying, his eyes fixated on the black void behind the dais.

I will not be leaving this damned dark castle without an army behind me and a queen leading it. I will wait. I will be patient. Vellar demands I be patient.

I'm done being patient.

At this rate, my legs are aching. I continue to stand with no more attempts at interacting with our escorts. Will has taken to a squat his propriety dissipating with each passing second.

We're an afterthought. One would think when meeting with their neighboring kingdom, animosity or not, that they would make it top priority. Clear she doesn't feel that way. But then again we never announced who we were, meaning she may not have any idea who we are at all.

"I'd heard we had visitors." Will jumps to a standing position at the intruding voice and I straighten the lapels on my jacket. A tall man aged about mid forties walks towards us from the side of the room. "I wasn't expecting ones of *your sort* however." He speaks out in a loud thick accent. He moves towards the throne stepping just behind it. I recognize him from the scrolls and a handful of trade meetings - Felix Grim.

"A-hem. I apologize for the informality of our arrival but—"

BAM! The doors to the throne room fly open.

My mouth gapes slightly. Will's too. "Gods help us all." He whispers.

Covered head to toe in blood, a small woman struts past us straight to the dais, an air of smug superiority blankets her.

She doesn't look the least bit phased at Will and I's twin faces of shock while she takes her seat.

Her head falls to rest on her left hand, her legs are crossed and eyes are narrowed on me. She has a striking gaze, *bright gold*, just like— *A small shadowy figure stands in the arch of it...gold glints at me from under the hood. Two eyes, stare back* - last night, it was *her* waiting for the guard.

"Felix dear." Gods help *me...that voice.*

Her annoyance cracks through the steady cadence. "There are two pieces of spoiled meat in my throne room, *why*?" She slowly slides her eyes to the man next to her. He looks bemused by her appearance despite the blood pooling beneath her.

She's a disaster, I can't stop staring.

When he doesn't answer I take that as my cue and step up to introduce myself, "Excuse me, your Highness if I may-"

"You may not" she says as she hops off the dais. In a startling quick succession of movements she now is directly in front of me, playing with a dagger between her fingers - *where she pulled that from I've no idea* - "Felix. Who, or rather, *what* are they?" Her head cocks at me, the dagger tip now poised against my throat. She's holding it casually, like it's an extension of her and not a weapon.

Felix looks up at the ceiling, his stance not much different from a tired father dealing with a rowdy toddler instead of a councilman addressing his queen. "Highness, this is His Majesty Prince Rorin of Vellar and his...lackey." Shock shoots through Will and I at Felix's knowledge of who we are. "They requested to portal here, you denied them, and it would seem they came anyway." His voice is monotonous as she sheaths her dagger back into a hidden pocket against her ribs.

Noted, the tiny queen comes with sharp toys.

"Hmm." She tilts her head, considering us. "They said you were desperate to meet me. But you don't look desperate to me." Her thin bronzed fingers lift towards my face, her sharp fingernails ghosting down my jaw line. She spins on her heel, ascends the steps to her throne and plops down into her seat. The still wet substance on her clothes squelches against the stone.

It's now or never, or I risk losing our one chance at an ally. My conscience reminds me.

"Queen Eveera," She lifts her eyes to look me at me directly. I bet just about anyone would piss themselves under her leveled stare.

I wait for her objection, but it doesn't come, so I continue on. "We have a...situation, on our hands, one I am sure you are aware of as it is fast approaching your doors." I pause searching her face for any indication she knows what I am talking about but she gives me nothing. "For years, King Baelor of Hadar, has waged a mass genocide on the outer kingdoms. The kingdoms of Mellant and Peverell have already fallen. The King of Evendell however has made a deal with him. Despite that, they still decline under his siege." Both hers and Felix's expressions remain still.

"The Kingdom of Vellar has been keeping him at bay but we won't survive much longer before his Guards overrun our borders." With a steady foot, I take a step closer to her. "My father thinks continuing to squander away our resources on these petty skirmishes will deter Hadar's Guards from invading. When all it will do is weaken us until they have no one left to block their way." I loose a heavy sigh. "Baelor is greedy, he won't stop at just our kingdom. If he succeeds in felling Evendell *and* Vellar then the Obsidian Kingdom will be next." I take another step towards her. Looking me up and down, she uncoils herself. Her position on the dais leaving her higher than me. "I am desperate. I promise you."

"Tsk tsk tsk. And what exactly are you desperate for, Vellaran?" She's circling me like a predator stalking its prey, the glint of something in her hands before cool metal brushes against my throat. *That's twice now she's had me at her blade.*

I tilt my stare down. Such a mesmerizing sight she is. In my court, if she approached me in this manner, she would be apprehended immediately and tried for threatening the heir to the throne. Alas, we are not in my court and so here I stand with a blade to my throat - *again*. Great.

Maybe Will was right to think this was a terrible idea.

"I have done research on you, your Highness. You have an extensive army made up of lethally trained men and women. Those are numbers we could only dream of having." I try to appeal to her, complimenting her armies, boosting her superiority complex. "Rumors would suggest you even have different creatures under your employ...Serpentes', Oriks, and Shifters." Her lips purse in contemplation. "My formal request is that your military forces join ours in common cause against King Baelor and Hadar's Guards. This fight isn't just one against my kingdom. As I said he will come for yours as well."

She stands still next to me, the dagger pointed at my throat unwavering. "I see." She lowers her weapon. Backing up towards Will, her head bobs up and down, assessing him. He tenses under her scrutiny.

"You see?" I ask, hearing the irritation now present in my voice.

"That's what I said isn't it?" She rolls her eyes as she circles Will. "This seems all very advantageous for you. But I don't see how this will benefit me." She sits down, crossing her legs on the ground, and stares up at Will. "Does it speak?" She asks, looking at me. Will, in all the years he has been my companion, has never lost the battle between propriety and rudeness. Especially not in the presence of royals - myself not included. In the span of five minutes Obsidian's Queen has plucked at every band of my man's restraint.

The muscle in his jaw feathers his teeth clenching together. "I speak, your Highness, I just don't see my need to interject between your conversation with his Majesty at this time." He keeps his stare ahead not meeting her gaze. Propriety won out it seems.

Her jaw drops as she gets back up to her feet, those golden eyes glinting with something. "Fascinating. Felix dear, did you hear that? It speaks!" She exclaims.

"I heard, Your Highness."

Will turns his head, his eyes pleading with me to step in and end this.

"Time is not in our favor. Not with the resources dwindling as quickly as they are. To repeat myself, at this rate we won't survive another season and then Baelor and his Guard will be right at your doorstep." I rest my hand on her arm. A forward move maybe but I hope it appeals to her better nature, if she *has* a better nature.

Her gaze drops immediately to my hand on her bicep. She takes it, grabbing onto my fingers and removing my grip as if repulsed.

"No."

No. Just one word and yet it slices through me like a sword. *No.*

I see a beat of relief mixed with disappointment pass over Will's face.

"Excuse me, did you just say 'No'?" The grip on what little patience I had has long since passed now. No was always a possibility, Will wouldn't shut up about it, but to still hear the word was another story.

"Do I need to spell it out for you? Here you go - N. O." Her attention switches to picking out the blood - that is now drying on her scalp - out of her hair strands.

"What is wrong with you?" The question slips out before I can stop it. "You'd let a tyrant continue, let two more kingdoms fall? Risk losing your own in the process? Do so many lives at stake mean so little to you, your Highness?" I've resorted to yelling at her it seems.

She turns to her councilman. "Felix."

He nods. "Of course." His arms wave out to Will and I. "I can show you both to your quarters. You must be exhausted from the outer lands." He descends the dais, motioning for us to follow him. Eveera offers us a sarcastic wave without looking back up.

"I'm sorry. But," I spin in place and walk back towards her wagging my finger, "no. You can't just say no without fully hearing me out." She stares at me, a smirk playing on her lips. She wants a challenge, a game?

Fine, I can do that. "You denied our request to portal here, but allowed us at the gates." My fists ball up. "You kept us waiting for gods know how long, parade around covered in gods know what, just to *dismiss us?* Your attitude is one that would have your pretty little head in most places. Queen or not." All I can see is red at this point. She is the ONE chance I have left to save my own kingdom and she rejected my request in a matter of ten minutes.

My last hope dashed in *ten minutes.*

"But we aren't anywhere else are we? So unfortunately my 'pretty little head' will stay seated right between my shoulders. The *horror*." She mock pouts in my direction.

"You, you, YOU!" I step forward. My feet are moving before my mind can stop me. I'm completely out of control and crossing too many lines. She sits there watching my fit with a stupid grin on her face.

"Me, me, ME." She taunts and magic flares in my palms.

Will's voice sounds behind me. "Rorin, back off. She's said her piece today and we need to rest." He steps onto the first step grabbing at my wrist, but I stay rooted in place.

"No, Will." My finger makes contact with her sternum as if to grind my point in, "we trekked for six fucking days. All the while, I had to listen to your complaining ass through those damn monster infested woods. We had one chance to convince her that this is worth her time. The least she can do is sit and have a proper negotiation with us." I look between the two of them.

"Rorin, you are out of..." he stops, voice trailing off. I turn my head to look at him but, his pupils are blown wide. Righting myself, my eyes follow where his were drawn. Everything has gone deathly still. Eveera starts to laugh quietly, that stupid smile turning feral.

"You shouldn't have touched me." We both look down to where my finger is still pressed against her. "It upsets her." Her voice is barely above a whisper.

"Her?" Will and I both say at the same time, as a pair of large golden eyes appear out of the cave mouth behind the throne and a black dragon's head moves into view directly behind the queen.

Oh *fuck*.

EVEERA

This is always my favorite part. Vada, as deadly as she looks, won't make a move unless I give her the directive. Not that they know that. But scaring them shitless is just as fun to me as watching her rip someone a part. The princeling will think twice before getting so bold a second time.

"He touches you again and it'll be a bonfire." she speaks down the bond while growling audibly for everyone. The fear spikes into his companion's eyes, his name slipping from my mind. *I'll call you Mousy,* I think. Much to my dismay, the prince looks less afraid and more awestruck.

"I'll handle it." I tell her.

She huffs a hot roll of steam, clacking her teeth in warning before retreating until once again only the glow of her eyes are visible. "Fine. You've made your point for today. I will meet you both tomorrow morning in the courtyard. You wish to converse and *negotiate* then meet me there and we'll talk. Felix," He looks expectantly at me, "handle the rest of this for me." I step past the prince forcing him to drop his hand from my sternum.

The blood has begun to dry on my skin and I smell like a butcher shop. "Thank you." His companion says quietly.

Cute, I say to myself. *Let them think this will get them what they want.* I turn, smiling pleasantly, "oh and *princeling*," he bristles at the nickname, "touch me again and I'll have to portal your ashes back to Vellar."

My feet carry me down the rest of the steps. "You can touch me but I can't touch you, huh?" He asks from over my shoulder. I ignore him.

Once out the door I slip into one of the passageways cutting through the castle and go straight to my bedroom. My shower calls to me the moment I am in the room. It was quick work removing the sticky clothes and hopping under the stream. My head falls back against the wall, rivulets of water tinge pink as they roll down my skin. *Bleeding gods, this day.*

KNOCK KNOCK!

If I have to entertain another person today.... "I'm in the showerrrrr." I groan turning the faucet off. My hands are fumbling my hair up into a towel on the top of my head when I whip open the left side door to my bedroom. "What?!" I snap.

Felix's face is stunned for a moment, before his eyes avert towards the ceiling. "The Prince and his companion are settled in at the end of this wing. I have Maxwell and Orem guarding their rooms." My hands move to pull the hem of my nightdress down a little more.

"Felix." He keeps his eyes fixed on the ceiling. *Snap! Snap!* "Felix. You can look down now." His head slowly lowers warily, both shoulders slouching in relief when he notices the dress is appropriately covering my body.

I walk across the room and crawl into my bed, the mattress sinking underneath my weight while Felix stands at the foot. "How long am I playing host for?" I ask.

"Six days." He replies and I groan audibly. "You have avoided these sorts of interactions for ten years Evie. There was bound to be a time when someone would come knocking on our doors sooner rather than later." He moves around the bed tucking my hand in between his.

I hate it. The softness of it too much, too overwhelming.

"He must be an idiot." I throw the covers back, standing and skirting around him to disconnect from the moment of familiarity. "Does he really expect me to help him?" I ask pulling my hair down from the towel. "Does he not understand the circumstances of *why* our kingdoms don't cooperate?"

"Evie, it is possible he is unaware, this could work to your advantage. It would seem the prince and his father may be on separate terms on how to handle this situation with the Kingdom of Hadar. I urge you to at least hear them out. Do what you're best at. Play your games, use your upper hand and eavesdrop, find their every angle. But do consider their request in the case they're being true." His gray eyes bear into the back of my skull as I drag the brush through my wet hair.

"And what would my own people think of that? The people who work in this court?"

"Our citizens only know the grief. Not the logistics. The respect will still be there, from both them and those that work for you."

His words bounce around in my head, "I'm going to the Room." I say curtly, walking to my doors to show him out.

"And dinner?" *Such a father.*

"Not hungry for food. Set the two parasites in the dining hall. Join them, converse and find out as much as you can. I'll be late." The door clicks shut behind him. I reach over, grabbing my weapons belts and slipping on my boots. My nightdress is a little unusual for my plans. But at least, it's black. Black always hides blood better. *I knew I should've waited to shower.*

Percy's whimper irritates every nerve in my body. The tattoos inked onto my skin writhe around, all of them eager to let go of the magic clinging to them. "Poor pathetic Percy…I thought we had an understanding? Didn't we? You were going to wait in your cell until I was ready to kill you. NOT, try to wage and barter with the guards or pretend to drink the vials given to you." He mutters incoherently as I tuck a shiv into his right hand. He tries to release it but I press it tighter into his palm. "Do not let that go," I whisper, "it's important."

I walk around him, tying my damp hair up into a top knot. "You've disappointed me greatly Percy. I could just let Vada sink her teeth into you, but I think you need a few moments to yourself. Don't you?" The crack of my knuckles loud in his ears. "Yes I think you do, I think you need a moment to confront yourself and see what a disappointment you turned into."

His desperation reeks as he fights miserably against the inky black tendrils of my magic. They enter every orifice on his body, infiltrating his senses both inside and outside — my Wield manifesting and manipulating the victim's biggest fear. A satisfying feeling warms through me as my magic sinks its teeth into him. Some might find this sadistic. I find it therapeutic.

My shoulders against Vada's right leg, I admire my handiwork, while tilting my head to look into the golden eye closest to me. . "*They want me to help.*"

"*Hmph. Everyone wants something eventually, little demon. You humans are constantly taking more than what you are owed. Greed is your biggest weakness.*" She huffs, turning back to the writhing man in the center of the room.

"*I suppose.*" I muse. "*Though I don't have that issue.*"

Vada snorts, "*No you, little demon, have a whole different set of issues.*" She lifts her imposingly large head and her snout turning up. "*Please end the man, his sniveling has become tiresome.*" She slinks backwards moving deeper into her cave, leaving me with the miserable son of a bitch.

"Oh come now. Shhh. It'll all be over soon. The worst is nearly over." I croon. He looks pitifully in my direction, his pupils dilating wider the closer I get to him. "Percy dear," I pat his sweaty cheek twice, "slit your throat please, your whines are grating against my nerves." At the will of my Wield he takes the shiv in his hand and drags it across his throat. Blood spraying along my face and neck. "*Release him.*" I whisper the subtle command that beckons my magic back into its serpent counterparts. I stare down at the gore. "Told you it would be over soon." I exhale letting my shoulders roll. *Finally some peace and quiet*, I think, clapping my hands together before kicking the dead Vellaran's boot for good measure and leaving the room.

"*Don't eat him.*" I warn Vada, her presence lingering closely in my mind.

The room shakes with a low growl rumbling through her cave. "*I'd sooner eat you.*"

RORIN

Felix leads the way towards our rooms leaving only a trail of two guards behind us rather than the five we were accompanied by earlier.

"Here we are." With his hands on the knobs of the double doors, he pushes, revealing a suite following the same color palette as the castle. The blood red drapes frame a wall of large windows, but the view outside is much darker than home. "There is a sitting room, a bedroom through that door there and the bathroom suite is to your left once you enter the bedroom." He paces around the room before turning to me, "Prince Rorin these will be your rooms during your stay here and Sir Will you will be directly across the hall. I will leave you both to rest now but if you would please join me in an hour for dinner. The guards," he motions to the two that followed us, "posted outside of your rooms will lead you to the dining hall."

He exits swiftly, leaving both Will and I to watch him move down the hall where his body simply vanishes into the darkness at the end of it. Will nods a thanks to our guards before closing the door. "This all feels very...odd." He says as he starts to fidget around the room - snooping.

"Sit down Will, no bogeymen is going to pop out of the stone walls." I pause looking around dramatically. "I'm pretty sure she's down the hall." When my eyes land back on him, he's frowning in my direction.

"I am your guard Rorin, it's in my job description to protect you, which entails checking all areas for potential hazards." He scoffs, continuing his investigation.

"It was odd though, you're right." I concede, waiting for his reaction. *Three, two, one...*

His body slowly rolls back up to straight, his head swiveling around like an owl to look at me. "What was that?" *And there it is.* "Did you just admit that I was right about something?"

"You are positively insufferable." I try to stop the direction of this conversation but it's already too late. His grin is growing wider by the second. He continues on with his taunts for several more minutes, before I start to feel annoyed. "Are you done, Will? We need to rest up, we have dinner with Felix in forty-five minutes." I fold my arms beneath my head leaning back to close my eyes. "Wake me up will you?" The sound of him getting up to head into his own quarters is the only indication I have of him leaving.

He mocks me with an, "*I was right*" and an, "*I told you so.*" before he closes the door.

With a few minutes alone to myself, I find my mind drifting back to the tiny queen. She took an audience with me drenched in blood - I wonder if this is a common sight around here or if it phased anyone else in that room besides Will and I. I don't think I've ever seen my parents in a state other than pristine. My father especially has a penchant for keeping up the "proper image" as he calls it. As a kingdom of healers and portal masons, we are meant to be seen as new age, brilliant, and peace driven. Little do they know what a hypocrite their king really is.

Will woke me up with an obnoxious greeting. Still riding his high of me conceding to agree with him three quarters of an hour ago.

As promised, the guards delivered us to the dining hall where Felix is already seated to the right of the queen's chair. Looking up from his papers, he nods at us in greeting. "Gentlemen, I see you found us alright. Rooms comfortable enough?" He asks.

"Yes, thank you. Quite the display, your court. And a dragon! Incredible you managed to fit it indoors." Will supplies. *Well that was subtle*, I think. I shoot him a quick glare for being so obvious.

Felix offers us a guarded smile as he sets down his paperwork. "Yes, well, our queen and her familiar prefer to be in close quarters."

"Of course." I interject before Will can blunder the conversation any further. "We only meant to imply that we weren't aware any dragons were still around. Let alone docile. Most of our scholars thought them to be extinct." Will gives me an apologetic look as he picks at his food in front of him.

"Vada is anything but docile I assure you." Felix states. His hands are placed in his lap and he makes no move to eat the food in front of him. "Now, the queen will be meeting you promptly at daybreak. I'll have clothes delivered to each of your rooms this evening for you to wear tomorrow. I trust that will be met with your approval?" He blinks at me, waiting for my reply.

"Clothes? I don't understand. It's a negotiation...what would be inappropriate about our regular clothing?" Will asks. Felix looks him up, down, and tilts his head, clearly contemplating whether he wants to answer that.

"The queen...likes to multitask. I thought it would be prudent for you both to wear comfortable attire. She prefers to keep things a little informal." He replies curtly.

"Informal?" Will's tone pitches up an octave.

Her head of council's shoulders sag. "Sir Will, I understand you come from a long line of noblemen in your family. Am I correct?" Felix's head cocks in the same predatory manner as Eveera.

"Yes, you're correct." He answers.

"And yet, you were chosen for military duty. To act as Prince Rorin's personal guard, quite out of standard procedures." I see Will's eyes flash.

"I was second in line. I'm proud to hold this position." I smile, for as much grief as I give him, he's never failed his role.

Felix wipes at the corners of his mouth with a napkin. "Mm. Oh I have no doubt you take pride in your work." He challenges again. I can see the gears working in Will's head as he quietly agrees, pleasing Felix with the answer. "You see, no matter how averse to formalities our queen may be. She is still our queen, making us quite proud to serve underneath her." His tone is even and steady as he lays that truth before us.

I use the moment to switch the inquisition back to Felix. "Speaking of Queen Eveera, is she not joining us tonight?" I catch he slightest crack in Felix's cool and professional demeanor.

"No. She has other...court matters to deal with presently. She'll be along later, I'm sure." He motions for the staff to come over and clear our plates. Will and I exchange glances. "Would either of you want a nightcap? I would very much like to hear more about your request for the use of our armies, if you don't mind?" *Here's your opening*, I think. If I can get Felix as head of her council to side with us on the matter he can usher her into the same direction.

"Yes, of course I..." Movement slipping out of the wall panels cuts off my line of thought - *do they just move through walls around here?* My gaze snags on the queen, clad only in an excruciatingly tight, short-sleeved nightgown and calf high military grade boots. She has on her hips a low slung belt filled with weapons - most notably throwing stars. *Interesting choice.* And despite having met her only a few hours ago somehow I am not even surprised to see she has more blood spattered all across her neck and face. The black snake tattoos coiled from wrist to shoulder ending at her sternum however, is a surprise.

She walks briskly past the table, not sparing any of us a single glance. Instead, she reaches for one of the exiting servants trays, grabs a few rolls and stomps out of the room.

Felix's brow twitches in concern. "Ezra." The name an order, and a built guard with blonde hair tied back moves off the wall. He nods at Felix, following quickly on the heels of the queen, ending the bizarre interruption. "Now, I believe you were just about to tell me your hypothetical plans for our military."

I straighten my jacket, sitting up taller in my seat. "Before we move on to that...is she always covered in blood?" I ask looking at Felix directly.

A collective "Yes" from every person in the room sounds. My stomach dips, the realization that being around her is most likely going to end up with my blood on her skin and clothes.

What have I done?

EVEERA

Felix has ordered Ezra to follow me. I just don't have the energy to acknowledge him yet but I don't bother closing my doors.

The shower turns on for the second time tonight.

I prefer not to sleep with someone's blood on me.

My skin twitches at the presence of someone at my back. The shower becomes a lot more claustrophobic than it was a few seconds ago.

"E..." he starts, his chin resting on top of my head.

"No thoughts." I say, turning around to face him.

His sandy blonde hair is already damp, falling around his face as he looks down at me. It's not hard to imagine how we ended up here. We got close after he was placed as my head guard. He took his job very seriously and I...did not. It's difficult to take someone meant to protect you seriously when you received the level of weapons and Wielding training that I did.

So, instead of respecting his role, I chose to charm and flirt with him until he either quit or fell into my bed. Clearly, based on his very naked presence in my shower, the latter won.

"I missed you." He whispers.

Obviously. The voice inside of my head chides.

His gaze drops to my lips, but it's not a look of heat or passion. It's a look of observation - like I am something to study. His hand moves to cup my cheek while his head dips down. Our lips graze together for a second before he presses his mouth fully onto mine. His kisses are quick to become insistent, his mouth searching mine desperately. My arms loop around his neck, our tongues warring for dominance. It feels sloppy, uncoordinated, and tired. For *me* at least.

He breaks away his breath coming in heavy pants as he sweeps his mouth down over my collarbone and then latching on my neck. Both of his palms have dropped to lift my ass. He lifts me up easily, my back connecting with the shower tiles. The edges of my nails leave half-moons on his slick shoulders. I dig them in hard to anchor myself against him.

From this point everything becomes routine. The same pattern and energy it always has, I'd hope with how infrequent we've been in this position together in the past months that maybe things would feel different. That it would be more. But as our bodies move against one another, it feels more unbalanced than ever, it feels like something is missing. Whatever burn there might have been five years ago is gone. His name used to tumble off my lips, now I force it out, "Ezra..."

"*I missed you*" he said.

Those three words settle sourly in my stomach. If only I could have returned the sentiment.

"Mom? Mommy?! Mom?!" I ran straight past my guards, running through the empty castle to search every room. My bare feet are loud as I sprint across the cold stone.

They said I was safe, they said she was safe - I have to find her.

"MOM!?" She isn't in any of her usual sitting rooms. Maybe they moved her to a safe room? I think. But no, she would have been with me then. I race down the hall and see the light glowing from under her and father's bedroom doors. She doesn't stay in those rooms anymore - not after he didn't come home. My hand reaches out in front of me, shaking as I grip onto the handle of her door.

I don't know why I am so nervous. I heard a guard shout "CLEAR!" not too far back. But the air feels off in this wing and there is a pit growing in my stomach as I slowly push the door open. She hasn't been herself lately, and I don't want to upset her.

"Mommy? Are you-"

My eyes fly open, my fingers clutching my chest as I gasp for breath. "It's just a dream..." I whisper, "just a dream." I blink away the sweat and tears from my eyes, Ezra is sleeping soundly next to me. My startled wake-up doing nothing to disrupt him.

So much for guard duty, I scoff quietly to myself, even though I know Armond is always posted outside at night.

I crawl quietly off, tiptoeing to the hidden door in my wall that leads into the passageways. My feet follow the familiar way down to my Room, the steps I take are silent against the floor. Vada's consciousness is present in my mind and I know she felt the dream, our bond doesn't allow her to be exempt from the more visceral ones.

"Little demon." She grumbles.

"No arguing." Even my internal voice sounds exhausted.

"*Torturing yourself is beneath you.*" Her gaze lowers to meet mine while slinking further into the room, steam rolls from her nostrils and coasts over my body, blanketing me in warmth.

"*I said no arguing. If you don't want to stay and watch then don't. Either way this is happening.*" I turn only my head to look at her. She lays her substantially large body onto the ground decidedly out of her cave. Her eyes narrow, her only further protest of her disapproval.

CRACK!

I take a shuddering breath in, the familiar sting and heat spreading through me, "One."

I wanted to avoid the domesticity of sliding back into bed with Ezra after tonight, so I took off in the passageways towards Axel's room instead. There's no point in knocking, I can already hear his obnoxious snores through the paneling. *Click!* I latch the door shut behind me. His room is dark save for the one dim sconce he left on by his main door.

There's not much to his quarters other than it looks like a smaller version of mine. Most of the rooms in this wing do, I could've chosen to move into the Queen's Suites when I took up my crown, but the thought of being in her wing of the castle churned my stomach. I chose to stay in my childhood bedroom instead.

"Shit!" I hiss, picking up my foot, pain lancing through my shoulders from the sudden movement.

"What in the gods?" Axel's groggy head peeks up at me from beneath his covers. He scrambles, to turn on the lamp on his bedside, illuminating his corner of the room. "Eveera, what the hell?" He blinks a few times before he takes in the full sight of my disheveled state, his face softening in the process.

I ignore the question and look down to see my foot's assailant was a rogue dart that never made it into the board hung above his wardrobe. "You should pick up your room." I note, hobbling to his bed.

He throws back the covers scooting over for me to climb in. "You should pick up your feet." I turn my head, glaring at his sleep addled face.

"Turn the light off." I snap.

"So bossy. At least buy me dinner first, before you start commanding me in the bedroom." Despite his graphic protest, he reaches over and turns it off. "Did you put the healing balm on."

I nod my head obnoxiously against the pillow, twinging a little as I do.

"Did you bandage them?"

"Yes." I groan.

"Are you avoiding Ezra again?"

I bury my face into the pillow. "I'm avoiding this question. Now go to sleep." He chuckles quietly, flipping over into a more comfortable position that shakes the small bed. "Injured." I whine.

"Self-inflicted doesn't count." He quips. *Asshole*, I think to myself.

My body sinks into his bed and his hand reaches across the mattress his fingers lacing with mine. The warmth he gives off lulls me into a deep sleep, this time the dream doesn't come back. In fact all of the thoughts inside of my head go quiet.

I don't wake up again until we hear - *BANG! BANG! BANG!* - on the door. I squeeze my eyes shut, pretending to still be asleep while Axel drags himself up out of bed to go see who is at the door. "You're not fooling anyone Eveera, wake up." *Felix*. My hands pull the covers back, and I sit myself up and face him. "Any reason there is an odd splatter pattern in your Room?"

He knows, he always knows. Even if I've never admitted it.

I grab the extra pair of shoes stored here I have from within Axel's wardrobe. "All the splatter patterns seemed normal to me. Is there a reason you were in there?" Next I reach for my extra pair of pants, slipping them over my curves and cinching them at my waist.

"Just curious is all." He hums. "You have a meeting, remember? You might want to..." He waves his hands in gesture around me, "get dressed."

Ezra is already waiting for me, sword in hand. "Ez, eager to lose?" I throw him a wink while pulling my sword out of it's holster.

His shoulders shake, laughing, "how many times have I won sparring with you, hmm?" He walks in a wide circle around me.

The hilt of the blade spins in my hand. "As many times as I have let you." A frown forms on his face and he lunges for me, his bulky armor slows him down with its weight. I swing my sword down towards his legs, pushing his advance back. We go a few rounds, swords clanking against one another. "Oh come on, you can do better than this!" I taunt, which only eggs him on to move faster, duck lower, and block harder.

He's here, the voice in my mind warns. The air shifts around me, disrupting my momentum. I don't know how I know it's him - but I do. Ezra charges at me out of the corner of my eye, trying to use the distraction as a way to one me up. Without sparing him a look, I swing at him, clashing against his blow and shoving hard. He loses his footing and stumbles to the ground. *Well that was lucky,* I think. My knee falls onto his chest plate, the new position allowing me to press my sword against his throat. "You're dead." Even through the metal of his armor I can feel him tense underneath me.

"Your" *Grunt.* "left side is open." His nose brushes mine while he leans up as best as he can.

I relent, climbing off of him and taking hold of his hand. "What would that matter? My sword would have sliced clean through your throat." I argue, the two of us still not acknowledging our guests.

He shucks off his armor and moves to the wall of weapons, selecting a few. "Well it matters, your Highness, because it gave me a few seconds when you were pinning me to stab a dagger right through your left ribs." He takes his fingers, grazing my side. I don't miss the fact his eyes drift up to look at the two men behind me, before he looks back down. "When leaning on top of someone you have to angle your body properly." I subtly push his fingers away, not allowing the touch to turn into something more possessive.

"I think you know well that I have no issues angling my body properly."

He rolls his eyes at me. "I meant when delivering the killing blow, Eveera."

I laugh and turn around. "You." I point at the prince.

"Your Highness." He and his companion both say in unison, Mousy tries to look everywhere but straight at me. The prince however, looks me up and down lazily, a smirk on his lips when his eyes finally make their way to mine.

"I need a volunteer."

"A volunteer?" His deep voice rattles something loose in my chest. I slip one of the throwing stars I've grown to favor and spin it between my thumb and fore-finger. "Well you aren't just going to stand on the edge all day, are you? You came here to talk, I came here to train. So, I need a volunteer." My empty hand beckons one of them towards me. The moment Mousy steps over the edge I pitch my arm back, launching the throwing star in their direction.

To my shock the prince stops the momentum, catching the star before it could find purchase. Before I have time to process, the sound of it whizzing by me and embedding in the wall, fills my ears. My gaze switches from the star and back to him. "It's not nice to throw things." He says, dusting off his hands.

I disagree.

"You can borrow from the selection on the table or wall." I note.

He clears his throat. "A-hem, I think I'll just use my own."

"Ha." I glance at him from the corner of my eye. "Scared I tainted the metal? Imbued it with something?" I back up onto the mat, sliding a dagger in tight against my chest. "Ezra, you're with Mousy here. And you…princeling, you'll be my volunteer."

Ezra appraises his opponent, waiting impatiently for Mousy to be ready. He'll launch himself at his new opponent as soon as he's given the command, and he'll fight dirty.

"Engage." I say.

Rorin and I both watch as Ezra pivots, swinging his sword hard. The move leaves his opponent with little time to recover or block his blow. "That was an unorthodox way to start a sparring match. Your boyfriend over there didn't even look ready."

"Never said we do things the orthodox way around here, princeling. Ezra can clearly handle his own, your man on the other hand…"

He glares in my direction at that assumption. I shift my stance to be in front of him. "You have until one of us lands a mock killing blow to explain your point and convince me why I should help you." He looks at me with a raised brow.

"If I lay one on you, will an army of men come through those doors and bushes or perhaps a *dragon*?" His head tilts in challenge as he unsheathes his sword.

"Mm, quite the suggestion." We start moving around one another, searching for openings. "Give me a good fight princeling, don't make it so easy that they think you've just let me win."

His tongue darts out, wetting his lip. My attention zeroing in on the unconscious habit. "Well since, letting their little queen win won't get me an army. I think I'll pass."

"Any day now, princeling." I bait.

He surges forward, sword angled and cutting low at my ankles. I jump out of the way, blocking his steel with mine pulling both our swords up. I turn with the momentum and bring my sword close to his stomach. A cheap shot and one he's unfortunately too quick for.

His brow is scrunched together with the effort he's putting into calculating the moves before I make them. "As I said, Hadar's Guards have already taken over Mellant and Peverell with forces in Evendell. My father's opinion is that we should keep pushing back on every small advance. But he's not the one on the front lines." *CLANK!* Our swords make contact, pushing against one another, dragging both the sword tips down.

"And you are?" I look at him before moving away from where we're connected. "I am not mocking you, I am asking. You were wearing a military jacket yesterday." He goes for another low shot at my knees. My feet barely moved me fast enough to avoid the impact.

In a flurry of quick movements I manage to land the hilt into his ribs, earning me a pained grunt. "*Oof!* Yes. I was made responsible for our military." He doesn't slow down though on his retaliation.

"You-" *Block* "Don't-" I duck under the next hit. "Sound too happy to hold that title." He lowers his sword a moment, panting. "Would you? If each skirmish or countermeasure led to losing dozens of men? Or if the towns saddled with hosting your men were struggling to feed their families. These are peasant levies, not the trained professionals like your military. They're healers, farmers, barely of age boys, and their fathers." His sword comes back up and - *Whack!* My weapon pitches out of my hands, clattering to the ground from his force. I lurch for it, Rorin's words stealing too much of my focus. The wounds on my back stretch, opening again. *Too much movement.*

"Something wrong?" He asks.

I grab my weapon from the ground and roll back up slowly, cracking my fingers and neck in the process. "Of course not. You haven't quite gotten to the part where I come into all of this." I spin out of his reach. "So blah blah you hate your job blah blah inexperienced soldiers blah blah your deaths are all imminent. If that happens then maybe I won't have such annoying neighbors." I chide.

His eyes narrow. "Didn't I though? This needs to be handled, your military knows how to handle it. I am not willing to risk more innocent lives under a tyrant."

"Just my soldiers' innocent lives."

He lowers his sword for the second time. "What?"

"You said, 'I am not willing to risk more innocent lives under a tyrant'. Do my soldiers not count as innocent?"

One of his thick hands drags through his curls, "I would consider them more contractual. Hired, they understand and choose to throw their lives into the throngs of war."

"Hmph." With my free hand I reach for one of my daggers, throwing it within inches of his neck. With astounding speed, he stops it just like the throwing star and advance on me in the next breath. His empty hand curls around my bicep and he leans down, sweat dripping down his forehead. "What did I say about throwing things?" I swallow thickly, feeling the cool tip of metal pressing into my side.

I smile, "that it wasn't nice." His throat bobs as his eyes drop down to the dagger I've replaced and now point at his heart. "But there was your first mistake. Assuming I care about being nice." I lean slightly to the right, feeling the prick of where the dagger is now nicking me. Not enough for him to notice yet, though. "Your second mistake, was thinking I fucking *care* about your kingdom."

The hurt flickers in his eyes. "You care so little about life, so little about mankind as a whole?" He asks, the sound of the spar next to us has stopped and I know they're watching our exchange.

"No I care greatly. But the lives I care for are only fodder for you. Remember? *Contractual.*" I challenge, leaning a hair more into the dagger at my side.

The frustration is growing in his eyes, the two of us standing so close we share breath. "So all this time in your precious isolation, avoiding what's really going on past your borders has left you above everyone else? What kind of a person wouldn't step in to stop, that would make you a mons—"

He's overwhelming. I close the distance and lean all the way into the blade. A gasp comes from one of the other men watching the two of us. My blood trickles down into the prince's hand, shock filling his face as he looks at what I've just done. I whisper low enough that only he can hear me, "I thought we were all under the impression that I was barely human."

Rorin yanks the blade out of my side, pushing me away from him. I stagger back, Ezra already behind me ready to catch me in case the blood loss happens too fast. My vision dances a little bit, but not before I see Mousy dragging the prince further away.

"That's enough." Ezra growls out.

The laugh I let out is weak. "Down boy, it's just a flesh wound." I reach the hand on my good side up, patting the broad shoulder next to my head. *Fuck.* "Ezra?" I have my gaze trained as best I can on the two Vellaran's faces as he hauls me backwards.

"You two," he points his sword at both of them, "I suggest you go clean up in your quarters."

"Giving orders now, Ez? I thought I was sovereign here?" I grit out while pressing my left hand to the gash. I struggle to get him to let me go wanting to make my exit without him attached to my hip.

On the trek back the staff darted out of my way, their focus fixing only on the blood left in my wake. Axel's mouth opens to ask what happened but I interrupt, "Axel dear, if you wouldn't mind please go get me Marjorie." He nods, letting me into the room and closing the door behind him.

"WHAT THE FUCK, E?!" Ezra shouts causing my head to spin. I lay back on the bed, my breathing becoming more labored. *Shit, why does this hurt so bad? It was a dagger in an area that wouldn't cause permanent damage, it's not like my body can't handle that.*

"The yelling Ezra. Please turn it down a notch." I wave limply in his direction making my best effort to shoo him.

"NO. No I will not 'turn it down a notch'. What is this insatiable need to harm yourself?!" He's still yelling, giving me the beginnings of a headache.

"Beauty isn't without pain, dear." I jest but he doesn't take the bait. "Besides I knew what I was doing."

"He *STABBED* you, Eveera! You are *queen*, you have to stop being so reckless!"

"Who stabbed you?" Felix asks, both his and Marjorie's stares drop to the bloody hand pressed to my left side.

"I did.", "The Vellaran did." Ezra and I say simultaneously.

Felix's eyes go wide. "You let him *STAB* her?!" He shouts.

"The yelling!" I snap cutting Ezra off before he talked himself into having one foot in the grave. "Rorin and I were sparring and I *leaned* into it." Marjorie's moved next to me her withered hands already glowing against me. I hate the feeling of her magic, especially the feeling of skin stitching itself back together.

"You *leaned* into a dagger?" Felix looks incredulously at me.

Marjorie makes good time, helping me to stand when she's all finished. "Yes. I thought it would be fun. I wanted to see his reaction when he drew blood, *my* blood."

I turn to Felix. "I am *fine*. I wouldn't have let him kill me, and I don't think he would have done it anyways if he needs me. It was simply a game. Have them meet me in the throne room in an hour. I'll give him his answer then."

In truth I could have told them I made my decision, before we even sparred, but I liked making him squirm. And squirm he did.

RORIN

She *fucking* stabbed herself with MY blade - her blade, I guess, considering she sent it for my throat.

"What's her angle here?" I whisper to no one but myself.

Will's voice filters into my tangled mess of thoughts. His head is in his hands staring at his feet. "You *stabbed* her. You stabbed the queen. What the actual HELL, Ror?!"

"I didn't stab her. She stabbed herself. She was taunting me, playing games, like she has been since we stepped foot in this damn castle." I pace across from him, his eyes going straight to my still bloodstained hand. His face lightens about three shades before he gets up, returning with a washcloth.

He extends it out to me and I take it gingerly, grumbling a thanks as he sits back down. "Ror, we need a game plan here. You have to watch your temper with her. They don't do things normal here." His expression is earnest.

My fingers pull at my hair in frustration, "nothing about her is normal. She's feral. Damn woman." I gripe. Will's chest is shaking out of the corner of my eye. "WHAT?!" I snap.

"I've just never seen you so worked up over a woman. Not one as uncouth as her." He laughs out.

I roll my eyes. "Oh fuck off, prick." A knock comes at the door. "You're getting that." I point.

He stands shaking his head at me, "Sure thing, boss."

We're both surprised to find her guard, Ezra, behind the door. His face revealing he'd sooner rather be anywhere else. "The queen has requested your presence."

The two of us trail after him to the throne room. It's noticeably clean of any real blood today, though the room is still bathed in red light from the glass ceiling.

Ezra leaves us in the center of the room to go stand by his queen. He leans into her ear, whispering something that I can tell makes her tense. If for not that nearly imperceptible shift in body language it would almost look like they're nuzzling.

When she raises her eyes, she locks in on me, moving off the raised platform to stand in front of us. She's nearly a head shorter than I am; but despite the height differences she still manages to make it feel like she is looking down on me. "You came."

"Did I have a choice?" I don't break our stare, instead I take note of her inhuman gold irises and the snake tattoos slithering under her sheer sleeves.

She tilts her head at me. "Mmm. I suppose not."

"And your thoughts on my proposition would be?" I challenge.

She sucks her lip in between her teeth, "Mmm. I'm not convinced. Maybe if you got on your knees and begged." Her face is smug, already thinking she's won this round. That damn mouth.

"Ha." I take a careful step towards her, making sure she knows it is *me* who is looking down on *her* - no matter how big and scary she thinks she is, "and that would convince you? Me on my knees?"

She shrugs her shoulders, looking disinterested. "Maybe."

"I don't know what more you want from me. This should satisfy both our causes as your people will never have to suffer at his hands like mine have." My hands curl into fists, trying to maintain the grip on my magic that her taunts bring out.

She points her finger up and down. "I just said. I like the idea of you begging me for something." The image of me on my knees in front of her flashes through my mind. *Fuck.*

My mouth curls up to match hers. "Your Highness, I assure you when I get on my knees, it is to do more than beg." *Two can play this game.* I hear Will choke on a cough behind me and Ezra's face goes red.

"Ha!" Her hands go to a slow clap. "Cute, princeling. Very cute."

My palms are clasped behind my back still holding tight to my Wield, "do we have a deal?" The clapping stops, but her saccharine smile stays put.

"For you to get on your knees or for you to use my army?" She's holding in a laugh, I can tell. Nothing to her is serious, everything is a game, a ploy. All of us pawns for her to toy with.

"Eveera." Ezra bites out in warning behind her but she ignores him. Felix, I see, puts a hand on his shoulder while subtly shaking his head at him in reprimand.

I sigh, trying to not sound exasperated. "For you to allow me the use of your army against King Baelor and Hadar's Guard."

A look of what I know can't be true disappointment flits across her features followed by an exaggerated yawn. "Pity. My idea sounded more fun." She moves her gaze to Will - who looks like he is about to pull his hair out from the exchange, then to Ezra, who looks about the same. Lastly, she looks at Felix. "We have a council meeting soon, do we not?"

He nods and says, "Yes, they're setting up for it now."

She sidesteps me, shouting over her shoulder, "are you coming?"

Will dips his chin to whisper in my ear, "does this mean she is agreeing?"

"Your guess is as good as mine." I have no idea what that exchange meant.

We follow her into one of the hidden passageways and are spit out into a small, well lit meeting room. Eveera takes her seat at the head, kicking her feet up. Her left leg is thrown over the right causing the slit of her dress to fall open and reveal almost her entire thigh.

She's already playing with her throwing stars, launching them at a cork board above the main doors. *Thwwwump*! The star lands perfectly in the center. *She managed that sitting down? No, correction. She did that reclining?!* I think in mild amazement.

She pulls out another one and lands another bullseye. The motion causes the arriving council members to duck and flinch. A woman who is as tall as I am, with long plaited white hair, has her hand pressed to her chest and her mouth dropped open in shock, "Your, Highness must you play with those in here?"

"There's a starboard above the door isn't there?" The woman tilts her head up to look at the board, disapproval settling into her features, "besides, Alina, it's too early for your complaints." The queen snaps. The woman, Alina, scowls and takes her seat at the end of the table, notably furthest from the queen. Felix motions for us to take two seats directly to the left of her as he takes up his own on her right. The rest of her council files in, leaving two gentlemen staring at us; I am guessing it is their seats that Will and I are sitting in.

"Frederic, Mose, you two are fine with standing for this meeting, are you not?" She asks.

They both mutter, "Of course, your Majesty."

With everyone situated she swings her legs down and stands, both of her hands braced against the edge of the table. "Fabulous, welcome to our weekly council meeting. I'd go through all the regular pleasantries where I pretend I care about your day to day lives-" I expect the council members to be insulted but they all just laugh - well all but the one councilwoman, Alina - Eveera throws them a wink and I can see the hint of a genuine smile on her lips which she quickly removes when she catches me staring. "As you all can see in Frederic and Mose's seats are two new people. I'm sure you have heard of the arrival of Prince Rorin and Mousy." Will's face heats at the nickname while nods and murmurs of confirmation rumble through everyone.

"Great, well, this is them." She sweeps her hand in our direction. Looks of disbelief cross some faces and some looks of anger enter others. "Prince Rorin, if you would be so kind as to explain why you're here and what you want from me to the council." She sits back down looking at me expectantly.

I clear my throat as I stand, "Of course." I look and meet everyone's eyes, "I've come to your queen with the realm-wide issue we are having from King Baelor of Hadar. He is wreaking havoc and committing mass genocide. We've already seen Mellant and Peverell fall. Evendell is suffering greatly under his regime as it stands. Vellar struggles as we continue to push against their invasion." I'm cut off by a short, dark haired woman sitting three seats down from me.

"I'm sorry," she says with the same accent I picked up on from Felix the first time we met, "but what does all this have to do with us? The Kingdom of Hadar hasn't made a move on us and he'd be foolish to try with the state of the outer lands." Everyone around the table nods in agreement.

"Foolish maybe, but he has his ways. My father is under the jaded impression that if we keep entertaining these petty skirmishes that eventually Baelor will give up on us. Move on."

Another councilman interjects. "And you disagree with your father, do you?" He asks.

"I do. My father isn't on the front lines with our men. But I am, I've seen first hand what Hadar's Guards level of force looks like and that is only from a fraction of them. By the time he sends his full military...if Vellar falls, the Obsidian Kingdom is next. War will be at your doorstep before you can blink." The councilman, who can't be much older than eighteen, looks up at me.

"So what is your reason for being here? To warn us?" He asks genuinely.

"No, not to warn us." Eveera turns to me and smiles, one that doesn't radiate kindness this time but has a layer of malice laced through it. "He wants to use Obsidian's army and me to defend Vellar." Arguments erupt out of every member in the council. She tunes them out as she keeps up on holding our stare. I hear someone saying her name but she doesn't react until Felix rests his hand on her shoulder. "EVERYONE QUIET." Her voice is loud and firm but the arguments continue.

Screams begin to erupt from the woman who spoke earlier. Her eyes are completely black as she thrashes in her chair. Will looks horrified. Eveera's own blackened gaze is predatory, focused solely on her councilwoman.

"Eveera that is enough, release her." Eveera doesn't move. The dark haired woman's screams turning so sharp blood could curdle. "Eveera. I said stop." Felix is in her face now bracing both hands on her shoulders until her Wield finally lets go.

What the fuck was that?

"Armond." she calls on a guard, the same one from the tavern. "Take her to the healers quadrant please." He nods scooping the woman's stunned frame into his arms.

Nobody moves, their heads all cast down. "I told you all to *be quiet.*" Murmured agreements spread through them. "Now, you can argue left and right for all I care. It won't make a difference."

I eye her, "okay...?" The word comes out slowly.

"Don't look so terrified, gods." I wait a few more seconds for an answer, "Fine." She says *fine* as if that is any clearer of an answer.

"Fine?" I ask, raising my brows.

"Fine, we have a deal. How much time do you think we have before Hadar's guards fully invade your outer cities?" She waves over for a member of her staff, who brings over a set of maps. The council is all still sitting there, some brave enough to look up and gape at her. She looks out towards the room. Her eyes widen at the full house like she forget they were here with us. "Oh, none of you are needed here anymore, you're dismissed."

Everyone quickly removes themselves. Alina, opens her mouth to speak but is pulled away by her wrist and forced from the room. Leaving just Will, Felix, myself and the queen.

"How much time?" She repeats.

It takes a second to find the words. "Uh, Will?"

"Bennett mentioned before we left that he thinks they have two maybe two and a half months." He responds. I grimace, *shit*.

Eveera nods, chewing on a nail as she thinks. "Will and I have already been gone six days, Your Highness. It will take us at least a week if we don't portal to get to the first post's front lines." I lean and gesture towards the route we would need to take on the maps.

"The army is too large to portal into one space without drawing attention." She bites her lip considering, "Felix? How many men and women do we currently have? I know we had some casualties after our last scourge with the outer lands." She looks back down to the maps and begins flipping through some paperwork that he hands her.

"25,000 humans and roughly 600 hundred from The Vast."

"And that's not counting yourself or the dragon?" Will asks. With the mention of the beast, Eveera's head whips to him, eyes blazing.

"Vada will *not* be coming with us." Will tries to protest, "Vada, will *not be coming with us*." She hisses again to emphasize her point.

"The knowledge is not lost on me that my father will notice a large army has arrived *inside* his territory. Which means I'll have to approach him with what I've done but I won't do that until we have a victory under our belt." I supply. She places one of the pieces of paper in front of me and I see that it's a contract. "You drew up a contract for this agreement? When?" I ask, looking at her surprised. That means at some point between her stabbing herself with my blade and this meeting she found the time to draw up a thorough contract.

"I do participate in some queenly duties." She rolls her eyes, "go ahead, take it back to your quarters and confer with one another. Those are the terms. Agree with them or don't. This day has been exhausting enough." She gets up and exits through the room.

I say "excuse me" in parting to Felix, running after her. "Queen Eveera!" I call but she doesn't hear me. *Damn this woman walks fast for having such short legs.* "Queen Eveera!" She finally stops right in front of the ominous blacked out end of our hall.

"Yes, princeling?" Fatigue is clear in her voice.

"Thank you. I just wanted to thank you." I breathe out.

She squints her golden eyes at me, "hold that thought." Her fingers wave over in the direction of the darkness. An unfamiliar Obsidian comes through with a large sack hanging over his shoulder. He throws it down unceremoniously which loosens the wrappings on it and reveals the contents. *A body.* My eyes snag on the seal branded into what's left of his clothes. *A sun.*

I try to speak, stunned at what's in front of me. "How the fu-" Looking up at her, her face is smug.

"I think that belongs to you." And with that she disappears. Horror claws its way through me as I stare at the mutilated Vellaran. The trance snaps when the sound of gagging finds its way to my ears. My head turns, Will is there at my back, retching onto the floor.

When he finishes he takes the back of his hand and wipes across his mouth. "Is that?"

I swivel back to the corpse, "yeah," is all that I can articulate.

"Rorin, what the hell have you gotten us into now?"

I have no idea.

EVEERA

No nightmares.

After delivering Percy back to the princeling, the satisfaction of seeing his face lulled me into the first peaceful night in awhile. That was until Axel crashed into my room scaring the shit out of me.

"Can I help you Ax?!"

His hand is pressed to his chest, trying to gather the breath to speak. "So you can barge into my room at night but I can't barge into yours?" He asks, his face is bright red from running in here. He hobbles over to the hidden door in my wall, slapping his free hand against the stone. "You need to get to Vada." Axel states, his words coming out winded. *What was he doing? Running a marathon to get to here?* I wonder to myself.

"Vada? What for?"

He pinches his brow together, "outer lands."

I don't need anything more than that, I sprint down the hallway struggling to lace up my leathers in the process. "*VADA!*" My words tear down the bond.

"*Yes?*" She replies groggily.

"Wake up sleepy head, I need an aerial view of the outer lands. NOW." Commands are flying out of my mouth to the staff as soon as I breach the throne room, my beast of a familiar meeting me in the center. "GET THE CEILING OPEN. NOW." I shout, they scramble towards the levers I have concealed behind the drapes. I don't waste any time mounting her back and clinging tightly due to her almost vertical take off.

The anticipation rises under my skin, my heart rate matching the steady beat of Vada's wings, her speed picks up the closer we get to the edge of Oriya. I coil my magic at the surface. For the creatures in range, it'll obliterate them. For those on the edge, it'll only pacify, unfortunately.

"The Vellaran's arrival seems to have disrupted more than just your state of mind. The creatures are restless." Vada growls. A migraine starts to form in my temple. If they're restless that means they're multiplying, simply appearing out of thin air. The threat of Hadar is laughable when I have much worse within my own gates already. My people are vulnerable enough just by living within these borders.

"I need us over the south side of Oriya. The villages over there are likely to have more anyways." Despite my best efforts, some places get more neglected than others, and the south side of Oriya always seems to take the brunt of that neglect.

"Calm your heart." She demands.

"OH. I'm sorry. I'll get right on that—" I start and she cuts me off.

"It's beating too loudly, and your mind is noisy - distracted. I cannot focus, human." I roll my eyes. She's reverted back to calling me 'human', an annoying habit of hers when she gets agitated. Sometimes it's because of me - the other times I think it's because she's a curmudgeonly overgrown lizard. *"The Vellaran is also noisy and distracting. I could eat him if you like, then there will be no more distractions."*

I laugh, *"I fear that would interrupt my plans to help him."* A growl of disapproval rumbles beneath me as I say the words.

"How very noble of you, human."

"*I can be accommodating from time to time.*" I say.

"Mm. I do hope I don't find you in the same state as you found your parents. It would be most unfortunate for me." *Ouch,* I think.

Finally the hills surrounding the south post crest into view. My eyes widening in horror as it does. *Why did nobody fucking tell me that half the south post was destroyed?* "Vada I need you to drop me just past the border."

"Absolutely not." She bellows.

My head shakes. "No time for arguments. Alert whoever is left at the post that they need to get out. You'll have to burn out the threats that have already breached the post and village." She wants to argue with me but I've already stood up, preparing to run in a dismount off of her.

OOF! My body rolls awkwardly against the hard ground. *They* are already in sight, creeping out towards me, their mouths gaping with black sludge. Some of them look nearly human, others look melted. Disgusting things. *Cursed* things.

"Good morning to you too, fuckers. No offense but you're kind of causing a problem. And for what? A little bit of hunger? How impatient you all are." I throw out one of my stars, finding purchase between one's eyes. Their heads slowly turning to see their fallen...*comrade?* I don't know the hierarchy very well, I'll admit.

I uncoil every tendril of magic and watch as the black magic leaches off my skin. *SQUELCH! THWUMP! PLOP!* One by one the bodies around me drop into a festering heap.

The smell of smoke filtering into my nostrils is coming from the village. "*Clear?*" Vada asks down the bond.

THE NIGHTMARE QUEEN

I nod as I turn, waiting for the steady beat of leathery wings to come within ear shot. "*For now. Are the threats that breached the wall and who ripped up my post dealt with?*"

"The village will need time to recover." She replies.

I sigh. "*They always do...we really ought to trade places when doing damage control.*"

Her skin ripples underneath me as we lift off into the sky. "*I'm sure I left someone alive.*" She argues.

"Let's go home." The words come out dejected and defeated. I nestle into my spot against her scales with the intent to close my eyes. I hope the wind will pull me to sleep, but the moment my eyes go dark, I see those fucking red eyes and I know that sleep won't come. These creatures plague my mind as much as they do my lands.

What the hell am I going to do, while helping Vellar?

Vada banks hard then angles us downwards as she makes her final descent home. "*Hold on.*" She snaps. "*It would be most inconvenient for you to fall off now and become splatter on the stones.*"

"You wouldn't let me become splatter anyways. If you did, you wouldn't have anyone to annoy any longer."

Rocks kick up towards her hind legs, no matter how smooth her landings are, the ground still shakes every time. Ezra is already waiting for me. Both arms folded as he leans against the archway. His face has two emotions fighting for control. Impatience on the one hand and concern on the other.

I shouldn't have let him sleep next to me so often, I think. *It's led to expectations and "I missed you's".*

I hike my leg over and slide down Vada's forearm giving her a pat on her thick neck before she lifts off again.

"Eve—"

My hand is up cutting off whatever sentiment or argument he had planned. "Don't start Ezra, I'm fine. The situation is...handled."

He tucks his chin down in deference. "Of course, Your Highness." We walk side by side into the castle and alone only for so long before I am apprehended by Felix and the prince.

"Taken care of?" Felix asks.

I nod, pushing my way through the wall in front of me. "Taken care of."

"Dinner in fifteen, Eveera." Felix shouts at my back. *Already?* The events of the day it would seem have swept away the hours. The answer I give him is a half-assed thumbs up, stepping into a side passageway as I do so to get to my room faster.

Fifteen, I say to myself. Fifteen uninterrupted minutes. Fifteen moments of quiet before I am bombarded yet again with pleasantries, questions, and *visiting*. I'd say the sooner I get them out of my court the better, but unfortunately I'll be going *with* them. I shouldn't have agreed. But the opportunity for something better forced me to do so. The opportunity for my own plans to come to fruition.

The fates had already decided, I had to say yes.

No one was in my room thank the gods, when I closed the passageway door behind me. My bed has never looked so inviting, it's the biggest thing in the room taking up the most space. I may not have wanted to upgrade where I slept when I became queen but I did want to upgrade what I slept in. I shuck my leathers off, tying my hair into a loose bun on top of my head, and rifle through my drawers to look for something less constricting to slip on.

Much to my happiness I find an old ratty t-shirt of Axel's to throw on. I practically throw my body into the bed with plans to bury myself underneath the covers and—

"OOF!" *THUD!*

"WHAT THE FUCK?!" I shout, tossing the covers back again to reveal not just Axel but Axel, Max, and "Orem are you on the ground?" I shout.

Three very groggy guards are all in my bed. Well one is now on the floor. "Yeah...that really hurt." He groans as he picks himself back up.

"Oh I'm sorry. Next time I'll check for my guards in my bed, before crawling into it. Because asleep in their charge's room is the obvious place my 'protectors' would be!" I shriek.

Axel props himself up on his elbows, looking me up and down. "Is that my shirt?"

I look down, "is this your— that is not relevant! The three of you," I point to my door. "OUT!" Each of them scrambling to their feet, protests spilling from their mouths.

I hold the door open for them with a scowl plastered on my face. "Next time the three of you want to have a slumber party, do not do it in my room or my bed."

Axel holds up his finger, "you know next time you break into my room to avoid sleeping next to Ezra, I'll remember this." He turns on his heel, "fuck."

Ezra and Armond are conveniently standing in the center of my hall, the former's face stricken. "Ha. Well, I don't know which I should be more upset about. The fact that three of my soldiers are napping, that they're napping in their queen's room, or that you avoid sleeping next to me..."

"I had fifteen minutes…" I mutter, "just fifteen." The door closes behind me, leaving the five of them out in the hallway. These men are getting too comfortable both with and around me. When my clock hits that dreaded fifteen minute mark I groan, and throw on a dress for dinner.

Felix, the princeling, and Mousy are already seated when I march my way up to my seat, plucking a goblet off the tray of the closest staff member while I do so. The weight of stares fall on me as the drink slides down my throat and into my stomach. "What?!" I snap.

Felix returns to the paperwork next to him, "you still smell like dragon Eveera." His nose scrunching as he turns the page.

"Well, that's because you gave me fifteen minutes to be here after a day-long trip on Vada *and* Ax, O, and M all decided to occupy my room for their own leisurely endeavors. So *excuse me* for not smelling like fucking roses Felix, dear." My hand flags over another staff member who hands me a second goblet. My eyes peer over the rim, while Mousy looks like he might throw up, the Prince is holding back a smile.

"A-hem well, I won't ask for you to explain that." Felix remarks.

"I'm guessing that's my cue to be diplomatic then?" He doesn't acknowledge my comment so I turn my attention to our guests. "So, are the terms suitable for you, princeling?"

"We found no issues to note." Polite answer while he cuts into the food in front of him, he's the picture of propriety, while I manhandle a roll.

Things settle into an uncomfortable quiet with only the sounds of chewing present. *Oy here we go.* "Since, I am playing the part of the diplomatic queen, I should ask if you have any questions."

"Questions?" Mousy squeaks.

I huff out a sigh. "Yes, questions."

The prince angles his body towards me, dabbing the corners of his mouth lightly with a napkin. "What had you and your dragon in such a rush earlier?" *Wrong question.* I should have clarified, I didn't even know he'd seen me fly off.

I narrow my eyes. "Nothing." "Not up for discussion." Felix and I both answer at the same time. "Just village issues." My answer is curt giving up very little.

"Village issues?" The disbelief is plain on his face and to my chagrin he presses on. "Village issues require a dragon?"

My lips thin, the smile tight. "I like a show of force. Keeps them in line." I say, pushing my plate back and rising to my feet. "Well, I'm just stuffed. Tomorrow, same time as this morning. You'll be meeting the army you came here for."

Armond and Axel are both at my doors, waiting for me after dinner. "What? No sleepover this time?" I mock.

"What? Wearing your own clothes this time?" He mimics, but his voice has some hardness in it. From what I know, he is from the south side villages with family still there and each time the outer lands press in it throws him on edge. It's probably why he chose to avoid his job and sleep while I was gone.

I think back on Vada's words suggesting that she must have left someone alive. Regret of not making her burn out the woods instead of the village fills my stomach, like lead. *Hopefully there were no Vada related Mecham family casualties tonight,* the voice inside my head comments.

I lean into him, "you *can* go check on Vernilla if you need to. Use Armond, you'll get there quicker. Maybe she'll be better today, there could be cakes!" He stiffens at her name, the soft reminder of how she used to be not helping.

Years ago when he first became my guard, his mother used to send him to the castle with blood orange cakes. I'll admit I had a bit of an affinity for them, and demanded I meet the woman responsible. He was hesitant at first and only kept refusing me, because I allowed him to. But finally, my more petulant teenage side won out and I stopped taking no for an answer. It wasn't difficult to figure out what his hesitancy around me meeting her was.

She was a Sight, it's a rare Wield that takes more than it gives.

The cakes were a hyper fixation for her that kept her lucidity at the forefront of consciousness. But *then* the cakes stopped coming and Axel stopped visiting her as much. When that happened I moved her closer into Oriya. The affects of Sight have left both her and Axel vulnerable and the threat of the outer lands has only made things worse for him.

His stance softens again and his fingers curl around mine. "Thank you, E. But no. I'll stay here." His eyes betray him. I know it kills him to see her decline and that he's avoiding her. His anger is both at her and their Wield. Unfortunately for me I already know that his worst nightmare will come to life when he loses her from this plane.

I give his hand a squeeze. "Armond, call for James to be posted outside my passageway door. I don't want any visitors tonight."

Once securely in my room my body sinks to the floor.

What will they do while I am gone? Will Vada be enough? The worry crawls into my subconscious, burying itself there. There's only one answer that I can come up with. *She'll have to be. And the cost of gaining my help will have to be worth leaving them behind.* I think. Too bad the prince didn't ask what the price was — his kingdom's king and queen for my help in winning him this war. I hope he's not as close to his parents as I was mine.

RORIN

"*Village issues*" - what village issues entail a dragon I wonder.

My thoughts refocus when Will looks me up and down and asks, "did you sleep at all?"

"Like a baby." I snark, patting his shoulder and grabbing my military jacket from the wardrobe.

He trails after me out into the hallway, voice low, "you're not regretting signing the contract are you?"

I shake my head, "No. I'm not. She was our only option left."

"Just remember, this is what you asked for. This is what you wanted. We will have to get used to the unpredictability." I nod in agreement. Leave it to Will to be rational at the moment.

"Though, apparently, she won't be sharing *all* her resources with us." I mutter, my brain circling back to her dragon.

Our two guards, Maxwell and Orem, are waiting outside to bring us to meet the ranks. They move in complete sync with one another. I'd guess they were fraternal twins if I hadn't overheard them through the door the other night - something about Maxwell being tired of being the more responsible one just because he was older.

The balcony they bring us to looks out over the courtyards and a handful of buildings I presume must be the barracks. Beneath us, thousands of men and women are all standing in formation, waiting for their next command.

"Good, you're on time" Her voice sends chills rippling over my skin. She seems to have appeared from thin air. "Max, Orem you may go. Thank you." They dip their chins at her, Ezra stands close at her side, greeting both the brothers as they leave. "We'll split the military into thirds. Each third will include those from The Vast, and a handful of common mages." Her explanation abrupt. *Okay...I guess we're just jumping into things.*

Will raises his hand, "You said you have 100 companies of men and women but this is only nine. Where are the other 91 companies?"

She smiles but there is no warmth in it, "I'll humor you, Mousy. In front of you stand nine separate companies. We don't have the space to house or train them all at the same time. We house only certain companies at a time and of course those who serve in our personal guard. The Serpentes' live on their territory, the Oriks on theirs, and the Shifters - well you get the idea." She moves to descend the stairs towards them, continuing to explain on her way down. "We train in a rotation. Their training rotations run on alternating days of the week every day of the year." She spins on the step to look up at Will, "does that answer your question, Mouse?"

He grunts in agreement which I guess was satisfactory enough. She walks up next to an older gentleman with bronzed skin and graying hair. Tipping her head to the crowd of soldiers she asks, "how are they looking?"

"They're honed and ready for battle. But then again, they're always honed and ready for battle." Eveera's lips purse while motioning for Ezra. Both him and the old general hoist her body into the air.

"SOLDIERS!" All eyes on her. "THE DAYS YOU'VE SPENT TRAINING AND BEING TESTED IN THE OUTER LANDS WILL NOW BE TESTED ELSEWHERE. WE HEAD TO VELLAR AT DAYBREAK." No one moves, breathes, or blinks for several seconds it seems. "Oh good, no mutinies yet. Thank the gods." Her eyes roll on that last part while Ezra and the gentleman put her down. As soon as her feet hit stone, keeping her hand on the older man's shoulder, she turns and stares at us.

"Prince Rorin, Sir Mousy, this is General Matthis. He heads up our human companies. He'll be one of our eyes and ears during this *rescue mission.*"

The man's face is stony much like his political counter-part, Felix. Will extends his hand, to be polite, but Matthis makes no move to shake it.

Eveera's eyes light up at her General's subtle rejection. "Don't pay too much mind to him. He's not used to working alongside...*your sort.*"

There is that "your sort" *comment again. What the fuck does* "your sort" *mean?* I wonder.

"Well—" she claps her hands together, "that's all I needed you for." Her words all the dismissal anyone seems to need. She pushes past us, marching her ass back up the stone steps. I give Will a look, one that he works out quickly but my feet are moving before he can stop me.

"Rorin what are you—" His words die down over my shoulder. I pick up my pace, taking two steps at a time to catch up to her.

"Is there a reason you're following me?" She shouts, turning down a narrow hallway. Finally catching up, I stop her by putting a hand to her shoulder. She looks down at my hand, then back to me. "Is there also a reason you are touching me?" The words coming out strained through her clenched teeth.

I smirk, "what? Don't like being touched by 'my sort'?" I ask, emphasis on the last two words.

Her fingers shove my hand off, dusting off where I touched her. "I don't. Actually. Makes my skin crawl." I glare at her and shove my hands into the pockets of my pants. Looking up and around I notice that we are standing in front of two stained glass doors.

"What's behind those?" I ask.

"Marjorie." She says it as if that should be answer enough.

"Do I get to meet this Marjorie too?"

She smirks, placing one of her tanned hands on the gaudy gold knob. "Hope not. She doesn't take to well to your—" I raise my hand cutting her off.

"Let me guess, 'my sort'." I say, throwing air quotes around what I've now figured is a slur. "Is this arrangement going to work with your inexplicable disdain for me?"

Her laugh is low and breathy, her eyes somehow growing brighter despite the poor lighting in this hall. "I'm getting what I want either way. Nowhere did it say I had to like you." My brows scrunch at her words, confusion etching its way in.

"Are you talking about payment? We never did discuss…" My words are silenced by the sound of the door clicking closed, and I'm left by myself, staring at colorful glass. "payment." I finished. "We *were* having a conversation." I huff out, turning on my heel and marching back towards my room.

Will's thrown himself on the chaise with a drink in his hand, it's an odd position for me to find him in, furthermore it's odd he doesn't acknowledge me when I walk in. I reach for my own drink and watch as he takes a long swig from his glass. He coughs and sputters, liquid dribbling from his lips. "Oh *shit*, what the hell do they drink here?"

I shrug, following suit and taking my own swig. The drink burns down my throat and I wince. "My guess? Blood of her enemies." Will rolls his eyes at my suggestion. "She wants to leave at daybreak, but we still haven't formulated a plan for what happens when we do leave." I take another swig of the acrid liquor.

He glances my way, "is that why you chased after her? To formulate a plan? Hey, did you catch that *"your sort"* comment? Both Eveera and her guard Armond said it."

"Yeah, more than once." I mutter.

"What was that?"

"I don't know, Will, she probably refers to everyone who's human with terms of endearment like that. As you've reminded me many times she doesn't have the best of reputations.

He snorts into his glass. "To be honest, I half expected her to have horns."

"Ha. She did you one better, she has a damn dragon," I lean back against the fireplace, "a damn dragon we can't use. Hell, if we had access to that kind of fire power, Baelor's forces would be wiped out in one fell swoop."

Will doesn't say anything to that, just closes his eyes, sinking further into the chaise.

"Daybreak." I murmur. "At daybreak we head back to Vellar. In just six days, we start to fix this mess."

"Of course the military will probably take longer, but at least we will be there to help Bennett." Will adds, bobbing his head up and down against the arm rest.

I have six days to figure her out before we're thrown into battle. I don't even know if she is planning on fighting alongside us. I know she *can* fight. But will she risk her own neck for mine? If Baelor weren't such an impending threat to us both I think she would happily hand my neck over to him.

EVEERA

"PLEASE. PLEASE STOP. PLEASE!"

I'm sweating, we've been at this for hours. "P-please." She sobs. "Ple..ase."

She wants me to feel pity, when all I feel is disgust. "Have to admit dear, you're not the type I prefer to have saying that word. Doesn't do the same thing for me." The tendrils I'm Wielding wriggle in and out of her body. It's a brutal assault to witness, can't imagine what it feels like. "Do you see her, Viv? Do you see her limp little body?" Her mouth quivers but no sounds come out. "See, yours is about to match."

Scarlet red blood pools at the corner of her lips as she sputters out another plea. Oh boo fucking hoo. My fist connects with her face, blood spewing to the side as the bones in her cheek crunch beneath my knuckles. "Did you listen when she begged you to stop, Viv? Did you answer her whimpers or pleas?" Her face is still turned from me, but even in the dimmed lighting I can see a bruise already blooming on her cheek. "Did you stop when her chest rattled with its last breath? What about the others, did you stop *them* when her heart finally quit beating, or did you just collect the cash? She was *nine*. She deserved better than you."

Oof. My fist lands this time in between her breasts forcefully. "Do you know what my power is doing? It's making you live out your worst fears. Funny enough your worst fear is death." My laugh is sardonic. "Probably don't even need to use my Wield on you if that's what you're afraid of." Sobs rack through her chest and I can hear the amount of effort each breath is costing her now, cracked ribs and all.

"P-pull it out."

"I'm sorry, what was that?" My hand cups around my ear. "I didn't quite hear you underneath all of that pathetic sniveling. I said I *probably* don't need to use my Wield, Viv. But you see, this is *fun* for me. Besides, your fate will stay the same."

"I didn't mean to. I didn't mean to." Like I said, *pathetic.* She begins muttering "no" over and over again. I grip her chin hard, forcing her to look at me.

"Yes. You did, Viv." My free hand strokes her bruised face, "shh...you did, dear. And that little girl paid the price of your selfishness. So now you get to pay the price for her life." Her screams ring out as my tendrils make their final assault, stopping her heart in the process.

Sweat drips off my brow, my peripheral catches sight of a looming figure in the shadows of the room, "bring the next one in, Ezra."

"E..." His voice is soft.

"Marjorie said I needed to do this before we left! I can't leave if I don't!" I snarl.

He looks at me desperately, his hands reaching for me. "Then don't go! We don't have to go." The thumb of his right hand comes up swiping at a droplet of blood. I turn my cheek, shrugging away from him.

Yes, I do. I think to myself. "Bring the next one in." He flinches at my tone, skulking out of the room to drag in the next prisoner.

It's going to be a long night.

Ezra brought in ten separate wastes of space after I dealt with *Viv*, all over the course of the past several hours.

With the most recent attack, I knew I would have to go see Marjorie before leaving. I just didn't expect the prince to follow me all the way to her study doors. Her well worn advice for me was to expel as much of my Wield as I could into the outer lands around Oriya and on my exit from the kingdom.

Best way to do that was to boost up my Wield - hence the prisoner's. Their fears feed into my magic. I'm strong as it is, but this is a lot of land to cover in not a lot of time. I left Ezra and other's to clean up when I was done. My familiar was watching from the mouth of her cave as always but there isn't an outside exit from the Room.

"Vada, I'll meet you at the edge." I say through the seal.

"Why not just meet me outside the gates?" She doesn't bother hiding her irritation. The "you're not coming with me to Vellar" conversation - after my meeting with Marjorie and before the prisoner's punishments - didn't go over too well with the words "insolent, insufferable, ignorant human" repeated several times.

I sigh, *"because I want to walk for a little while."* Her deep laugh rumbles back down the bond.

"HA. You'll be walking for days little demon. I will fly you to do this." She argues.

"It's really not necessar—"

I'm cut off by her roar echoing through the castle. *"I will fly you."* I guess that settles that, I head back into the passageways to grab a few extra handheld weapons from my bedroom.

I walk out into the hall to find Armond at attention per usual but poor Axel is slumped down on the floor, asleep. I crouch down winking at Armond as I whisper into Axel's ear. "You know, you really suck at the whole 'guarding' thing."

His bloodshot brown eyes snap open. "Well, I wasn't really planning on making it a lifelong career or anything." He quips.

I grab his hand to help pull him up. "Of course not. At this rate, if anyone succeeded in assassinating me on your watch you would be out of a job anyways with the only person willing to write you a recommendation - dead. So." He huffs out a groggy laugh. "Don't wait up. I'll be gone until we need to leave. We have a long six days ahead of us with the two spoiled meatheads."

Armond's mouth slips into a frown, "make that a long 'until Baelor's dead' time with the Vellaran trash." The words clipped as he says them.

I smile. "Attaboy Monty. Keep up the positive attitude." He gives me a weak smile back. "Go. Sleep. Both of you. I will be back to meet you all at the barracks for departure."

"When are *you* going to sleep, E?" I pat Axel's cheek twice, ignoring the question.

I stalk down the hallway, leaving them to hopefully get rest while I handle the creatures. *SMACK!*

"OW! What in the...gods?" Pressing a hand to my forehead I look up to see a startled princeling. *Talk about bad timing.* "Do you always roam around in the middle of the night giving headaches to queens?" My free hand gestures at that skin covered stone wall he calls a chest.

A smirk settles on his face, "not often no. Do you always walk around in the middle of the night in…" His eyes drag up and down my body…slowly. But when his eyes find mine again they're filled with confusion, "fighting leathers?" A warm feeling slinks up my spine at the eye contact. I shake it off as I take in my outfit. He's right, it's not exactly middle of the night attire.

Irritation replaces that warm feeling quickly enough when I remember what I am supposed to be doing and who exactly I am talking to. "Well at least I'm dressed." I snap. "Now if you'll excuse me." My shoulder checks his arm, my hand moving back up to rub my temple. *I think I'm going to get a goose egg from this exchange.*

"Wait! Queen Eveera, wait up." He yells from behind and then steps into time with me.

My stomach sinks. "Gods, why are you so awake right now?" I ask looking up at him briefly, that stupid smirk still present. "An insufferably annoying prince was not on my agenda." I grumble.

"You have an agenda?"

Shit you weren't supposed to hear that, I say to myself.

"Where are you going in fighting leathers?" He repeats.

I sigh, "None. Of. Your. Fucking. Business. Now go away. You'll have plenty of time to annoy me starting in four hours." My fingers wave him off but he doesn't relent.

His next words stopping me short. "Can I come with you?" I spin so fast on my heel it almost propels me back into his chest.

"No, you cannot come with me." *Is he dense?* I wonder. "Why would I let *you* come with me?"

He shrugs, rocking back on his heels, "because we have four hours to kill. You're helping my cause…maybe I could help yours."

HA. "You can't help." I say turning back around.

"I could." He argues.

"You can't." *Unless you too have magical energy absorbing tendrils that live underneath your skin and can feed or kill the waking horrors that surround this kingdom.* I snap inside my head.

"I could."

I drop my head back groaning, the headache I figured I would get is already forming. "You can't!" If he suggests one more time that he can help? I'll kill him.

If I couldn't still hear his feet I would assume he turned back and dropped the issue until his damn mouth utters again. "I could." He repeats a third time.

"AGH! Alright princeling, you want to help? Fine. But I don't want to hear another sound out of that godsforsaken mouth of yours." He grins ear to ear, certainly thinking he's won the upper hand here. I turn away from him heading towards the exit where I know Vada will be waiting. His steps grew quieter and when I looked over my shoulder he was no longer with me. *Hmph, good. He changed his mind,* I think. Vada dips her forearm down as she always does to make it easier for me. I'm preparing myself for take off when my ass begins to vibrate, I look up to see what's set off Vada when her words slam into my mind. *"You brought a snack with you?"*

I guess he chose to come after all, and oh look - he's found a shirt, I mock to myself while ignoring her question. *"He says he can help."*

As if the growl of disapproval wasn't enough she's clacked her teeth every time he attempts to climb up her forearm. "You coming? We don't have all day!" I bark.

He gives me a wary look. "Well, I would love to. I don't think your pet agrees with it though." Vada snaps again, this time I'm sure it's for his use of the word *pet*. My hand strokes down her scales. "*Easy Vada, can't eat him yet.*"

"*Debatable.*" She grumbles.

I roll my head to the side, eyeing down at him. "Hurry up, princeling! Burning night time here." The look of concern in his eyes stays as Vada finally concedes, allowing him to sit behind me.

He shifts uncomfortably, his hands awkwardly out to the side. "Uhm, not to state the obvious, but there isn't much to hold onto back here." I stare up at the sky, begging the gods, *why me?*

"Well, she's a dragon, not a fucking saddled horse. So if you don't want to fall the moment we take off, you're going to have to grip around my waist." I grab each of his hands from their distended positions and lock them around me. The contact sends electric shocks into my skin.

"A-hem and what exactly are *you* going to hold on to?" He asks, as I try to create as much distance as possible between us.

"Nothing."

Nervous laughter rumbles against my spine, "I'm sorry - *nothing?!*"

Vada takes off in the next moment, answering his question for me. "*This is going to be one hell of a long night with him.*" I grumble into her mind.

The flight will probably take about an hour.

Unfortunately, it's only been maybe twenty minutes and my back is already cramping. I've never had to sit ramrod straight on Vada before, but with Rorin and I awkwardly hooked together, there is no shot in hell I am going to relax back.

"Just so I have an idea...what exactly are we going to do?" My mouth stays clamped shut, my body shifting forward again. He sighs, annoyed. "Fine, don't answer me but at least stop sitting like you have a sword up your ass."

Excuse me?

"You're the one who wrapped my arms around your waist. So before you end up pulling us both off to our deaths from your squirming, I suggest you lean back."

He's right, my conscience sings. I concede and lean into him. "Don't enjoy it too much, *princeling*." My back relaxes and what was originally a stone wall suddenly seemed a lot more soft. *Dammit.* I try very hard to ignore how he doesn't feel like I hoped he would. Quite the opposite in fact, he feels *better*.

RORIN

I was screwed the moment she grabbed my arms and if she weren't so obnoxious this would be a lot easier. "Don't worry, Your Highness. There is nothing about this I am enjoying." I catch her scent and have to stop myself from breathing her in.

Liar.

The only response I get from her is an ungraceful snort. "I might suggest the same to you but, you're more into blondes." I say, making her tense. The dragon makes a sudden decline causing me to squeeze her waist tighter.

Her lungs suck in a sharp breath. "Oh my *GODS*. You don't have to grip the life out of me! You're going to leave bruises and *not* the good kind." The words come out in a snarl, and I nearly choke on whatever I had planned to say. *This woman and her mouth.*

"Are we landing this thing anytime soon?" The stiffness in my legs from flying is going to make me look crippled. *Maybe she ought to have a saddle,* I think. Not that it would matter, I probably wouldn't ever be on the beast again.

She moves her head to scowl at me. "This *thing*, has a name, you idiot."

"Right. Of course, how could I forget that you've named your pet dragon." The beast banks heavily to the right putting us parallel to the ground. My already sore legs do their best to squeeze tighter and hold my place against Eveera. Her right hand loosely grips onto Vada's spines, while the left keeps me tightly against her.

The heavy draft from Vada's wings causes the forest floor debris to pitch upwards around us. For the first few moments after landing the two of us sit there somewhat clinging to one another.

When sense crawls back into her mind she breaks out of my hold, sliding down the scaled flanks. Following suit, I swing my leg around; while mid slide the beast decides she's had enough of me. She angles her body so that the rest of my descent sends me tumbling to the ground where the queen stares down at me, lip curled.

My hands dust my clothes off as I take in the surrounding ominous woods. We're not too far outside the expansive city, but you'd think we'd entered a wasteland. Bare trees with their grayish bark are far as the eyes can see. The shadows dance around, their horrors hiding within them.

"Is this your idea of helping? Sitting there still as a statue?" She smirks and reluctantly extends her hand towards me. "Oh, thank the gods, how would I have ever survived without your help?" Eveera turns in a circle, scouting the area.

"See anything—" Her hand comes up to clamp against my mouth.

"*SHH!*" Her body pushes at me, backing us into a tree. Startled by the sudden change, it takes me a moment to notice the dozen pairs of red eyes that surround us. A twig snaps to our left and, *swish!*, one of her coveted daggers flies out of her hand burying itself in an eye socket. The dozen quickly turns into *dozens* after that.

I peel her hand off my mouth and reach for my sword. My left hand grips her shoulder, inching her to the side. When I glance down I see that her eyes are that inhuman black. No trace of gold remaining.

They're moving in quickly towards us. She's already broken away from me, beckoning the horde to close in, her Wield stretching out to coil around multiple beasts at once. My own magic flickers to life under my skin as the unaffected ones run towards me. My sword makes wide swipes cutting down any of the beasts that get too close.

What in the gods are they?

Even now, after fighting them as we made our way to Oriya, I still couldn't figure it out. Some look humanoid and others I can't make sense of how they even stand on their...*feet*? The question disappears as my blade spears through another. *SQUELCH!* "EVEERA!" I shout.

Eveera's diving underneath them, slicing and stabbing all while Wielding. I finish off the ones she leaves behind in her wake of magic. Her moves are fluid and quick. What she lacks in stature she makes up for in speed and flexibility. It's astonishing. *She* is astonishing, her power is like a heavy blanket of darkness.

I would hate to be on the receiving end of it, I think to myself.

My own power tries to respond to hers. *Tainted, broken, cursed*. My head twitches as the words rattle around in my head. There's too many of them. Mist starts to seep from my palms, control always was difficult for me. With no one wanting to help teach me my Wield, I had to learn on my own. If I use it now, I won't be able to single her out and the Wield will take everyone in it's path.

Tainted, broken, cursed.

Her scream pierces the air. I whirl on my heel to find five of them are circling her. One of the creatures has it's gnarled hand wrapped around her hair. "PRINCELING!" Her eyes are no longer black as her Wield snaps back into her. I can tell she's losing her grip. "LITTLE HELP HERE!" She shouts at me.

My feet pick up their pace, "I THOUGHT YOU COULD HANDLE THEM." *SLASH!* "JUST." *UGH!* *"FINE."* My sword slices clean through the hand and then the neck of the one yanking her hair as I finally get to her. We fight back to back for while, getting through the horde. By what I hope is the end of it - there are bodies littered around us. "Next time, just ask for my help first." The words come out breathy and choppy.

The familiar smell of smoke starts to encroach all around us accompanied by a loud roar. She must have taken care of a different location from ours. "Next time?! There will not be a next time! You insufferable—" her eyes black in and out just as—

-

SMACK! "*Stupid boy!*" *My lip stings from the cut his ring has opened up again.* "*What a dishonor you are to this kingdom! Poisonous mist! An omen if there ever was one.*" *My vision goes black and I can feel my eye start to swell and that the bones in my nose are broken.* "*P-please don't lock me up here again. PLEASE.*" *His laugh rings out through the room.* "*Please don't lock me up here again.*" *He mocks before landing a kick in between my ribs.* "*P-please.*" *I sob out - no NO!*

-

I push my Wield out back against hers, not allowing this memory to continue. I can't see where the hell she is as my mist rolls freely out from my palms. It isn't until I feel myself slip out of the nightmare that I hear her gasping on the ground next to me, clawing at her throat. "What..." Eveera pants. "The..." Another gasp. "*FUCK. Rorin?!*" Her gaze is liquid fire.

I grip the soil underneath my palms, my head spinning as nausea crawls up my throat. "What the fuck yourself! Could you control your Wield?!" I shouts.

Her eyes are filled with malice as she stands there accusing me. "And you?!"

Both my shoulders shrug; feigning nonchalance. "We'll call it self defense." My nostrils are flaring, my ribs straining as I pull in breath after breath. "You aren't the only one, Your Highness, who has a Wield to be afraid of." The words are pure venom dripping off my tongue.

Why did it have to be that memory?

The ground shakes as Vada lands next to us. The fire that radiates through the dragon's body and scales is molten, but somehow not near as hot as the anger brewing between the two of us. The queen begins walking to the beast, her back to me. I stalk off after her, my feet forcing me to catch up. The closer I get the easier it is for me to notice she's nursing her shoulder, dark liquid leaking between her fingers. "You're bleeding." I note.

Her mouth opens and closes a few times, looking down at the open wound.

"Thanks for noticing." Without missing a beat she climbs up the dragon, taking her seat.

This damn woman.

EVEERA

"*Why are you bleeding?*" Vada growls.

"*It's nothing. One of the creatures got me.*" I say, while settling on her spine.

"*I thought the* snack *you brought was here to help you? Instead he lets you bleed.*" Her agitation isn't just felt through the bond, it's making her skin and scales twitch.

"*He did help, sort of, and he isn't letting me bleed. I am letting myself bleed.*" I argue back. She slams her mind closed to me while he climbs up, winding his arms around my waist. The motion accidentally brushes against my open wound causing me to hiss at the contact.

"Shit. Sorry." He grumbles, loosening his hold.

I push my shoulder forward to create more distance, "it's fine."

"You're going to have to see a healer mage before we leave." He adds.

"No, really? I thought I would let it fester and get infected." *Obviously,* I need to see a healer mage before we leave, this would be murder to travel with without seeing one.

He clears his throat, his discomfort evident. "I'm just making an observation is all."

"Well stop doing that." I snap.

"Stop doing what?!"

"Observing me. It's annoying."

Stop speaking while you're at it, the voice inside gripes. My shoulder screams at me as we take off. This is going to be the longest hour of my life.

Apparently not for Rorin, however, he nodded off fairly quickly against one of Vada's spikes. After so many minutes and making sure he was truly asleep, I tried to loosen his grip. His hands are locked around me like iron and my struggle causes me to bump the injured portion of my shoulder into his collarbone. "AH! Dammit!" I shriek, pain racing up my arm.

"Gods you're loud." His tired voice reaches my ears.

My lip curls up into a sneer that he can't see. "Oh, I'm sorry. I'll be quieter next time you're around while I bleed out." I peer over my shoulder at him.

"You're not bleeding out." He says his eyes closing again.

"No?" I ask.

"No, you were bleeding out when you chose to stab yourself on the blade you so graciously threw at my throat. This is not that. You're not bleeding out." He peeks open one eye, assessing me. "But, it does look like that hurts." He lazily lifts a finger and pokes at the bite.

My breath hitches sharply. "*Ouch!* The venom is acting quickly." My teeth grind together as the warmth of the toxins seep deeper into my bloodstream. *And this is why you don't bring other people with you to do that, too much of a distraction.* My conscience chastises me.

His body straightens and two broad arms push me back into his chest. Careful to avoid my shoulder. "What in the bleeding hells are you doing?" My voice is shrill, pitching up an octave.

"Shut up and lean back." I gape at him, looking again over my good shoulder. "Come on, you did it on our way here." He pushes a second time so that I am snug against him.

"That was different." I argue while trying to bring distance between the two of us again.

His head shakes, chin lightly ruffling my hair. "No, that was not different, if anything you were better off sitting straight as a board on the way towards the outer lands. But now you're injured. So shut up and lean back, the tension from holding yourself upright the whole hour is only making your shoulder worse."

"But—" One of the wide hands locked around me unhooks itself and clamps over my mouth - just like mine had done to him just a little while ago.

His lips graze my ear. The deepness of his voice as it dips to a whisper makes my stomach dip with it. "I said, shut up and lean back."

A growl rumbles beneath us. *"Both of you stop talking before I decide to eat him and cauterize that wound myself."* The corners of my mouth twitch, making me force a frown to counteract the smile that wants to break out at Vada's snide comment. I can't risk the princeling thinking there is a smile on my face because of him.

Castle spires and red glass finally come into view. "We don't have much time to get ready to leave, and you still need a healer." The statement is the first he's said since he forced me to use him as a human pillow. If Vada's irritation at me wasn't obvious enough, her landing was anything but graceful. The turbulence of it sending the prince and I knocking against each other.

He tries his best to avoid my shoulder as he untangles himself. My eyes drop down to where his hand is extended out, offering me his help off of her.

My nose scrunches up, "no thank you, I can get off *my* dragon *myself.*" He holds both hands up in mock defense. I move to dismount but the venom has worked too fast and instead my limbs fail me, my body tumbling off to where I land directly on my ass. "MOTHER-FUCKER." I shout, pain racing up both my tailbone and my shoulder.

Slow clapping sounds above me. "Very graceful, Your Highness."

Vada steps back from the two of us retreating into her den. *"You're on your own. Don't die."*

ARGH! The fist of my good arm balls up, punching the ground next to me. "*YOU CAN EAT HIM NOW!*" I shout through the bond to her.

Her laugh carries through the cave walls as she descends deeper. *"Not hungry, little demon. As I said, don't die. It would be most inconvenient for me."* The line between us going silent. *Dragons.*

My attention refocuses on the princeling. He's bent down in a position that suggests he's about to scoop me up. I squirm aiming to get away from his grip. *I don't need to be in his arms a third time today.* I warn myself.

"Keep doing that, Your Highness, and you'll end up on your ass twice this morning." He growls. Ignoring him my body continues to struggle, there is a sudden absence of pressure on my muscles and the ground meets my ass for the second time.

"*OW!* YOU BASTARD!"

His face is smug, both of his arms crossed. "I warned you. Now, will you stop acting like a petulant child and let me get you to the healer mage? Because your shoulder looks disgusting and we really don't have time for all of this."

"Fine." I reach out my hand for him to help me, but he slaps it away, choosing instead to throw me over his shoulder. His thick arm bands across my thighs. "Excuse me but I didn't say 'Fine. Carry me like a fucking sack of grain!'" I beat my good arm against his back. But it only serves to make him laugh, loudly.

He thinks this is funny.

"Actually. You didn't specify how I had to carry you at all." He comments.

"I hate you."

"Tsk tsk tsk. Such sweet nothings you share with me." The words coming out of him in a croon.

Oh bleeding hells. This is humiliating. On every level.

"You!" Rorin points to a younger boy, Seth, the son of my head staff. "Go get the healer mage and tell them to meet us at Queen Eveera's rooms immediately."

"Uh..uh.." Seth stammers.

"NOW!" Rorin roars and Seth breaks off into a run.

I shake my head. "Great. Now you're ordering my staff around."

Rorin winds down the halls stopping short between his and Mousy's rooms, the latter of which happens to stumble out and quickly take in the sight of the princeling and I. Maxwell and Orem look equally as horrified.

"Um." Orem squeaks out.

My hand waves out to cut him off, "If *any* of you mention this ever again. I will personally rip out your vocal chords with my bare hands." Max blanches. A swift SMACK! hits the back of my thighs and the men's eyes bulge, "what. the. *HELL. RORIN!*"

"Stop threatening people for five seconds and tell me where your room is before you die from this venom." I groan. "Only twenty minutes." He reprimands.

I'm sorry, I was wrong before, *now* I am going to kill him. If I wasn't wanting to before I really am now.

"Straight down the hall through the pitch black." Orem offers.

"Thank you." Rorin nods moving us quickly down the hall with Mousy trailing behind on our heels.

"Did you just say *venom?!* And why are you two even together?" He asks.

"Not now Mousy, the adults are handling things at the present moment." I sneer.

His face screws up in a scowl muttering, "*I'm older than the both of you*," under his breath.

The prince kicks open my doors, neither Armond or Axel are outside, meaning they must have taken my advice and gone to bed. He lays me down gently, a sharp contrast to him smacking directly under my ass a few moments ago.

"Tsk tsk tsk. Oh Eveera, what have you done to yourself now." Marjorie's voice chimes in my ears. I watch as she shakes her head.

"I'm fine, Marjorie." I grumble. H

er pointed look argues differently as she waves her hands upward at me. "Come on. Up, up, up."

My arms lift up as best they can. She peels off the shredded tunic, having to pick at certain parts that are glued by blood to my body. *"Gah!"* I hiss again, *gods it got me good this time,* I say to myself.

"She has to be shirtless for this?!" The prince's companion, shrieks.

Marjorie's face turns pained in annoyance. "You do not have to be here, Sir Will." He flattens his lip at the clear reprimand.

"Yes, why *are* you here, Mousy?" I grit out while Marjorie's gnarled hands work to get every last piece of fabric out of the wound.

"Because *he's* here." He replies, pointing at Rorin, whose face is stoic while he watches Marjorie work intently.

"Clearly an oversight." I mutter before gasping at the warmth and pulse of Marjorie's healing magic working on the bite. It draws on the venom, stinging the whole way as it's pulled out.

The passageway door in my wall busts open, Axel tripping out of it, "EVIE WHAT THE HELL HAPPENED!" His face is wide with panic, Ezra and Armond filing in behind him. Before I can answer they all turn taking notice of the prince - who's still staring at me. "Scratch that." Axel shakes his head, "what the hell are *they* doing here?" He asks gesturing towards the two Vellarans.

"And why is he staring at you?" Ezra snarls. I roll my eyes, *because that's the most important part about this situation.*

I grimace instead of answering right away as Marjorie pulls out the last of the venom. My head tilts a little to look at the old woman. "Almost done there Marj? Time's not on our side here."

"Impatient girl." She mumbles while wrapping up my shoulder. I move to stand when she holds up her finger. "One more thing."

I groan. "Marjorieeee." *THWACK! Ow.*

Her gaze falls to the prince and I, "*You.*" She says, jabbing a gnarled finger at him. "Your kingdom does not deserve the help she offered. Bring her to me broken, battered, or bruised again and I will remove that pretty head of yours from your shoulders."

"Understood." He replies, but he doesn't look at her, he keeps his eyes locked in on me.

Marjorie swats at him next, "I wasn't finished. The way you will assure me of this, is through a blood seal. Which you both will perform. *Now.*" She starts rummaging through her kit.

All eyes whip to the mage, Axel and Mousy's mouths dropping open. "Absolutely not." They all say in unison.

"Hold out your wrists." She commands, ignoring their protests.

Rorin's companion steps forward, voice low as he speaks to the prince. "Ror- you're not seriously going to make a blood seal with her are you?" He looks to me desperately, "you're her queen. You can stop this."

He's right, I could, but there is a glint in the prince's eyes. One that reads more as a challenge, and a tug inside me dares me to back down. When neither of us answer him, Marjorie takes out a small knife. There is a brief sting as she begins carving the runes of the seal into our skin. She mumbles ancient words that cause the rivulets of blood to rise. The droplets merge and hover over our wrists in the same shape as the mark she carved. Our gaze doesn't break, with his hazel eyes burning into mine. A feverish feeling spreads through me as the ritual finishes followed by a sharp sting as the seal snaps into place.

"I'd suggest adhering to the agreement you signed. The blood seal is a magic that does not take kindly to broken promises." She warns before turning her attention to my three men, next.

"We don't have to perform a blood seal too do we?" Axel's asks, his expression wary.

She ignores him. "It is *your singular* duty to protect *her*. She made an - albeit foolish - agreement to this Vellaran but—" she points a finger at each one, "you made an agreement to keep her safe. Over your own lives. Is that understood?" They all give her a small nod.

She takes one last long look at me, "we lose you, you damn us all. If they begin to fall then you let them."

Noted.

Ezra's furious with me. Everyone left the room after Marjorie except for him. He chose to stay and sulk in the corner, not speaking a word to me from room to hall.

"Whatever it is you're assuming, I'll bet you're wrong." I state, trying to throw a bone.

"You're being ridiculous." I add.

He scoffs, stopping in his tracks. "I'm being ridiculous?! I thought you were going to *bed*. You failed to mention that you were going to expel the energy right away!"

"When else was I going to do it? I don't owe you any explanations." I argue.

His eyes flare with anger. "NO! See you do! I am your *HEAD OF GUARD, EVEERA*. It is my job to know where you are so I can protect you. I could have gone *with you!* But you let him instead? And your explanation for the blood seal? You had nothing to say when she suggested that?"

Unbelievable. "I didn't let him and it wasn't like I had a choice with Marjorie."

"YOU DID LET HIM AND YOU DO HAVE A CHOICE! YOU ARE QUEEN, YOU ALWAYS HAVE A FUCKING CHOICE. Did you even bother telling him *no* to accompanying you?!" He's yelling now, making the soldiers passing us duck and avert their gazes.

"I said no originally, but he is very persistent." The anger sloughing off of him has my magic twitchy.

Ezra's fists clench while he takes a step closer to me. "The big deal?! Do you forget—" My power juts from my fingertips materializing into claws that rest against the pale skin underneath his chin.

"Do not finish that sentence, Ezra." I threaten, the claws pressing in. Defiance flares to life in his stare. "I forget *nothing*. You are out of line." He jerks out of my hold, stalking away from me the minute Axel comes into view.

"OOOO claws were out, what'd he do?" He asks, while his arm falls clumsily around my shoulders.

I stare up at Axel from the corner of my eye, "Don't you have something you're supposed to be doing?"

"Just came to grab you. Make sure you're still all in one piece." He says - turning me around - picking and prodding.

My hands swat him away. "Okay! Okay. I'm good. I'm good."

"Well, you seem to be all there. But I won't lie." His eyes swinging to look at Ezra's retreating back. "That looked intense, E." He mutters low into my ear. *I know*, I want to say. But the words get trapped in the back of my throat. Instead, I let him lead us on the rest of the way to the stables where General Matthis is planning on meeting us.

There are a few final things to confirm before we head off to modern day Helys - also known as the Kingdom of Vellar. I glimpse down at the new addition on my wrist. It looks no different than raised, pink scar tissue. But something in me feels different since she carved them.

General Matthis is standing by the horses, right where I expected to find him. His eyes have darkened circles shadowing underneath them and his weathered face is filled with concern. Concern I don't have time to entertain today.

"General." I greet. He gives a curt nod before making his way towards me. Rorin quickly takes up the space next to me and my wrist twinges.

"Your Highness. The first round of soldiers will be following behind you. It will take them longer due to their size but, Prince Rorin," he motions his hand towards the princeling, "has assured us that they'll be able to move them quickly into place without too much disruption. Unfortunately that amount of people will be noticed. Be prepared for...*interruptions*." His eyes flick back again to the prince before continuing on. "Based on the maps he's provided we need to decide quickly which routes the second round will be taking to aid the post in the northeast."

"Each company has 250 men and women? The beings from the Vast are somewhere around that number as well?" Rorin asks General Matthis.

He nods again. "Correct."

"Including my personal guard, we'll have soldiers with us. Then of course, your man, yourself and I. That makes the head count for your southern post, a little over 500." I supply.

"We should reach Bair in six days, with full forces they're probably going to be a week behind us." He points to the map of Obsidian and Vellar. "We are getting beaten heavily both at Bair and in the northeastern city of Piram. I'd like to have your armies on standby. My father isn't currently aware of what I am doing here, so—" Ezra cuts him off.

"Prince, if your father isn't aware of any of this." He snaps. "What exactly do you suggest we do? Matthis wants us to be aware of 'interruptions'," he throws quotes around the word, "but we could be killed on sight as invaders."

Frustration blooms on the prince's and his companion's features. Mousy ignores Ezra choosing to babble on to General Matthis that one of their commander's will meet and lead us in, then do the same for the soldiers when they reach the same checkpoint. It's unclear what state Bair will be in when we arrive but their conversation left off with Matthis stating he would wait for word from us before sending the second round of military. Their trek would of course be much longer, so the sooner we let him know the better.

I grin, "I hope it's a bloodbath." I mutter over to Axel while mounting my horse. He laughs nodding to Felix as he walks away from me to get onto his own horse. Felix's hand brushes down my animal's mane before landing on my knee.

"This is what we've trained for, Eveera. This is what your parents built you to be, what I built you to be." He reminds. "You both wear the blood seal. You understand what this means, yes?"

I smile, "Oh, you know, Marjorie was as explanatory as always." He groans.

"Do not be stubborn. Now is not the time for your self sacrificing recklessness." His eyes soften on me, his grip turning shaky as does his voice, "You - my dearest one - are our salvation. Whether you ever wanted to be or not. Be who they need, but if they begin to fall, you let them." His final words are exact to what Marjorie said in my bedroom, striking a chord in me as they hit my ears a second time. My focus only breaks from him when Seth comes running at me along with a very important parcel in his hand.

I mouth a thank you at Felix, snatching the parcel up and winking towards Seth.

My horse settles into a standard pace next to Axel, "he tell you not to be stubborn?" He asks.

"Mm-hmm."

"He tell you not to be reckless?" He adds. I turn to glare at him, a smirk pulling at the corner of my lips.

"I'm offended to hear you would think I'd be reckless and stubborn at a time like this. I happen to be very flexible." I reply. Axel coughs out a laugh before very loudly stating, "Just ask Ezra." That earns him a few snickers from the brothers while he earns a scathing glare from Armond, Ezra, and myself.

Remind me why I thought traveling with a bunch of men would be a good idea.

RORIN

We've been riding silently for hours. And during such quiet time, I've mulled over every possible outcome to the reaction my father will have once he figures out that I've gone directly against his orders. None of them turn out positively.

To ease the churning in my stomach I center my mind on something other than him. Instead I focus on my win, earning the Queen of Obsidian and her army. Or at least I hope it's a win. Her army trails a few miles behind us. Their group is about fifty times the size of ours, slowing them down significantly. I wonder how they'll fare with the creatures that live out in these lands. The gray tone of the trees and overcast sky make for a perfect camouflaged setting for the beasts that I know lurk somewhere within them. They'll have to endure them much longer than we will. But, surely, as trained professionals who are native to this kingdom they should be able to handle themselves.

SNAP!

The hairs on the back of my neck rise, unease weighs over us like a blanket. Our horses halt pausing our trek as we sit in silence long enough to be sure that nothing would come of that snap.

When we started moving again, I sidled my horse up to Eveera's. "How's your shoulder holding up?"

She keeps her golden eyes forward, the muscle in her jaw feathering. "Fine. Marjorie took care of it."

"And your wrist?" I pry. She looks down at it and shrugs.

"That was nothing. What about you?" She asks keeping her eyes straight ahead still.

I smirk, "I've endured worse, Nightmare."

Her nose scrunches up in annoyance, finally meeting my gaze. "*Nightmare?*"

I laugh. "Sure, I figure if you get to nickname me and my companion, then I get to nickname you. Queen of Nightmares - Nightmare. It works."

"It's 'The Nightmare Queen'." She corrects. "And don't nickname me."

My lips tip up at the correction. "Oh, I'm sorry, so you get to nickname yourself *and* the two of us - but I can't nickname you?" *I think I'll ignore that demand.* The voice inside my head sings. I decide to switch topics by asking, "You seem on edge, you're not nervous are you?"

It was meant to be lighthearted but by the way she turns to glare at me, she didn't take it that way. "Do I look like the type that gets nervous?" She snaps.

I raise my hands up, "just asking is all. Checking in."

"Don't do that."

"Don't do what?" I ask.

She waves her left hand around haphazardly, "*that*. The checking in."

I neutralize my expression, choosing to look away from her this time, "don't check in? Why can't I check in?" I ask, trying to seem aloof.

"The reasons are endless as to why you cannot check in on me."

"Well, we have a long ride ahe—" A whistle rings through the air followed by Armond flagging our group down. With the sky so cloud covered and gray nighttime came quicker than I had expected, so quickly that I hadn't even noticed how dark it was getting already.

The redhead jumps off of his horse. "We camp here." He has a gravelly lilt to his voice making his demeanor all that more imposing. Most of her men *and* women are intimidating to look at and I'm slightly ashamed my own army isn't as hardened as they are, I suppose they each mirror their sovereigns in that regard.

The rest of us follow suit jumping off our horses and unloading our packs. Again the group goes silent. The tension and unease from earlier has returned now that we aren't moving.

Will's anxious energy is palpable, the two of us have memories of these woods not too far removed from the present, and I can tell he isn't too sure about being ready to face them again. He's muttering quiet words and assurances to himself to ease his nervousness. Eveera at some point in setting up camp overheard him and barked in his direction that we are, "going to war and the creatures out here should be the least of his problems".

Will lets out an irritated sigh, "must you Obsids always be so vile. Everything has to be a threat?" he snaps.

"Hey man, no offense or anything, but you're probably safer with the creatures than you are with any of us. With us being so vile and all." Axel offers his less than helpful commentary, throwing Will a wink.

Will looks at me desperately. "Ror-"

"Go set up the mats." I say. His eyes narrow at me, distress seeping into them as he turns around. I hate pulling rank, but the more back and forth arguments there is between our two sides, the less I can make this work.

Looking around the small camp I observe everyone settling down for the night, with the exception of one person. The queen. She's not anywhere where I can see her, my head spinning around like an owl looking for her in the firelight. It's not until I hear leaves rustling straight ahead of me that I see her small shadowy form slipping deep into the woods away from camp, *alone.*

My feet move to go follow her when I feel my wrist catch. "Where do you think you're going, princeling?" Ezra growls, his fingers wrapping tightly around the rune of the blood seal.

"I think your Queen has slipped off into the woods unprotected." I snap.

"She's got it covered, Muscles." Axel pipes up from his sleeping mat, *great another nickname.*

I yank at my wrist, pulling Ezra toe to toe with me in the process. "No offense, gentlemen, but my kingdom made an investment in *her.* So I think I will go ensure that said investment doesn't get herself killed before we leave your soil."

Axel props up on his elbows. "Actually," his lips curling into a sneer, "you invested in *us.*" He motions his finger in a circle indicating the group, "she'll be pissed you followed her out there anyways."

Tearing my arm away from Ezra I flash my wrist at all of them. "I don't see anyone else with one of these. Meaning my deal is with *her.* I'll take my chances." I say taking off in the direction she went. Axel's parting words of "it's your funeral" die down behind me with each step I take.

It took me several minutes to find her. She's sitting with both palms pressed into the dirt. Rivulets of her black magic splinter through the ground around her. I rest my back against one of the barren trees witnessing her Wield work, not wanting to interrupt but wanting to watch her.

It's interesting to see her tattoos go so still, frozen in whatever position they were in before the magic started leaving her. So much power pours out of one small human. It's suffocating bottling in a Wield, I can't imagine what hers would feel like if she didn't expel it so freely.

"You're not very discreet when you're stalking someone." Her voice rasps. But the sound of it as it leaves isn't her usual voice. The voice she is speaking to me in is distorted. It sounds like she is battling between herself and her Wield.

"I wasn't stalking, I was ob—"

"*Observing*. I know. I told you to stop doing that." She doesn't turn around to address me. She stays prone on the ground with her hair out of its loose braid falling around her face. Her eyes - from what I can see at this angle - are as black as ever. "Didn't they tell you I don't like being followed?" She growls.

"They did. I didn't listen. I have an investment to protect. And they all seem to forget that they're meant to be guarding you."

She plays with a small tendril of her magic. *Fascinating*. I look her over, paying closer attention to those tattoos. The women in Vellar aren't quite so bold with painting their skin. "Why the serpents?"

"Got a thing for reptiles, I guess." Her reply is toneless, but it's returned to her normal, raspy and sultry voice.

"A thing for reptiles?"

Her head lifts up, the gold of her irises peeking through cracks of black as the last of her magic is absorbed. She hops up to her feet, somehow she still manages to look her nose down at me no matter how much shorter she may be. "That's what I said." Her hand comes up and pats my chest, the touch leaving behind a burning sensation.

I skulk behind her the rest of the way back to camp where most everyone has gone down for the night. She walks over to the fire and with a swift kick she snuffs it out, waking Will. "What the hell did you do that for?" He groans pulling the blanket up to his chin.

"Light will only draw attention to us. And I'd rather not draw attention out here, Mousy."

He purses his lips, "I thought you said that the war and yourselves were more dangerous?" He asks, his tone mocking as he flops back down.

Across from the fire, Ezra shifts on his mat, leaving a very blatant amount of excess room on it. My eyes flick between him and Eveera who glances at him and then glances over to her own mat. For a brief moment I swear she meets my stare, before casting her gaze down. She turns and walks to her mat next to Axel who's already snoring. Ezra's face contorts, the rage clear on it.

Coincidentally it would seem Will laid out my mat between hers and Axel's. I can't help the smirk that grows on my face. She chose being closer to me - her enemy - than her own lover. Whether she realizes that or not, Ezra seems to. At least that's what I'm assuming based on the murderous look he gives me before flopping over and giving me his back.

I lay down next to her. She's created as much distance between us as possible to the point that she's practically on top of Axel who remains asleep despite his queen fusing her chest to his side.

Her long dark hair blends into the night, the curls spreading across her mat behind her. In this state they look nearly identical to the tendrils of her Wield. Her side lifts up and down matching the rhythm of her breathing as she falls asleep.

Screaming, who the hell is screaming?

I'm standing in a dark hall the screams echoing off the stone. The pain vibrating with the sound. I follow the noise, weaving around the bodies that are in pieces and littered everywhere. Their blood splattered all over the walls.

The screams lead me to a set of doors. The markings and carvings in the wood seem familiar to me, but I can't recall why. I peer through the crack in the door, looking into the room. In the center is a small girl on her knees, hair a sea of black flows down her back, blood covering her nightgown, legs, and hands. There's magic pooling around her black as her hair.

Eveera? It can't be...she can't be older than maybe eleven or twelve...

My hands push the door wider which allows the smell inside to overwhelm my senses. More of that thick, coppery, scent of blood enters my nostrils. My eyes follow to where her blackened gaze is trained, all the way to where I see—

Oh fuck. Oh no, no, no gods no. I fall to my knees next to the younger Eveera, horror clawing up my throat as I stare at the body hanging above the both of us. Her mother, Queen Ayla, is completely disemboweled. She's strung up by her innards from the posts of her bed.

It's a gory and hideous display and Eveera found her.

I gulp down the bile building in my throat.

"This was the night of the assassination. It has to be." I whisper, my voice coming out garbled, like I were speaking underwater. But I wouldn't dream this-this isn't my memory...this isn't my nightmare...it's hers.

-

My eyes fly open, a fiery sensation tearing up my arm. The sky is still pitch black, shadows dancing around us. The only visible light is coming from my wrist, it's glowing red. Whimpers and rustling fill the otherwise silent camp.

Eveera -tosses and turns in her sleep -no doubt from the living hell I just witnessed in her mind.

In her *mind.* I think. *Oh this is going to piss her off.*

Her hair, that same sea of black is no longer spread out across the mat but wound around her now, *"No, no, no, no."* Tumbles from her lips.

I move over to place my hand on her shoulder. I pick up her wrist, it's glowing the same red as mine, further confirming that another facet of this seal isn't just binding our agreement - but binding *us*.

"Eveera. Eveera. Come on." She doesn't budge, but her whimpers have started to turn into wails. "Wake up before you alert the whole damn outer lands." I hiss into her ear.

Both eyes snap wide as she gasps in a mouthful of air, her hands clawing at her chest. "What the hell?" She whisper shouts. Next to her Axel groans out a barely coherent *"Evie, shut up"* in our direction, his hand flailing out to smack at her.

"Don't yell at me, you were the one making all the fuss." I snap. She shoves me away from her, sprinting off into the darkness. "Damn woman." I grumble, darting off after her. Armond - who's on guard - lets a slight snort out at the display. *Why the fuck didn't he wake her?* The want to turn around and confront him instead of Eveera rises up in me but I tamp it down and settle for a scathing glare in his direction.

"Must you follow me?!" Her attempts to shout are dwindled by our need to be quiet.

"If you insist on stalking off into the middle of the night then yes, *Your Highness*, I must follow you." My frustration matching hers.

Why does she have to be so difficult? She knows how dangerous these woods are, and yet she still is choosing to storm away. The thought sits in my mind, the voice in my head begging to materialize. "You can't take off out here." I argue.

"Ha. I'm probably the only who can take off out in these woods, thank you very much."

A sigh heaves from me as I rub the scruff on my chin. "Well last time you got bit."

She glares, an accusatory finger poking into my chest, "because you distracted me! And look here you are, distracting me. *AGAIN!* Poking your nose into something that isn't your business, *AGAIN!*"

"I was just trying to help."

She leans her head back against a tree. "It was a nightmare, Rorin. I would've woken up eventually. You don't need to try and help me with my dark and twisty head. Okay, princeling?" Something tugs inside me when she says my name, before she switches back to that insipid nickname. I pace back and forth in front of her.

"I'm not. I-I wasn't." The words stammering out of me. My body moves in front of her, caging her against the tree. "My mind...and then my wrist." I whisper.

Her eyes go dark, "what about your mind and wrist?"

"I saw things. I saw memories. I think you pulled me into them." My voice is barely audible. If my words weren't, then my position was the only thing holding her in place.

"Pulled you into *what, princeling.* Words." She asks her tone on the brink of turning violent.

"I saw you. I saw...*her.*" Her eyes start to bleed black at the corners as she loses the grip on her control. On instinct I grab her throat and pin her in place, the proximity putting our faces close enough that our noses brush. My lip curls into a snarl that just barely grazes her top lip. "Don't do it, Nightmare. Don't throw my own demons at me just because someone saw yours for once."

Her eyes slip back into that mesmerizing gold at my words her voice cracking. "Why?"

Why indeed. With the threat of her Wield lashing out sated, I place some distance between the two of us. "Our wrists, the seal. I think it links more than just the terms of our agreement. I think it links us. You were panicking, your mind was throwing you into chaos - into danger. The seal *reacted*. I think it pulled me in to protect you."

She huffs out a quiet incredulous laugh. "Protect me? *You* are who I need protecting *from*. Fuck whatever the seal does. Stay out of my head, princeling."

For the next day and a half, Ezra scowls at me. If his glares could kill, I'd be dead ten times over already.

We kept the routine from our first night. Armond whistles out, we make camp, Ezra glares, Eveera stalks off to release more energy, I follow, Eveera glares *and* Ezra glares, we fall asleep, we wake up, and naturally, Ezra glares. There were no nightmares on the second night, but Eveera hasn't looked at me since the first. She hasn't spoken to me either.

"We are about a day and a half's ride from the border." Armond's voice booms over the sound of hooves clamoring through the terrain.

Orem's head pops up. "Who's meeting us at the wall again?" He asks.

"Commander Bennett - will greet Rorin and I first. Then he will let all of *you* in." Will answers.

A collective snarl rolls through the group at the tone Will takes with them. The closer to the border we get the bolder Will has been with his demeanor. "Get your foul remarks in now, because once we are back on Vellaran soil no one will tolerate your treatment of the prince."

"If that was your version of a threat Mousy, you might want to work on your delivery, dear." Eveera says. Her voice shakes something loose in me. A tendril of hers pats his head as she passes his horse. For the first time ever, I see a murderous look flash through Will's eyes. He's a damn good head guard, but violence, murder? Not his thing. He prefers to detain and deal with people through the justice system. He's only ever killed when protecting an innocent.

"Ror." He calls, waving me over to him.

"Yeah?" I ask.

I bring my horse closer so that he can lean over and keep his words quiet. "Notice how there's been a lack of some certain possessed beings so far?"

I nod, chewing on my lip. "Yeah, I have."

"And?" he presses.

My shoulders shrug. "And, I think the queen must have it under control."

He laughs at that. Not as quietly as his words clearly had been, because we get a few stares from the Obsids around us. "Where was that control when she got herself *bit* the other day?" I don't have the explanation for that, I don't know when in that fight she got bit exactly, just that I noticed her bloodied shoulder after we pulled back our Wields from one another.

"You guys can stop talking about me now." We both startle at the sound of her voice. It's the first time she's acknowledged me verbally since our last conversation. "But, you're right, princeling. I *do* have it under control." I give Will a look to let it go. We already have a fragile enough relationship with them.

She returned to her silence after popping into Will and I's conversation. Her next acknowledgment coming in the form of her hand reaching out to stop us. We all pull our horses up to where she's stopped. To where there is a deep fissure running through the ground. *That wasn't here when we entered the kingdom,* I note. "Shit. How are we supposed to get across tha—" Axel's mouth drops open as Eveera's horse backs up and then takes off at breakneck speed, the two of them jumping across the expansive gap.

The rest of us stay put and stare at her dumbfounded. "You lot coming?" She shouts. Unease trickles through while a few of us look around for any possible way around this. When one can't be found, each of her men take off in a run, meeting her on the other side. Will shoots me a nasty look before making the same jump. I'm the last to do it, my horse landing with a grunt.

"Armond, Void to the others, the armies will have to detour around as best they can." Eveera barks. Within a blink he winks out of existence, leaving his horse behind.

Axel is panting, his hands planted firmly on his hips. "E? Have I ever told you that you make terrible decisions. I could have just *died* right now." He shrieks while pointing a shaky - *dramatic* - finger at the fissure.

She tips her chin up. "I do not make terrible decisions." She argues.

"No. No, sweetheart, you really do." He says breathlessly. "You really do."

Sweetheart? He calls his queen sweetheart? I mull that information over in my mind as the voice in my head suggests, *maybe he was a lover too.* That thought and their familiarity with one another sends an ill feeling twinging through me.

As she passes his horse up, he leans over to thwack the side of her head. *Another person who hits the queen upside her head? How bizarre.* She gives no other reaction than yelping, "OW!" and shoving him back. Armond blinks back to his place on his horse interrupting the queen and Axel. He gives her a nod that she returns as she takes the lead.

The closer we get to the border the more anxious the energy around us seems to get. Will is the only relatively unaffected one, his mood steadily improving.

CRACK! An eerie sensation of déjà vu creeps up the back of my neck while my horse stops in its tracks. The rest of the horses slow as well, all eight of our heads looking around us. I urge mine forward to line up with her and Axel.

She hands her reins to me, standing quickly in her stirrups. Just as I think she's about to get off of her horse, she instead climbs up onto her saddle using the new vantage point to survey the area. Her irises go from gold to black in an instant just as a dozen pairs of red eyes appear on either side of our horses. Black tendrils explode out of her hands and both Axel and I lunge to grab a leg and steady her. Our eyes lock, the look saying the same thing to each other.

The tendrils secures tightly around the creatures' throats. She pulls her hands down, forcing the creatures to collapse with the motion. She then whips both her hands out to the sides and their heads roll from their shoulders, black sludge pouring out into the ground from the stumps.

The air is still for a moment until a scream rings out from deep in the forest. What was a dozen pairs of eyes has now tripled. Panic briefly crosses Eveera's face just before she dives towards the ground, her ankles slipping from our hold. We both scramble off our horses after her.

"WHAT DID I TELL YOU? SHE MAKES TERRIBLE DECISIONS!" He shouts while unsheathing his sword and cutting through the closest creature. *This damn woman.*

I *had* eyes on her but now she's disappeared into the masses. *Again.*

My wrist both glows and burns and if I were to guess, I would bet that it is my indication that she was at least still with us. The sign that proved she was okay came from the wave of bodies dropping to the ground at our feet.

"SHE'S SOMEWHERE IN THE MIDDLE OF THEM, AXEL!" I call out.

"Eveera." I reach out to her mentally. It's a long shot that the link will work this way but I want eyes on her. No, I *need* to have eyes on her.

A new voice pipes up. "CAN SOMEONE MAKE SURE SHE DOESN'T GET HERSELF KILLED, PLEASE?" *Maxwell.* "IF SHE DIES, MARJORIE WILL SKIN US ALIVE." He shouts.

"How about" *Grunt.* "nobody" *SLICE!* "DIES," Will yells back to him. "I thought you said she had this *HANDLED*!" He directs those words at me.

I dive under the hands of the creature closest to me. *"EVEERA!"* I try again.

A strange feeling washes over me as a feminine voice barks into my mind. *"I SAID STAY OUT OF MY BLOODY HEAD."* I don't have time to respond as I stab another beast, sludge splattering all over me. I see her head pop up in the middle of a group of creatures.

She screams out slashing in all directions. "Where are you all coming from?!" Her throwing stars are seated snuggly in the throat of a beast that I pass while running towards her. I urge my legs to move faster when I see a deformed hand grabbing at her back.

"NO!" I scream, yanking her chest into mine, my sword coasting over her head and cutting clean through the creature's face. She slumps against my chest for a moment both of her hands fisting into my bloodied clothes. My free arm comes around, hand cupping the back of her head. I hold her tightly to me as our breaths sync together.

After a short while she stiffens, taking in our position and the bodies littered around us. We hear another branch break in the distance and her head whips to the side, *"what the gods?"* her words echo into my mind. She points her finger but keeps the arm close. I squint in the direction she's turned her head in, trying to see what she's pointing at.

Distantly, I see a shadow and then two red eyes. There off in the woods stands a lone creature. He makes no effort to charge at us. He just stands there, staring the same as we are.

"*Is that?*"

"*A creature that looks almost cognizant?*" She breathes out. Meanwhile my hold tightens on her, fusing our bodies together, as I move us back.

"*What the hell do you think that means?*" I say down the seal.

She shake my head. "*I don't know.*"

"IF YOU TWO ARE DONE SNUGGLING, WE'D LIKE TO GET GOING BEFORE ANY MORE OF THE WALKING DEAD SHOW UP." Axel's voice carries, dumping over us like ice cold water.

"You okay?" I ask, my hand stroking down her hair absentmindedly. "No venomous consequences this time?" I rove my eyes over her. *No injuries this time.* Her chin lifts in defiance but how she looks at me when she notices us holding onto one another...makes my head dizzy. And it only clears when she slips from the position I put us in and saunters off back to the group.

We all look like shit. We decided as a whole to stop for the night shortly after the fight. If I thought we were quiet before, I was wrong. It is more silent than the dead now. Looking over each person the only ones with injuries sustained were Will and Orem. Orem, has a cut through his eyebrow that's still bleeding and Will's lip is busted. Other than that, the only things that really sustained any damage were our clothes. They're all soaked through with the creature's sticky black sludge.

With how exhausted I was and the tension from earlier, I hadn't planned on following Eveera tonight. Until she got up and looked in my direction. I've either deluded myself or there was an almost imperceptible look of expectation on her face when she did.

When I caught up to her I take note that she is sitting again in a small clearing, palms to the earth, her black magic veining through the soil. Her shoulders are slumped, giving way to her exhaustion.

"*This is becoming a habit, princeling.*" *That voice.* It's like a siren's call, luring me to sit down next to her.

"*I thought you told me to stay out of your bloody head.*" I remark.

She snorts, "*I did.*"

"What happened out there today?" I ask, this time vocally.

She shakes her head, sighing, "I have no idea. The way the lone one looked. It looked like he was—"

"Studying us." I finish for her.

She lets out another long sigh, "yes. I have never once in the years we have dealt with them, encountered one that seemed to be aware of itself. Mostly they seem mindless, slaves to their bloodlust. I've even witnessed them turn on one another if they aren't satiated from the energy or killed off quickly enough."

"How long have you been dealing with them?"

Her fingers dig deeper into the dirt. "How old am I? Twenty-five? That would make it fourteen years, they showed up after..." Her voice trails off, gaze bleeding from gold to black. The seal in our minds slams down sharply, sending my presence against a mental wall. *Whatever she's working out in there she doesn't want me to know.*

I lean forward trying to get her to look at me. "After what?"

She pulls her lip between her teeth, biting down gently. "Nothing, it will be fine."

Putting my hand to her shoulder, I try to shake those eyes back to their golden hue. "Eveera."

"I SAID IT WILL BE FINE!" A wave of black rams into me.

"P-please don't lock me up here again. PLEASE." His laugh rings out through the cell. "Please don't lock me up here again." He mocks before landing a kick in between my ribs. "P-please." I sob out to nothing. I'm dirty, broken, bleeding. I will kill him. I will kill them all the moment these mage shackles are taken off.

I gasp, clawing at my throat as I suck down the breaths.

"*Did you kill him?*" Her voice comes quietly from inside my mind.

I look up at her, rage overwhelming. "What?!" I snap.

"The man. Did you kill him?" Her voice is soft and her eyes are gold again.

I take a few more breaths to calm myself down for good measure before answering. "Yes."

"Good." Her stare is as pained as mine. "Next time, don't push me for information. Or I might grow to enjoy your fears." She threatens.

She takes off towards camp. Dread was already pooling in my stomach, like it does every time I think about my time in that room.

I'm going to have to build better mental blocks if she is going to continue sending me into that nightmare. I already killed the man once, I don't need him coming back to life.

EVEERA

The nightmares keep getting worse.

And to add more kindling to the fire, the blood seal allows *him* to experience them with me.

Every day I look at him it's like I am looking at her killer. I suppose it's a healthy reminder. My eyes apparently *like* looking at him.

You should remove them and get new ones, I think.

I am consistently having to redirect my thoughts to spend most of their time combing through old memories, pushing on the recesses of my mind in an attempt to get back to when we first noticed the creatures. *It was right after they died.* The voice in my head supplies. The whispers around court said it was like Obsidian was revolting against the loss of it's King and Queen. The harsher rumors whispered that maybe Obsidian wasn't just mourning the loss but *rejecting* it's new Queen.

From the start the creatures appearances have had variation among them. The humanoid and the non. How appropriate that the kingdom whose sovereign held such an unsavory Wield was surrounded by the most foul of beasts. The one tonight, however, superseded humanoid.

It was *present - sentient* as it locked eyes with Rorin and I. Thank the useless gods for the one mercy that none of the other men noticed. We don't have the time to diffuse panic.

Once we made camp, I commanded Armond to Void himself to the army again. We needed to warn them of the hot spot. It was easy for the prince and I to ignore what happened and resume what little activities we can while waiting for morning to come. Making me a culprit of avoiding two things tonight as my mind refuses sleep. I'm not the only one wide awake though. Ezra is off to the side of camp, standing guard and doing a poor job of it as he stares into the fire.

"You should go talk to him." The voice startles me at first. "

Vada?" I ask. She grunts into my mind, confirming. "*You're snooping.*"

"*I do not care enough to snoop, little demon. I can feel his toxic masculinity all the way here, in Oriya. Deal with it.*" As quickly as she came she was gone again from my mind. *She's right*, the little voice in my head sings. *Fucking annoying conscience.* My shoulders sag as I make my way to him, leaning up against his tree. "You're angry with me." I say.

He chuffs at the statement. "I am frustrated, there is a difference."

"Is there, Ezra? With you?" My head lolls to the right. Not close enough to touch his arm but enough that when I look up I see his blonde hair loosely falling from the bun it's twisted in.

His blue eyes look sideways at me through the rogue strands. "With *me?*"

"Yes, with you Ez. You've been acting insecure since right before we left." I state, picking at my fingernails.

He lets out something between a growl and a chuckle, "Insecure." He repeats.

"Did I stutter?"

He holds his hand up, cutting off any further reply from me. "No, let me speak now. As your Commander, your Head of Guard, as your...whatever I am, I have a role to uphold." Oh *brother*. "But since dickhead princeling showed up, you have completely disrespected that role." His expression warns me from opening my mouth to argue. "Which means not only have you disrespected the significance of my job but you've disrespected me. *Humiliated* me. More so than you have before." His body moves so that he is standing almost chest to chest with me, one arm placed above my head. "Imagine *my* panic, when I get word you're being *carried, YOU of all people,* into your own bedroom by *him.*"

His teeth are clenched, the vein in his neck bulging. "You were hurt. You needed *Marjorie* for gods sake, twenty fucking minutes before we're supposed to leave. You've enlisted all of us in essentially a suicide mission for the kingdom that murdered your parents - and that fucking blood seal?! You. Are. *QUEEN*. Eveera. You can always tell Marjorie no. No matter how many times she swats at you because of it." He breaks eye contact with me, instead choosing to look at the sky. His body is rigid, tense. "He doesn't even give you the space to Wield out here so that maybe we can travel safely. But that's not the worst part. No, no, no. The worst part is you *allow him to be there*. You would never let me do something like that, hell, you don't even let Mecham go with you and he's your best fucking friend. But *him?*" His face screws up in disgust. "I know you don't owe me anything for whatever we are, Eveera. But it's extra salt in the wound when you won't even lay by me at night. You choose to be over there. And if it were just Axel, I might understand. But it's not - it's Axel plus the princeling and his rat."

"Mouse." I correct, drawing an eye roll out of him.

"It's disgusting. I'm only entertaining this mission for your sake. Because I'm obligated to keep you safe." He growls the last bit.

"OBLIGATED?!" I snap. "Let's get one thing straight here, *Ez*. You are not obligated to do anything. Last I checked *we* don't share a blood seal that ties you to this. You don't want to be here? Go. Home. You don't want to serve as Head of Guard? Quit. You're angry with me over the fact that Rorin doesn't know how to respect personal boundaries. I'm not *allowing* him to do anything, I just don't care enough to put up an argument with him. It's not like my powers are a secret. They certainly wouldn't be one after helping the Vellarans." I spit, pressing my chest up against him. "Find a way to deal with this or go home." My palms flatten, shoving him off of me.

"That's right, go storm back to the princeling." He mumbles.

My fist tightens around cool metal before I have time to think about what I'm doing. "AGH! YOU INSOLENT BASTARD." *Schwoop!* The hilt of my dagger shakes by Ezra's head where it sinks into the bark of the tree I just stood against. I feel my power leaking from my fingertips as I struggle for control. He shakes his head walking away from the tantrum he coaxed.

Axel's familiar scent fills my nostrils before I feel his hand clasp my shoulder. "Evie? We okay there?" He asks tentatively. I take a deep breath regaining my composure.

"Just…I need to go." I say storming off into the dark woods. This time no one followed.

When dawn crept up I made my way back to camp. Everyone was just barely waking up when I walked over to the mats. Ezra's stare burning a hole in me the entire time, but I refuse to look at him. His accusation that I've forgotten our roles is laughable. I will never forget what and who we are. He doesn't get to put the prince's annoying and invasive behaviors or Marjorie's desperation on me.

"Your Highness." I jump at the intrusion, my hand clutching at my chest.

"Shit, Monty you scared me." I rasp.

He nods towards where my head guard stands. "You and Ezra have it out?" He asks, his face and tone serious.

Not you too. "UGH. Please, Monty, I am begging you - and I never beg - for this conversation to be over before it starts." He nods while tacking up my horse for me. "You're not mad at me too, are you?"

"Your Highness, I don't have any place feeling anger when it comes to you." *Highness.* His tendency for formality makes me laugh.

"Mond. The title." He glances down at me. The look in his eyes is tender, so much softness these men hold for me. It's disconcerting.

"Eveera." He says slowly, testing it out. "I don't think I need to tell you how proud I am of who you have become. For the queen you are now," I smirk, "but even with the growth you've made these past ten years - you're still at times that same headstrong, *obnoxious,* and reckless young queen I was forced to train." He laughs to himself, "I still remember the rage you came at me with. Your powers were in full swing, you had zero control. You were terrifying. Maybe more so back then. And I was your magical punching bag, trying to navigate the both of us through all of that. But we did it, because you chose to have a clear mind with everything."

My brow cocks at him. "Are you saying I am not in control? That my mind isn't clear? Or that I am behaving like a twelve year old with no manners."

He drags his hand across his chin, thoughtfully. "I am saying - we are here for *you.* Not him. You made this deal. We simply follow." My gaze narrows at him, this speech sounding eerily similar to my argument with Ezra. "I am saying, do not lose *control*. Not around them. He is sneaking us into his own territory to fight a war that is not ours. You can't afford to slip or to have a clouded mind." His hand falls to my shoulder. "I trust you. Find that control. Nobody believes in you more than I do, little serpent."

Little serpent. At the call of that name, the serpents on my skin slither slightly, a memory of him taking me into Oriya after my Wielding nearly killed us both surfaces and I smile. His hand has slid down my arm, tracing one of the markings. The same look of reminiscing flits across his features. He was the first person aside from Felix to show me familial love after my parents died. Someone I can count on still to be willing to do anything for me. Even if it's walking directly into the mouth of a beast we aren't prepared for. I shrink away from the tender moment, not wanting to dwell in it for too long. At the shift in my demeanor he switches back to his professional persona and leaves me and my horse.

Rorin and Mousy announced they'd be leading the rest of the journey. Not giving any of the rest of us a choice in the matter. Apparently their faces need to be seen first to prevent any "*accidents*" as Mousy says.

I've been keeping my eyes peeled for any other hordes that may have decided to become self-aware and attack. So far in the few hours we've now ridden there has been no issues. The terrain is starting to get more unfamiliar the closer we get to the border. The only times I have been out this far have been with Vada to deal with the outer land situation.

I've tried reaching out to her since last night but it's been silent. *Big lizard baby.*

"Where's your head at, Evie?" Axel asks, sidling up to me.

"Oh you know, just the impending shit storm we are probably walking into. I'll kick ass, of course." I wink at him.

That same goofy grin of his spreads across his face, "Of course."

"Who's ass are we kicking?" Orem's voice pops in.

"Yours." We say in unison earning us a frown from him and a laugh out of his brother.

He puffs his chest out. "I could kick your ass, Mecham!" He points back and forth between Axel and Maxwell. "*Both* your asses!"

"Nobody is kicking anybody's ass. Enough with the immature banter." Ezra barks.

Axel lets out an exaggerated gasp. "Evie, I think he just called you immature." He looks over to his head of command mischief already brewing behind those deep brown eyes. "Hey Ez! Does the immature banter include the queen? Because if so, I wouldn't count on keeping your head for too long."

Ezra doesn't respond - resuming his sulking at the back of the party. Petulant bastard. The two brothers and Axel chose to continue their argument of who would kick who's ass while my attention switched to a very silent princeling and his comrade. A dangerous idea plays in my head as I saunter up to the two of them. "You're both very quiet. No snide comments, no gasps of disgust or disapproval?" I hum.

Mousy's jaw clenches at the sound of my voice. "I'm going home. So no. Today there is nothing you or your lot could do to irritate me."

I smirk, "oh?" I ask, leaning down and reaching into my saddle bag. He eyes me warily as I fish around for the package Seth handed off to me before we left. "Absolutely nothing?"

He tilts his chin up and stares straight ahead. The prince gives me a dark look as he watches my hands deftly unwrap the parcel. With the final piece of wrapping falling away, the item rolls around in my palm, revealing itself. Rorin's eyes widen and he gasps causing Mousy to whip around his head and look. I fasten the string of the item around my fingers, allowing me better mobility and access to dangle it near Mousy.

He shrieks so loudly he almost falls off his horse. "WHAT THE BLEEDING GODS IS THAT?!" His voice shrill as the tone of his skin goes from beige to green.

"I thought it obvious?" I play dumb as I hook the item to my saddle. When neither party gives me a response, I sigh, "well, traveling with the full-sized head would have been preposterous. So I had it shrunk. Now Percy is travel sized! It's so convenient!" I wave my wrist around, shaking the now shrunken version of their fallen comrade's head around violently.

Mousy gags, his face can't decide if he should look enraged or disgusted. One thing is for sure, his hatred for me has deepened. "You could have done literally anything else. Burned him, buried him, but to desecrate a man's corpse?!" He shrieks.

Looking down I pat Percy's head with my opposite hand, the action causing the soldier to gag a second time and speed his horse up to move far away from me. My chest rumbles with amusement. Much to my disappointment however, Rorin barely gave me much of a reaction. He quickly resumed his broody silent ride once Mousy's horse was out from between us. Naturally, with the gap now there, our two animals gravitate closer.

"*I'm guessing your father won't appreciate my handiwork?*" I ask, testing out our newfound telepathic capabilities. His shoulders roll backwards, the tension rippling through his back.

"*Probably not.*" He replies, the words curt and unfeeling.

I roll my head towards him, "*not even after I save your sorry kingdom?*" He doesn't give me a response. Those two hazel eyes fused to the sunrise.

"*So I can forget the thank you dinner when we're all done then, huh?*"
I thought the jest fell flat until he laughs.

But the laughter has no humor in it, it's the precursor to his snap. "Is everything a joke to you?"

I shrug, "not everything, no."

He glares in the direction of Percy. "You had to do that?" He stares at it as it bounces against the buckle on the side of my saddle. His expression is stormy. I can tell he's deciding whether or not he wants to let the situation go or to fight for the Vellaran's honor - not that it matters, he's already dead. You can't raise what's already dead.

"*You irritate him.*" His deep voice floats into my mind but his chin jerks in the direction of his man.

I smile. "*Really? What gave you that impression?*"

"*Call it a hunch.*" He says dryly.

He's suspiciously tense. I'd say it's because of me or even Percy but it feels unrelated to my morbid display. "So, why the brooding lone wolf persona today?"

Rorin grunts. "*You're not the only one with a kingdom to worry about.*" My mind rattles at his words. His voice is teeming with fear, the kind I am all too familiar with. This is the fear of losing something, disappointing someone or *someones*.

"You know if you keep making that face it'll freeze like that. Then you won't be so pretty anymore." I say down the seal.

He laughs, again, this time with some levity. Unfortunately for me, it's not a sound I hate hearing. Even if I hate him. "*You think I'm pretty, huh?*" He jests.

I roll my eyes, "*You know you're pretty, princeling. Just not as pretty as me. Obviously.*"

The prince purses his lips, a slight smile resting on the corners, *"Obviously."* He replies. The rhythm of the hooves beneath us is the only sound reaching our ears. The men behind and in front have no idea a whole conversation is happening between us.

"I know I'm not." I say.

He looks at me, finally. His face scrunched up in confusion. *"What?"*

"I know I'm not the only one with a kingdom to worry about. You have your own men you worry about." He's quiet for a moment, contemplating what I said. "How much time do you think before we reach your commander?" My voice carries out loud, available for everyone to hear.

"Ah-hem. We'll be there right at nightfall. Should give us enough time to go through the wall and rest before heading to the post." He replies.

We stay riding next to each other the rest of the way. No more words were exchanged, verbal or mental. Armond came up quietly behind us at some point and fell into step with Mousy's horse. My anxiety mixes with my Wield creating an unbalanced level of control inside of me the closer we get to the border.

The stone structure of the barrier wall comes into view as the sun begins setting. The realization that I will no longer have the royal upper-hand becomes readily apparent. Mousy looks back at us and tilts his head, signaling for Rorin to take his place next to him.

The prince listens and I follow.

His companion bristles as line up my horse with theirs, barking orders at me to back up.

"Fuck off, Mouse." I snarl.

No way in Helys was I going to retreat behind them to meet this "commander".

"He meets me at your side or not at all, princeling." I growl into his mind. He doesn't argue - he doesn't respond at all, actually, his arms

tightening on the reigns and his jaw ticking in anticipation. Or maybe that's agitation. Hard to tell as we wait.

The agreement from what I recall was that the man, Bennett, would meet us several yards away from the gates. Supposedly, others know we are coming but for now we will try to keep a low profile. After meeting with us, he will usher the group in. We'll have to organize someone to do the same for the men and women traveling behind us. Their numbers will be noticed no matter what precautions we take.

"*Where is he?*" I hiss, getting impatient.

A low vibration hums through me as his voice sifts past the chaos of my brain, "*Slow your heart, Nightmare. It's putting me on edge.*"

"*You put me on edge!*" I snap.

A whistle trills out into the wind and Mousy perks up. He sends back what I can only assume is the return call and then a shadow moves towards us at break neck speed.

On instinct all of my men and I reach for our weapons, "HOLD. It's only Bennett." Mousy yells.

"Oh that makes me feel better." Axel mutters.

Slowly the shadow materializes, the last light glowing behind him and illuminating his golden armor. Bennett grins brightly, "Prince, welcome back."

He drops off his horse, Rorin and Mouse doing the same, arms extended out to embrace each other.

My men give me hesitant looks that I ease with a mischievous wink. As the three of them break apart I palm one of my throwing stars, sending it flying directly for the new man's face. As if Rorin already knew my plan, his hand snaps out and stops the star mid flight - that's the third time he's done this - directly before hitting its mark. "*Again? That wasn't very nice.*" His rough voice barrels into my mind, *damn that voice.*

His tone is a strange mix of exasperation and amusement, maybe even a little feigned disappointment. *It's anticipation in his voice you're hearing. He's learning all your tricks.* The voice built into my mind says. Desperately, I wished it were Vada's voice mocking me instead of my own but she's kept quiet. I'm beginning to think her most recent chastisement about Ezra was the last time I'll hear from her for the next however long I am out of Obsidian.

"*I'm getting impatient, princeling.*" I sing back to him. Our brief words are exchanged in the same second it took for shock and panic to register on the other two Vellaran's faces.

Mousy's panic wears off as profanities escape his mouth - along with some compliments to the tune of "you completely insufferable, horrid, *violent* disaster of a queen! He is here to *help* us."

"Shove it, Mousy. Your..." I wave my hands to gesture at the three of them, "reunion is taking far too long. Can't save you if we are still in my territory." My hands, now empty, are on my hips.

The gilded guard, steps forward, "you must be the Queen." He states giving a swift bow.

"Really? I for sure thought I saw her running around somewhere. No? Oh well then I *must* be her." He blinks slowly, taken aback by my brashness. "And here I thought I didn't need an introduction." I push my horse past his standing figure hearing Mousy mumble, "no, you need a warning label."

My fingers flick for my men to follow me, not wanting to dawdle any longer.

Behind I hear faintly, Bennett whisper, "well she's certainly something" followed by a noncommittal noise from Rorin and Mousy's reply of, "she's a headache."

Glad to see I've made such a stellar impression on the three of them, I think.

We made it through the gate under the cover of darkness without any hiccups.

For the first time in fourteen years, Obsidian is left without a sovereign behind castle walls. And it's again at the request of Vellar. My horse has grown twitchy with the feeling of my emotions much like Vada would be. Just without the mental link. It doesn't help that Rorin keeps casting concerned glances my direction.

"*Keep giving me that look, princeling, and your new fear will become blindness.*" I gripe.

"*You're tense.*" He replies.

"*Were you not? When on my lands? I'm simply returning the favor.*" His laugh enters my mind and damn the half-dead butterflies in my stomach for thinking even for a second that they could flutter at the sound. *We hate him*, I remind them.

The now nine of us stop a few miles north of the wall to make camp.

My hands are idle now knowing that I won't have to expel any energy here. Axel comes up behind me, his arms looping around my shoulders. He rests his head on top of mine. "Enemy lands, Evie. Guard up, always." He whispers. I give a single bob of my head in answer before disentangling myself and laying out our mats.

My Wield is itching to search and find any weaknesses in our newest companion. Giving in a little to it, I send one tendril to slither his way. "*Pull them back.*" Rorin's voice commands in my head throwing my concentration. His hazel eyes are narrowed into slits when I look up to see him leaned against a very green tree.

I raise my hands half way in a sign of mock surrender, *"just feeling out my enemy."*

His tone deadpans, unamused. *"My wrist isn't burning, you aren't in danger. Don't toy with him."* I redirect my tendril to Rorin then, allowing it to explore up his leg, his chest, and finally settling around his throat. I try not to shiver as his stare burns into mine while he allows my Wield to search his skin. No one else noticing our silent battle.

"Then I guess I'll play with you." I muse, it comes out breathier then I had intended.

That same rough laugh echoes against the walls of my skull again. Assaulting my every sense. *How many times is that now?* I wonder.

"Careful, Nightmare. You might enjoy that." I let out a weak, disgruntled noise, but it saves me from him noticing the mad flush creeping onto my cheeks.

The tension has minimally eased without the threat of the creatures. But now the threat lies with us being off Obsidian ground. Bennett tried to make curt conversation but I shut that down by flopping over onto my mat. My men following suit.

As snores sound, I strain to hear the three Vellaran's conversation. I don't understand a word with Rorin's baritone voice somehow soothing me to sleep. I'll blame it on the pure exhaustion of the past few days - it's certainly not due to my comfort level being here. His scent is the last thing I remember sensing as his body laid down on the mat next to mine.

Bourbon and citrus.

Of course he would be the sickeningly perfect combination of bitter and sweet.

RORIN

Being in our own territory seems to have relaxed only Will.

I could feel the unease radiating off of Eveera as well as her straining to hear our conversation so on a wild gamble I laid next to her to see if she'd fall asleep. By the grace of whatever gods are out there she did, I try not to let the fact that my presence seems to have helped her somehow go to my head, but even in her sleep she's still tense.

I sat up only when I was sure she was really out and returned to my conversation. Bennett filled us in on the current state of things and then redirected our talk to ask more of our stay and travels with the Obsids. Questions both Will and I narrowly dodge, the full truth of. Truths such as Percy's head and the fact that in order for us to get a fully equipped military we also get their sadistic queen and her team of misfit men.

When there was nothing left to say or update the other on, I lay my body back down next to hers. Sleep however doesn't find me so quickly. Instead, I stay awake listening to her uneven breathing, hoping that at some point her emotions will ease and stop wrecking havoc on both our minds. The seal leaves her open when she's in a vulnerable state like sleep.

Bennett takes up his spot next to me, not bothering to try and sleep either. He rests his arms on his knees, peering around me to look at the tiny queen next to us. "So she's who you defied your father for."

I roll my eyes. "I didn't defy him for *her*. I defied him because he was being dense. Her forces are some of the largest and most skilled in battle."

"Yet they've not been in battle for how long?" He asks me.

I adjust my sitting position, "you haven't seen what they've had to fight behind their own walls Bennett." He shrugs fixing his stare on the fire. I don't need to justify why I defied my father. It's us who see our men dying. Us who see their wives and children weeping. Only we know the calamitous effect this is having on our kingdom. If I have to play dirty against him in order to save the rest of them, I will. I will fight for them all in spite of him. Whether they want me as their prince or not.

"So what's her story?" Bennett's voice draws my attention back to him. My left hand drifts to wrap around a few strands of her hair, not obvious enough for anyone to see under the cover of darkness as I think about my answer.

"I haven't figured it out yet." I state quietly.

He coughs, clearing his throat, while moving to lie down. "Well, you better figure it out quick. Once morning comes Vellar will never be the same."

Great, that notion makes me feel, just...great.

Bennett's words stuck in my head all the way until morning actually came. Eveera for most of the night slept in a ball, a ball that drifted closer and closer to my body heat until the point we were almost spooning. I pretended to be asleep and stifled my laugh when she woke up and realized our nearness. She practically leapt off the ground, bumping up against Axel in the process.

Ezra has chosen to be on speaking terms with her behind "enemy lines". He's been fused to her from the moment he woke up. She's ignoring his imposing proximity while bobbing her head in agreement to whatever Armond is whispering in her ear. She moves her fingers deftly through her dark hair, plaiting it into a braided crown. There is dark kohl smeared onto her eyes accenting those inhuman gold irises.

She makes eye contact with me but her ear remains fused to Armond's lips, listening. Her brow quirks up, a silent question in the motion. "Does anyone have any idea what the hell we are walking into when we get to Bail?" Orem asks.

"Bair" Will corrects him.

Orem snorts, "well we are *bailing* you out of this fucking mess. So Bail sounds pretty accurate to me."

Will grumbles, "you didn't have to agree to aid us."

"We didn't, she did." Rings out in unison from every one of her men as they all point a finger at Eveera.

Bennett looks around confused, "they didn't all agree?" He asks, Will lets out a long sigh instead of answering, pulling himself into his saddle and trotting away from the mocking.

The ride was bound to be a boring one. It's mostly just bare fields all the way up to the post – a result from the strain our presence has put on the residents. Strain that is only going to grow more heavy with the addition of the Obsidian troops.

I look over to Eveera, still as a statue as she marches her horse slowly on the path. *"You're not breathing."* I chastise.

"Stay out of my head." She snaps.

"*You're anxious and you need to breathe. I know it's difficult seeing the devastation our presence and Baelor's has brought but—*"

Her head whips towards me at the insinuation. "*I am* not *anxious. These are your people, not mine. Their hardships are none of my concern.*" The apathy in her words stings.

I drop my head back and sigh trying to tamp down the frustration building in me. "*I know that. But think of them as yours for a time and Hadar's Guards as the creatures of the outer lands. Except every soldier we fight is completely sentient. If we don't kill them before they kill us, they'll be onto your true people next.*"

"*My issue is not with killing them.*"

"Right. Just with the people you're killing beside."

She nods her head in agreement. *Damn woman.*

The fields start to die down as Bair's post grows closer. Bennett takes us on a detour around the town, leading us straight to the keeps stables. We pass our horses off to a few stableboys and follow Bennett through the halls to The General's Wing, where I instructed him to set up rooms for everyone.

"So who all stays here?" Maxwell asks.

Ben looks at the brunette a warm smile on his face as he answers. "Only men of rank and servants stay up in the keep. It's not big enough to house all of the men we've enlisted."

"You don't stay with your men? Outside the battle zone?" Ezra asks, his tone disapproving.

My man looks to me, then back at Ezra. "We do, during active pursuits. For the past several days things have been quiet, I told the uppermost ranking officers to retreat here and greet your party. We need to develop a strategy." Bennett answers.

We wind around the last limestone hall which ends with us in front of the large wooden doors that access the General's Wing. "The servants already brought up your things. You three -" he spins around and points at Axel and the brothers, "will be in this first room here on the left. You two -" Ezra and Armond next, "door up the hall on your right." He nods at each of them, satisfied with his tour but nobody moves a muscle.

"Ha. I guess I'll be sleeping outside then?" Eveera asks.

Bennett gives me a stressed look. "I assumed Prince Rorin filled you in on where you'll be..."

"Well you know what assuming means." She bites.

I step up, saving Bennett from receiving any further ire. "You'll be in my apartments."

"Like hell she will." Ezra growls out, pushing her back with his arm and into Axel's chest.

I tip my head back and pinch the bridge of my nose. "Call off your dog, Eveera." She does no such thing and when I bring my chin back down I am met with six blazing stares. "She won't be in my *bed* for gods sake. I have more than one room." The stares don't falter. My answer wasn't good enough apparently. Eveera sighs, stepping out from behind Ezra and away from Axel. "Men." She hooks her finger into my collar, "I'm taking the bigger bedroom." She claims, dragging me behind her towards the end of the hall.

It's difficult to hold back my smug smirk as I look over my shoulder towards the group of fuming men. "You don't know where you're going." I laugh.

"Shut up." She snaps. My hand comes up carefully to wrap around her finger, pulling it off the collar of my shirt, and securing it in my palm. Her feet stop. She drops her gaze to where our hands are joined and then looks back up to me. This time I don't try holding back the smirk. "I'll take the lead from here." Before she can argue, I pull on her hand and lead us the rest of the way to where the doors to my apartment lie.

The moment I close the door behind us she drops my hand like a hot coal. She makes her way to the settee and flops down into it. Ignoring me again. I head straight into my office, less than thrilled to be doing damage control after a few weeks away. *Weeks.* It sinks in how long we were actually gone and I'm surprised to find the place still standing.

There is the suspended feeling of both relief and fear hanging over me. A tumultuous combination, really. There is the relief that we haven't been invaded yet followed by the fear as to *why* we haven't been invaded yet. Looking down, I find there are stacks on stacks of intel and correspondence piled high on my desk.

I grab an iridescent glass and pour myself two fingers of bourbon. If I'm going to be looking at the proof of my father's failures, I need to be less sober. From Bennett's guarded words it wasn't difficult to figure that things had only regressed in my absence. It's been too long that my soldiers - my people - have been forced to suffer under the constant pressure of war.

KNOCK KNOCK!

"Come in." I groan.

"Catching up on the latest bloody bullshit, Ror?" *Bennett.* He's leaning in the doorway against the frame and behind him, I can see Eveera. She's slid half her body over the armrest of the settee with both hands planted down onto the floor, staring at the wall opposite her.

"That cannot possibly be comfortable." I murmur shaking my head in disbelief. As if she heard me, her head snaps in my direction.

"I took the room to the left!" She shouts, kicking her leg over and walking out of view.

"That's my bed—" SLAM! "oh...kay..." I sigh, taking a long sip of the alcohol. The burn doing little to sate my brimming anxiety. Bennett snickers, stopping only when I give him a pointed glare. "You didn't tell me things were decreasing so rapidly." I say, switching the focus back to the papers in front of me.

"Well, then it's a good thing you and the brigade of death showed up just in time." He quips.

"Your humor is ill timed, Bennett."

He shoves his hands into the pockets of his pants. His lips is pulled between his teeth. A nervous habit. "A lot happened in a short amount of time." He says quietly.

"I thought you said things had been quiet the past several days?" I ask, recalling what he'd told Ezra.

Dark brown eyes raise, the shadows underneath them evident. "Well what did you want me to say? Did you want me to scare them off within the first few minutes of working with us?" I'm at a loss for words as he continues on. "Because here is how I envisioned that conversation going, 'Hi - thanks so much for coming to save our asses. I regret to inform you that you'll probably all be dead by morning.'" He sticks his hand out in a obnoxious demonstration.

"I'd rather you be honest." I grumble. His arm drops down to his side, defeat on his face. "I'm sorry. It's been overwhelming." I state.

"Looks like we both have been dishonest since your return." He's right. We didn't tell him the whole of what happened in Obsidian yet either. My reaction wasn't very fair.

The two of us stare at each other, "we've been at this too long." He says helping fill the silence. I nod my head and drink the last sip in my glass before filling it another two fingers.

"Hey princeling — oh, you're still here." My eyes widen when a very damp queen appears just to the side of my friend. Bennett's mouth drops slightly as he scoots out of her way. When her back is completely to him he looks over to me and mouths, *"Oh my gods."*

Indeed...I say to myself.

"Didn't realize *our room*," She gags saying the words, "involved other people coming and going as they please."

I prop my leg up on top of the opposite knee, reclining in my seat. "As you can see, Your Highness, this is an office. That means people often come into it seeking me out."

She rolls her eyes at my tone. "Right...well I am seeking out food. So can we wrap this up, and go fix that scenario?" She folds her arms over her chest, her breasts threatening to burst out of her towel at the new position. Bennett's head rolls against the door jam as he avoids looking over her shoulder like an immature schoolboy. His blatant ogling in front of me spurs an unsettling feeling of discomfort. I push up from my desk, slyly adjusting an unwanted reaction to her toweled body. *Fucking thing has a mind of its own.*

"We have a brief to go to first."

She groans, her head dropping back, further threatening the integrity of that towel. Bennett's eyes finally pinch shut at her brazenness - but I fear that's more because he doesn't want her to catch him staring and less because he feels uncomfortable.

"Fine." She spins on her bare heel, pushing her finger under Bennett's chin and closes his mouth that is still open, "you dropped this."

I slap Bennett upside the head following after her. "Ow." He yelps, rubbing the backside of it. "I guess, I'll just leave you two..." His words trailing off as he waggles his brows at me.

"Out." I say, pointing to my doors. He leaves making obscene hand gestures on his way out while I stick around waiting for Eveera and nursing another bourbon. She finally comes out of my bedroom with her hair wound into two loosely braided plaits and a green and black gown that might as well be another layer of skin it's so tight. The slit in her dress is nearly to her hip bone, leaving her thigh holster clad with two daggers and a throwing star visible. The serpent tattoos her skin boasts are on full display tonight. I cover up my dropped jaw by taking a large gulp. She walks over to me and props up her foot in mid air.

"Planning on holding that position all night, Nightmare?" I ask, still hiding behind my glass.

Her expression feigns innocence, "help a lady out, will you?" She throws in a bat of her eyelashes and a smile. Anyone who didn't know her, would probably swoon.

Devilish woman. I chide. Moving slowly towards her to close the gap, her chin raises to keep the eye contact. I drop down on one knee, my hand fitting around her right ankle and guiding it to rest on top of my pant leg. My fingers make quick work on the laces and switch to her other foot. "Satisfied?" My head cocks up at her, my hand settling on the back of her calf. It takes conscious effort on my part to not rub slow circles on the incredibly soft skin with my thumb while I hold her into place.

She tilts her down head at me, her grin turning mischievous. "With you on your knees? Very."

I shove her foot off my knee, the tension cutting through like a knife. She stumbles a little due to the lack of stability. It takes all of my self resolve to walk away from her and out of my apartments. *You are anything but a lady by the way.* I quip into her mind.

We made our way outside and back to the stables. I notice her saddle is lacking a certain new adornment, which can mean one of two things, she either put him away or he's sitting in my apartments. *Where I have to sleep...great.*

Eveera doesn't bother waiting for Bennett and Will to lead us towards camp, taking off on her house at maximum speed.

Blasted woman doesn't even know where she's supposed to go. I gripe to myself.

Our group chases after her, Bennett racing to get ahead. We could hear the camp before actually seeing any tents. The noise of all the soldiers overwhelming. *I'd forgotten how raucous war camps could be.* Soldiers mill about in between the different tents barely sparing us a glance as we dismount from our horses. That is, until they catch sight of a *woman* in their midst.

Bennett doesn't allow us to stall as he winds us through them and deeper into camp. The further we move through the base, the closer I find myself moving towards Eveera. Armond does the same, taking it one step further and pushing her directly behind him, sandwiching her between the two of us. His push knocks her off balance and my hand grips underneath her ribcage, steadying her.

She shoves off my palm once she has righted herself, whipping her braids back into my face as she struts in front of me.

The large eight paneled briefing tent is hard to miss at the center of camp. Once inside of it we all fan out around the table, the four different captains filing in shortly after us. "Captains, thank you for meeting with us." I greet, my voice carrying loudly throughout the canvas room. They all murmur their hellos, only one of them raising his eyes to look at me. "It's good to be back, gentlemen. And this time I came home with something special. The army of Obsidian." At that, the other three snap their heads up eyes narrowing on the queen beside me.

The captain closest to Bennett flicks his stare from the queen and then back to me, "Sir, I mean no disrespect in asking this question, but where in the hell are we meant to house another military force?" Bennett places a hand on his shoulder and pushes him back to his place in line.

"We come with our own provisions. You won't have to worry your gilded heads about a thing." She answers for me, not bothering to look up from picking at her nails.

I had the captains reprise us on recent events, giving Eveera the shortened version of what we've dealt with for years. Hadar's Guards continued to test our resolve by inching their soldiers closer to the border which lead to a few night ambushes. The men however, seem to have recovered as far as I can tell.

"I want to go to the front lines." She states into my mind not leaving any room for arguing as she takes off out of the tent. Axel and I drop our heads in defeat, already hot on her heels. We find her standing at the edge of the trenches. A focused expression planted on her face.

"They've been advancing closer and closer every few days. Some bizarre intimidation tactic." One of the soldiers who'd taken notice of us shares.

Eveera leans forward. "It's not bizarre. It's bold, but not bizarre. The way your camps are set up you can see each other clear as day. Very little room for any element of surprise or ambushing. See that ridge over there?" She points over to a steep hillside overgrown with trees and bushes. That area bridges between the two militaries. "You're not using that enough to your advantage. But *they* are. By the time they're on you with their full force, it won't be a simple ambush. You'll be so distracted by a direct hit on your front that you'll never see the rest of them coming from behind that ridge. They'll envelop your camp from two sides and you won't stand a chance."

His mouth drops. "How are you sure?" He asks.

"Because I've studied this tactic." She states blandly not taking her eyes off of them.

The soldier's eyes bulged, "You?"

I groan, not wanting to explain that another lovely aspect of my father's *peaceful reign* - meant no women soldiers. No woman should grace a battlefield in his opinion, too risky. Really what he means is, women are a distraction for men who don't know which head to lead with.

Axel chuckles quietly from my side. Her lips curl into a sickly sweet smile as she extends a hand out and fixes the soldier's lapel. "Yes. Me. And you'll be grateful that I know how to get your sorry asses out of it." Her close proximity has him shrinking back until Will pulls him away.

Smart move to grab him instead of her. *We have to stay on her good side - or whatever the equivalent of good is for Eveera - just long enough to rid ourselves of the Hadar leeches.* I remind myself.

"Can you for one second be polite?!" Will hisses.

She shrugs, returning the fullness of her attention onto Axel. "Whatever you want, the answer is no." He says quickly.

"Axel, I need you to punch me."

We all shout, "WHAT?!", in unison and she rolls her eyes. "Come on, Mecham. Right here." She pats her right cheek while her left hand folds his into a fist. "Just..." she mimics the motion, "right here."

Axel is staring, blinking slowly at her, "Evie I'm not going to—"

"You are." She affirms.

His lips flatten as he violently shakes his head. "I'm not."

"He's not." I add in.

She shoots me a glare before insisting again while still making that goofy mimed motion of punching herself in the face. "Just right here."

"Eveera this is madness. He isn't going to punch you. No one is going to punch her." Ezra says. *That's going to be the only time the two of us agree.* I think.

Her arms flail out to her sides in an exaggerated display. "Fine. None of you are any fun."

"Someone *punching* you sounds fun?" Will exclaims.

She doesn't answer him, grumbling under her breath that she'll just do it herself. Before any of us have a chance to stop her she takes out her dagger and slices clear across the cheekbone once and again through her eyebrow.

Axel presses his palms into his eyes while she starts ripping her dress and smearing the blood from her new cuts onto exposed skin. "What are you—"

"See you guys soon." She winks and walks quickly over to Armond who's just joined us and touches his arm. In the next instant she's gone, simply, *POOF!*

I whirl on him, "what just happened?! Why did touching you make her disappear?"

"She Voided." He says blandly.

My eyes narrow into slits. "No shit." I growl out. "Why the fuck was *she* able to Void when she touched you. Her Wield doesn't do that."

He sighs, looking out at the field. My eyes follow to where his are and out there in the distance is Eveera, tripping and running into the belly of the beast. "No but mine does."

Max steps up next to him his hands planted on his hips as he stares at her shrinking shape, murmuring, "always a plan of her own."

"So she just leaves you all. She gets to throw herself on the enemy's sword and have you lot clean up the aftermath of her recklessness?" I snap.

"No." Maxwell answers. "We make her clean up after."

Bennett looks over to them voicing the one question I've been asking myself for days, "you're not the least bit concerned she'll get herself killed?"

Her men laugh. "Of course we're concerned, but—" Armond says.

"But she's going to do it anyways." I finish for him. "*Eveera. Next time, include me on your fucking one whim plans. Don't do anything* else *stupid. We need you. I need you.*" The last part may have been a bit too much, but it's the truth. Without her, her armies won't answer to anyone else, and if her men lose her they'll cease to assist us. They made that very clear.

It's been an hour with the eight of us staring at the edge of Hadar's Guards encampment. We watched as she succeeded in flagging someone down but we haven't had eyes on her since. I keep trying to get her attention down the seal but no response. "I'm going in there - Will get me my horse."

"Absolutely not!" He shakes his head at me in disbelief. "Their queen and her stupid choice, *they* can go after her." He points to the line of her men, all standing with their arms folded across their chests and gazes still trained on the spot where she disappeared.

I glower at him, "I said get me my horse Will." He's ready to argue with me but Orem's frantic pointing steals away my attention. Across the field where their camp should be is a large tangled mess of black tendrils; moving not unlike a pit of serpents coiling around its prey.

"*Eveera? Are you okay?*" Nothing but silence meets me. "*Eveera?*"

"*Don't worry princeling, everything is just dandy.*" My shoulders relax slightly when her little form steps out from the sea of her slithering black magic with something gripped in her hands.

"ROR!" Bennett calls from behind me. I look back at him and see my horse's reins in his hand. *Well at least someone listened when I asked for my horse*, I gripe to myself while tearing the reins from him and hoisting myself up on the animal as fast as I can. I spur my horse on into a full sprint out towards where she is.

By the time I get close to her, I notice her magic flowing back into her skin. "*Can your horse run any faster than that?*" Her voice echoes in my mind.

"*Why?*" I ask, signaling to my horse to increase in speed again.

"*There were a lot of people and I may have pissed a few off.*"

I roll my eyes. "*So what are you saying?*"

"*That if we don't move quickly—*" GROAAANNNNN!! A loud and thunderous noise rumbles through the field. My head follows to what the sound was and that's when I notice not one but three large apparatuses housing equally large spears. *Apparently not everyone suffered the full brunt of her magic.*

"ARE THOSE FUCKING BALLISTAS?" I scream down the seal.

She nods frantically catching up to where I've stopped my horse. "*It would appear that way, yes. So does this horse go fast or...*" She asks again. Our hands clasp together so that I can hoist her up. Much to my chagrin the close proximity has brought into view the odd object she brought back with her.

"Is that another head?!" I shout over the sound of the wind.

"General Thornbirk's." She leans down, throwing it into the saddle pack. The head makes a sickening wet noise when it lands. *What is it with her and heads?*

BAM! One of those spears embeds itself into the dirt a little too close for comfort as I jerk my horses reins to pull us out of the way.

"You going to shrink that one too?" I snap. She rolls her eyes while twisting around on the saddle. The new position makes it so that we're chest to chest, legs straddling on top of mine. "Could you please stop wiggling?" In a few minutes if she keeps up this friction, dying isn't going to be my only problem.

"Excuse me for trying to get into the best position here to handle this." She grunts, wiggling her hips again, her thighs tightening around me. The scent of her is all consuming as the wind whips around us. My right hand secures against her, closing any gaps that are allowing her wiggle room.

"This is not my best position, Highness." I snark.

Her hand connects with the back of my head. *THWUMP!* "*You focus on riding, I'll take care of loose ends. Unless you prefer to become fertilizer for this field?"* The force of her Wield flows from her body and through where we're connected. The Wield seeks out any vulnerable mark. In this case, thankfully, those marks are the men in charge of weapons set on annihilating us.

WHAM! Dust and dirt kick up, I look to the side to see a sinkhole forming with a circular boulder at the center. "That's not the work of a ballista."

"No it's not. I don't know what the fuck that's from." She grits out.

The moment we are *barely* safe and sound back behind our own lines she untangles herself from me.

"Don't forget your friend." I grumble down at her. Her eyes light up at the reminder as she turns back around. "*Your eyes shouldn't do that when you're thinking of someone's head you just decapitated.*" The words come out in a snap and per usual she ignores me and snatches the whole pack off the saddle. Though, I don't think I'll be wanting it back afterwards anyways. She saunters right past her men heading for the tent we met my captains in earlier.

There is an air of uneasiness and tension circulating around her, the feeling worsening when she chucks the pack onto the briefing table. The general's head rolls out, face up and eyes open wide. A gagging noise sounds from the corner, familiar enough to me that I know it's Will who has broken the tension. He struggles to compose himself as he asks, "what in the gods is *that*?"

"*Who* is that, is the better question." Bennett adds, his jaw dropped in shock.

Eveera gives them both an annoyed look while flicking her hand towards the remains. "It's obviously a head." *A head indeed.*

"Seriously? Another one?" Will whines.

Bennett looks at me from across the room, mouthing, "another?" I dismiss him, thinking that now's probably not the best time to let them know our supposed savior shrunk a fellow comrade's head down into a decorative saddle ornament.

"Why is it on our table?" One of my captains squeaks out, his look of disgust similar to Will's.

She gives me a desperate look. "Ugh, it's like explaining something to children isn't it? That is General Thornbirk." She says it as if that should answer the question as to why he now rests on our table and why she killed him. "Look, the fastest way of getting into that camp was to make it look like I needed asylum from Vellar."

"So the cuts and the torn clothes…" Bennett supplies.

She nods her chin. "I took a gamble on the small chance they wouldn't refuse a beaten woman. They took me into their camp under the impression that I was kidnapped and whored out by your men." *Lovely.* I grimace. She gestures again to the general's head. "They took me to Thornbirk and we had a conversation. When he caught on too quickly to my ruse, I took care of him. So," her thumb drags across her throat and she sticks her tongue out in a dramatic display, "no more General. We'll need to act quickly, tonight even. Your prince and I have already endured part of what they have to offer and that was only minutes after I retracted my magic. I don't doubt with hours to recuperate we'll have a fight on our hands." A mixture of awestruck and dumbfounded looks are plastered on each of my men's faces in the room. *It's taken us years to chip away at those soldiers, and she does all of that in a matter of an hour give or take?* I don't know whether I should feel pride in myself for making the right call with her or if I should feel jealous that I didn't get to that point without her help.

Bennett steps up to the table avoiding the soulless eyes of both Thornbirk and Eveera. "Okay, I'm sorry but just to recap here. You cut yourself and tore your clothes on the hope that they would let you into their camp feigning being a damsel in distress? It worked for awhile until it didn't and then you decapitated their general? All while assaulting everyone else in range with your magic?"

She nods, "that is what I said."

"And you still want us to act now? We can't have a few days of planning at least?" He asks carefully.

Eveera sets her hands on the table contemplating his request. "You can have a few days." She says and sighs of relief echo all around the room. All the way up until she opens her mouth to finish what she was saying, "if you want to be dead." Their mouths hang open one by one. "I just committed a *huge* offense by killing off this Thornbirk guy. They're going to retaliate." She looks up at me with an incredulous expression. "Honestly, these...these are what I am working with? I'll be out there whenever you decide that living is better than dying."

The moment she exits the tent with Ezra trailing dutifully behind her, arguments begin to break out. I can't be bothered to participate as I watch the two of them, and an ugly feeling coils in my stomach when his hand curls around her bicep to pull her off somewhere he feels is private.

This is a war camp, nothing is private. My conscience reminds me. I can see their shadows wind around the tent and when they stop I lean against the canvas, straining to hear them.

"You risked yourself." Ezra starts. "You risked yourself, Evie, and for what? For them...these...people? You can't be reckless here! We could have lost you...I could have lost you, E." The last part comes out desperate even for him. Of course, I'm speculating. I only met him a little over a week ago. But I assume that whining to get her to comply is substandard for him.

Her shadow's body language gives away her feelings and her lack of interest in his complaint. "You'd do best to mind your place, Commander. I gave you your options the other day. If you are so distraught by my moves to fulfill my end of this deal then you can take your leave. No grudges held." Her tone is clipped, bringing a smile to my lips until the voice of our newest captain pulls my attention away from the discussion outside the tent.

"So um, not to point out the head in the room or anything. But what do we do with it?" He asks.

My lip curls up at the severed head. "Burn it."

The moment I stepped back into my apartment my bottle of bourbon was practically singing for me from within the office. I planned to spend the rest of my night holed up with paperwork while trying to come up with some sort of plan. If we're supposed to retaliate by tonight, we're going to need something more powerful than their bloody weapons.

The burn of the alcohol slides down my throat. There are mountains of missives, complaints, requests, and directives. A headache forms at the sight of all the papers in front of me.

My father - when gifting me this oh so honorable title of General - neglected to inform me that the job comes with cities full of people ready to jump down your throat. Unfortunately most of their grievances I share, and can't do a fucking thing about them. But as long as I am in any of my posts hosting our military effort I will do what I can to lighten their plight. Even if it seems futile.

Despite having Bennett take over while Will and I went out to retrieve more manpower, the simple truth is no one else can do the job of a royal. I recline back in my chair, picking up my glasses and the top parchment, while my drink sits precariously on the edge of the arm rest.

"You look like a tutor." Her raspy voice startles me from my reading. Glancing up over the rim of my glasses I see her leaning against the door frame clad in a black nightdress. She's twisting her still damp hair into one long braid that hangs off her shoulder. The dress, I notice, is the same one she wore on our first night in her court.

You should not *remember what clothing she had on.* I reprimand myself.

My hand raises the cup to my lips, tipping the amber liquid back. Her nose scrunches up in disgust as she watches me take a drink, "your liquor tastes like shit."

I smirk, swallowing the mouthful, and set the glass back down. "Maybe your palate just isn't refined, Highness."

Her face falls flat, unamused, while she extends her hand out for the bottle. Holding the bottle by the neck I wiggle it back and forth at her, letting her know if she wants it she has to walk over here and get it.

She broaches the short distance to my desk, letting both of her tan hands land with palms down on the edge of it. Her body leans over putting her directly into my personal space. Lithe fingers snap out and snatch the bottle from my grip. Those soft and stoic features of hers, contort in discomfort as she chokes down a swallow. "I don't think my palate is the problem. *Blech!* How can you drink that?"

I shrug. "Guess it's grown on me." She moves around the desk, setting herself on top of it. The smooth bronzed skin of her legs is on full display and if I were a worse man, I'd be tempted to run my hands across them. Thankfully the alcohol hasn't worked that quickly. "You could have gotten yourself killed today." I say.

Her head bobs up and down as she grimaces down another drink. "Scared you'll lose your little investment? Wouldn't want to disappoint daddy any more than we already have, would you?"

I glower up at her, "no. I just would rather not deal with your blonde boyfriend trying to slit my throat because you died helping me." Her eyes spark at the mention of Ezra.

"He's not my boyfriend." She snarls.

Defensive are we? I think to myself. "He certainly seems to think so." I bite, the words coming out harsher than intended and she bristles at my tone.

"I don't care what he thinks." Another drink, another grimace. She shoves it back into my hands and leans back onto hers, aimlessly flipping through the papers next to her thigh.

My thumb and forefinger rub across my chin as I watch her turn each page, "he seems irritated at the time we spend together." I note, bringing him up again.

"We aren't *spending time* together, we are working together. For the time being."

I hum, rubbing my lips together. "Okay we're *working* together. While also sharing the same living space."

She ignores my tease and crumples one of the missives. "Your battle plans suck." She states.

Yes, they do. "Dear old dad's classic ways. Write out the path he has to interfere with the least. The *peaceful* path. As if peace has ever won anything against brute force in war."

She looks at me, eyes curious, "sounds like you and King Eiser don't get along much."

I shift my chair forward, my arm brushing against her exposed thigh. "Let's just say I'm not his proudest moment."

"So what am I? Your ticket to earning 'Best Son of the Year' award?"

I huff out a rueful laugh. "No. No you are a giant 'fuck you'. You are the slap in the face he needs."

Her mouth tilts up. "Ah. I see. And I was so looking forward to meeting him and being welcomed into his loving embrace."

"He doesn't embrace much of anything. We'll both be lucky he doesn't cuff us in mage shackles the second he has a moment to." The thought of those shackles sends chills down my spine as I shake off my memories with them.

Her hand pushes back against my shoulder returning me to my reclined position as she hops down from the desk. I figured she'd choose to walk out of the office, but she surprises me by stepping in between my spread legs. It's taking more effort than I'd like to admit to keep my hands glued to the arm rests, especially when her finger trails down my jaw to grip my chin. Her scent invades all of my senses as heat courses through me with each inch closer she brings our faces. "Make no mistake, *princeling*. We may be playing nice right now. But I am every bit the monster the rumors claim me to be."

There is only a sliver of space between us, so much so that the air she breathes out is the air I am breathing in. "And who's to blame for that, Eveera?"

Her golden eyes narrow into two slits as black edges into them, "you should ask the King and Queen that question." She shoves my chin back and steps out from between my legs. All the heat between us is doused within a second as I process her words. "Figure out if you want my help or not. If we don't go after them again, my bet is that we'll be met with their forces by tomorrow." She says keeping her back to me as she saunters out of my office, leaving me in a uncomfortably *hard* position, with little focus or desire to return to the paperwork sitting on my desk. I'm not sure how we're supposed to work together if this is going to be my reaction every time she gets close to me.

EVEERA

I've no idea how I am meant to sleep here.

The ceiling and I are becoming really acquainted at this point. It started getting awkward after a while of me staring up at it, so I introduced myself. It didn't give me much back but it's served as a decent distraction from my headache. I thought I'd be fine here. I thought that my purpose would supersede these asinine fears I have.

I thought, I thought, I thought.

All this thinking hasn't droned out the pounding or the panic rising in my chest of being in a room meant for *them*. In a bed they've potentially peacefully slept in. The scars on my back have become itchier the more I lay here and without a thought my hand reaches haphazardly for my belt my eyes staying trained on the ceiling. Finally my fingers find a small blade. I run my thumb along the edge of it to see if it's dulled. *Thank the gods,* I think when I lift up the blade to inspect it. *Sharp.* My fist closes around the handle and I swing my legs around to rest on the edge of the bed. I take one more look up at the ceiling, "you're a shit talker, but a good listener." I whisper. My eyes drop back down to the blade in my palm and a few thoughts cross my mind.

Vada would chastise me, Ezra would ignore it, and Axel would hold me. *No one is here for that now.*

I suck in a deep breath and dig the tip into my exposed thigh, dragging it across an already scarred patch of skin. Blood beads up at the cut as I exhale, "one." Again. "Two." It burns this time but I don't let that stop me. Another breath, another drag, "three." The tension in my chest starts to break up as my body hones in on the pain.

"Four." I hiss - my left hand curls around the bed sheets with the sting of that one. *One more*, I think. "Five." Dropping my head back I let the knife clatter to the floor. My vision dots with stars that flick and bounce all around and warmth spreads through my body. In my last moments of consciousness I re-position myself back to lying down and wait for the pain to black me out into the most devastating sleep.

-

"Mommy please. No mommy. MOM! NO! No no no no no." *I want to get up. I want to put her back together.* "Mama!" *I wail out. But her face is lifeless. Her gold eyes glassed over and the brightness usually held within them is nothing but tarnished and dim now. I'm crawling across the floor to where her blood has pooled.* "Mama please. Mommy come on, don't be dead. Please don't be dead." *How could she not? Her entire body has been ripped apart in a sick display.*

I reach for her hands and her fingers are so cold...

"Eveera?" *There's someone else...someone shouting. A man.* "Eveera?!"

The voice tugs on my arm. "No. No, don't take her away, don't take her away." *I beg the voice.*

-

Hushed whispers come flooding in, "Eveera...it's just a dream. Shh, it's just a dream." The voice is no longer in my head but my ears.

"It wasn't just a dream." I whisper my voice sounding garbled outside of my body. My eyes snap open, finally registering that I'm being rocked back and forth. Blinking the sleep away I notice two tanned arms holding me. *Definitely not Ezra.* I'm hot all over, sweat plastering the hair framing my face to my skin.

Rorin clears his throat, stiffening before letting go of me and scooting to the other side of the bed, "the uh- the flesh on my arm suddenly felt like it was melting off my body which was a...startling way to wake up and so I came in here...and you looked like you were having a fit. Flailing and—"

My cheeks heat. "I wasn't flailing."

"You were flailing and kicking. I didn't want you to hurt yourself, but—" His stare drops down to the obvious bloodstain on his sheets, "looks like you already did. Why are you bleeding?" I reach for the edge of the sheet, throwing it off my body quickly so I can stand. But unfortunately for me my diced up leg doesn't cooperate with the motion and my knee immediately buckles. I stumble forward and his hand snatches my wrist angling my body towards him in the process.

Hazel eyes zeroing onto the bloodied mess overlapping faded silver scars. "Did you – did you do that to yourself?" He asks, his voice flabbergasted.

I don't have to answer to you, I think and point to the door, "out."

"Eveera, did you do that to yourself?" He asks again, harsher this time the tone of his voice dropping an octave.

I shrug. "Fell on my weapons. Now get out."

He moves me out of his way and slips off the bed. It's as he crouches down that I notice he's shirtless. His muscled chest, dripping in sweat that I can't tell if it's mine or his reaction from the rune's effects. He grips my ankle and forces my leg up. "You fell," he says dryly putting his face closer to the flayed skin. If his voice didn't already give away that he doesn't believe me for a second, his eyes do as they look up at me through thick dark lashes. "Falling made these precise slits in your thigh? What did you do? Line up all your blades face up next to your bed? And because if that doesn't sound stupid enough, you mean to convince me that you just what – rolled off? Tripped maybe and landed on top of them?" He's angry. An emotion that isn't his to have, so I point at the door again, clearly indicating what I want him to do.

"You didn't answer my question." He growls.

It's because of your people that I do this. Because of those memories. Because of you. The words rest on my tongue. I don't want his anger, I don't want his pity, sadness. "I don't have to." He doesn't move. If anything his grip tightens on my ankle. "We are not friends, *princeling.*" *I snarl, leaning down.*

He huffs out a laugh with no mirth in it. "No, we aren't. But I cannot have my...*leverage*...mutilating herself." *And there it is,* my conscience whispers. *He's not angry because he cares, he's angry because he think's he'll lose what he bought.* "Maybe I'll just go tell Axel or *Blondie* what their queen has been up to. See if they can get a better explanation than '*I fell on my weapons.*' out of you."

My lips flatten together. "You won't."

He drops my ankle like a hot coal, "they know?" his spits, the words pure venom. Rorin stands abruptly, finally listening and storming out of the room. I feel relieved for a moment until I hear the door to the hall open.

I limp after him as fast as I can, furious the nightmare came anyways and that he felt it. "Rorin." I shout but he ignores me, continuing to stomp down the hall. I finally catch up to him, colliding into his back as he stops short. "EVERYBODY UP!" *Dear gods, hear we go.*

"Rorin!" I hiss. "What do you think you're doing?"

I am met with silence once again, his hand coming behind him and clamping over my mouth and nose. "Having a discussion with your guards." Wield is leaking out of his free hand. The mist floods onto the floor and under the doors of our men. His hand covering my mouth shakes as he tries to keep control on the mist.

"Why the hell do you care?!" My words are a muffled mess behind his calloused palm, while my nails tear down his forearm trying to remove it from my face. But with preternatural strength he keeps it secure against me. I try to summon my own Wield, hoping to break his concentration, but it's mine that breaks with the sound of men coughing and heaving. Doors slam open as they all spill out into the hall with us. He doesn't pull the Wield back until every one of them is doubled over – Mousy and Bennett included. He lets go of my face but only to move his grip to my chin.

He stares coldly into my eyes. "I *don't* care." He says, "but they—" his left hand points at each of my men, "should."

"What in the fucking bleeding gods was that about, asshole?!" Axel shouts, the first one to regain his breath.

A sardonic smile spreads across Rorin's face as he continues to stare down at me. "Asshole, sure. But you five have got to be the dirtiest fucking scum to allow *this* to happen." All of them bristle at the insult, the two brothers with defensive Wields, flare theirs. "Someone better have a damn good explanation for *this*." The grip on my chin vanishes only to return around my upper arm. It's a power move as he drags me from behind him so they can all look at my bloodied thigh. Axel's face frowns and Maxwell and Orem won't even look at me, their gazes turning down.

"Rorin." I say a third time, this one a warning.

He shakes his head turning to look at the men. "You have one job. Protect her. And by the looks of the scars resting underneath the fresh ones, you've failed."

Mousy takes a step towards the prince, "Ror, maybe this is none of our business. There is no need to concern yourself with another one of her unsavory behaviors." Axel opens his mouth, and by the look on his face I know exactly what he is going to say.

It's too soon! The voice in my head screams. "Axel, mind your place." I snarl.

"*No.*" He growls at me, sticking a finger out at the prince. "Don't tell me I'm shitty at protecting her, you self important dick. You want a damn answer for that? Look no further than mommy and daddy." He takes a step forward, Armond and Max lunging out to grab hold of him.

"Axel, enough." Armond warns. Axel's head whips back and forth between our men and myself. "He honestly wants us to believe he has no idea what his own kingdom did? What his parents had a hand in?"

I rip my arm out of Rorin's loosened grip. "That's it! Reminder for you all that I am a fucking *queen*. I don't answer to any of you." A door slams closed and I notice Ezra has stormed off. I follow suit, turning my back on the rest of them and limp my way to any exit back to my room.

Rorin came back after some time slamming closed every open door in his wake, I could feel his frustration through the seal. I sink against the stained glass window trying to block out Rorin's emotions. By the looks of it outside, there are a few hours left until dawn breaks. I make myself comfortable on the cushions of the window seat knowing that sleep won't come for me again. On nights when it got really bad, Vada would coerce me into riding on her back as aftercare for how I handled things. What I wouldn't give to be on Vada's back right now, gliding alongside the stars.

The princeling's velvety voice trickles into my mind. "You're still awake." *Apparently, I wasn't very good at blocking him out.*

"You're slamming and general asshole behavior kept me up." I tell him.

"I'm not apologizing for it." His voice meets my ears instead of the walls of my mind and when I turn there he stands in the shadowed doorway. Those two hazel eyes are glued to my bloodstained leg as he walks my way and takes a seat on the floor. "She's the reason, right? Your mother? What I saw..."

"You already know that answer." I whisper into his mind, hoping maybe he won't really hear it. But when he shifts uncomfortably on the ground, I know he heard. Rough fingertips reach back and graze the fresh cuts lightly. "Do not pity me." I bite out.

The touch is gone as soon as its there and his hand back in his lap as he stares blankly ahead. "I don't." I bite my lip to keep it from quivering. I am not about to show any other kinds of emotion in front of him again. "You should get a healer mage for that." He suggests and all I can do is shake. He can't see me, but he gives me a quiet grunt of understanding anyways. "Then let me at least bandage it up." He gets up and walks into the bathroom returning with a kit in his hands. I squint my eyes at him, unsure of the idea until he angles his head at me with a plea in his gaze. My face tilts back to the window and he starts dabbing at the cuts I've made. Thankfully, the healing balm he's applying numbs the area fairly quickly and he finishes by setting a patch bandage on top of the cuts.

"You never got back to me or your captains on what you want to do. I'm guessing my going rogue again is out of the question?" He dusts off his hands and packs the kit back up. After putting the kit back in the bathroom he snags two blankets and a pillow off the bed. Handing me one blanket he keeps the other and the pillow for himself and stretches out on the floor underneath the sill.

"We'll discuss it in the morning." He finally says.

"It is morning — wh-what are you doing?" I ask.

He folds his arms behind his head and snuggles deeper into his spot. "Keeping an eye on my leverage." He says matter of factly. Irritation flares in my chest at the reminder that I am on loan to him right now, a tool to be used.

If only he knew the only reason he has access to me is because I need access to Vellar. Then we'll see who's being used.

RORIN

I left the room after only a few hours on the floor.

Exhaustion took me under again once I was seated at my desk until Bennett woke me up. According to him, Eveera's military had arrived. They'd managed to speed up their travels thanks to Armond making them aware of the hot spots to avoid. I quickly throw myself together and we head down to the stables. I want eyes on the two armies cohabitating with one another.

The door to my bedroom was still closed and I figured after the night Eveera had it would be best to not disturb her, figuring that someone would come to get her eventually. Imagine my surprise when I come down to the stables and find her already in them. From where I stand I can hear parts of the conversation she's having with Ezra. I'd love to say it was hard to eavesdrop but the blonde's voice carries, "—hide it better next time, Eveera. I don't want to be woken up a second time by your new toy bitching about something he has no business knowing."

Her head falls back, a laugh rattling her chest, "unbelievable. So the only reason he could have possibly noticed is because you think *I'm fucking him?!*" She shouts.

"Wait—you slept with him?!" Axel exclaims, his finger landing on me as he walks into the stables.

I step out around the corner of my horse's stall, leaning against the wood. "Slept with who, again?" I ask, smugly.

Axel points again for emphasis, "YOU!" He shouts.

Eveera grabs her guard's hand dragging it down to his side. "No, Axel, I did not sleep with him!"

I can't help the grin that twitches at the corner of my mouth. "Well...I mean technically last night after everything..." I tease.

She shoots me a scathing look before snapping. "Stop it." My mouth breaks out into a broad smile as Axel's jaw drops. The fact that she is so offended only makes me want to drag this on more.

Ezra huffs and hoists himself in his saddle, looking down at her. "All I know is we were woken up, raked over the damn coals and there you were being paraded around like some half naked animal clawing at his arms and back. Looked like you were in some sort of sick lovers spat."

Even from several feet away I notice her hands are flexing in and out trying to control her Wield enough to climb up on her horse. "Well thank you for thinking me a whore, Ezra. Truly. But I am not sleeping with him," she shoots me another scowl, "not that that would be your concern. Secondly, we are here for a job and you are *repeatedly* diverting from it with your need to claim me like I'm some prized broodmare!" He looks so stricken it's like she slapped him across the face. "Set aside your personal grievances, I am tired of your hysterics, Commander Wake."

He huffs again and swivels his horse around, storming off towards base alone. I mount my horse and sidle up next to her. *"They think we're sleeping together?"* I ask.

She rolls her eyes, *"that's all you gathered?"*

"Let me be clear," I start my horse passing by hers, *"if we were sleeping together – there wouldn't be any confusion around it. From anyone. Least of all you."*

She snorts from behind me. *"Good thing we aren't sleeping together then."*

"Good thing."

The briefing tent is a full house; my captains, Bennett, and Will were all standing with as much space between them and our guests as possible. The Obsids stand off by the tent's exit. Their stand stoically, her captains looking just as fearsome as their Vast counterparts.

Where I have common folk fighting our battles, these men, women, and beings are hardened soldiers. Battle-worn soldiers. The years of fighting the outer land creatures evident on their faces and in their eyes.

"Ah-hem. I trust you've all had a moment to acquaint yourselves." I ask, followed by a round of nods. "The reality is—"

"The reality is," Eveera cuts in, "the battle plans you Vellarans have are shit." *Subtle,* I think. "Truth be told I don't have any idea how you're all still alive. Especially with those weapons they pulled out on us yesterday. What would you have done if we hadn't come in to save your asses..."

The room goes still, awkward tensions rising at her brazenness. I lay my hand on her shoulder leaning down to whisper in her ear. "I think they get it, *Nightmare.*"

She straightens at the nickname peering up at me through her lashes. "Well, I'm just saying. I mean honestly the plans are laughable and—" I grab her chin between my thumb and forefinger, raising her gaze to mine.

"Stop telling us what we've done wrong and tell us what to do next." Her face is full of contradictory feelings. A war between irritation and compliance. She opens her mouth to speak when one of my infantrymen bursts in the room.

"THEY'RE—" He takes a sharp breath as his hands wave frantically behind him, "THE FRONT LINES." An explosion sounds off close by and everyone in the room ducks down out of instinct. I wrap my free arm around her pulling her to the ground with me. "I fucking told you we should've already retaliated." She snaps.

The two of us are a tangled mess on the ground for a moment before she's wiggling out of my grip and barking orders at everyone. She's out of the tent before anyone else is, leaving the group to scramble after her and into the throng of chaos. Once outside, Eveera looses her Wield freely. Her tendrils are leaking from her palms, flooding the ground where she steps.

Based on her Wield's residual path she's headed straight for the fields with no horse and only a few weapons on her. I don't need to tell Eveera's men what to do, they've already taken off ahead of me.

"*Would it kill you to wait for backup?*" I snap, the words are thrown into her mind as Bennett passes my horse off to me.

"*Wasn't a part of my itinerary for the day.*" She retorts.

My horse follows the river of black magic leading towards the explosions. The field looks like it's been bruised. The purple of Baelor's military is a stark contrast against the gold and black of our men and women. I grip the hilt of my sword freeing it from the sheath at my hip, my horse and I taking off at a breakneck speed, my blade at the ready.

Once down in the battle the wails of the injured, the squelching of a blade slicing the skin, and the clank of metal on metal ring throughout my ears. *THUD!* I land a kick in the face of a soldier aiming to gut my horse. My steed swivels back to trample over him the before I run back towards the thick of battle.

Pain laces up my arm almost costing me my sword, "Fuck!" I look down to find where I've been struck only to see the rune engraved into my flesh glowing a bright and angry red. *Eveera.* My eyes don't have the luxury to scan for her long before my sword is meeting flesh again. What's left of my kills continues to meet the hooves of my horse and as the pain intensifies I lose my grip on my Wield. The panic to find her has superseded the need to control it and soon the familiar symphony of those choking on air echoes out. Bodies drop to the ground one by one around me, fighting for their breath.

The little wraith is still evading my sight so instead I try reaching for her, mind to mind. "*Eveera?*"

A few seconds pass and her breathy voice filters in, "*LITTLE*" Pant. "*BUSY*" Another. "*HERE!*" Relief at hearing her response gives me enough reprieve to pull back my Wield. Unnatural screams erupt from the left of me so I take off in the direction of them. The closer I get the easier it is for me to see that there are a few soldiers lucky enough to be a little more resistant to her magic. Their swords are poised at her back. From my right, a distant flash of blonde rushes towards her. The larger of the two Guards closes in on her first she spins on her heel at the last second her concentration snapping on her Wield as she narrowly blocks his blow. I can't make this damn horse go any faster. Ezra is at her back fighting off the second Guard. The Guard takes a slow swipe at Ezra's knees, I watch in horror as he jumps back colliding into Eveera. The next moments seem to go by almost in slow motion. Ezra's body knocks her off her balance and in that same moment the Guard she's fighting slices his sword across her abdomen. "NO!" I shout. Against my will an image of her mother's gutted body flashes through my mind.

"*How poetic.*" Her voice echoes quietly. I scramble off the back of my horse, running to her. Ezra having finally slain his opponent notices her bleeding and torn body in a heap on the ground. Rage clouds both of our faces at the Guard who gutted her looks down proudly. A whistle whips through the air followed by a, *THWWUUMMP!* Her assailant's body crumples next to hers. From the corner of my eye I see Bennett breathing heavily and lowering his crossbow.

I hold a vice-like grip on my Wield as I watch Ezra fall to his knees next to her and drape his hands over her body. His wails echo as he presses down on her stomach trying to keep her together.

"GET OFF OF HER!" I shout, dropping down opposite of him. With a shove I tear him away from Eveera and gather her into my arms. Those golden eyes are already glassing over and her breaths are getting shallower. My foot lands a blow into Ezra's side, keeping him down on the ground. My Wield is volatile underneath my skin, desperate to be allowed out as I carefully put her across my horse's back, doing my best to hold her stomach closed. "Come on, Nightmare." I mutter over her. "You've got to live, so you can tell me how much you hate me. You've got to live long enough to do that, to say that, okay?" I don't know why I say it, if it's more for myself or for her. But I repeat the words over and over again as we power back to camp. I *should* be concerned with the casualties, I *should* be concerned with what this will mean for further attacks, I should be concerned with anything *but* Eveera. But right now, looking at her splayed open - nothing could be of more importance than her.

"WE NEED A DAMN HEALER MAGE!" I carry her limp body into the nearest tent. We're both soaked through with her blood. My eyes are trained on the rise and fall of her chest where her breaths are still too shallow. *"Come on, Nightmare! DO NOT CLOSE THOSE EYES."* I scream through the seal, I'd shake her if her organs wouldn't spill out at the motion.

Mages rush around us. They pull at my hands, but my grip only tightens on her body not wanting to release her. They settle on shoving me in the direction of their work table for me to lay her on. Relenting, I step back from her and let them work. My teeth saws my bottom lip between them. The commotion around me sounding like nothing more than white noise. I stare at her face - her eyes are closed now. I don't know when they shut, if her body gave out or if the mages closed them.

"Oh, E..." Axel whispers, I glance back at him in enough time to see his face fall. His hand outstretched towards her but he doesn't move from the entrance of the tent, no doubt to avoid getting in the way of the only people who could fix her.

I dip my head, turning towards him as Armond joins us in the tent. "Where is he?" I growl out.

"He feels bad enough, princeling." Armond snarls back at me.

"I assure you, he doesn't." Axel's eyes are glassy as he looks at his queen cracking something in my chest. The looks he has on his face is...that look...is pure devotion. Which is why gives up the answer for Ezra's whereabouts.

"Sitting with the brothers outside. Berating himself." His gaze never leaves her torn body. I peel out of the tent so fast I almost knock over

Will who is standing outside. He opens his mouth to speak but thinks better of it quickly as he follows my gaze towards my target.

Ezra - is sitting out with Maxwell and Orem just like Axel said. His head is in his hands, blood dripping from the blonde strands. "Get up." I bark. Both the brothers stand up and move in front of their commander who doesn't budge from his spot. I ram the hilt of my sword into Orem's shoulder pushing him out of my way. "I said. Get. Up."

He reluctantly looks at me. His stare is red and his cheeks have tear tracks down them. *Pathetic,* I think. *This is the man she had a relationship with?* My stomach twists at the thought, anger bubbling in my chest.

His words come out in a low hiss. "Excuse me, *princeling?*"

"Did I fucking stutter, Wake? I said— get up." When he doesn't move quickly enough after the third command, I grab him by the nape of his neck and drag him along with me. I drag him all the way into the tent where the mages are still frantically working. "Look. At. Her." My hold on his neck yanks his head upwards but he fights to keep his eyes cast down. *The coward.*

My hand moves up from his nape and tangles into his hair. With a swift tug I yank back hard, jerking his chin up. "I SAID LOOK AT HER!" His eyes finally snap up. "*You* are the reason she is like this." The struggle to get away from me intensifies. I loosen my handle on him enough that he spins himself into my chest putting his knife against my throat. "ME?! I'M THE REASON? She was on that fucking field because of her stupid damn agreement with you! *You* are the reason, *princeling.*"

I dig my throat into his blade, "she knows how to handle herself, and you hate it. So you treat her like a petulant child. In fact, she *was* handling herself and *you*" I stab my finger into his breastplate, "you cut her concentration."

"She was open and vulnerable!" He shouts back at me.

I shake my head, "you were supposed to have her back! Not collide into it! Gods, do you know how to fucking fight spine to spine? Should've left that to me we do a great job at it." I taunt, his face contorting into rage. "You're callous mistake left her impaled on someone's blade. You want to blame me for her being here? Fine, but you only have yourself to blame for her being on that table." I'm spitting into his face at this point.

"He took a sword to my knees!" He shouts as if that's a good enough explanation.

"Then you take that fucking sword to the knees. Better your lose your legs than she her life." He's at a loss for words, the knife dropping down to his side as he backs away. The smell of tonics, antiseptics, and ointments fill the air along with our silence. The mages are tense from the outburst their combined mists glow so brightly it almost hurts as they work to stitch back together what they can of her abdomen.

It's going to leave a nasty scar with a wound that deep. His eyes flick to her for a moment as regret washes over his face. I snatch his wrist before he can take any steps towards her. "Back outside, *dog*. You don't deserve to be near her right now."

He stalls, glaring at me instead of moving. "Wake." Axels snaps, "go back outside."

Once he's gone I resume my role staring at her counting each of those, painfully slow, shallow breaths. "*Open those eyes, Nightmare. You weren't supposed to close them...please open them.*" She doesn't say anything back, her body laying as still as a statue, while the rest of us wait.

Three hours later and the three of us are still here watching her. Waiting. Will and the rest of her men wait outside. Ezra tried to come back in at one point only for Axel to chuck one of Eveera's stars at him. I appreciated that, I won't lie. Saved me from doing something similar. *Except I wouldn't have purposefully missed.*

"Ror." Bennett steps in, briefly glancing at the queen in her state. "The captains, they all want to speak with you. Breakdown on casualties, resources, and whatnot."

I shake my head, "can it wait?"

"I'll go." Armond speaks up. He places a kiss on Eveera's head, mumbling something meant only for her ears.

Axel speaks quietly once Armond leaves. "I told you she makes terrible decisions." He mutters.

"She didn't choose to be sliced open across her waist." I snarl.

He lets out an agitated sigh. "Not the wound." He snaps motioning towards the opening of the tent. From the slight crack I see the blonde's head. *Ezra.*

Now that we can both agree on, I say in my head.

"I have to tell you though if she dies while on this escapade for you? I'll split you open, balls to chin." I nod threading my hands through the sweaty mop of hair on top of my head. *If she dies, I'll let him.*

"Only fair." I grunt.

"Then we understand each other." He says, satisfied with the threat.

I understand, alright.

Armond came back another hour later, the three of us sitting in silence again until a shallow rattled breath gasps out in the tent. All of us jump up to our feet at the noise.

"E?" Axel asks tentatively. .

"Ugh, bleeding gods that hurt." A strangled sort of sob left her man as he threw himself on her. "*Oof.* Easy there you big softie." She pats his shoulder as best she can from her position.

"Axel, if you add to her pain, you'll be the next one needing healer mages." I gripe. Her piercing gold eyes flit over his shoulder to me. "*You had me worried there.*" I say.

Her brow cocks, "*scared you're shiny new toy was busted, were you?*"

"Glad to see being almost disemboweled hasn't affected that mouth of yours."

A dangerous smile graces her face, "*thinking about my mouth now, too?*" This damn woman.

Axel looks between the two of us, confusion marring his dark eyes. "Uhm, not to interrupt whatever..." He waves his hand between the two of us, "this is. But, she just got fucking split open. Can we do the weird stare off contest later?" He strokes a hand through her hair, his eyes going soft again. "How are you feeling, sweetheart?"

Sweetheart? An uncomfortable feeling flickers to life in my chest at his use of the endearment.

"I feel like I almost died. How the gods else am I supposed to feel? You try being gutted and then hauling ass on a horse with your insides dangling from you."

He grimaces just as Bennett comes in to find me again. His face grim from whatever news he's brought with him. He motions for me to follow him and I look back at Eveera. "I'll be right back." I say to her.

Her face screws up into a frown "I'll come with." She states matter of factly.

"You were *gutted.*" I argue.

She gives me a pointed look, "I am not a child. I can walk a few fucking feet. Besides now I'm all fixed up. See, your kingdom is worth a damn for something."

The briefing tent was just as chaotic as earlier, only this time the smell of death and disappointment hangs over everyone. All of us are still bearing most of the blood from earlier too. Whether it's more our own or others I am not sure.

"What I want to know is how the hell they retaliated so quickly." Will barks sparking arguments to break out all around the room. Accusations are thrown Eveera's way by one of my captains who questions her on why killing General Thornbirk didn't buy us more time.

"It didn't work because none of you listened to a damn word I said. I *told* you they would retaliate quickly. Never mind my battle knowledge or my military's. Never mind the fact they've bested you guys almost every time. Of course they launched an attack." She snaps.

I rest a hand on her shoulder. "According to Queen Eveera they have some newfangled weaponry. Ballistas...and others I need to look into. Baelor is...resourceful we all know that already." I wouldn't be surprised if Baelor were just sitting back accumulating soldiers. What he lacks in a Wield he wants to make up for in brute force and numbers and now apparently in ammunition.

A voice I don't recognize takes a turn, the boy it came from looks around nervously, "maybe this is all a lost cause." He says quietly. He wears captain's colors on his armor but they look too big for him. Mentally, I count my captains noticing one missing and then my eyes fall to the kid. Regret blooms in my chest, realization dawning that the kid probably just got promoted thanks to his commanding officer dying.

"Snap out of those thoughts Captain or you'll end up dead or wishing that you were." Bennett orders.

Nobody talks for awhile until I hear a slight gasp from Eveera. "Oh gods." She says quietly. "How did I not realize?"

"Realize what?" I ask low into her ear.

She looks up at me, her hand smoothing across her bandaged stomach. The motion sends a twinge of guilt through me. Ezra's right, *I am also a reason that she ended up the way she did today.*

"We have a leak." She answers.

"What do you mean?" Another captain of mine asks.

She falls forward, bracing her hands on the edge of the wooden table. Her face is twisted in pain as she finishes her thought. "I *mean*, yesterday, I saw someone. Someone in a very noticeably gold armored uniform."

Will sputters, "and you didn't think to mention that yesterday?" His answer is the swish of the tent flap as she walks away from the conversation. "Great. Off she goes, again." He grits. The captains begin arguing, trying to work out a plan so I signal for Bennett and Will to take over, while I step outside after her.

Following her has become a recurring theme, you realize that right? The voice inside my head chastises as cool air hits my cheeks. "Eveera!" She stops and slowly turns back around. "Hey, where are you going?"

"Ugh, why are all of the men in my life so needy." She pouts as I frown down at her. "I'm going to go handle our leak."

I'm stunned for a moment, shocked that she feels healed enough to do whatever it is she's about to. "Do uh- do you even know who it is?"

She smiles, walking her fingers up my arm and then patting my cheek with as much condescension she can muster, "of course I don't. That's the fun part. I get to figure it out, and then I get to play."

Oh good. My base camp is going to become Eveera's little shop of horrors. Perfect.

RORIN

"What does she mean she gets to play?" Will whispers in my ear.

Eveera demanded that I line up the remainder of our men for questioning. I didn't know exactly what was up her sleeve, but I could guess the culprit won't survive whatever she has planned.

Looking over the formation of soldiers all I see is exhausted and confused men and women. Already beaten, bloodied, and bruised. Eveera's pacing in front of them, clad in nothing but the bandages wrapping her torso and a pair of leather pants. Her sword tip drags along the ground while she scrutinizes them.

She stops and slowly her tendrils begin leaking from her. I search for who she's zeroed in on but her eyes are at their feet not their faces.

"There." She points and a blood curdling scream rings out. "Him."

Her moves are lithe, winding through the crowd to crouch before the soldier. She takes the collar of his undershirt and drags him out of formation. We leave the rest of the soldiers to stay still - waiting for a dismissal that won't come until we have the answers we need.

The man kicks and screams while her tendrils bind around him, dragging him along. The way her magic manipulates and moves between both material and non is strange even for a Wield, she looks more like a demon reaping the earth than a human queen.

With a flick of her wrist her tendrils secure the man to the back of her horse. "She's going to pull him behind her? Aren't you going to do something?!" Will shrieks.

I shake my head. "If he's the leak then he's part of the problem. There's nothing I want to do for him."

Will's mouth drops like I've struck him. "S-so you're just going to let her—"

"Yeah. I'm just going to let her." I say, stalking away from him to mount my own horse. His screams became deafening, to the point that I begrudgingly let out my own Wield and knocked him out for the rest of the ride. By the time we got to Bair's post his skin was so torn he looked like ground meat.

Will tried arguing with me the whole ride about how inhumane it was but I ignored his protests. If the soldier wants to leak information and risk all our necks, I won't regret severing his. "This isn't right. This isn't the way we do things Rorin!" He tries again once we get down from our horses, but I push past him, guiding the queen and the captive to the cells.

Eveera had Bennett chain his limbs in an "X" position against the damp stone wall. His head hangs in front sweat and blood drip from his hair and pool at his feet. "Bennett?" She calls out. He steps up behind her, the dim light illuminating his gold armor and bronzed skin. "What's its name?" She asks.

"Baron Wriercliff, Your Highness. He's a second lieutenant in our ranks. 34 years old. No family of note." Her head tilts at the man. His prone position places him more at eye level with her. She taps her chin while pacing in front of him, mulling the information over.

"No family of note. That means no wailing wives or weeping children." Bennett retreats back to stand next to Will and me. Only the three of us followed her down here. The rest of her men, she ordered back into their rooms. Apparently she doesn't like too much of an audience during these...interrogations. But I want to know everything, the how, the why, the when. My men feel similarly, or at least Bennett does. Will's down here based solely on his moral compass. "*We do this my way. If I require you, you'll know. Keep Mousy at bay. Understood?*"

My eyes flick to my friend briefly while I move around the wall to quietly bring myself closer to her, "*understood.*"

I see the corner of her mouth twitch, a magicked claw extending from her finger to lift his chin up. "Tsk tsk tsk. Baron, dear, you've made a very *grave* mistake. Do you want to tell us about that?" Her voice is an octave higher, feigning sweetness. His upper lip curls in a snarl and he spits at her face. Her eyes glass over into the inky black as her Wield builds beneath her skin, the wave of power pulsing through the room.

"Wrong answer." she growls, stabbing the tip of the claw up and into his lower jaw. Blood drips down her finger in a thick stream and then the screams start again.

The interrogation, if you can call it that, has been going for hours.

Every orifice on Baron's face has a trail of blood dripping from it.

"Come on, Baron. Give me something here."

"What exactly do you expect him to give you? You're melting him from the inside out!" Will snaps.

"*Control him.*" Her bark rattles through me.

He looks to me desperately. "Why are you not stepping in here? You're sovereign, Rorin." His voice is tired, laced with both anger and fear.

"I told you why already." I snap.

He takes a step towards him, shaking his head. "He's one of ours."

A dark laugh rumbles out and I push him back against the stone. "He isn't." Will grunts against my hold. "He isn't." I say again, lower this time, my eyes bearing into his. "When he crossed the line over to Baelor's men, he disgraced himself. He dishonored Vellar. He *betrayed* Vellar."

Will scoffs struggling against me still, "and what do you think we did when we crossed the line over to Obsidian, hm?" His tone matching mine.

CRACK!

Will's eyes dart over my shoulder at the noise. The man hooked to the wall now has his right arm bent at an unnatural angle. "Do you want to answer me now, Baron?" Eveera taunts, her voice taking on that distorted unnatural lilt.

"You've damned us all, Prince Rorin. Bringing the likes of *her* behind our walls." The words are raspy and raw from his screaming. I shove away from Will moving to stand behind her.

Almost imperceptibly I feel her shiver when my chest brushes up against her back. "How's that lieutenant?" I ask.

"Does the King know you've brought her here?" Baron asks, blood sputtering out of his mouth as he speaks.

I grit my teeth together, "that didn't answer my question, traitor."

His body shakes twinging from both laughter and pain. "Ha. Oh, they have a plan for us, Prince. What side will you be on when that snaps into place?"

"Why did you turn on your own men, soldier?!" I shout, the rage consuming me as I look down at Eveera's bandaged chest and stomach. Her arms are folded and she's taken to leaning slightly against my chest. From this angle I can see that her eyes are still fully blackened as her Wield slinks beneath her skin, the black magic spreading across it like veins. I enter her mind, probing for her, but all I am met with is a black hole - her magic fully consuming her mind as she works to manipulate him telepathically.

His back arches pulling the unbroken limbs taut against the chains. "The Wield you're experiencing is not so different to say your Vellaran Illusionaries. However, I will admit that it's better. It's specific. It's mental, emotional, *and* physical. Do you know what I see, Baron?" He whimpers and she rolls her shoulders back, settling more snugly against me. "I see you cowering in front of Hadar's Guards. Selling out your friends, your Prince, and your home. And I know it's not just because of me, oh no. You've been selling information for *months.*" Her words are low, low enough that I'm not even sure Will or Bennett can hear her. "And like a coward, you feared them more than us. What a mistake that ended up being." His whines grow louder as she assaults his mind.

"*I think this kill is yours.*" She whispers through the seal. Her body turns slowly so that she can look up at me through her lashes, the gold returning to those irises. Her hand lays lightly on my chest. At her touch my Wield slinks out of my hands curling around her body and seeping directly into Baron's lungs. I could make this quick - so quick he wouldn't feel a thing. But he doesn't deserve to die quickly. There is a strong urge inside that begs me to stop. To not use the cursed magic so frequently, but as her icy palm burns my chest the decision to keep him suspended in this agonizing pain for as long as necessary wins out.

A minute for every life he cost us. And not just for today, but for every day he was complicit in his sin.

Eveera was face down in the chaise's pillows the moment we stepped back into the apartment. I drifted by her and into my office where the pile of paperwork still waited along with the faint reminder of the queen and I's previous interaction here. Despite exhaustion threatening to pull me under, there wouldn't be any sleep for me. Not when there was so much to fix, so much to change, so much to clean up.

The sun was rising when we'd left the cells but it burns brighter now, streaming through the windows and the orange glow that casts throughout the room warms up the space.

Knock knock.

I look over my glasses to Bennett peeking his head in. "Thought you could use this." He states placing a glass full of bourbon in front of me. *Unexpected but I'll take it.*

"I expected this to be coffee." I say, lifting the drink up to my lips.

He takes the seat opposite me dusting off his pants as he stretches out. "Ah. Well, *that* drink is waiting in front of the very sound asleep queen out there. Coffee didn't seem strong enough for you." His face is as hollow as I feel at the moment. I'm not ignorant to the fact that the hit to Bair's post affected him the most. Being the Commander over this post while I was away hasn't been the lightest job, and I would bet money he's feeling responsible for Wriercliff.

"You look tired, friend."

He chuckles, "so do you."

My head drops into my hands, "Fuck Ben...I don't know how to get us out of this. I thought by bringing the Obsid's here we'd tank them quickly. A massive show of force, an immediate win. But..."

"But?" He asks softly.

I suck in a deep breath, "but...I've only cost them their lives. Men and women who don't trust me but are willing to fight on the word of their queen. They trust her enough to gamble their lives for people they hate. But my own soldiers, my own men, don't trust me enough to not fucking betray us." His body shifts to lean forward resting both arms on the desk.

"They're my men too Rorin. And they were under my control while you were gone. How many times have we had to flip flop the roles of command due to your responsibilities in Valen?" I groan into my palms. "As for the queen...not to be insensitive but you contracted them. They're getting paid to be here. Which is more than I can say for our men, unfortunately." Anger crawls up my neck as I think about the hand my father has had in all of his citizens' lives and they don't see a dime for it. "Gods, this is all a bloody mess." He grunts in agreement, reclining back in the chair again to stare at the ceiling. The two of us ruminating in the silence.

"Will's furious with me."

"Ha. When is he not?" I know it's meant to be a jest, but the barb stings all the same.

"Right." I mutter.

He gives me a soft look, "we're not boys anymore Ror. Tough decisions have to be made...and Will well, he had an easier time growing up than we did." *Maybe.* I think. *Or he was just better at staying out of trouble. Maybe if we'd been a little more like him we all would've avoid the haunts of our pasts.*

A quiet knock and a young voice grabs our attention, "prince?"

Ugh. "What now?" I ask. The page's face goes white before I wave him in, he apologizes quickly for interrupting and hands me a missive with the royal crest on it.

"Please tell me that isn't more bad news?" Bennett asks tentatively.

I shake my head, "it's not." He starts to sag in relief until I add, "it's worse than bad news."

"Greeeaaat." He says.

"Apparently we have pressing responsibilities to take care of before the Valen Celebration in two weeks. They want us home, now."

Not exactly great timing. War is encroaching on our doorstep but sure let's keep our regularly scheduled programming at court. Gods forbid we don't spend another dreadful evening together dressed as gussied up show ponies. I snip inside of my mind.

He peers over the edge of the paper. "Anything about the queen in there? Do they know you're working together?"

I give him another shake of my head, "if they do they aren't letting on. For now we still have that element of surprise but…we'll have to prepare Eveera." I hand him the document to read over himself.

"Prepare me for what?" A very sleepy-eyed and mussed up queen stands in the doorway. Something tugs in my chest at the sight of her. If she greeted people like this all the time some might confuse her with being innocent, sweet, and harmless. No one would guess the tiny woman with a bird's nest of tangled curls on her head and a coffee mug in her hands finds enjoyment in watching people's brains melt. I slip back into reality when I see her stepping towards the paper Bennett waves in her direction.

It takes her a moment to read it. She sets down the mug and holds the paper closer to her face, reading it a second time. Her eyes peek up over the edge of the page, looking a little more awake now, as her lips curl into a feline smile. "Hope they don't mind you bringing a plus one." She quips before tossing the paper back to Bennett.

Oh *they'll mind*, my conscience says. *They'll mind.*

EVEERA

Not everyone was as eager about the news as I was.

Rorin's been puffing about the apartment since last night, slamming doors and drawers, and snapping at his men.

His feelings towards returning home are obvious and while I could feel pity for him, I don't. Meeting the king gets me one step closer to ridding this realm of the two Vellaran leeches responsible for my early rise to power. It honestly couldn't have worked out better, us getting a summons. "You're going to burn a hole in the floor from all of your pacing." I comment. Watching him spiral at first was humorous - now it's just annoying.

He stops mid pace to look at me. So much palpable discomfort rolling off of him. "I committed treason by bringing you here. They could string me up and then you'd be left to fend for yourself. And how would the tiny queen fare if it came to that?" He barks.

Irritation pricks underneath my skin. "Oh quit your whining. You *chose* to commit treason. You aren't ignorant, or maybe you are, and I've been trusting an idiot all these days." He seethes at my harsh words. "You want to break the rules for your own cause? You want people to listen to you? Grow a pair and deal with the consequences of your actions. Untuck your tail from between your legs and go confront them like a real General. If it costs you the noose then, well, at least I'll get to go home early." I snap, slamming the door behind me.

The hall at first was a bit dizzying to navigate, all the winding turns, but before I knew it I was spit out in front of my men's bedrooms. I knock twice on the door and Orem answers. His face is surprised as he steps aside to let me in. "Boys! She's here." He shouts, looking at me nervously, his feet shifting underneath him. "I'll uhm. I'll go get Armond and Ezra."

"Good plan, O." I murmur wandering over to the window.

It's not long before a heavy arm drapes over my shoulders. Axel doesn't say anything, instead the two of us just stare out at what we can see of the post. Golden rays of sunlight filter throughout the room, highlighting parts of the crystalline glass. "Eveera?" Armond's voice echoes through the suite. We turn around and I detach myself from Axel, clasping my hands in front of my stomach. "Is everything alright?"

I bob my head up and down, "oh it's better than alright." I state, their faces twisting in curiosity. "We're going to meet the king. Tomorrow."

For some reason I thought my men would share my enthusiasm about going to Valen, then I remembered I didn't share with any of them my secular ambitions for this agreement and the arguments started almost instantly.

"We agreed to be here." I explain again.

"*We* didn't agree to anything." Orem grumbles.

My fingernails dig into my palms as I hold back most of my irritation. "Orem, dear, if you're going to try and have a backbone I suggest you do it without hiding behind Maxwell." He scowls, but makes no move to step up in front of his brother.

"Leave him alone E. He's not wrong." Axel tries to mollify me.

"Oh my *gods!*" I shout, my fingers pinching the bridge of my nose. "Can you all please stop the damn *whining*, this is not negotiable for me. This is what I am doing. It doesn't have to be what *you* are doing. And if I have to hear this 'we didn't agree' thing one more time I will lose my fucking mind." I don't know how many more times I can express this. I am not keeping any of them here, regardless of their quote unquote bound duties. "I know you have an order to protect me, but as queen I can release you from that. You don't want to follow me into this madness? Then don't."

Ezra laughs darkly. "You think we have a choice? If we stay we'll probably die. If we leave they'll hang us for abandoning you. You act like you're giving us an out just because you're sovereign but we didn't make these oaths to you out of friendship or kinship." His words sting as he steps closer to me. "We made them out of necessity. We made them to the crown." Maxwell reaches out his hand, tugging on his commander's shoulder.

"Speak for yourself." Axel snaps, his tone sharp, stepping in front of me.

"What was that Mecham?" He bites.

"I said speak for yourself. Not all of us took the oath to climb the social ladder. Just because you fell from her favor doesn't mean you get to talk to her that way. She *is* the crown, whether you like it or not." The two of them stand nose to nose, steam rolling from both their ears. Armond steps up to separate them, looking at me to continue.

I back away from Axel, lifting my chin to look over the five of them. "You're right. You no longer have a choice, how silly of me to offer it." I keep backing up until my heels hit the wooden door and I grab hold of the doorknob. "One more complaint." I say over my shoulder, giving them my profile. "One more deflection of orders. Just one more - and I'll do the work for the council and hang you myself." From my peripheral I can see their faces shadowing over. "You all have gotten too comfortable. A mistake, I see."

The conversations with Rorin were no less pleasant when I returned. We spent the better part of the afternoon arguing between going on foot or portaling.

I hate portaling, it makes my head turn fuzzy.

He, however, doesn't seem to care about that fact and is adamant that he wants to be in and out of Valen as quickly as possible. When I prodded him as to why the rush he began griping to himself about the summons. Something about not wanting to be a "trussed up swine" for this Celebration that the court throws every year.

Since I didn't really want to know what that meant and I knew we'd be coming back here anyways, there wasn't much to do in terms of packing. I decided to fill my time and impatience with training. No harm in sharpening up my skills.

Winding through all of the obnoxiously lit halls was like taking a tour of the sun. Everything here in this kingdom is bright and glowy - another difference between Obsidian and Vellar. There are windows that line most of every hall that keep the daylight flowing in. It's all very open, trying a little too hard to show that they're a passive people in my opinion. But I can't argue that it would seem that - should the gods be real and actually care about us - between our two kingdoms Obsidian is not the favored one.

I shuck off my weapons belt while walking out into the ring to set the targets. My body is anxious to sweat off the pent up tension from the past few weeks. I choose one of my ruby hilted daggers and with a swift throw I launch it at a horizontal angle. The trajectory allows it to slice through the "neck" of each of the targets in one fluid motion, lodging itself in the side of the final one.

Ready to go again I pick up another one of the rubies and throw it directly into the "head" of the second target. Repeating the maneuvers, I keep going until my hands feel raw and I'm out of breath. By the end each target is filled with daggers, knives, throwing stars, and arrows made of Obsidian steel. Sweat is rolling off me in streams and the towel I brought does very little to fix it. Lining myself back up I ready myself to go again. The movements are routine enough that my mind loses focus and drifts off to a memory of Armond and I.

-

"Pick your feet up! You're shuffling! You'll never best an opponent with feet like that!" I want to slap the smug grin off his pale skin. I charge again focusing this time on my feet, too hard apparently because he checks my shoulder and I land on my back.

"ARMOND! YOU INSUFFERABLE BASTARD!" I snarl. He never lets me have the upper hand. *"YOU'RE TWICE MY SIZE YOU MIS-ERABLE OAF!"* His laughter ringing through the room only serves to anger me more. He Voids in and out of the place. Leaving me to only hear that blasted laughter.

"Such harsh words from such a tiny queen. Little venomous serpent." I whip around to face him but he isn't there.

"Stupid Voiding powers." I say to myself.

My laughter slips out into the present.

"Daydreaming again while training?" Armond's voice startles me.

My brow creases in annoyance, "just thinking of one of our first spars."

"You were such a venomous little serpent." He says, moving out onto the floor in front of me. "Hope you pick up your feet better now than you did then." His sword is ready in his hand along with mine that he kicks towards my feet.

"I'm training." I argue, lazily picking up the sword. He lunges for me, metal glinting in his hands as he aims low for my side as I'm crouched over. I barely block the blow, rolling under his next swipe. "That wasn't fair." I shout back, readjusting my stance and placing equal weight on my legs for balance. My knees are bent slightly ready to pounce on him. The butt of his hilt meets my sternum before I have a chance to leap at him, throwing me back down. I roll out of the way of his incoming heel and grab onto one ankle, my legs swinging out to kick into the other. His leg buckles on impact which allows me to pull him to the ground next to me. We tussle on the floor for a moment while I try to pin him. I ready my knee to kneel into his chest and hold him in place. "Prepare to yield, Monty." He shakes his head giving me a lopsided grin as he Voids out from underneath me. I tilt forward, losing my balance. *Damn Voiding powers.*

He Voids back in right as I am vertical again. I run at him, and he swings his arm wide. There's no sword present anymore, only his fist. My metal clatters to the ground and I duck at the last second barely missing his hit, landing a solid blow with my elbow into his gut.

He goes down with a grunt and quickly my legs wrap around his shoulders, locking him in. "You want to play dirty and use your Wield? Two can play that game." He claws and grapples at my shins when I connect my fingers to his temples, shoving my Wield into his mind.

He slaps the ground three times yielding almost immediately and I release him, pulling my magic back. Both of us lay there a minute. He gets up first, extending a hand my way. "Like I said, venomous little serpent." I smirk, still not wanting to be friendly yet. "Are you prepared for tomorrow?" He asks cautiously.

I suck in a deep breath wiping at my skin, "is anyone ever really prepared to meet the two people responsible for their own parents deaths?"

He rests his clammy palm on my shoulder, "you're sure you want to go through with going?" I turn to look up at him, my gaze hardening. "I'm not arguing. Don't get my noose ready just yet." He says, trying to get a laugh from me. But it doesn't work. The gravity of the situation settling on me.

"I meant what I said."

He nods, his face growing solemn. "I know. Just remember who's on your side here. Your anger shouldn't be with us."

"And are you on my side out of obligation or choice?" I ask.

He raises his brow. "The truth of it?" I nod, but inside I'm hesitant to hear his answer. "Both."

The doors to Rorin's room and office were both shut when I walked in. He's nowhere in sight, giving me a moment's respite from having to interact with another person.

I move to peel off the damp leathers the minute I am in the bedroom, struggling as I try to climb in the shower. My hands fumble with the temperature dial to turn it as hot as it will go until the steam rises off the droplets on my skin.

It's a fast shower for once. Knowing we have to be up and out of the post early, I peek out of the shower to grab one of the gray towels sitting on a shelf next to me. It's soft against my bare skin, a slight chill running down my spine as I step out of the steam. Combing through my wet curls, I wrap it loosely in a smaller towel on top of my head while I go through my clothes, looking for something to wear tonight. I settle on dark leggings and a fitted tunic, pulling on my boots and winding my hair down from the towel and into a knot at the base of my neck.

Knock knock.

"Come in." I don't bother to look up from the vanity, I already know who's walking in by the scent alone. "Princeling."

"Food's ready, you can join us or not." He says curtly.

"Well if I hadn't planned on joining I would be stark naked under those sheets." I look at his face in the mirror's reflection for a reaction but his expression is stony. "And that would have been quite a scene for you to behold." I boast.

His eyes widen a but that's all I get from him and he clears his throat. "A-hem. You can hurry and leave with me. Or you can dawdle more and find your way there by yourself." He leaves the room briskly, not bothering to close the door behind him. *Dick.*

Rorin waits outside the room - leaning against the wall. He's clad in all black, his shirt opened at the collar. His hair is mussed up, the curls splaying wildly against his forehead. Tension lines through his face as he picks at his nails only looking up when I move to stand in front of him.

Those two hazel eyes narrow on me for a moment before he pushes off the wall and stalks off in front of me, leaving me to trail behind him.

The noise of the room was hard to miss as we got closer to it. Rows of tables and benches line the center of the room. Higher ranking soldiers and captains filling nearly every seat. There is a lingering sensation of fear mixed with curiosity when we enter the room, all eyes turning to us. My men, I notice are up at the head table with Rorin's. Orem is chatting Bennett's ear off and at a brief glance one might assume them friends, not pacified enemies. I stalk around Rorin's looming form marching up and over the table before plopping myself on the bench.

"Must you always be so...irreverent?" Mousy snaps quietly.

"Yes." I quip as Rorin takes his seat in between us. The staff comes around with the same simple dish for all of us. A blatant example of their low resources. They cast an apologetic look towards the prince and his commanders which none of them acknowledge.

My men are uncomfortably quiet as I settle into my spot, Orem stops chattering off to Bennett and Ezra and Maxwell keep their eyes downcast on their food. Axel was the only one to look down the row at me but even that was tense. *I guess my words hit their mark earlier.*

The dining hall resumes it's normal commotion but our table eats in silence.

WHAM! The doors to hall slam open, disrupting everyone as a woman rushes into the room, charging towards us.

No...not towards us. She's charging at me. I realize quickly.

She points her narrow finger in my direction. ""IT WAS YOU! YOU KILLED HIM. IT WAS YOU!" Rorin pushes up from the bench hurriedly and braces an arm in front of me. He signals his soldiers, several of them getting up to apprehend her. "YOU TOOK HIM YOU MISERABLE BITCH!"

I stand up slowly behind his arm, and slowly move it out of my way. "I'm going to need you to be more specific, dear." I call out. "I've killed a lot of men in my years." Stepping up, on, and over the table again I place myself in front of her. When I get too close to the distressed woman she spits directly in my face.

Ooo so we want to play tough girl do we? "Tsk tsk tsk. That wasn't very nice."

Her lip curls, "YOU TOOK BARON FROM ME."

Ah, there it is. "So the little traitor had a little whore." I croon, egging her anger on. "How sweet." She's struggling against the soldiers' grip on her biceps. "Oh it's fruitless to fight against them. Funny they hold you back, one of their own, instead of me. How the tides have turned." She lets out a snarl, saliva foaming and collecting at the corners of her mouth. She's winding up to spit in my face again but before she can I let one of my tendrils snap around her head sealing her mouth closed. "I wouldn't do that a second time if I were you."

Her eyes widen in shock at my magic. "What should we do with her, General?" The men detaining her look over my head and to Rorin.

"I'll take her, gentlemen." I say. They don't respond, the wariness in their expressions deepens. I crane my neck around to see Rorin nod his approval and allow another tendril of my magic to slip out from my skin and bind her wrists together. "There. Much better." The guards shoot Rorin one more look before passing her over to me.

"You're really going to let *her* handle this?" Mousy's voice shrill and loud enough for the entire room to hear. I stop in my tracks, waiting for the prince's answer.

"She has a method, who am I to stop her?" He says disinterested. A small smile tries to slip across my face as I push the woman further out into the hall. Leaning in close, my breath brushes the shell of her ear.

"Hear that? I have a method. Of course, Baron didn't seem to like my methods too much. Let's see if you do."

I brought her back to the same cell I held Baron in. Her blood and snot have created a grotesque pool underneath her hung head, dripping on top of the stain her lover left behind. We've spent most of our time together with her fighting to push out my Wield, to block me from accessing her fears. She didn't do a very good job because it wasn't long when I figured out that abandonment is her biggest one. Little did I know last night I brought that one to life.

She's now gone quiet. Her whimpers matching the drip of her blood. I tune in every so often to see if her fears are changing. If she has anything interesting about her at all, only thing that I found was the memory of her welp of a father leaving her mother and her to rot on the streets, followed by her mother whoring herself out. I applaud the entrepreneurship her mother had, if only she hadn't taken a turn for the worse hanging around a little too long with the cretins that crawl about brothels. From there the little snotty wench grew up and met a little traitor. Only he abandoned her too. Albeit at my behest but still.

Poor poor little traitor's lover.

I'd feel worse if the man she so bravely defended hadn't sold out all our men with the intention of getting us ripped apart by Hadar's Guards. I'd stay out of their court business but the one she's devoted too is the reason I was flayed open on a field. And that is not how I plan to go.

My Wield pulls back just enough for her to catch her breath, maybe give me something other than sniveling. "Are you ready to talk now?" I hum. "I'll admit, you've held out longer than most. You must have really loved him." I purse my lips together considering her. Her rosy hair is drenched in sweat and hangs limply around her face.

"You r-really are as c-cruel as they warned." She says, her words slurring together.

"That just might be the most interesting thing you've said so far, dear." Her whole body shudders as I slink closer. "Not that I'm expecting a heart to heart or anything. But woman to woman? It's not my fault I am this way. But I'll take full responsibility for the fact that *I like being this way*." My finger slides under her chin forcing her to keep holding my stare. "Now sweetheart, answer me this and I'll make it all stop."

"I'm n-not telling y-you anything, *somnia maga*." *Dream witch.*

I give her a disapproving look. "Oh dear. Name calling and the wrong answer. How unsurprising." A tendril spears right through her, her scream loud enough it rattles the rickety metal bars around us.

"Haven't you had enough?! Just put her out of her misery already."

I snap the tendril back into me at the intruding voice. "Sir Mousy Buzzkill, everyone." I throw my arms out to the sides. Unfortunately, he doesn't take the bait. "Fine." I concede, dropping my arms back down. "She was getting boring anyways."

He stares at me dumbfounded. "You're just going to leave her there? Not even end her life with whatever respect she has left?"

My head jerks towards him, "she lost her respect when she sidled up with a traitor."

"News flash, Your Highness. We're all traitors. What makes them so different?" He shouts. There's a glint in the corner of the dank hall outside the bars, and a pair of green and gold eyes flash my way.

I jerk my chin towards the prince. "She knows information, but she refuses to give it despite my efforts." My head turns towards Mousy again, "you want to put her out of her misery? Be my guest; I'll leave you to it." He pales at the suggestion, yanking open the cell door and stomping past me to unlock her chains. Her body thuds into the pool of mucus and blood on the cement.

Her weak voice barely carries her last hiss in my direction, "*Somnia maga morieris a malo in ossibus tuis.*" *Dream witch you will die from the evil in your bones.*

Lovely. I send a little wave in their direction while calling out over my shoulder passing up the prince on my way out.

The chaise up in the apartment has been calling to me for the past hour and once I'm finally out of the cells and face to face with it, I collapse. My eyelids fall heavy the minute my head hits the plush velvet. I'd drift off to sleep if not for the incessantly noisy thoughts filtering in from Rorin's head. "*Your mind is very loud.*" I send down the seal.

"*Then ignore it.*" He snaps.

"*If it were that easy I wouldn't be talking to you. Believe me, I don't like you enough to voluntarily have a conversation.*" I snap back at him, and just as everything starts to numb and drift again, the scent of bourbon and citrus fills the room. I crack an eye open to see a scowling princeling standing over me. "You're staring." I note while trying to close my eyes again.

He places both his hands on the edge of the chaise caging my head in when he leans down. "Mm. Merely observing, Your Highness." *These proximity run-ins with him are becoming more and more frequent.* "We need to talk."

I raise my brows, "about?"

"Vellar."

My interest piques. "Oh?"

He stalls for a moment, pulling his lip between his teeth and chewing on it. "There is going to need to be a plan." He says.

"A plan for?" I ask.

He taps the rune on my wrist "These."

"Care to elaborate?" I press.

He huffs, lifting his chin up so that I'm staring at the stubble on the underneath of his jawline. "We have red angry runes on our wrists. At some point someone is going to notice."

He doesn't give me anymore than that, forcing me to chime in. "Oh-kay...so we need a plan for what? To explain it?" His head bobs up and down. "We can't just tell them to fuck off and mind their own business?"

Rorin tilts his face back down, his expression disapproving as he says, "no."

Damn, I think. "Alright...any suggestions?"

He tilts his gaze back up. "One. But you'll hate it." When I don't answer, he takes that as his cue to keep rambling. "We'll have to be convincing, they're not easy to conceal, and if questions are raised...well it's just better if we stick closely to one another. And that closeness will most likely raise other questions—" Alarm bells start going off in my head as he explains this plan.

"Don't you dare suggest we *sleep* together, princeling. Please tell me you aren't suggesting that?!" I shriek.

He shakes his head giving me a moment of relief, "well no not *literally*. But I think it may be in our best interests to make them think we entered into an agreement as a result of...passion."

Disgust churns in my stomach. "A result of *passion?* You're right. I hate this idea." He mumbles something along the lines of "*I knew you would.*" But I can't be bothered with the snide comment as I'm still stuck on the suggestion that we did this based on our being romantically involved. "I don't make decisions based on...passions."

"You do too. Just a different kind of passion. If anyone asks about the runes we can spin a story of us falling for each other. That we faced death during our travels and in the heat of the aftermath we made promises to one another. Or after I almost lost you when on the battlefield we decided to commit then, as a means of reassurance to one another."

He sounds completely ridiculous. If his parents believe it, they're denser than I assumed. *Oh gods, what if my own men start to believe it.* "Will it keep them from retaliating for you bringing me into your kingdom? Into your battle?"

"No, but it may delay them long enough for me to get you back on Obsidian soil."

I look at his face. *His stupid chiseled face, that has his stupid smug smirk on it.* "I hate the idea and I hate you for suggesting it." He stares down at me, waiting for a yes or a no. "Fine." I state pushing out from underneath him.

"You concede so easily?" His tone surprised. "You realize this will mean a bit of acting on both our parts. They'll need to be convinced that we are mad for one another." I grunt in understanding. *Obviously.*

"Bleeding fucking gods." I groan. He takes a seat on the table in front of me, resting his forearms on the tops of his thighs.

He looks at me intently, his face growing serious. "I have to ask. What made you so..."

"Charming, exciting, alluring..." I suggest.

Rorin's brow pulls tight, "no." *Oh.* I think. "Pitiless. Merciless. Heartless. I saw her life too, through your mind. You did a shit job at keeping me out." His words wash over me like cold water it's such a drastic change of the subject.

"Did you want me to have mercy on the woman?" I ask.

He shakes his head. "I didn't say that."

"Then what are you saying?"

Rorin doesn't answer me, so I choose to invade his space this time. I move off the couch to stand in front of him. His face is at chest level for me with our height difference. "This is what you asked for." I murmur, dragging a finger against his pulse. "If you wanted merciful, if you wanted compassionate, or even a peaceful way to handle things you would've never knocked on my door."

He swallows thickly, his throat bobbing with the movement. "So you tortured her for being affiliated? For being a potential threat? Or because she came after you?" He looks at me earnestly his rough hand coming up to his throat and wrapping around my fingers.

"I tortured her for a few reasons. To find out how much Hadar's Guards know thanks to her lover, because I could, and because you let me." His face drops at my words. I smile as I back away from him, letting him stew over that fact, the fact that he could've stopped me and didn't.

RORIN

Again another sleepless night came and went. Her words plaguing me the entire time. *"Because you let me."*

I did, and the problem is, I would again. The things that damn woman does to my head. I was accosted by Bennett and Will after she left the cells. Panic rising between the two of them over how she'll behave in Valen. I simply reminded them of who's responsibility she is and that I would handle it. But she makes it difficult. Everything about her disrupts my sense of reason.

I can't figure her out. There are times I think things are getting more comfortable, that we are bridging across whatever tensions our kingdoms have but then she slams those walls down again. When I saw her on that field, when I waited for her to wake up, I couldn't explain that the emotions that ran through me at the sight of her torn body. How could I explain to my men that I didn't care what the traitor or his lover suffered at her hands because they almost cost me her. Maybe I could have convinced them that without her Baelor's army with destroy us, but I didn't think that explanation would hold. So instead I said I'd handle it, and the quickest solution I came up with to handle it was to have us play the part of lovers.

My Wield pools in the palm of my hand, the mist twisting and turning. Anger and disgust fills me as I watch the cursed magic move. The Wield clouds over the seal's rune the glint of it's own magic glows under and through the mist. I've studied my magic in these controlled states for years, trying to understand why my mist wouldn't be the same as my mother's. My father's fury over it led me to my lessons - but those lessons weren't to learn it, adapt to it, Wield it. They were to contain it. I've worked so hard not to let it consume me but around her...around her I have no control. Yet another frustrating development since getting her involved.

THUD! THUD! THUD! "COME ON GENERAL WAKE UP!" I snuff the mist out, pulling my Wield back to me.

"If you've any good sense you would shut the hell up!" I grumble, burying my face into the pillow. There is a muffled sound of metal meeting wood before my door bursts inwards.

"She is apparently not a morning person." Bennett quips. He rips the pillow out from under my face and throws it across the room in the general direction of where the queen must be, "we know you aren't too excited about going back to court, but your appearance is unfortunately required. So get up and dust that crown off, Prince. Otherwise the creepy queen might eat us for breakfast as penance for the wake up call."

Will rounds the bed without making eye contact with me, the both of them each take an edge of the covers and pull them back off my body. *Good thing I decided to sleep in pants last night.* My body flinches at the stark contrast in temperature. "I think right now I would let her." I mutter.

I dress quickly and pass off the last of my things to one of the servants. While walking out of my room I noticed one of her throwing stars embedded in the door frame outside my room. *That must have been what was used as the precursor to her thank you this morning.*

Strangely enough she had found her way to the portal room without me or one of my two men guiding her because when I walked into the room, there she was already standing with her men, Axel was tying her hair up for her while she worked on the buttons to the front of her corset. The position has them nearly fused together, whereas the rest of her men stand a bit away, eyes focused forward on the portal.

I place my hand on the portal, imbuing it with my magic. "I am sure you all are aware of how to use this?" I ask. The only people to shake their heads are Maxwell and Orem. "Right, so for those who don't know, repeat exactly what Will says and then follow quickly behind one another. You don't want to risk ending up in the wrong place. For the future - if you can envision the portal location you want to go you won't need to say it out loud, but today as you all have never been to Valen Court it'll be safer to say the words."

Will steps up loudly stating, "VALEN COURT, SUN PORTAL" and then steps through. They each follow suit and step in one after the other leaving Eveera and I alone. Her face is tight as she attempts to conceal her unease. *"Nervous?"* I ask through the seal.

Her eyes flit to mine before settling back on the swirling portal, *"should I be?"* She retorts.

"Don't forget. Play your role." My hand drifts to hover over her lower back as I say the words aloud again and then we step letting the magic suck us in. The magic spinning our bodies through the ley channels that the portals work off of. It spits us out in mere minutes.

The attendant working the room looks at our group with a stricken expression sputtering and stumbling his words together. "Now what?" Axel asks as Eveera and I straighten our clothes.

My lips flatten into a grim line. "Now we go make our entrance."

The servants scatter at our approach down the gilded halls. They have somehow managed to become even more ostentatious than usual in my absence. Eveera and her men keep tight-lipped as we make our way through the castle towards the two arched mahogany doors leading into the council room. Tentatively, I reach for her through the seal but her walls are locked down tightly preventing me from seeing, feeling, or hearing any of her thoughts right now. The guards as we approach gape in confusion before switching over to a defensive stance that blocks our path.

The guard to my left speaks up first, his eyes drifting towards the added members to my entourage. "Prince. Welcome back."

"Gerald." I greet, stepping up to move him out of the way.

"Prince, the council is in a meeting." He warns, hand going to his hilt.

My knuckles press into my palm cracking as I stare down at the man. "Am I not a part of said council?"

His feet shift underneath him in nervousness cracking through his resolve. "Uh-uhm. Well yes."

"Then get out of my way." He looks over to his fellow guards, the one to my right giving him a nod as they move. Gerald ducks his head down and reaches for the handle.

The doors pull wide and we position ourselves so that myself and the men are the only visible people upon our entry. All heads turn towards us. A few mouths drop while others frown, but my focus is only on the individual directly in front of me. My father rises from the table, his expression guarded, "Son. I see you've returned. How is Bair?" He asks while looking down at the papers in front of him.

My magic thrums in my veins at his nonchalant tone. "Shit." I say flatly. "But that shouldn't come as a surprise."

He hums feigned concern, "and you've brought new men with you. New recruits for your personal force?"

A smile twitches at my lips. "Sort of."

My father looks up at that, "sort of?" He asks while everyone else at the table exchange a look. From the corner of my eye I see a curious black tendril curling around my ankle.

"Yeah. See, they're more of an experiment. On loan to me if you will, to see if we work well together." The furrow in his brow deepens.

"On loan?" My father's right hand councilman, Lord Birk, pipes up just as Eveera's presence slips into my mind. Her magic grows as it slides up my body and coils around my neck. An odd sensation rolls over my skin as her fingers graze down my back, the soft touch feeling far more intimate than I am sure is intended.

"What is this?" Lord Birk speaks again, waving his hands around to gesture at me. I look down and my body looks like it's been wrapped in macabre ribbon. "Who *loaned* you these men?" Birk pushes while my father's eyes flash at me. I notice my mother inch closer to him and her hand curls around his bicep.

Eveera carefully steps out from behind me, her hand position mimicking that of my mother. I dip my chin down to gaze over her as her magic slinks back into her tattoos, her fingers gripping a little tighter as they do so.

A wicked smile forms on her rosy lips. "I did."

She didn't hold that position long, her hands now folded more professionally behind her back. *"That's one way to make an introduction."* I whisper down the seal taking the opportunity to reach behind her and lock a finger with hers, showing her that in this room we are still on the same side as she did for me only moments ago.

Her voice is still and calm as she replies. *"Just playing my role, as you reminded me."*

"What have you done?" Lord Birk shouts, whipping his head back and forth between our brigade and my father. "Your Highness, they've they-it's TREASON!"

"Arrest us then." Eveera says, her shoulders shrugging.

I snap my head down at her. *"Want to clue me in here?"* I press into her mind but she's quiet in there. I let go of her finger and move my hand up to cup her shoulder. Absentmindedly I find my thumb drawing lazy circles on the exposed skin. "You would arrest your own prince?" I dare, Birk's eyes narrowing in on me.

My father's hand scrubs down his clean shaven face, "it's an intriguing thought. Might serve you right - I could've sworn I told you *not* to seek out their help. And yet, here you are joined at the hip with whom I can only assume is the elusive Queen of Obsidian."

I huff. "It was a mistake to dismiss my suggestion. The directives Bair has received have left us wide open for attack. You gave Bennett and I practically useless formations and faulty instructions. It was no wonder Hadar's Guards had almost infiltrated our borders and without the Obsids they would've succeeded only a few days ago." My words come out in a shout.

My father taps his finger against his chin, "bold of you to assume my directives were useless. Even more bold to seek help from such a notorious royal."

Eveera's shoulders straighten. "I'll take that as a thank you." She quips. His eyes cut sharp, "take it as you will. You'll fit right in with my son who seems to be interpreting my words as a great many things these days." He looks at Eveera and her guards before leveling his gaze on my two men. "You two are very lucky I am feeling merciful today." Will sucks in a breath. "I should strip you both of your rank for going along with my son's antics. But I won't - this time." Both of their heads droop and they take that as their cue to exit the council room and wait for us outside.

"We will discuss things later." My father says, his words a command not a suggestion.

"Can't wait." I mutter, gripping onto her and pulling her back with me all the way back out in the hall. I was anticipating that to be more eventful than it was. "Bennett, will you take Eveera's men to where your quarters are and find them rooms. Have one of the servants set them up accordingly." He gives me a nod corralling her men around to follow him. I grab her by the elbow and start dragging her down the opposite way, towards my room.

She yanks at her arm trying to loosen my hold, "is there a reason you are manhandling me, princeling?" She snaps yanking at her arm again, "could you- *UGH!* Let go of me?" I shake my head, pulling her up the white marble stair that will spit us out into The Glass Hall. Looking over my shoulder I see she has her free hand up to shield her eyes. "Must everything be so bloody bright? Have you people never heard of curtains?"

I laugh. "Don't ask me, ask my mother."

She grimaces, "rather not." The frosted glass doors of my bedroom come into view, the glass shaking as I slam them closed behind us.

"There." I say letting go of her arm and walking into the space that looks as untouched as I left it. "Now before we talk about our next steps.

Bedroom is to the left and the bathroom is through there." I point in the direction of the two rooms as I take a seat on one of the gaudy couches.

She folds her arms across her chest, my eyes darting up to avoid staring at how little coverage she has in that position. "I don't understand." She says.

I stretch out across the couch, "well considering the circumstances, and my father's...reaction, I didn't think it would be safe for you to have your own quarters."

"All apart of your plan to make us look romantically involved?" She gags on the phrase, while tilting her head to peek in the bedroom and back at me. "There's only one bed." A statement not a question.

I move my head up and down in exaggerated motion. "Mhmm."

She scoffs, "you didn't mention that a piece of your plan was us sharing a bedroom." Her voice turning accusatory.

"Told you we'd need to be convincing." Turning on her heel she marches into my room and shuts the door behind her. I pat the cushion underneath my head. The couch is comfortable enough but...I peer up at the closed doors. *I'm going to have to convince her to let me stay in the room somehow.*

My eyes close, resting and waiting for her to decide to come out of the room. A knock sounds outside and Bennett peeks his head in accompanied by a blonde that I actually like, "how'd she take the news of you sharing a room?" He asks.

I hop up reaching for my bourbon on the mantle. I pour each of us a glass, "she was pissed. How did you think she'd respond to the news." Millie - the blonde - covers her mouth, smothering a laugh. "It is *not* funny."

"A girl immune to your wiley personality? Even with your reputation you've had girls pawing at you since we were children."

I roll my eyes and Bennett loops his arm around her shoulders, sipping his drink. "That woman doesn't paw, she mauls, so it's probably better that she doesn't want to sidle up close with you brother. Good luck with her Millie."

Millie looks between all of us and then at my bedroom door before whispering, "is she really that bad?"

At that exact moment, Eveera decides to come out, her eyes landing instantly on Millie. "You're new."

Millie straightens and extends her hand to introduce herself. Eveera looks her up and down, "why does she have that face?" Millie's smile melts quickly while Bennett fails to hold in his laugh.

"*Be nice.*" I reprimand.

"*Why?*" She wonders.

"*Because she is being nice.*" I smirk down into my empty glass. Forgetting for a moment that no one else knows about the mind link side effect of the blood seal. The three of their faces are filled with curiosity. "Ahem," I clear my throat, "this is Millicent. She will be your lady in waiting while you reside at court."

The queen gives her another once over, Millie's hand still suspended in the air. She reaches out, pushing Millie's hand back down to her side and looks directly at me, "I just came out here to ask where you put my men."

I nod to Bennett who backs up towards the door. "That's my cue." He mouths and guides Eveera out of the room.

I pat Millie on her shoulder, "that answer your question?" She shakes off my hand before going into my room and unpacking the queen's things. "She's a means to an end, Mil, don't worry!" I shout but as I say the words a part of me doesn't believe them.

EVEERA

I thought the hallway to Rorin's room being completely glass and having a view over the gardens was obnoxious enough until I learned that they actually named the hall, and nothing original either, they named it "The Glass Hall". *Foul.*

Bennett takes me down a separate marble staircase different from the one that Rorin dragged me up. This one spilled us out into a less see through hall - no less gaudy though. The ceilings have golden arches that curve across them, forming panels with different displays of artwork above us. We have something similar in the king and queen's wing in my own castle. This artwork is somewhat less impressive however.

When we reach an alcove that opens up to a corridor lined with doors, he motions for the door closest to my left, "this is your men's apartment. Mine's just across the hall. If you, you know, need anything." He states, throwing a wink in for good measure.

"I'll pass." I say and watch as his eyes dim at the refusal and he slips quietly into his own room.

BANG BANG! I knock and when no one answers I let myself in.

The room opens up to a foyer with four doors facing each other, doors that I presume lead into bedrooms. A hearth is nestled in between the two doors to my right and the back wall has a wide expanse of windows. Golden upholstery glints at me from the couches, the same mahogany wood throughout the castle - or from what I've seen - is in the chairs and tables. I step further into the apartment, stepping up to a tapestry of what looks to be one of Vellar's legends.

My hand strokes down the fibers, tracing the threaded linework. "When did you get in here?" Ezra's voice breaks my line of thoughts. I turn to see him, his blonde hair is damp and his lounge pants are hanging low on his hips. It wasn't that long ago seeing him like this was one of the heights of my desires, and now...well now it's just Ezra.

"Bennett let me in only a few minutes ago." I tell him.

He's leaned up against the hearth, his arms folded across his bare chest. "I see. I'm assuming you've been given rooms somewhere else then?" He asks, his tone guarded.

I nod. "Mmm. I have. The princeling thought considering the circumstances I would be safer—" I throw air quotes around the word - 'safer' - "near his quarters."

He rolls his eyes tilting his head to look out the windows, "I'm sure he did."

"You don't trust me."

"Is that a question or a statement?" Ezra asks.

I sigh, combing my hair out of my face. "Both."

His expression softens as his arms drop to his sides, regret flashing across his face as he looks to me. "I said some...uncalled for things."

"Ha." *That's it?* I think. *They were only uncalled for?*

"You're more than just the crown to me—"

I raise my hand to stop whatever heartbroken sob story he's come up with. "What's been said has been said." Both of his shoulders slump down even further than I thought possible. He hangs his head back bringing up both hands to drag down his face.

"What are we doing here, Eveera?"

"That's a loaded question." I say but he doesn't look satisfied with that response. "We are here for a purpose and then we are going home."

"Please be more vague." He groans, frustration filtering into his tone. "I deserve to know, E. We all do."

I toggle between telling him or keeping him in the dark. Telling him puts me at risk for him trying to stop me, but not telling him puts us at risk for not being able to work together behind enemy lines. He waits patiently for my response and after several minutes I decide to give him at least an idea of my real reasons here.

"Justice."

Ezra's stare hardens on me. I can see the gears turning in his brain trying to piece together what I meant. I plop myself down on a chair where I can recline into it, my right leg crossing over my left and he takes the seat adjacent to me. We sit in silence for the next several minutes during which I figured out the rest of my men must be sleeping. Finally he looks up at me, "jus...tice..." he says slowly.

"Justice." I repeat.

"That all I'm going to get out of you?" He asks. I nod, my fingers dragging across my lips pretending to seal them shut. "Hmph."

"You don't trust me." I repeat the words hanging heavy above our heads. He doesn't say anything as my feet carry me away from him. With my hand on the doorknob, I turn over my shoulder to look at him once more. "That was a statement."

I walk back through the painted hall, Rorin's staff averting their eyes as I move past them. I follow the same path I took with Bennett a little more slowly this time. My eyes snag on the entrance into the gardens we'd flew past earlier. At the time I was only interested in finding my men and making sure that they weren't locked away in some dank cell. But now, now no one is here to stop me from perusing them.

Can't hurt to look right?

The doors open out onto several paved pathways, each one lined with different flowers. I take the path straight out in front of me, the hedges filled with white gardenias. The deeper in I go the more I realize it's a labyrinth complete with hidden alcoves that no doubt are filled with secret debaucheries. The walk ends at a stone circle, looking around I see the mouths of the other pathways framing the center stone. *The heart of the gardens*, my mind figures. From where I stand, If I look up, I can see clearly into the suspended glass hallway that leads to Rorin's room. And if I look down I can see that the center circle showcases the Kingdom of Vellar's sigil - a bright six pointed star.

A shiver ripples through my spine as it stares back at me, the gold glinting harshly in the setting sun. I shake it off, not allowing my fears to settle in. They'll have to kill me before I allow my own fears to overwhelm me while in the home of Eiser and Mareese. Ahead of me there is a stretch of hedge that catches my attention. It's devoid of color from this angle, looking like a black hole, beckoning me. On my way to it, I notice an inscription on the stone surrounding the sigil, warning people to walk around it and not over it probably to prevent the metal from tarnishing.

Fuck you, I say in my mind, spitting on the sigil as I stomp over it. Not as satisfying as it will be to kill the king and queen, but it settled my discomfort for the moment. Entering the dark path I notice that the flowers crawling up in a chaotic display are black baccara roses.

That's a funny choice of flower to have in a Vellaran garden. My fingers run lightly across the petals of the flowers native to my kingdom. One's that are usually showered all over my court. Their darkened hue makes the hedges appear like they're bleeding in the evening light. "I see you've taken it upon yourself to explore our court." My heels ground themselves onto the cobblestone while I tilt my chin over my right shoulder. *Queen Mareese.* She's in the same iridescent dress as earlier that hangs loosely on her tall and frail figure. She stands a few feet from me, turning to face the flowers as I am, her hands folded behind her back. "Rorin always did prefer the darker side of things. Even flowers." She adds. I've still yet to verbally acknowledge her but she doesn't seem bothered as she continues speaking, "I thought it such an odd choice when he requested the black baccara, but seeing you here now it all makes sense."

I pluck one from the hedge, "does it?" Her dress swishes on the stone as she moves to stand next to me.

She has a tight smile plastered onto her face. "They're native to Obsidian, are they not?" She asks.

"Obsidian's native flora are not why you came to talk to me." I reply, keeping my response curt.

Irritation flickers on her face. "Clever girl. After your little...display in the council room I found it imperative to know you. My son has, after all, just let a rather unpredictable force inside of our walls. I'd like to have your assurances that we won't regret this."

You won't have time to regret it – you'll be dead. I want to say. My hand comes up to tuck a stray hair out of my face and behind my ear. With the barest tilt of my wrist I flash the rune in her direction, as I'd hoped it would, her gaze snags on it. "Don't worry. I'll keep the promises I made to the princeling—" Her hand darts out, snatching my wrist and cutting off my words.

"He d-didn't..." She stammers and I can feel the heat pricking underneath the rune where her grip has tightened. "What deal did he make with you witc— *AH!*" With a hiss she drops my hand like a hot coal. Her attention switching to where she's been burned by the seal's magic.

"The promise I made to the prince is for his knowledge alone. You'll have to find it in yourself to trust me. Or don't - up to you. But," I let my Wield take over just enough to blacken my eyes, "as you saw from my 'display' earlier. I have no issues taking the situation into my own hands. In case you need a reminder of Rorin's and my privacy." Her fear is palpable, her magic useless against me.

"Eveera?" My power pulls back at his voice and the queen and I both look up to see Rorin standing a few paces from us. His face filled with mild worry. Who that worry is directed at is a mystery to me, but I imagine it's for her.

Vitriol fills her gaze. "Maybe your mother was right to hide you. If I had a monster for a child, I'm not sure I would want them out in the world." She snarls.

Rorin moves to my side standing close enough that our arms brush against each other. "How lucky you are that your court is so...bright. I hear monsters enjoy the dark...I'd hate for them to seek you out." Her face pales while I turn into Rorin's chest, our fingers on instinct locking around each other's, his free hand comes around to my lower back and I raise on my toes putting my lips against his ear. I speak mind to mind, but to her it'll look like I'm whispering. *"She knows about the runes."*

He leans into my touch, the position on my back turning more possessive as he holds me. *"Does she?"*

I nod against him slightly, *"Funny - she thinks I am the one who manipulated you into this agreement."* I lower myself back flat on my feet, flashing a cloying smile her way before pulling her son and myself out of the gardens.

Rorin paces the length of the room while I tilt the bottle of this sickeningly sweet wine to my lips. My arm extends the bottle up and out to him which he snatches from my hand and takes a long swig of. He drops it back into my lap and continues his pacing. The motion is serving to only make me dizzy at this point.

"How did she find out about the runes?"

I shrug, taking another languid sip of the acrid wine. "She caught sight of the rune when I was tucking my hair behind my ear."

"So you flashed it at her." It wasn't so much a question as it was an annoyed realization.

I shrug. "Mmm. If you want to think of it like that, sure. I flashed it at her." He slumps down next to me reaching between my legs to take the bottle of alcohol back and finishing it off.

"Are you trying to get us killed?" He asks, his voice hardening.

"You were the one who said they'd notice eventually." I argue.

Rorin looks at me incredulously, "that doesn't mean go and show it off! You can't just tempt fate here with my parents, with my-my father." His yells his words stammering together.

Interesting. "You're afraid of them." I say.

"Don't use your Wield on me." He growls.

"I don't have to. You reek of it, you're afraid of what they'll do to you, and yet you defied them anyways. I honestly didn't think you'd care based on your previous lack of care for their opinions."

The expression he gives me is a mixture of anger and pain. "Don't do something like that again here without discussing it with me first. Make all the power moves you want in your own court, but here you wait for my say so." He stalks off out of the room leaving me alone so I walk myself into his bedroom. Where it would seem the words avant garde should perfectly describe the whole of Vellar - they don't even begin to cover the obscene furnishings that are housed in this glittering palace - and yet the decorators must have skipped Rorin's room. The walls are the same marble throughout the castle, but everything else is a variety of grays, blacks, and greens. The gold filters through lightly, his tan military uniforms hang in the armoire next to his regular clothes, and his gold general's armor stands in the corner next to the large mahogany desk but that's about all of the noticeable Vellaran touches in here.

Slipping off my shoes I feel the chill of the marble flooring. I walk around to the desk my fingers gliding along the sleek wood edge. It isn't as large as the one in his office at Bair, but it still swallows me up as I sink into the leather seat. The idle time I have gives me a moment to hash out a letter with all of the updates, including this ridiculous *fib* that Rorin has concocted, and send it off to Felix. Quickly I scribble the updates I have for him on a piece of paper and fold it, pulling out my wax and seal. Lighting the candle in front of me, I warm the wax and drip it onto the folded edge, pressing the seal down into it. The now embossed wax glints at me in the firelight as I set it aside to be sent off tomorrow. My head falls into my hands as I think of all the things I have to do. *Heavy is the crown one wears.,* my mind coos. I swapped one war for another but this time

I have no Vada, and no Room to privately work out all my stresses. So showering in a scalding hot stream of water will have to suffice.

I stalk over to the bathroom and strip out of my clothing. I twist the knob all the way to right until steam billows up and out of the shower. Much like that night in Bair, the realization of where I am and who I am sharing a roof with hangs over me. It's like I've signed my death warrant already by simply being here...

"I know you're not listening to me. But if you were...you'd probably tell me what a fool I am for taking this deal. Or what a fool I am for not bringing you along. And you're right, I am - a fool that is. On both counts." I wait for the steady thrum of Vada's presence to run through my head but it never comes. I slide to the tiled floor, pulling my knees into my chest. The serpents on my skin slither and blink up at me as I empty my mind. Out of boredom I summon the Wield, watching the tendrils wrap and tighten around me. They brush against the scars on my thighs triggering the urge to add new ones. Unwillingly, the words the queen said tonight drift into my brain, *"Maybe your mother was right to hide you. If I had a monster for a child, I'm not sure I would want them out in the world."* I used to envision hearing Mareese, if only to hear her screams as I killed her. But, in this moment at least, I think I would have lived a much happier life without ever hearing it. Because now there is a voice to my nightmares...one that isn't just my own. *They'd like to think of us as weak and vulnerable. They rightfully think of us as a monster - and if a monster is what they want, then a monster is what they will get.* My conscience reminds me.

A soft knock sounds at the bathroom door interrupting my thoughts. "WHAT, princeling?!"

"Er - not the prince, Your Highness." A soft feminine voice comes muffled through the wood – *Millicent*.

Turning off the water I step out of the shower and open up the door finding the taller blonde standing on the other side with my dinner in her hands. She smiles. I grimace back while snagging a towel for my hair off the shelf. "You can just set that down on the desk." Her gaze follows me all the way to the clothing rack set up with my things, the sensation making me uncomfortable. "Oh don't tell me you do it too." I say, selecting a silk set off one of the hangers.

"Do what?" She asks.

I pull the chemise over my head and secure the slip robe around me tightly. "Stare. Rorin calls it *observing* but he really means staring." I turn around to see her draping her hand across her mouth suppressing a laugh. I twist my long dark hair into a messy knot on the top of my head.

"I'm not, I was just—"

"If you dare say *observing*, I *will* rip out your vocal chords where you stand." Her face pales slightly but the smile doesn't falter.

Taking the somewhat lighthearted threat as her cue to leave she pushes off his desk that she's leaned against and only turns back towards me when she reaches the door. "I *was* staring." I eye her curiously waiting for her to finish. "You're an enigma. You are...an elusive creature we've only heard horror stories about or rumors of. A monster that was meant to hide under our beds and in our wardrobes. Yet here you are now, albeit shorter than I imagined—" I snort at that, "—in the castle helping your supposed enemy with a war that isn't yet yours." My mouth opens to interject but she raises her hand stopping the words. "I have no doubt to the King and Queen you *are* that monster. They are expecting you to act as a caged feral animal. Don't give them the satisfaction." We hold the others' stare for a moment as I give her an almost imperceptible nod. The door clicks behind her.

Grabbing the food I crawl into bed and lean back against Rorin's absurdly comfortable headboard. *Of course his bed would feel like this.* I grumble to myself while I mull her words over. I hate that she makes a good point, only people who *care* make good points. I don't need another person who doesn't know me, *caring.*

As for the 'caged feral animal comment' that was exactly what Mareese was intending to do in the garden, bait me until I snapped. I won't give them that satisfaction. Not yet. Not until I have them wound so tightly in my web that they will be begging for me to kill them. Only then will they see how truly monstrous I can be.

I was curled up in the large silky bed drifting to sleep when I finally heard Rorin come in. Barely glancing in my direction he slipped off into the bathroom and turned on the shower. The white noise of the water seemed to go on forever before he finally emerged back out.

His dark curls lay damp against his forehead, beads of water dripping down the corded muscles of his back and absorb into the fabric of his towel. I watch the muscles flex in and out as he picks out a pair of navy pajama bottoms and starts to...*oh hell no.* I bolt upright in his bed. "Please to all the gods that might be left, tell me you are not about to strip down right in front of me." *As if the loosely tied towel slung low on his hips wasn't enough of a distraction, the thought of what a sight his bare ass would be.* I stop the imagery from materializing in my mind.

He doesn't bother looking at me, chuckling lowly to himself. "Why, your Highness, think you might find something you're...*interested* in?" I glare holes into the back of his damp head and cross my arms over my chest.

"No. I don't feel like burning my retinas into blindness at the sight of you naked." He has one hand on the waist of his towel holding it in place. The towel shifts precariously as he walks over to the edge of the bed. Leaning his arm on the headrest he lowers his face towards mine, "most women gape in awe when they see me naked, but no one's burnt out their own eyeballs before."

"Well then let me be the first." I huff out in frustration trying not to inhale too much of him. *Why the hell does he have to smell so good?* I duck under the covers putting distance between us and to offer him some modicum of privacy. That low laugh grows distant as he abandons my bedside. I hear the soft thud of his towel and against my better judgment I can't stop myself from imagining what that bare ass looks like this time. My fingers squeeze the fabric tighter around my head before I lose all sense and actually look. "Are you done yet?"

"I guess that means you didn't peek. I was done nearly five minutes ago." I throw the covers off my head. He's grinning while standing at the vacant side of his four poster bed. My eyes widen. "You're not seriously going to..." His smile falls and his shoulders droop, both hands grabbing the pillows from that side. With an annoyed vigor he haphazardly sets up a cot on the floor. It takes a shameful amount of pointed effort to not gawk at noticeably scarred bare chest or those silk navy bottoms that are slung somehow lower then the towel was but not low enough to *release* anything.

This is a punishment; it must be. Not only do I have to endure him in the same room but he has to be half dressed? And look good half dressed?

He flops onto the makeshift bed, punching the pillow a few times to get comfortable. I guess if I have to convince people we are in love, his appearance alone will make it easy. His personality on the other hand...

The stillness of the room is only slightly disrupted by soft snores filling the silence and for a moment it all feels very mundane. Then I remember where I am and who I am with and all my torrid motions come rushing back.

I get up letting my feet hit the cold floor and rush into the bathroom to splash my face, the temperature shocking my system. My head hangs between my shoulders, with my stare planted on the basin in the counter top. *Little demon...* drifts through my mind jolting me from my thoughts. I search my mental channels for her, for that voice, but nothing else comes. Just a figment of my imagination, I guess, so I send another splash up into my face.

"No. No please don't do it. Don't lock..." I whip my head towards the sound of his voice. "Don't lock..." Tiptoeing back into the room I peer around the bedpost. He's thrashing around on the blankets and there is sweat plastering his hair to his brow while panicked mutterings escape his lips. I hate to admit it but the tortured look frozen on his face highlights how beautiful he is, raw and unfiltered.

A part of me wants to reach into his mind and watch the nightmare - but I know already what I'll see. It'll be that same boy on the same dusty floor with the dead man spitting threats at him. The same thing I saw in his mind in the outer lands.

Wake him. I flinch at the sound of my conscience. *Wake him!*

Fine, persistent bitch. I hiss. I hesitate before closing the distance and crouching next to his twitching form, my fingertips ghost over his cheekbone. "*princeling...princeling, it's not real. Wake up.*" I let my hand rest on his cheek fully. His face is burning up underneath my palm. "*Ror—*" my feet flip out from under me. Rorin's eyes are glazed over as his face twists in rage, his hand squeezing and pressing down into my windpipe. The full weight of his body digging into my freshly healed gash on my torso. *"Rorin, let go of me!"* I struggle to break into his mind. *"I would really rather die in a much more valiant way than being choked out on the floor."* I tell him but it does nothing. The dull burn of the rune on my wrist progresses to full third degree, *"RORIN!"* At my shout, his pupils shrink back down to their normal size and air starts flowing into my lungs. Familiarity and then confusion enters his hazel eyes as he looks down at our position and then at his hand, realization dawning in his face.

"Oh my gods, Eveera." The rasp in his voice a result from all of his earlier muttering. His hand flies off of my neck and in a quick succession he grabs my waist flipping me over and on top of him. His right hand spears into the hair above my nape while he cradles me against his sweaty chest. "I am so sorry…" I am struck dumb in my place as he rocks us back and forth. I'm torn between considering staying here and catapulting him across the room.

The latter wins…thank the gods. My elbow connects with his ribs as I push him away as far as his body weight allows me to. "WHAT THE ACTUAL FUCK!" My voice is broken and hoarse and he reaches towards me, lightly brushing the bruises that match the shape of his fingers already forming.

"Gods, Eveera. I didn't realize…" the tenderness and concern in his face is enough to make me want to vomit. I tear my gaze from his, scrambling to stand and move over to the mirror where I can get a closer look at the purple marks blooming across it. *That's what you get for listening and waking up the damn swine.* I didn't notice he'd moved until I felt his chest brushing against me. He drops his forehead to my shoulder with each of his hands wrapping gently around my biceps. Electricity sparks under his touch and I withhold the shiver that threatens to run through my body at the contact. How utterly ridiculous and pathetic the both of us look. Bruised, sweaty, and winded; *usually in my book these would all be positive signs of a male and female interaction, but tonight it's just…unsettling.*

We stand here for awhile. Finally, his palm reaches around my front and finds my chin. He forcefully tilts my head to the side as he looks over the marks. "You're overstepping." I hiss, yanking my chin out of his grip. He spins me in my spot until it's both our chests that are brushing against one another. "Next time you're squealing like a pig in your sleep, I'll throw a pillow at you. That'll leave less marks."

His eyes narrow and I swear the muscle in his cheek twitches as he ignores me and continues his appraisal of my injuries. From the corner of my eye I can see the sky brightening. "The staff will be in soon to wake us with their chores." He says breaking away from me to pick up his disheveled bedding off the floor. We wordlessly climb into the bed and instantly the heat from his body warms the covers, fatigue ramming into me like a bull. His arm reaches over, fingertips lightly brushing my throat before he flips around to face the windows. I swallow thickly, ignoring the discomfort as I stare at the wall.

"This plan better work." I whisper into his mind before everything fades to black.

RORIN

She fell asleep almost instantly once I crawled under the covers. The curve of her backside is barely nestled into me, I flipped back over once I heard her breathing even out and I knew she was out, now I've been staring at her for the past two hours painfully waiting for someone to disrupt us. My fingers reach over to trace the imprints they left behind. I fucking choked her. *Dammit.* How ironic that we are in the kingdom of healers and I can't even fix the damage I caused.

One. Breath. *Two.* Breath. *Three.* Breath. *Four.*

I've fallen into a routine of watching the rise and fall of her chest. I'm not sure when exactly it started but with this being the second time I've inflicted an injury on her - intentional or not - I'll either need to sneak a healer mage, that isn't under my father's thumb, in here to fix the bruises or she won't be able to show her throat for several days.

I fucking choked her…if it weren't for that same fucking dream. It hasn't haunted my mind in years but since her…it's like her presence brings out the very demon in me I've worked so hard to suppress.

"An omen if there ever was one." The man's grating voice echoes around in my head. *I am broken. My Wield is broken. I am a dishonor to this kingdom.* The chant goes on a loop as my chest aches with guilt. She shifts, her body inching closer to mine if that's even possible. And another pang of guilt spears through me as I add a verse to the chant.

I am a dishonor to her.

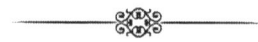

It's been a few days now since that night. The guilt never subsided, but we got into a routine. She didn't wake me from any of the other nightmares and other than the moments where we share a bed, we've been narrowly avoiding one another every time we are alone. The only words we've uttered were when I suggested to her that she should wear a high neck for those bruises. Her response? "We'll call it foreplay."

No one else has said anything yet to us. For the most part she's stayed holed up either in my room or in Axel's. She thought it was best if she told her men our plan alone. Based on the looks they've laid on me every time I am near them, they didn't take to the idea well.

By the morning of the sixth day, her bruises had begun to fade and there was still no word from my parents other than to say I am currently not required to be at any council meetings. Which means one of two things:

One - my mother has chosen to not say anything to the council or my father for some undisclosed reason, but knowing my mother, I am sure it serves her in some way.

Or two - they know and they're biding their time, waiting to see how Eveera reacts when cornered.

A soft knock sounds at the door followed by Millicent walking in holding the new linens. She makes her way around me and strips the bed. She must think I don't notice the reason she is doing housekeeping as a lady isn't just for good housekeeping but in hopes she'll find something of interest on Eveera's bedside. *The little sneak.* She shuffles behind me - carefully sifting through the drawers. I laugh while lacing my sparring leathers up and grabbing the dagger sheath from the top of my wardrobe. "Millie - if she catches you doing that, I won't stop her from putting you in your place." Her incoherent grumbles are the only response I get but she makes sure I understand, *prick*, come out of her mouth. I pull my boots on last and move to my desk, rifling through the notes of importance on it.

"Any summons yet?" I jump at the proximity of her voice.

"Gods, Mil don't you know not to sneak up on someone?"

She raises her brows at me, "didn't know you scared so easily...what are you looking at?" She asks while snatching the document from my hands.

"Sure help yourself..." I mutter, my arms crossing over my chest.

Millie's brows furrow as she flips the paper over. "These are all just updates on the border outposts." I nod. "Hmph, well, guess that's better than a summons from daddy dearest."

I scoff. I think I would rather it be a summons. All these notes updating me on Bair and Piram are grim at best and if Will and Bennett haven't seen them already then I'll have to brief them with hopes that we can get word quickly to the troops.

Permission from my father be damned.

"Mil, let the others know I'll be in the sparring room. We have to adjust the plans."

"You're going sparring?" Eveera's voice floats over from doorway of the bathroom. She's clad in only a towel that is very loosely tied around herself and it's as distracting as the first time. She looks around the room before her eyes land back on Millie, "you went through my stuff." A statement, not a question.

Millie's cheeks turn pink, quickly she drops the paperwork and scurries from the room. I grab the missives from where they scattered and extend them towards Eveera. Her expression quickly sours as she reads the newest updates. "Hopefully the girl will have the good sense to grab my men too." I nod grimly. "Although, I can't commend her subtlety when snooping."

She reaches for her fighting leathers and weapons and when I don't move fast enough out of the room she turns back around to me, "if you'd like to see a naked woman, I suggest you go to a whore house."

"Tempting." I say, her eyes widening and then darkening at my comment. For some reason I have a feeling that if I chose the whore house option, she'd skin me alive.

I wait outside in The Glass Hall for her. She comes out of the room still tying her hair up into a tight braid on top of her head and keeps her eyes straight forward as we walk through the halls. I look over to her and there's about a foot of awkward space inbetween us. *"Stand closer."* I hiss into her mind.

"What?"

I reach for her elbow in an empty stretch of walkway and haul her into my side, securing her hand tightly into the crook of my arm. *"Someone is always watching. Play your role remember?"* She growls through the seal at me while keeping a neutral expression onto her face. Most heads stay down as we pass them. Finally we round our way into the empty sparring room and Eveera wastes no time breaking away from me.

Picking the weapons she plans to use from her belt and a bow off the wall she moves onto the floor. Her golden glare finds me again as she empties out her arsenal into the target, hitting her mark every single time. The hate filled stare deepens as she moves to retrieve the weapons and start again.

Slowly our men trickle into the room, keeping their distance from the queen as they do. The brothers, Max and Orem, step onto the empty section of the room meant for sword and hand to hand combat. The two of them moving swiftly in time together each parrying and blocking the blows of the other with their broadswords while Armond is off to the side refereeing their fight.

Bennett comes in next, making his way to me reaching for the missives in my hand. He flips through the pages, turning them back to front a few times to make sure the words he's reading are correct, while shaking his head in disbelief. At one point his fist lands in the cork wall behind us drawing everyone's attention.

"Your father isn't even bothering to stop these deaths." He snaps quietly. His voice is strained showing me just how much control he has to exert over his anger. I have a feeling if he let it all out, there would be more damage done than just a dent in the cork. He crumples the page, casting it down onto the floor.

Will's jaw drops. "I wanted to read that!" He whines.

"Too fucking bad," Bennett snarls, snapping his head in Will's direction. "Will, if you don't stop pacing I swear to the bleeding gods I'll ask the resident psychopathic queen to shoot her next arrow through *you.*" I'm stunned, I haven't seen Ben this angry in awhile, he's not usually one to bite the heads off of others.

SWISHH! THWUMP! Will ducks as an arrow whizzes overhead of us sinking into the cork next to the dent Bennett made. He shoots a scathing look in Eveera's direction, who can't be bothered to apologize.

"Careful now" I send through the seal. Bennett's tantrum persists as he stamps a foot onto the crumpled piece of paper almost as if its destruction will put an end to the ever present war. But it won't. The war is on our doorstep and my parents have us here, playing courtier with the rest of the lazy noblemen and women. The Valen Celebration is almost comical to have at this point when there may not *be* a Valen in a matter of weeks.

I unsheathe my sword and motion for Ben to take up a weapon and use some of that anger a little more constructively. Will acts as our referee signaling for the match to begin. Bennett is an exceptional fighter, just as good as me if not better. Growing up training side by side it was no question who would become one of my commanders, Bennett was an easy choice. His moves are precise and sharp. The only problem is after sparring with him for the past twenty some odd years, he has become predictable.

He lunges to the right extending his sword forward, a blow I narrowly dodge. We continue this dance for a while, I swing and he ducks. He comes for my side and I go for his neck. Will eventually calls it when I knock Bennett flat on his ass and pin him with my knee.

"Oh shit." He mutters while standing to dust himself off, his eyes locked on something behind me.

"What?" I ask, looking over my shoulder.

Eveera and Axel are locked in a hand to hand fight on the adjacent mats. Blood is pouring from both of their faces. *"Damn woman."* I growl through the seal but her focus remains honed in on her guard. Her movements are quick and defined against Axel. She pauses to crook a finger towards Maxwell and just as I think she is going to tap out he joins Axel in the spar. Two against one.

They throw every combination of punches and kicks I can think of. They land more than half of them on her body. I step up to intervene, thinking they've taken it too far, but her face has a broad and bloodied smile stretching ear to ear. She's *enjoying* this.

From the corner of my eye I see sparks popping at Max's fingertips.

"Reign it in Abrams." Armond snaps, a warning in his voice. Max pulls back his Wield and uses that warning as an opportunity to remove himself from the fight and tag another into it. Ezra enters the floor, taking up a place next to Axel. He stares her down, before turning and tapping Axel out.

Eveera's deranged look only makes her appear more lethal. Despite the bruises blooming on her bronzed skin. The sensible side of me knows this isn't abnormal for them - *even if it is for us*. That this woman was raised to be as formidable as she could be if only to make up for her lack in size. But seeing her so small against them as they lunge for her, has a much more primal side of me screaming to stop the fight. Ezra charges after her the glint in his eyes telling me he plans to fight dirty. His swings are wild and uncoordinated. The momentum behind them feeling more personal than it does professional.

His elbow rams into her cheek, sending her head at an awkward angle. "*Ugh.*" She yells, spitting blood onto the mat. Another bruise starts to form at the base of her eye and the rune on my wrist begins to warm. Eveera ducks the next blow, sweeping a foot out to trip Ezra and he lands on the ground with a thud. She uses the opportunity to lock his head between her knees.

"*End the bout.*" I snap, pushing at her through the seal. The rune heats up past warm when a scream tears out of her, he thrusts his hips up tipping her over onto her back. The change in position putting him on top with her braid wrapped around his hand. I notice her fingers digging into the mat, black magic pooling from beneath her palms.

"Eveera. No magic. You Wield, you yield." Armond shouts at her.

It may be their rule to not Wield on one another but last I checked that doesn't apply to me. Another scream tears out of her as she bucks and flails from her position but Ezra only tightens his hold, pulling her ear to his mouth, whispering in it. Her hand flies up and scores down his cheek, Ezra lets go with a wild yelp, shoving her away. The nerve I had to use my Wield vanishes the moment he lets her go just as her will to use her flares, her black magic spilling out of her and wrapping around him.

"YOU YIELD EVEERA!" Ezra barks at her but that doesn't stop her advance on him. Each of her tendrils twist and tighten against his limbs, effectively mummifying everything but his neck, face, and the hand clutching his marred cheek.

She's turned predatory and whatever humanity hangs on inside of her has completely succumbed to the magic. Her men watch stoically from the sidelines. No one making a move to stop her right now. So I do. Not for him, but for her. We don't need her murdering her own right now.

I step up behind her, carefully reaching out. "*Nightmare...*" I whisper, as my left hand gently wraps around her wrist. My right comes up to close around her throat so that I can pull her flush against my chest. My chin rests on top of her hair, narrowing my eyes at Ezra who's struggling against her magic. "*Whatever he said, whatever he did. We will take care of it. But not this way. Not here.*" The palm of my left hand comes to rest over her heart. The muscle beats rapidly against it. "*Pull it back. Pour into me if you need to. But I have a feeling if you don't let go of your commander, your other men will have to step in.*" No response flows back into my mind, but her form starts to melt into me and her magic retreats.

Slowly. *"That's it. Good girl."* I purr running my thumb up and down the column of her throat, feeling her pulse calm under my touch.

I back up with her in tow, thankfully, she doesn't fight against my grip. Maxwell and Orem fall in front of us, hauling their commander up from the ground. His eyes are aflame with rage. "Traitorous bitch." He snarls, spitting at our feet.

Axel comes up next to me and I gently shove her into his arms. I take two steps at a time towards Ezra. My hand flies out to grab the nape of his neck pressing my blade against his carotid. I drag his face to me putting my mouth right at his ear - just like he did to her. "You've caused problems from the moment I met you." He jerks against my hold but I dig the blade in harder until copper hits my nose. "Whatever you said to draw that out of her should've cost you your life. Next time I won't be so generous with saving it. Speak to her like that again, call her any more names, *spit* in her direction and I'll cut your tongue out myself and wear it around my neck like a fucking trophy." With a hard push I send his body back into the brothers standing behind him.

"We're done here." I growl, grabbing Eveera from Axel to usher her back to my bedroom. Surprisingly she doesn't protest - not on the walk up or when I sent her to the shower.

She's been in there long enough now that the hot water has probably run cold. Axel wordlessly joined me on the couch as I waited for her to finish up. I keep hoping with every swig of wine I swallow that he'll leave me be. If he thinks my ire doesn't extend to him as well for being a part of that exhibition, he's grossly overestimating my patience for him.

"You should know—" His voice breaking the silence we've been sitting in the sound of it only serving to annoy me more, "—if you plan to play the part of her lover, you should at least be giving the illusion you're in the shower with her. She takes them a lot, sort of helps recenter her thoughts. It's also a favorite spot for her to spend *quality time* with her lovers." He waggles his brows at me.

"I'll go join her then." I snap, abandoning him on my couch that he doesn't bother moving from. "You're not planning on staying are you?" I ask my annoyance a little more evident now.

He shrugs giving me a lazy smirk. *Great*. I shove my empty glass into his hand and stalk off to our bedroom - *my bedroom* - letting the door slam behind me, Axel's deep laughter drowning out behind the wood.

I knock on the bathroom door but no answer comes from the other side. Based on how beat up she was I make the executive decision to peek my head in there. The door creaks open under the weight of my hand not allowing me a more quiet entry. The shadow of her small frame leans against the back wall through the foggy glass.

"If you're checking out my ass I'll gouge your eyes out with my thumbs." Her voice is gravelly and low. It sounds a lot like the voice that takes over when her Wield is in control.

"Mm. Noted." I say to her, deciding to fully allow myself in the room.

"Is there are reason you're fogging up the other side of this glass?"

I tap my finger against the shower door rhythmically. "Assumed you might need a hand in there. You barely made it up the stairs."

"Bold of you to assume that I want your hands anywhere near me. And I had a difficult time with the stairs because you practically dragg—"

"Eveera." She sighs in defeat, relenting much to my surprise as her hand reaches back to slide open the shower door. *I guess that's my invitation in.* I step backwards onto the slick tile keeping my front facing the glass instead of her. "Apparently showering with a lover is a favorite pastime of yours." It's the only thing I can think of to say to break the awkward tension swirling around us. Why I thought this would be a good idea is beyond me.

Astonishingly she laughs. "I have a lot of favorite pastimes. But you could say showering is one of them. Though, I'd be shocked if you came in here just to fuck me." The carnal side to me perks up at that idea. To distract myself I look down at my boots, noticing that the water swirling around them is tinged pink.

"You're still bleeding. You've been in here for at least an hour and you're still bleeding." I take a deep breath before speaking to her. "Eveera. You have two options here. One - I can turn around and assess the damage while you let me or two - I can...no no there's only one option." I say lifting my head and turning around slowly. I keep my eyes looking up to the ceiling, because if I focus any lower... "I turned around."

She shifts the weight on her legs, hissing at the movement. "I figured as much." We stand there like this for a moment. "Well aren't you going to nurse me back to health?" She asks, her tone anything but permissive.

"I think it would be rude of me to do so without your permission."

She scoffs. "And it wasn't rude of you to just waltz in here during my very private, very naked shower?" *Fair point.* "Well go on. Nurse." Very slowly I drop my gaze and find her facing me already, glowering upwards. Her tattoos have strategically moved to cover the more intimate areas of her body.

"Eyes up here princeling." She grits out. Her face is puffy; whether from crying or the fight I'm not sure. The more severe injuries ended up being her black eye, the cut in her bottom lip, and the gash in her hairline. Any other scrapes or bruises I take note of are superficial, but the cut in her hairline continues to weep.

She could have easily dodged every one of the punches, kicks, and slaps her men threw at her. She chose not to. She chose to be their punching bag. "You let them get those hits in."

She shrugs. "Boosts morale."

"Fuck that. Allowing yourself to be beaten in a spar you can clearly win, isn't boosting morale. It's masochism." The scars on her legs should be proof enough to me that she savors her own pain. Even if her men tolerate it, doesn't mean I have to. I grab the rag from the shelf above her to soak under the stream. I bring it up to the cut on her forehead the contact has her wincing slightly before relaxing under the touch. It takes a few dabs at it until the blood flow lessens. It won't scar but it'll give her one hell of a headache. I continue the dabbing motion on every one of the cuts, careful not to press on the swelling under her eye. "We ought to get a healer to look at you before dinner. People may question why you look like a human pincushion. And by people, I mean the court nobles."

Her nose scrunches in disgust and she pulls back from the cloth. "Fuck your nobles."

"Ha. I wouldn't recommend it."

She rolls her eyes. "I wasn't afraid to wear the collar you put on me. What makes you think I am afraid to wear the marks from a fight?" With her chin raised, she decides she's done and slips past me to leave the shower.

"Eveera I—" The words catch in my throat. Large, puffy, red and white scars peek out of the edge of the towel she's wrapped around herself. "Eveera." I breathe, the words still lost. Her head turns to the side as she peers at me from over her shoulder.

Her puffy, purple eyes are exhausted. "I think that's enough show and tell, *princeling.*"

EVEERA

Rorin stays behind in the bathroom. I wasn't afraid of him seeing my scars, but I didn't feel like answering any questions either. He can figure it out himself.

When I walked into the sitting room I was surprised to find that Axel was draped across a lounge chair with a drink in hand. He looks up and eyes me up and down. "You look terrible, E." Usually that sentence would have some levity to it, but today his voice has none.

He gingerly offers me his drink that I gulp down in one go, wanting to avoid the taste. "You're so sweet." I quip. "You should go—" I wave my hand around, "—go change or see if Armond needs you. He probably does."

His deep brown eyes flit towards the bedroom door. "What, you're not worn out yet?" He says that one as a joke but unfortunately the mood hanging over it causes it to fall flat. "Evie...what are you playing at here? You spend a few days with the guy—"

I groan, interrupting him. "I already got this speech from Ezra. I don't need it from you too."

His arms cross over his broad chest as he looks over at me. "So just like that you're all done fucking Ezra and now you're crawling into bed with the heir of Vellar?" I open my mouth to correct him. "If you're going to say that you're not actually sleeping with him then fine. That's not the point. The point is you're *comfortable* even pretending that you are." *I am not comfortable with it.* I want to argue but his face has a look on it that prevents me from doing so. "I mean, Evie...you're putting everyone in a tough spot here. You're putting *me* in a tough spot here." His stands up, his hands brushing up and down my biceps. He pulls me into a familiar hug placing my head right under his chin. "I love you. But I don't get it. You hate everything he is. Or you're supposed to at least."

I let out a long breath trying to process those words. "Yes." These are the moments when I hate *him* most. I hate how well he knows me, how well he reads me. He switches out his chin for resting his cheek on the top of my hair.

"You don't have to. Get it, I mean. You just have to trust me. If you can't do that then..." His body tenses against mine and he pushes me out away from him making me a witness to the hurt on his face.

"Don't threaten me, E. We've moved beyond that. You don't think that we know how powerful you are? That you don't really need us? You spent nearly the first half of your life training to be THE weapon, *of course* we know. But you're not just our queen, you're our family, dammit. We aren't about to leave you here. I don't care what fucking deals you make with *him*." His finger jabs towards the doors behind me. "We made our oaths to you and we will uphold them." He's practically shaking with frustration.

"I thought you made them to the crown?" It's mean and I know I shouldn't have said it. Not to him at least, but I couldn't help it.

Hurt turns to anger as his grip loosens on my arms. "Not me. I made them to *you*." I give him a nod and he's gone from the room without another word and I'm left with all of what he said hanging above me.

I knew I couldn't avoid these dinners for very long. However, the longer I sit here the better the idea of stabbing myself between the eyes with the fork in my hand sounds as each of the different lords drone on. I thought I'd already made a shocking impression on the court's nobility until the other night when I walked in wearing the hand print necklace their prince left on me. I must be losing my luster though because tonight I barely got any reaction at all.

Millicent has a place at the end of the table sitting next to a few of the other ladies, she gives me a once over and when our eyes lock she shares an expression I've become familiar with, one my men wear often. There is concern and a look of protectiveness in her eyes - I can only assume it's not for me but rather because of my proximity to the prince.

"Can you please make her stop?" Lord Birk's obnoxious voice pierces my ears, drawing my attention to him, his knobby hand is pointing at my fork and plate. "The noise is positively grating, your Excellency." The endearment draws a laugh from Orem who's standing behind me.

"Something funny, boy?" He sneers.

"A-hem, excuse my soldier. I am sure his slip of laughter simply came from your use of the word 'excellency' when referring to your king."

The lord cocks his head, his beady little eyes narrowing at me – scrutinizing, "you and your men find it humorous that I believe my sovereign to be of excellence?"

I drag my fork against the plate again staring at him for added discomfort. "Merely a difference of opinion is all." My response has him slamming his hand down on the table and jabbing that knobby finger at me a second time. Before I can react, Rorin pushes me back.

"Lift that finger at her a third time and I'll slice it clean off. Give her the respect she is owed, Lord." Birk's face turns into a rather unattractive shade of red. I can feel Rorin's magic pulsing under his skin begging to be let out until I place my hand on his forearm, nudging him back into me. I expect him to tense up when I do it, but he plays his part well moving his arm protectively across the front of my waist and hooking my body into his.

A throat clears from the other end of the table where we see Mareese's face scrunched in annoyance. "If you wouldn't mind, could we save the rather grotesque threats for somewhere a little less civilized than my table?"

Lord Birk's face flushes a bright, a litany of kiss-ups leaving his mouth and heading straight for the asses on both the king and queen. Rorin and I sit back in our seats, his arm sliding from my waist but keeping a protective hand draped across my lap.

I wasn't surprised when at the end of the dinner - we were asked to stay afterward. The palace guards usher us into the council room and while everyone takes their seats, Rorin and I stay standing. His hand resting gingerly next to my side. "Have a seat son, no one's going to hurt the girl."

Rorin bares his teeth. "Queen."

The king waves his hand. "Yes, of course. *Queen.*" The way he says it makes my stomach turn. As if my title is a stain on the realm. "There is a plethora of details to discuss until the Valen Celebration in eight days." He looks openly between the two of us, "the most important of which seems to be your infatuation with the young, *queen*." His lip curling up again when he says it.

"I'd rather talk about the war we're currently fighting."

"Hm." The king taps his finger against his chin in contemplation. "You received the directives updating you on the status of Piram and Bair, I presume."

I nudge him through the seal. *"Don't let him bait you."*

He ignores me. "I did. And you have nothing to say about what was in them?"

"Princeling." I warn, but he ignores me again and for the next half hour Rorin and his two guards take turns arguing the importance of our return to Bair and then to Piram. The council interrupts every so often to deliberate amongst themselves, most of them too lost in debate to notice the silent stand-off between the four royals among them. My eyes are trained on Rorin, Rorin's on his father, and his mother's on me.

"If you continue to clench your jaw like that, your pretty teeth will break." I say leaning into him casually. "We are going in circles here, ladies and gentlemen." I say aloud.

The council members look startled at the sound of my voice, including the king who leans back in his chair. "You're quite right. We really don't need to be having this conversation at all. Do we, son? I believe we've already had this discussion." I can hear Rorin screaming inside of his mind containing the desire he has to throttle his father. "I've let you dally and play, you had your fight in Bair and *barely* won. Now you have responsibilities here, you are the heir to this kingdom not just a general."

Laughter slips past my lips and a stubby withered man sitting next to Mareese looks up at me from his stack of ledgers. "Forgive me, your Highness." He says to the king as he levels a glare on me. "Queen Eveera. The laughter is becoming inappropriate, from you and your men. Do not forget yourself or that you are a guest in this court. Our generosity and peaceful natures go only so far."

"Excuse me..." I start.

"Chancellor Finnigan." He finishes.

I nod. "Chancellor Finnigan. Thank you for your...insight." I feign a look of thoughtfulness. "You're right. We're guests in your court and you may choose to rescind our invitation extended by the heir here at any time. I nearly did the same when he and Sir..." My mind blanks on Mousy's name, "when he and his companion showed up at my doorstep. They were willing to do *anything* for our assistance. It was out of the goodness of my heart that I entered into diplomacy with him. He was a destitute general suffering the loss of too many men thanks to your king's battle directives." The council's eyes bounce around to one another as I continue. "The reality of your front lines has surpassed grim. They are being decimated and without the Obsidian army you won't even be *barely* winning the fight against Baelor." My eyes lock on the king, who has a smug smirk pasted on his face. "It is clear the war has not touched you here in Valen or you would'nt be having your little party. I hate to inform you that war will always find a way to your doorstep. Just because yours are gilded does not make you exempt from that. If you like the thought of ending up dead, well by all means, my troops will put out and you can see how far that gets you." My hands are laced together in front of me, my serpents slithering wildly along my forearms as my Wield tastes the fear emanating from so many of the members.

Queen Mareese rises from her seat, mirroring my pose at the opposite end of the table. "Our 'little party' as you call it, is a tradition. Maybe you do not have those where you are from, Queen Eveera, and that is why it seems so uncouth to you that in times of war, we find times to celebrate." Her gaze challenges mine as she gives me a cold smile. "Forgive me for my boldness but I must ask. If you care so little about what happens here to us in Vellar, is the assistance you offer us *really* out of the goodness of your heart as you said? Or is it out of my son's lack of control for what is between your legs?"

Rorin's mouth drops to say something as he slips behind me. I stay my hand at him, *"whatever you are about to utter to be my virtue's knight in shining armor, don't. You're playing into their hands. We want them playing into ours."* He clamps his mouth shut and presses a whisper of a kiss into my hair, with the weight of his stare a shiver goes up my spine.

This is all a ruse. It is all a game, my conscience reprimands.

I lean into the kiss absentmindedly while I meet the every pair of eyes staring at me. *"You wanted me to be convincing right?"*

"Wha—" I turn in my spot while my magic forms into my favored claws. They watch my hand rise to Rorin's face where I trail a fingertip down his cheek, dragging the claw across his bottom lip. He doesn't flinch at the cut the sharp point makes or at the blood beading up from it. Heat flares in those hazel eyes, his tongue pressing hard into the inside of his cheek. The burn from his stare finds its way down into my stomach.

You're only reacting this way because everyone is staring. It is not *because of the look he is giving you.* But for some reason the heaviness of his eyes tracking my movements seems to make time slow down.

I'm not sure this will work to convince them. But from the kiss on my head to my magic marking him in front of the most important people in all of Vellar, our ownership has become very obvious. I break the stare between us, my eyes landing on Mareese, while I bring the blood covered finger up to my lips, wrapping them around it.

"I'll let you decide Queen Mareese."

Save for a few gasps the room was completely silent.

Time only resumed its normal pace once I step out of the direct line of Rorin's heated stare and leave them all in my wake. None of the men seemed to follow my exit, and if they had I would've been far too preoccupied to notice. When I stepped back into the apartment, Millicent was there working on a plate of sweets while reclined in Rorin's desk chair. She freezes when she sees me. "Do not say a word." I warn.

She lets out a low whistle, "you two put on quite the display at the end there."

I shoot her a frustrated look, "what did I say?"

She shakes her head, "you look like you need a drink."

I collapse on the bed and stare at the ceiling. "I do but all of the drink in this court is absolute shit." I clamp my eyes, pinching the bridge of my nose.

Millicent's moves had been so silent I assumed she wasn't in the room with me any longer until I cracked an eye open to find her standing and leaning over me. Her hands are placed squarely on her hips. "*Gods!* Do you make it a habit to sneak up on people?" I snap.

She shrugs her shoulders, "I think I can solve your shitty alcohol problem." As soon as the words are out of her mouth she is up and marching out of the room and I have to bolt after her. She's taller than me and takes significantly longer steps. Finally, I fall into step with her, winding through the halls and down sets of stairs. All of which end with us in front of a rather nondescript door.

"Where are we going?" I ask, partly curious but mostly aggravated. Millicent looks towards me before giggling again. *Why the hell does she laugh so much?* I wonder.

The door she opens, opens up into a very busy and steamy kitchen filled with people moving frantically about with pots, pans, and trays of food. She takes my hand and weaves us through the commotion. A few stray glances land in my direction, but nobody says anything about my being here with her. "Is the less shitty liquor somewhere in here?" I yell out over the boisterous noise. She doesn't give me an answer, just continues barreling through the busy workers.

Low and behold in the center of the kitchen and chaos sits a disheveled Rorin, a peeved Mousy, and Bennett who is shamelessly flirting with one of the maids. She looks down at me and winks before calling out to the three of them.

"Well well, Millie, what pray tell caused you to drag her Highness into the belly of the beast?" Bennett flashes me a toothy grin. *Flirt.* Rorin's leaned back in his chair, both of his sleeves are pushed up to his elbows showing off his corded arms.

"*We* are going to get drunk. In the city. She says our alcohol in the castle tastes like shit."

Bennett pushes out from his chair and loops a lazy arm around Millicent's shoulders. "So what you're saying is you need some male escorts?" She rolls her eyes and gives him a shove but he only holds onto her tighter, ruffling her hair.

She slaps his hands away, "I am *saying* - before you started messing with my hair, you asshole - that we are going to get drunk. Whether you choose to join us or not is up to you. But I wasn't about to get in trouble by broody over there," she hooks a thumb in Rorin's direction, "for not telling him where she went." With a grip on my bicep, she drags me past them and into a hallway I actually recognize. The three of them must have followed us because I can hear Bennett arguing a few feet back with Mousy. As we get closer to my men's door, Orem peeks his head out of their door, probably to see what all the noise was about.

"Evie? What are you doing down here?" He asks, looking genuinely confused.

Millicent waves him off, "oh, we're just walking through." She smiles at him and I can see Orem's cheeks turn pink when we pass him up.

He ducks back inside, and in the next few minutes three of my men tumble out into the hall. Axel is hopping on one foot trying to get his boot on while a sleep addled Max straightens his clothes.

She groans at the six of them, continuing her hot pursuit for the exit that leads out into a courtyard. We cross through until we reach the gates and that's when Mousy begins his whining again, "Millie, please tell me we aren't going to *walk*?!" She pointedly ignores him making me like her just a little more. Her pace stays quick until we cobblestones.

Axel catches up and loops an arm around me, looking out and around our surroundings before extending two fingers to tap Millicent's shoulder, "where exactly are we going?"

"*Goldfinch*." She and Bennett answer at the same time. "To get drunk." She adds again and a boyish grin spreads ear to ear across Axel's face.

"Oh thank the gods. You know your alcohol in there tastes like dragon piss right?"

Max - more awake now - joins Axel in throwing an arm around me from the other side, "have a lot of experience with Vada's piss, brother?"

THWACK! Max's arm lets go of me and goes straight to rubbing the back of his head. "Ow." He mouths.

Millicent turns around to look at us, "Vada?"

Max's eyes go wide at his slip up and Axel gives him a look while redirecting the conversation. "Let's just hope this Goldfinch redeems you all."

Loud drunken voices start to drift our way from the end of the next street we turn on. It's not long before large lights come into view. Beaming at the end of the alley is a bright sign that reads "GOLDFINCH" hung above a set of swinging doors.

Our bodies press tightly together as patrons shove past and through our group trying to make their way outside while we try to make our way inside. A few whoops sound through the crowd at the sight of Millicent, Bennett's face souring at their brazenness. He drapes a protective arm around her while flashing a crude gesture at one of the callers. The two of them argue quietly, heading towards a table in the corner of the room. It's raised on a platform giving us a view over the lively crowd. Rorin's body bumps against mine as we pile into the booth. His arm moves around my shoulders to lay against the back of the bench. The position caging me in place. Which is *not* what I planned on doing tonight.

I slap my hands down on the table and push myself up. "Move, princeling." He looks up at me his expression annoyed, not bothering to listen to me.

"We just sat down." He argues.

I nudge him again a little less gently this time. "*Move*. I need a drink, that's why we're here isn't it?" Thankfully Millicent bounces up from her seat exclaiming that she'll come with me. When Rorin still doesn't stand I swing my leg over him, practically sitting down in his lap to get out of the booth, his hands come up to my hips pulling me snug against him and anchoring me onto his lap for a millisecond - the movement sending shocks through me - his hazel eyes darkening before he lifts me up and over him. Orem gets up next helping Millie down like a gentleman, unlike how Rorin just handled me.

Millicent takes off into the crowd and I follow, keeping an eye on her blonde head bobbing through the crowd. I realized halfway through that Orem didn't sit back down but in fact came with. "I don't need a babysitter, Abrams." I gripe.

His answer to that complaint was his finger looping through my weapons belt keeping him locked into his side. *So they think I need a babysitter* and *to be leashed?*

We find Millicent leaning over a sticky bar top that's set in front a colorfully lit wall. The shelves are all lined with different bottles that glow in the fluorescence. She's chattering with a gangly man covered in gold paint who flashes a bright smile at us when we join her. "And what can I get you, loves?" He asks, his accent thick and noticeably not Vellaran. "Three pitchers of ale." Millicent slides over a few pieces of Vellaran money that he doesn't hesitate to swipe up quickly, winking at her. Before he leaves to go gather our pitchers I slam down my hand startling a few patrons in the vicinity.

"Is that the strongest thing here or is there something else I can add to that?" The bartender looks me up and down as if to gauge by my size how much of a lightweight I might be. He chuckles behind his gold teeth and lips then turns away from to pour our drinks, not answering my question. I hop up on the stool and place both elbows behind me on the counter behind me. Orem unfortunately is blocking most of my view with his bulky frame. He keeps both eyes trained on the man behind the counter making our drinks. Every so often though I notice, he switches focus, and his eyes wander over to a unaware Millicent.

"Let me know how that drink goes, love. You make it through that and I'll make you one on the house." I spin around in my chair and find the man laughing while he passes off the tray to Orem. Millie smiles again at the bartender and hops down from her seat, looking up Orem she pats his chest, softening his otherwise icy expression. He jerks his chin for us to walk in front of him so he can keep an eye on our backs, ordering Millie to hook her arm through mine and not to let go until we're back at the table.

Axel and Bennett cheer when they see us approaching. Orem sets the tray down and I reach for my drink, pushing it towards Axel. "Here. Try it in case it's poisoned."

He gapes at me before picking it up grumbling, "sure, I'll just be the expendable one."

I smile. "When you become a royal, I'll test your drinks for you. But for now drink up."

Axel smirks, tipping the drink to his lips, "are you proposing?" He teases before swallowing the sip. His face twists in discomfort. He passes it to Orem next who takes a sip as well and ends up coughing and sputtering afterwards.

"Bleeding gods, Eveera, if you wanted to be lost to Oblivion you could've just asked." Orem chokes out, his shadowy Wield hovering over the pads of his fingers.

I raise my brows, reaching for the cup. "Can't be that bad." I mutter, decidedly ignoring the looks that are passing over the Vellaran's faces.

"Well...it's strong." Axels adds.

I gulp it down in one go, the contents of it singing the back of my throat. I drop the empty glass harshly in front of Rorin. "Child's play." I snark, slinking back into the crowd before anyone can stop me.

The mass of sweaty bodies sucking me into itself, my body flowing to the rhythm. I feel the sensation of a wandering hand graze over my skin. My head starts to loll along with the music as the alcohol does its job and I sink into the stranger's touch. Unfortunately the distraction is short lived when I feel the annoying sensation of being watched. I tilt my head to the side and see two dark, stormy, hazel eyes boring into me and my new dance partner. My smile widens as I listen to my impaired judgment and sway my hips against the man behind me.

"*Problem,* lover?" I croon.

RORIN

She slipped away from us easily with the distraction of her slamming her glass down. It took us a moment to notice she was gone at all. I restrained myself from running after her out onto the floor and dragging her back to the table but now, as I watch her, I wish I had. I'm irritated at how unbothered she is with the amount of sweaty bodies moving around, grazing against, and clinging to her when she usually seems to be so averse to touch.

"*Problem,* lover?" She asks, her voice sweet and sour all at the same time.

"Only with the ceaseless gyrating of the idiot behind you."

Her cold laugh trills down the seal while she presses herself further into him and the others surrounding her. Her arms drift up into her hair and her head drops back a little. *"A little early to get territorial wouldn't you say, princeling?"* My eyes rove all over her body and I think I hear a distant Will attempting to get my attention but it's like I'm frozen, refusing to take my eyes away from her until a set of fingers snap in front of my face.

An all too knowing look from Axel comes into view. "You're ogling, princeling."

"I am not *ogling*. I am watching your charge to prevent her from getting herself into any trouble."

Axel looks over his shoulder and shrugs. "She's the Queen of Obsidian, if the drunken fool is unaware of who she is then he is no better than a unsuspecting fly roving too close to a spider's web." He snags my ale mug from me. "This is better than the shit at court, I'll give you that. Look she makes terrible decisions. I think I've mentioned that before and if she can get herself in them then she can get herself *out* of them."

"Most of the time." Maxwell chimes in from behind me.

Axel bops his head to the beat, agreeing with Max. "Most of the time. So with that concern out of the way, we resort to the fact that you *were* ogling. Understandable after the performance you two gave earlier." His eyes glint with suspicion.

"Are you always this annoying, Axel?" I ask.

"Only when I'm right." He replies. When I look back out to where Eveera is on the floor, I see only random patrons in varying degrees of drunkenness. My eyes scan the room for her, but the damn woman is so fucking small it's like finding a needle in a haystack. That is until the crowd parts just enough for me to see her sitting back at the bar, taking shots of suspicious blue and gold drinks. "That can't be good." I grumble mostly to myself. If she blacks out, I have a feeling she will find a way to blame me for it, which does not bode well for the star-crossed lovers ruse we are managing.

The painted bartender behind the counter skims his hand across her lower back. I wait for her reaction but nothing happens, she remains either unaware or purposefully ignorant of his boldness. The image of him suffocating from the the poison that courses through me flashes in my head, catching me off guard. *Who touches her back should be none of your concern.* I think, but at this point...there is a sinking realization that's settled into the pit of my stomach. That from the moment she walked into her throne room - drenched in blood - I knew she would somehow become the center of every single one of my concerns.

"Oh boy." Max murmurs into his drink. "You seeing this?" He asks, nudging Axel. Axel gives him a nod, shifting on the bench to stand.

"What? What's wrong?" I question.

The three of them give each other a look before Orem bursts out into laughter. "Her little hip swaying and the sitting on bartops are going to be the least of your problems." He comments, his head jerking towards the floor. In the two minutes I turned from her she made her way back onto the floor and completely tangled herself up with the same dancing idiot as before, who's hands have dropped precariously low on her hips teasing the slits in her dress.

I groan. "What's my biggest problem then?"

"She tends to like clothes a lot less when intoxicated." Axel's snickering does not help the next thought I have, *of course she fucking does.*

I feel a knot starting to form in the back of my neck from this woman. "So you three figured she needed an escort when she went to get drinks, but you're just going to casually let her drink herself until she gets naked?" The words are sharp, their expressions turning defensive. I don't give them the time to argue back their bullshit explanation. The table wobbles as I storm away from them, making my way out to her on the floor.

Whatever the fool has said into her ear causes her head to fall back onto his shoulder her chest rumbling with laughter. His wandering hands drift up from her skirt and skate along her ribs. His first mistake was touching her to begin with, his second was where he thought his fingers were headed next. "What the he—" his words stop short when I grip both of his wrists in my hands, a line of poisonous smoke snaking up his arms and straight into his nostrils. I don't often take pleasure in the sound of someone choking for air, but this time the sound calms something down in me.

Her big golden eyes lazily look up at me caged in between me and the man gasping and struggling in my hold. She drags her fingers down my chest, "aw, sucking the fun out of things are we?" She glances over her shoulder at him, his expression urging for her help that she won't give him. I let him go before he passes out onto the floor and creates an even bigger scene, he gives us startled looks before darting off into the crowd gasping for his breath.

Her lip exaggerates into a pout and her words are loose from the alcohol. "And he was being so devout."

"Is that what you want? Someone devout? Someone to worship you?"

Her hand drops from my chest, her gaze darkening. "Who needs worship?"

I chuckle stepping closer to her, her hand quickly going back up to put some space between us. I knock it out of my way and grab her chin between my thumb and forefinger her breath hitching slightly as I bring her face to mine. *Gods when she does that...* "I didn't say *need*. I said *want*. Plenty fear you, Eveera. But if you want someone to worship you? You need only to point me to the altar."

I can feel her heart rate quicken through her pulse as my other hand comes around to cup her nape, pulling her into me. The walls she is trying so hard to maintain in her mind are faltering. "You once said you wanted me on my knees begging. But what if I were praying?"

She swallows thickly, scanning my face for something. "Are you praying, *princeling?*"

A smirk tugs on my lips, "am I on my knees, Nightmare?"

"I could bring you to them." She suggests, that heady stare drawing me in.

All teasing aside, I dip my face low. The alcohol mixing with her scent overwhelms me our lips skimming one another. *Gods this damn fucking woman.* "Is that what you want?"

She pulls back the look she's giving me now has the same hatred in it that she held the day we met in her throne room. The truth to her feelings regardless of her body's inclinations are written all over her face. "Torture truly is your specialty." I mutter.

"I've hardly tortured you, Rorin."

I drop my hands from her, the loss of feeling her warmth beneath my fingers is immediate. "What do you think this is?" I didn't stick around to see the change in her face. But I don't miss her words that hit my back.

"A game."

I step outside, the warm air sweeping over me.

The alleyways are crawling with serviceable women and the men desperate and drunk enough to pay for their company. I tug at the ends of my hair, the curls wrapping around my fingers still caught up in our exchange I briefly think of her fingers being the ones my curls wrap around.

What is wrong with you? My conscience hisses. *She puts on* one *show in front of everyone and that's enough to have you panting after her?* Gods. I've never been one to trail after women for more than a night, but apparently if they hate me and tries to kill me as a fun daily activity then they'll have me tripping hand over foot.

Drunken patrons stumble out of the tavern some searching for a basin to vomit in, others looking for a dark corner in which to debase themselves, delirious laughter rings out all around me. My head drops against the stone behind me staring up at the night sky. I have no idea how we are going to pull all of this off. The hand portals and written correspondence have kept us up to date with the front lines. Since our last update things have been eerily quiet. Certainly not because of my father and his orders, no, he has something up his sleeve and the prickling sensation under my skin warns me it's nothing good.

I'd caught them off guard with my initial suggestion to obtain Obsidian's help, and I threw them off further when I showed up, Obsidian soldiers and queen in tow.

For a kingdom with magic that Wields in healing and not in defensive measures you would think they would have a more efficient military base. And we did at one point, but he's whittled them down to the bare bones. Now I'm whittling her men down too, something that I wouldn't have to do if we had brought her dragon with us. Fuck, she has a dragon and we can't even use it. With force like that we'd have taken Baelor's men within the day and my father would be forced to admit that getting them on our side was the right thing to do.

"There you are." Bennett stares at me from under the glow of a street light.

"Here I am."

The crunch of the stones under his feet echoes in the alley. "You're hiding, Rorin Collier. Course I can't say I blame you. The woman is downright terrifying. Guess that's how she got her nicknames." He smiles crookedly at me and for a second I see the same boy I met in the courtyard as kids, wooden sword in hand.

"*Hi. I'm Bennett Haid and I'm going to be a soldier one day.*"

Will came along after and the three of us - much to his chagrin - have been tumbling on a path together ever since.

Bennett blows out a breath, "they seem more relaxed."

"Are they drunk?" I ask.

I can feel the weight of his gaze on my profile. "Probably. Ror – just curious but...what's her endgame?" My brows draw together and my lips flatten tightly against each other. *I wish I knew.* "I could believe she is doing this because she's clearly infatuated with you but I don't think that's the only reason."

"Bloody hell, Bennett. In what gods forsaken world does she seem *infatuated* with me?"

He rolls his eyes down at me. "Oh come on, Ror. Why else would she be doing this? Why else would she bait you the way she does? Unless it's because of course she already knows that *you* are the infatuated one and is one hell of a manipulator."

Probably the latter, I want to snap at him. But instead I tell him, "It's a part we both are playing. One that will get us the outcomes we each hope for." *If only I knew what her outcome she hoped for was.* He looks poised to argue with me further but a scream comes from inside the tavern quickly followed by a few more screams and people fleeing from the building. "*Fuck.*" I mutter under my breath. We both bolt back into the building, shoving and elbowing the mob of patrons to get to the source. I could just barely feel it before Eveera's magic slams into us at full force.

"P-please don't lock me up here again. PLEASE.", "Stupid boy. An omen if there ever was one."

The wave of power knocks her off her balance just enough for one of the unaffected Guards to slice his sword through her stomach. "Open those eyes, Nightmare. I need you to give me those eyes..."

-

The nightmares both new and old assault my minds eye. I hear Bennett's wails next to me the most over the screams of everyone else. I push against her Wield, fighting through the crowd to get to wherever she is at the center of the floor. When I reach it, I find her standing over them magic out and wrapping around two separate men who flail about in her grasp. Her uncontrolled Wield fights for control over my mind, Bennett's screams rising the closer we get to her.

If I were to guess, I would say the alcohol she drank is playing a part. The lack of inhibitions causing it to leak past her two initial targets which causes the rest of us to suffer alongside them. I see Max from the corner of my eye the electricity zapping at the ends of his fingers drawing my attention. His gaze keeps bouncing back and forth between the queen and a heap on the floor. It takes me a few seconds to realize the heap is Millie and Orem and Orem is cradling her unconscious frame.

I look around for Axel and Will but can't find them. "MAX!" He doesn't acknowledge me at first. "MAX!" I try again, his head turning towards my direction. "What happened?" I shout over the commotion.

His face is grim, "after seeing the two of you on the floor. They figured out who she was. They must have spiked her drink with something! Millie took a sip of it before Evie could and started seizing almost immediately. Orem caught her as she went down and now we're here!" His voice is strained, well practiced as he may be against Eveera's power it's evident it takes effort to keep her out of his head.

I feel around her mind through the seal, her walls are fractured as all the focus goes into tormenting the two fools in front of her. I don't have to look at her face to know her eyes are completely black, her serpents depth of color pales in comparison to the darkness flowing out of her in droves. Both men are writhing on the floor, whimpering and sputtering. Stepping away from Bennett I move behind her. "Eveera." I whisper against the shell of her ear, my hands falling onto the triceps of her arms. She doesn't respond to my touch but a slight twitch in her scowl let's me know she heard me. "You're drawing quite the scene here."

"Am I?" her words are tight, clenched between her teeth.

"Mmhm." I drop my gaze watching her work. "We'll bring them back with us. Doing this here is only going to worsen our position. We need them playing into our hands, remember?" Her eyes flit to the left towards where Millie and Orem are. "She'll be fine. But we need to go now. I need you to pull back." Her body tenses at that request.

I move around her assailants and cup my hand over the first man's nose, my magic filtering through his nostrils until the twitching stops. When I moved onto the next man I recognize his face as the idiot who danced with her. A rage was already building for what they tried to do to her in the first place and ended up doing to Millie. But now that rage was close to boiling over when I think of his hands and body having been pressed against Eveera's for half the night.

Her magic dissipates, her eyes returning to their gold hue. I meet them for only a second before dropping the second man's head. The tavern has completely cleared out save for the gold-painted bartender whose pupils are blown. A state of shock is plastered over his face.

Orem is still cradling Millie, her blonde hair spilling across his arm. Max gives her a brief once over, concern etched across his face before looking to me.

"We should go." The five of us startle at Will's voice. He and Axel approach us, both of them looking perturbed. "Before it gets out further, who she is. We don't need another..." He waves his arm to gesture at us and the now empty tavern, "this happening."

Entering court without alerting anyone was a tricky enough task, but then we had to go about getting a healer mage in here. Armond and Ezra join us in my rooms while Millie is being worked on. They determined it was ragroot that was used and by this point it had drained all the color from her already pale skin. Her blue veins stand out in stark contrast. We all sit or pace quietly as the mage works on her. The glowing warm pulse of magic radiates over her. By the end of it, her color has brightened slightly, but she still looks half-dead.

I thank the healer mage for their help and discretion on their way out of the apartment. "Keep an eye on her. That concoction was strong, but she will recover." The woman looks warmly at Millie.

Bennett and Orem haven't moved from her side. The question of when Orem and Millie became so acquainted crosses my mind before Will bursts into the room. "Does anyone want to explain what the bleeding gods happened down there?" He looks directly at Eveera. "Well?"

"I think it's pretty obvious what happened." Max says his voice raw.

Will's jaw slackens feigning disbelief, "no it's not pretty obv—"

"Where are they?" Eveera's voice startles us.

"That's all you can think about? Those men?" Will yells. "Millie could have died!"

A bitter smile crosses her face as she walks over to him, "well, Mousy, you asked what happened down there. Why don't we go find out exactly what did happen." His shoulders slump slightly in defeat but he moves to show her the way.

Looking over to Bennett, he shakes his head, his hand clasped around Millie's. "We'll stay here with Mill. In case she wakes up." I nod following after Will and Eveera to the dungeons.

Despite their overall damp feel, they match the same gaudiness throughout the castle. Most of the cells are empty and look almost completely unused. Will quietly leads the group to the end cell. In the dim light two heaps - caked with dirt, gold, and sweat - lay unconscious. The door to their cell yawns open, the brass hinges screaming in protest at the motion. Eveera sweeps in, hovering over them. Her foot swings out and presses down on the larger of the two men's throat. His body jolts from the pressure on his windpipe, both eyes flying open. The man's hands dart up to try and grab her ankle but she is too quick for him. She repeats the process on the second's throat. They try to scramble away from them but the poison in their system however makes their movements choppy and uncoordinated.

"Oh, stop your squabbling." She barks, making them flinch at the sound. Taking a seat on the bench adjacent to them, Eveera looks over expectantly to Will, "well go ahead. This is your interrogation not mine, Sir."

He clears his throat, stepping up to the men on the floor. "Last night or this morning, whichever way you choose to see it, the both of you decided to commit not only a crime against a Vellaran but an attempted crime against a guest of the crown and the queen of Obsidian—"

He's cut off by Ezra's growl. "Who sent you?" He asks his eyes vengeful. Armond pulls him backwards, muttering something into his ear that gets him to back off. I nod at Will to continue who sighs and turns back to the men.

"While I don't appreciate the outburst from Commander Wake, his question stands. Who sent you?"

The larger of the two men spits in the direction of Eveera, his saliva splattering on the stone floor. "She's an abomination." He snarls.

"Flattery will get you nowhere, dear." She coos, making him spit at her again.

We do this back and forth for a while and the interrogation takes up most of the day with neither of them willing to give us an explanation as to why they spiked the drink. "I am *bored* with this. Is this really how you lot get information from people?"

Will huffs and glares at her, "you said this was my interrogation."

"Well, that was when I thought you would actually incentivize them to answer."

"I do not think your idea of incenti—"

"ENOUGH!" Both of them turn to me stunned. "If I have to listen to the two of you argue for another second, I'll put the both of you out." Eveera's lips press in disapproval but at least she quiets. I crouch down in front of the accused men. "Let me be very clear here, gentlemen. You can give us the information we want, or you can die." I wait for an argument from Will that surprisingly doesn't come.

The bigger one of the two, who's named we found out is Zekiel, starts to laugh. His ruddy brown eyes are bloodshot and locked onto Eveera. "How did we miss you?" He asks. "You should have died the night she did."

Eveera's eyes flash and then something hot and sticky splashes across my face. I look down to see Zekiel's head now on the floor at my feet. She is panting heavily in front of me, her eyes blackened and her magicked claws dripping with blood. I stand up and wrap my arms around her, pushing her back a few steps. The second man, Ryel, gapes in horror at his decapitated companion. "There." She gasps her face turning into my chest for a moment. "Maybe we can turn him into a friend for Percy."

She half heartedly jokes while I switch the weight of her fully onto my left side.

I slip my hand down into the slit of her dress and reach for one of the daggers attached to her thigh. "I so wish I could have taken my time with you." The words are low, he stutters trying to put together some half-assed argument to get out of this but those attempts are thwarted when the dagger sinks into his chest.

"Well, that was productive." Ezra snaps storming out of the cell.

Once back in the room, Bennett had questions for us. Unfortunately, we had no answers to give.

Will rushed to the bathroom sick from the blood that splattered onto him. But I was less concerned about him and more concerned about the queen next to me. Her face is stricken, a mixture of hate, pain, and confusion. *She didn't bother closing her mental walls to me, those five words on a constant loop in her mind. 'How did we miss you?'* What in the gods is that supposed to mean? I wonder. When Will returns, his skin has taken on a green pallor and he is wearing one of my night shirts.

We all wait in hesitation for her to say something as she paces back and forth the length of the room. "We end this *fast*. I want what is owed to me for my end of this deal." Her voice is shaky as she says it.

"What exactly is owed to her?" Will asks quietly.

Her head cocks to the side, "I'm going to make our prince here a king."

EVEERA

I left them with their jaws gaping and information I hadn't planned on sharing yet. Millicent I found asleep in the bed, her skin color finally pinking up again. "Stupid girl. Didn't anyone ever tell you not to drink from a cup that wasn't yours?" I mutter.

From my peripheral I can see my reflection watching me through the crack in the bathroom door. Blood is stuck in my hair and my face and chest are dotted with the red spatter pattern from Zekiel.

"You should have died the night she did."

I wanted to scream at him, that I did die that night. That they killed me the moment they gutted her. It wouldn't make a difference. Just like his death my feelings mean nothing anymore and after tonight? The king and queen's blood will never be enough. No, now, I want every fucking individual connected to their deaths.

My hands grip the lip of the slate counter top. Like a dam breaking all at once the wave of emotions tears out of me. I can't find it in me at the moment to care how loud I might be. If my feelings truly mean nothing, then who cares who hears me? Right?

Let them hear what they've driven me to. Let them hear what they've created.

With each sob my back pulls tight, the familiar itch to overtake the pain is restless under my skin. I've nowhere to place my rage and against my better judgment I hurl my magic into the mirror.

Glass shatters everywhere, over the counter, onto the floor, onto my skin where tiny cuts now make themselves comfortable.

My hand closes around a larger shard and I watch the blurry eyes as I bring it up to my shoulder. I reach as far back as I can and press it hard into the scarred skin. The burn from both the jagged slice and the rune steal my breath. "One" I gasp. Two arms rip the shard from my hand and wrap around me before I can make another cut. "NO!" I hear myself scream, the sobs racking through my chest as we stumble back, falling clumsily to the floor.

Rorin's voice starts whispering in my ear, and whole whatever his words are, comforting or not, all I can do is shake my head rapidly as I yell. His arms put pressure around me, keeping me still in place until the sobs stop.

I don't know how long we've been sitting here for. But, the words I try to speak come out in a hoarse quiet croak. "I broke your mirror." Is all I manage to get out. Rorin's hand brushes down my hair as he squeezes me a little tighter against him, mumbling into my hair.

"Shhh...it can be replaced." I nod slowly. "I did die..." I whisper as pure exhaustion takes over and my eyelids start to droop. He's body stiffens around me momentarily before he repeats himself, not acknowledging the vulnerable admission.

"Shhh...it can be replaced. It's only right before sleep takes me that I hear him whisper, a kiss pressing into my hair, *"but you cannot be."*

The light streaming into the bathroom assaults my eyelids, stirring me awake.

My ass is completely numb from spending the entire night on the hard floor. I blink trying to clear the sleep from my eyes when I hear soft snores come from behind me. I peer over my shoulder, trying not to disturb him.

Rorin's head is back against the wall. His arms still locked in a tight embrace around me. I try to tip forward enough to see Axel's body come into view - he's contorted in a horribly uncomfortable position against the door frame.

I start to move out of Rorin's grip as subtly as I can but his arms flex in response, pinning me to my spot. "Can't we pretend for just a little longer?" He asks. His voice is heavy with sleep and his eyes remain closed.

"What?" My words are a whisper.

One hazel eye peeks open, looking right at me. "I said, can't we pretend for just a little longer? You can go back to hating me and wishing death upon my head when it's not only daybreak."

I'm at a loss for works and, "are you not uncomfortable?", is the only thing I can think of to ask him. He readjusts his shoulders against the wall and brings a hand up to my forehead, pushing me against his collarbone. "Well, I wasn't until you started moving around. Now shh. We'll talk in the morning." I open my mouth to argue that it is, in fact, already morning but he can hear the thought forming, his voice drifting into my mind, "*in the actual morning, Nightmare. Just a little longer.*"

"Okay...a little longer." I sigh.

The three of us didn't officially wake up until Axel yelped. Rorin and I both startled looking over to see Ezra standing over Axel.

"Get up, Mecham." Ezra's voice a command. A scathing look skates over Rorin and I, the two of us still wound around one another, "we have things to discuss."

Axel rubs his side and flips his middle finger up at Ezra's retreating back, "didn't have to fucking kick me, man. Gods." He shakes his fingers through his hair before looking at the both of us, eyebrows raised. His gaze drops up and down, a sleepy smirk curling up.

I cock my head at him, mouthing, "don't say a word." He raises his hands up defensively and scrambles out, leaving us alone to untangle our limbs. Rorin stands first reaching his hand down to help me up. I refuse the gesture. *I am perfectly capable of standing up,* I think to myself.

I pick up a shard of glass, examining the damage. Cool fingers touch the new cut on my shoulder. "You should get a healer mage to fix that." His voice is quiet and our eyes lock in the fragments of the mirror.

"No. It stays."

He takes a step back, moving towards the door his hand rubbing the nape of his neck as he stares at the marks. "Part of me is hoping that I am wrong in the thought of who made all of those scars. Part of me is hoping that there is someone responsible, someone that I could make pay for subjecting you to that. But I'm not wrong am I? I'm not wrong in thinking that the person who is...who..."

My head dips down, furiously blinking tears threatening to slip. "It will never be an answer that you like." His fist connects with the frame as he walks out. I can't bring myself to look back at him. I've never been ashamed of my habits, of how I choose to cope. But when he acts like he actually cares...*no.* I think, *he doesn't get to care. He doesn't get to feel any way towards how I deal with the festering wound his family left in me.*

Millicent is sitting up in the bed fully awake when I step out of the bathroom, but she keeps quiet while I take my time walking to the wardrobe. I twisted my wet, sink washed hair up into two buns at the base of my neck on my way. There is a pair of brown leathers hanging that I slip on over my legs grabbing my thigh holster off the vanity and securing it around the slippery material. I tuck a few daggers into the holster and a pocket sized one in between my breasts. All I need now is a shirt, looking through the rack I come up dry.

"You could always wear one of Rorin's, I doubt he'd mind." Millie says from behind me. I look over to Rorin's wardrobe, closest to me hangs a billowy white undershirt. Throwing it on, I see that due to our height difference the shirt hits at the top of my thighs. I button and cinch up my green embroidered waspie corset or the shirt to tamp down some of the wideness of it. The collar is equally wide, hanging easily off my narrow shoulders and exposing my tattoos and scars.

My lips thin when I spin around to face the girl in the bed. "You almost died."

Her face turns sheepish, as she shrugs "Sorry?"

I roll my eyes my hands rolling and pushing up his sleeves. "Yeah well, I would really hate to be responsible for your death simply because you drank a drink that wasn't yours."

"I heard you, last night." My lips turn down in a frown. I grab my boots slipping them on and reaching for the doorknob. "They won't go down easily." I freeze in my spot, my head swiveling around to look at her.

"What did you just say?"

She sighs, sitting herself up straighter. "I said - they won't go down easily. If you plan to make him king you better have a damn good way to do it. Trust me."

I tilt my head, considering her. "And why should I do that, dear?"

"She didn't always used to be like this." Her voice quiets, her focus on her fingers twisting in her palms as she looks down. Anger flares to life in my chest at the mere mention of the queen. "You're the product of something terrible that they did. But I have lived alongside them for eighteen years. And I am the product of something great they did, and because of that, I know everything. You'll need me." I'm at a loss of what to say, too many mixed emotions swirling around in me. "So just trust me, if you want them dead? Be ready for a fight."

"And will *you* fight me? When the time comes?" Her features turn cold, her gaze glazing over.

"No. The woman I knew is gone now, never coming back. And for what happened to Rorin...they deserve to hang."

Our conversation comes to a close when I decide to leave so that she can get some rest. Walking out into the common area the tension is thick, icy stares wandering all over me. It's not hard to find Rorin amongst the men, he's leaning with his arm against the fireplace. He gives me a very slow once over from where he stands a smile twitching at his lips, my stomach sinks a little at the heat of his gaze on the nearly see-through shirt of his. . "*Nice shirt.*"

"She's awake." I announce and the three of them - Bennett, Max, and Orem all leap up from their seats.

"Hold." Ezra's hard voice rings out causing my men to freeze begrudgingly in place. Bennett however walks away from what him, muttering, "you're not my fucking commander."

Max and Orem lower themselves back down and Ezra's hand swings out towards me, "explain, Eveera." He orders.

"Explain what?" I ask, my arms crossing to mimic the way he is standing.

"You're joking. What do you mean 'what'?" His hand juts out at Rorin. "You're marrying him?!"

The prince and I look at each other, unable to help the shock on both of our faces. "Marry?" We ask at the same time.

"You said you were going to make him a king!" Mousy exclaims.

Oh. Well, I did say that. I can't help myself against the fit of laughter that bubbles out, the emotion so violent that tears spring from my eyes. "Oh, you foolish, *men.*" All of them, including Rorin, stare at me confused. "He will not be king because I am marrying him." *Although what a thought.* "He will be king, because soon he will be the only royal Collier left standing."

Rorin chokes and before any of them have a chance to say something we're interrupted by Armond who charges into the room, the look on his face is solemn. "Obsidian or Bair?" I ask, his eyes shadowing over. "Obsidian or Bair?!" I shout.

"Obsidian." *Fuck.*

The entire room goes into an uproar. My men are trying to figure out from Armond what exactly happened while Rorin's men are trying to figure out what exactly I meant. At the current moment I can't find it in me to care, my head was already spinning with all sorts of grave thoughts.

"What's wrong with Obsidian?" I practically growl at him, my voice cutting through all of the noise.

He shakes his head. "I received a missive from Felix yesterday."

"Yesterday?!" I shout.

"I would've come to you sooner but you weren't in any state to hear it."

My feet march over to him putting us chest to chest, my anger radiating between the two of us. "You do not get to decide what state I am or am not in to hear news about my own fucking kingdom, Armond!"

His eyes are soft, that blasted empathy of his surfacing, "the situation is severe, Eveera, and you were volatile last night."

The situation is severe. "How. Severe." *My patience has already snapped, I'm already imagining the worst, how bad can it really be?* I wonder. Armond takes a deep breath in, his eyes flicking over to where my men have clustered together. "Don't look at them. Look at me. How. Serious."

"The three towns that border Oriya," *Oh gods,* "they're gone."

"Gone? Th-they can't just be gone. Towns don't just disappear Armond." I'm struggling to put the words together as well as keep a handle on my magic. "Wha— how?" I can feel the panic crawling up my throat and my heart is beating too fast in my chest. It feels like the air is being sucked out from my lungs, making my vision blurry, and my nerves tingly.

He braces a hand on my shoulder, "outer land creatures have overrun them." He tries to explain.

"But...isn't Vada?" Orem starts before, *"oof!"* My head whips around to see him rubbing his ribs, Axel's elbow still hanging in the air. I look back to Armond, searching his face to see if he's going to tell me the truth or try and spare my feelings.

Thankfully he has some self preservation skills, but I don't know if it matters because the overwhelming feeling of dread that comes from a single word.

"She's gone." I nearly pass out as he says it.

"Dead, gone? Or disappeared, gone." Axel asks the question for me.

"Disappeared." He replies. We've run out of time - *I've* run out of time and Vellar is going to cost me yet another thing, except this time I don't even have the satisfaction of blaming it all on them. I chose this. I chose my revenge, and now my people are suffering.

Rorin tries to reach me through the seal whispering my name, but I slam my walls up, shoving him out of my mind. "We can send some troops back. We can work with half the military, if necessary." He suggests.

Everyone looks at me for a response or approval. I shake my head, "no." My voice coming out quieter than I'd intended.

"No?" They all repeat back in unison.

I nod my head. "No. We don't send back troops. She wouldn't respond to them anyways."

"Uhm-I don't think Rorin meant to send the troops back for *her*, Evie. He means to send them back to defend the citizens." Axel says. I shrug both he and Rorin off. My hands reach to unwind the low buns on my neck and restyle my long locks into a high pony. "No one goes back—"

"You can't be serious?" Ezra shouts.

I bare my teeth at him, "no one goes back but *me*." Reaching for Armond I think of the portal room we entered through on our first day here and Void out of the apartment.

The attendant's eyes grow wide at my magical intrusion. He stands with what I can guess was the full intention to stop me. "Excuse me but—" A tendril of my magic tightens around his throat, silencing him and my right hand rises to the iridescent flicker of the portal.

The door flies open, I don't have time to look over my shoulder and see who it is so I focus harder on the iridescent shimmer and start to push my hand into it. His scent hits me first bringing me a complicated mix of relief and anger. "*You can't escape me that easy.*" He says.

"*You all were going to argue with me. We don't have time to debate.*" He stands tall next to me, briefly glancing at the man wound in my magic, before lacing his fingers through mine.

"Where to?" He asks out loud. I don't say anything, instead, with a hard yank I pull him into the portal with me. We land fast, tumbling into the hard dirt.

Fuck. I didn't think that would actually work. Quickly, I pull myself up. Rorin is twisted at an awkward angle on the ground, coughing as he gets his breath back from the fall.

"WHAT THE ACTUAL BLEEDING FUCKING GODS WAS THAT?!" He yells. Good question...I didn't know if it'd work, but I figured it was worth a try. I pulled on the portal's magic like I do when I manipulate Armond's Void powers but instead of calling to the Obsidian portal and landing in Oriya, I called for Vada. But, looking around us, it doesn't *feel* like Obsidian. The air is too warm, and the trees aren't right.

"Where the hell are we?" I ask.

He turns in place looking at our surroundings. "We're on the outskirts of Valen...what did you do? How did we end up somewhere other than another portal?"

"I didn't think of another portal..." I whisper. "I thought of Vada. But why in the gods' name would she be here?"

I reach for her but she still ignores me through the bond. Her usually familiar presence, still absent. I decide to just choose to head in one direction to look for her. He reluctantly follows after me muttering the whole time we search about how he spent years studying the ways of the portals. Not only the magical element to them, but the technological and industrial elements as well and how a normal person should not have been able to overpower the latter two components and alter the trajectory. I can't be bothered to explain something I myself don't really understand when my mind is swimming on how she managed this and how I missed my own dragon just minutes outside the city.

Sweat begins beading on both our brows from the warmth and the density of the moisture in the woods. I've lost count of how long we've been out here, but by the looks of the sun setting, we've been out here awhile. He stops in moving, spinning around to look at our surroundings a frown forming on his face. "What? What is it?" I ask, annoyed that we've stopped moving.

"Uhm, well. We're right back where we started." He says cooly.

"What?"

"We just walked in a giant circle, look," I turn around in place, "this the same clearing you somehow portaled us into."

I groan. "Oh not this again."

He lifts his arms up and down, flabbergasted. "Well, I'm sorry but I don't know how the hell you managed to get us out here, it just doesn't make sense!" He shouts.

"That is not the biggest issue here!" I shout back, wanting nothing more than to just leave him here and go look for my damn dragon myself. A loud rustling sound comes from the trees distracting us and both of our heads snap to the noise.

Thwump! Thwump! Thwump! Thhhhwump!

Each sound finds success hitting their marks. "Oh, gods." I choke. It's too little too late when I notice that they're arrows protruding from our bodies. He looks to me stunned and tries to say something as my body thuds to the ground and my vision blacks out.

RORIN

The smell is dank and damp in whatever hell hole they've brought us to. It takes my eyes several seconds to adjust to the lighting and notice that I'm bound up against the wall. Both of my hands are chained above my head and with the darkness I can only make out maybe five feet from in front of me.

Despite all that it doesn't take me long to notice the dangling figure across from me. *Eveera.* There is a steady dripping sound, and while I would like to believe it is from some sewer or tap nearby, I know it isn't. Her body was riddled with arrows when it hit the ground - I don't even know if she's alive.

I can hardly feel my magic, guaranteeing that whatever those arrows had on them to incapacitate us, it also incapacitated our magic. If she is alive she will be pissed once she finds out. *"Nightmare."* I call into her mind. She doesn't answer me right away and a sinking feeling forms a pit in my stomach until she chokes out a guttural groan.

As if our captors knew we were both starting to come to I hear the sound of feet approaching. Fear strikes through me the closer they get to us. But it's not fear for myself - it's fear for *her*.

They'll reach her before they will me.

The voices stay low and their faces covered. The figure to my right takes the back of his scabbard and hits her torso with it. She yelps out at the impact and I lurch for her, forgetting for a minute that I'm bound.

"Oo-hoo-hoo. Someone's awake. Look, Gribly." The man to my left says, knocking elbows with the man to the right - Gribly apparently. They both laugh before cutting at Eveera's shirt, exposing her tan and bruised skin. From the little stream of light I can see gashes on her sides and chest that have contributed to the pool of blood underneath her.

"Let's see if we can make him squirm." The first man chucks his chin at me as a he takes out a knife and digs it into an already weeping wound on her side.

"*AHHHHHHH!*" Her scream vibrates off the walls as it turns into a sob. I pull on the shackles again.

"Don't. Touch. Her." My words are gravelly. The first man turns towards me - only his eyes are visible from the coverings on his head.

"Too late for that, isn't it." The sound of fabric tearing and then her flesh echo in the room but she doesn't scream this time. If I didn't know any better I'd say she passed out from the pain.

I reach for my magic again, and try to Wield it in their direction but nothing comes. They continue to make tiny slits in her skin and clothes adding to that pool. Their laughter grates on my last nerves as I jerk towards her a third time, my muscles screaming against the wounds and the shackles that they have me in. "I said not to touch her."

The man Gribly turns to me, "what, don't want to watch us play with your little girlfriend?" He takes a stubby finger and tugs on the waistband of her underwear snapping it against her skin. The touch has me seeing red.

"I'll have your hand for doing that." I growl. The man steps in close to her taking a deep inhale.

"She smells so sweet prince, I can see why you like her. I wonder if she tastes as sweet as she smells." I can hear the smile in his voice as he paints a grotesque image in my mind. He nicks her spine with the tip of his knife, slicing at the thin layer of skin.

"Nah, Gribly. She's as nasty as they come this one." Damn these fucking restraints. I'll kill them. "One things for sure though," the first man growls, stalking over to me, "you won't be awake to see if we test that theory out."

Before I can ask what he means, he rears the hilt of his sword back and rams it into my skull. Stars spin in front of my eyes before the darkness takes over again. I reach for her mind to mind desperately. The feeling of completely helplessness surrounding me.

"I'm so sorry..." I whisper down the seal before going unconscious again.

A cool sensation wraps around my weakened limbs as I come to for the second time.

What little light has leaked through casts a faint glow on Eveera's hanging body, now in ever worse shape than it was before. I look down at my feet, surprised to find her tendrils of magic are loose and leaking out from her. They wrap around my legs and torso, tentatively exploring me, almost seeming sentient.

I've heard the stories of shadow magic and its...benefits. But her magic is something else entirely, more corporeal than shadows. These when being used so gently, have a similar feel to silk. A smug part of me relishes in the fact that an extension of her has sought me out, and is *cautiously* feeling me up.

"*We are in a fucking torture cell. Please stop thinking of me groping you.*" The interruption of her voice in my thoughts is like a slap across the face, startling away any rogue fantasies my delirious state may have conjured up.

"With all due respect, Your Highness, your magic sought me *out*. My mind simply went along with your Wield's friendliness." My voice feigns innocence. "Besides I would have thought this environment would be a turn on for you." I tease attempting to lighten the mood.

A humorless laugh is all I get out of her, *"the irony is not lost on me."* Her shadowed body twitches causing the chains she hangs from to rattle and rustle.

"Eveer—" *Thud.* I freeze as I watch her body hit the ground hard, knocking the wind out of herself. She rises to her feet slowly then hobbles her way over to me, as she gets closer I'm better able to see some of the damage inflicted on her. The coppery scent of her blood filling my nostrils as she raises a clawed fingertip up to undo my chains.

"I guess whatever they used to drug us wore off." She says flippantly.

I guess. I rub my wrists where the chains left an unfortunate mark over top of the blood seal. Eveera's eyes follow to my wrist, "think they saw these?"

"The glowing insignia on our arms? Yeah. I am going to say they noticed." I grunt.

She nods grimly, and sighs. "Let's just hope they're too unimportant to know what the runes mean."

"It won't matter." I say. "They'll be dead before they can figure it out." My eyes roam from the top of her head on down to— "you have no pants." I say dryly.

Eveera tugs down at the frayed hem of my shirt that she borrowed, "evidently not. Can we go now?" Without giving me time to respond she turns to where the doorway is and limps towards it. The fools keeping us here, did us a favor by not only leaving the door unlocked, but by leaving it ajar too.

SQUEAAAAKKK!!

I cringe at how loud the rusted hinges are, hoping we don't end up getting caught before we're ready to make our move. Eveera doesn't seem to notice the noise however, and wastes no time leading us out of the dark and into a sconce-lit hallway.

The deeper we walk into the belly of the building, the more we come to notice it must have been a manor at one point. But whoever lived here in this estate, no longer does, the adornments and pictures on the walls are all covered under a thick layer of dust and the plush velvet walls are torn and stained in different places. Abandoned would certainly explain how our abductors have access to it.

Men's drunken laughter filters towards us as we come up to two large oak doors at the end of the hallway.

The doors are cracked open and through that opening I can see four men sitting around a dining table. They're tossing back and forth what appears to be a woman's undergarments while slurred and lewd comments leave their gnarled mouths. I look hard at the undergarments that are clearly bloodstained and then I look back to Eveera. I scan over her bare legs, the slits in her clothes, and to the bare hip bone peeking through one of the holes.

Fucking gods. I mutter in my mind my stomach feeling sick. Red clouds my vision. Her face gives away nothing, only her hands as they grip the handles and whip open the doors. All four men's heads snap to the two of us. They look dumb struck as a cruel smile dances across her lips before she switches it to a mocking pout. "Oh. *Tut tut.* Don't tell me we're late."

The four of them stumble to their drunken feet, "how the hell did the bitch get out?" The man furthest to my right shouts while pointing at Eveera.

Her steps forward are slow, both hands twitching while she summons her Wield. "We would've been here sooner but we were a little...tied up." The man who spoke only moments ago struggles as she slides closer to him. "I must say—"

Her hand flicks and the tendrils wind around his torso, he claws at himself but it's no use, the tendrils squeeze until his eyes pop out of their sockets the two rubbery orbs dangling down his cheeks. She places both hands on his shoulders allowing her Wield to slink back into her skin. She cracks a smile again and looks over her handiwork, "you really aren't very good hosts." The three that remain look around nervously as she walks around them all. "I mean—" she plucks her tattered corset from the lap of the largest man. It takes me a moment in the light, but I recognize him as Gribly. Rage boils inside of me at the memory of him digging his dagger into her side. The obscene things he said - *bleeding gods if he truly touched her...*

Gribly glares up at her, his nerves replaced with newfound confidence. *Damn fool.* "You won't beat him, you know."

She looks to me exasperated. "Why is it that that's not the first time I've heard those words? Does everyone have so little faith in me?"

My eyes wander to his hand where a glint of something flashes. *A ring.* "How's the wife, Gribly?" The others whimper while anger etches onto the man's face. Eveera looks up at me - confused. "Do you think she'll miss you?" I press.

He pushes off his chair, "why you—"

Eveera thankfully quickly catches on to where I am going with this. "Maybe not, by the way he was handling another woman's undergarments. She may not miss the bastard at all."

"Should we pay her a visit?" My full attention now onto her, using this as my window to scope out her injuries. She is covered in blood, dirt, and bruises. Her knee wobbles just a little as she tries to cover up her limp.

I move over to her side my arm securing tightly around her waist while my head rests on top of hers. What to the three of them will look like a protective lover's embrace is really more to support her weight.

"Don't you touch 'er." Gribly slurs, spittle from his lips landing on the table.

"Why not? You thought it was okay to touch what's mine. Why can't I return the favor?"

Gribly bares his teeth at me, "I didn't touch nothing."

My brows rise, a hand fanning over the exposed skin of her ribs. "Is that not my woman's torn undergarments strewn across the table and chair? Why else would her corset be in your grubby hands?" The men's eyes flick down. I might almost believe the other two were remorseful if I hadn't seen them drunk with the fabric pressed to their faces. "If that weren't evidence enough, your men's faces are full of guilt. So…you must have touched something on her."

They didn't have time to argue any further, the two of us broke apart from our hold on one another, and made sure that the remaining three wouldn't be able to maim or hurt any other unsuspecting people. With our weapons nowhere to be found, I sat there with a dinner knife hacking at their heads until they were no longer attached to their shoulders. "Rorin." Eveera says softly, her blood spattered hand pulling at my shoulder as I severed the final head. "Rorin." She says again. I look over my shoulder at her. My arms wrapping around her bare legs with my head resting carefully against her stomach, she sits back onto the edge of the table, a hand tentatively tangling into my matted curls. "I—" she shushes me, her fingers stroking as best they can through the knots. "It's not your fault." Her voice shakes a little. I lift my head gently to look at her but she's staring straight ahead.

Carefully I ask, "did they..." She shakes her head violently back and forth and my thumbs stroke circle onto her thighs. Her throat bobs as she swallowed thickly, the black edging into her eyes, and I can feel her pulling away. "I don't know." I stand up slowly, my hands careful not to touch any injuries or anything that might be sensitive.

"Better you don't know." I whisper. Her Wielded eyes snap up to me while her brow furrows. I tuck a strand of blood soaked hair behind her ear. "I can't kill them a second time. And if you knew and you told me, then I'd feel like their deaths weren't good enough. That they would have needed to suffer more. And I'm afraid with our injuries we don't have that kind of time." My lips tip up sadly.

She said it's not my fault, but I think that's the shock talking. I have a feeling I am at fault for a lot more than I know.

We walked in silence the whole way back to the city.

Eveera keeps her head down, staring at and spinning Gribly's ring finger between two of hers, eyeing the jewelry attached to the digit. I carry the men's heads in a makeshift sack over my shoulder,

The dark streets keep us hidden from any wandering or curious eyes as I pull us around to a set of stairs that descends down into the street itself. The stairs empty out into a narrow alley that has a single door at the end.

Knock knock knock!

I hear feet shuffling behind the soggy wooden door before the creak of the peephole opening enters our ears. A soft glow shines on us from the peephole in the center of the door before quickly disappearing. It doesn't take very long for the metal hinges to yawn open, revealing a stocky little man.

"Murph." I grumble. His peculiar eyes gleam at us as he shuffles out of our way and lets us in. Eveera takes her eyes off the severed souvenir so that she could glare at me.

"I have been stabbed, shot at, nearly drugged, actually drugged, and now kidnapped one too many times for my liking since arriving in your gods forsaken kingdom, princeling. And now you've brought me into the home of a troll man." Her barrage of words rattle around in my mind.

Our bodies are still supporting the others weight and her skin has now turned a grayish color as opposed to it's usual deep olive tone. *"No need for the verbal reminder of your plight saddled to me. I have it physically seared onto my arm."*

"Who is this troll man anyways." She asks, her tone filled with disdain.

"He has a name."

She scoffs at me and winces. *"Murph is hardly a name."*

The smaller man stops at his work table - it's a gnarled piece of wood that's seen better days sitting square in the middle of the back room. His stubby body waddles around, knocking on shelves, pulling down tonics, salves, and other unidentifiable liquids. I can feel the scrutinizing weight of Eveera's gaze flicking between the two of us.

Murph pats the table and before Eveera can argue I lift her up and set her down on it. "What in the bleeding *gods,* Rorin? I am not an invalid."

Laughter spills out of Murph, "the gods do no bleeding, Queen of Serpents." The cadence of his stumbling voice clutters his words against each other.

She looks at me incredulously, "it's an expression, *troll man.*"

Another roar of laughter floods the small workspace. "Is that what you were calling me to the Broken Prince?" His snicker continues while he grinds something down in his mortar and pestle. When neither of us respond, he looks up. "You thought I did not notice?" His hand gestures side to side with a finger pointing to Eveera's wrist. "You bring your bloodied selves here and thought I would not notice the Lady in the Black's handiwork on you?" He sighs, turning back to his mortar and pestle.

Eveera stares hard at me. *"Lady in the Black? He can't mean Marjorie."* I simply shake my head beats me what the old man is talking about. I only understand about half of what he says. Once finished with his grinding, he starts to work on her wounds. She grimaces at the bright light of his healing mist and the scent of the salve he whipped up.

Murph flits around the table, huffs of frustration coming from the both of them as the shirt tatters get in his way. "Oh fucking hell!" She exclaims loudly before stripping off the shirt's remains. My mouth drops open to object but her serpent tattoos slither quickly and cover her bare chest as best they can. Murph doesn't seem to take notice other than to breathe a quiet 'thank you' in her direction. He moves through each of her wounds - stabs, cuts, nicks, and arrow holes alike.

She asked him to leave the puffy scar from Gribly's first stab - a reminder of "the time she was almost bested." Which he begrudgingly agreed to before moving on to me. My wounds were significantly less extensive comparatively but it still took a few hours for him to finish both of us up.

He gave each of us a tonic to filter out any remaining traces of poison while we readied ourselves to head back to court. Eveera hands her cup back to Murph their small height difference giving her the advantage of actually looking down on him. "You said The Lady in Black. Explain, troll man."

His face splits into a large grin as he gingerly takes back the cup. "I like it, the name. Very good, Queen of Serpents. I do believe I have troll on my mother's side..." He begins rambling, Eveera gives me an annoyed side glance.

"Explain." She repeats.

His eyes glint with mischief at us as he piddles around his home, "you know where healers hail from, do you not?" He turns in a circle, dramatically gesturing around the room. "The Lady in Black...very clever, very smart, and very unforgiving." His gaze lands on me at the final remark prickling the hairs on the back of my neck.. "I'd ask our Golden Madame the remaining questions on your tongue. She knows better than I."

He shoos us out, the door locking in place behind our backs. We both look at each other, with more questions than answers waiting on our breath. *Golden Madame*, doesn't take a genius to know who he means. *My mother*. Which will bring nothing good.

We were about halfway back to court when I realized Eveera was still shirtless, some wounds on her were deeper than others and required wrapping, Murph's healing was still good but he was old school and his Wield out of traditional practice. "Do you want my- uh, do you want my shirt?" I ask? Tugging at the hem of the dirtied fabric.

"Why? Are you embarrassed?"

I fumble around for the right words, "no I just—" my eyes shamelessly drop to the curve of her breasts. Her serpent tattoos strategically placed. "Murph only gave you pants?" I ask, looking at the high waters she's currently donning.

"He did, said it was better to let the deeper wounds breathe with only the bandages on them currently. And you know what?" She stops in her tracks, pointing her finger into my chest. "I just almost died. *Again*. And while I like to court death I'm not sure I want to enter in a long term commitment yet. I'm sure your pride will survive my semi-nudity."

It's not my pride I am worried about surviving. I want to snap at her, but I don't have the energy tonight. Instead, I grab her elbow, ushering her into one of the old tunnel passageways. At one point it was meant for getting people out of the castle if needed, but for today it will help us get back in.

Thankfully the castle was dark and devoid of two much activity, allowing us to slip back in unnoticed or at least unrecognized. That was until we walked back into my room.

We were immediately accosted by our men and Millie. There was a mixture of relief, confusion, and anger across all their faces at the sight of us. Bennett and Will's eyes darting everywhere but towards us after noticing Eveera had nothing covering her upper half except for various bandages. She limps away from me towards the bedroom with Millie trailing after her.

"How many days?" I ask, breaking the silence.

"That's all you have to say?" Armond snarls at the same time Bennett answers, "three days."

I blow a long breath out. *Three days.*

No one said much while we waited on the women. With how long it was taking them I started to worry that something had happened, that Murph had messed something up until the door creaked open and she waltzed back in. She's cleaned up and dressed in a floor length black gown that catches in the light revealing a deep green and purple iridescence. On top of the fabric is a gold metal corset fitted around her waist and bust, if you look closer at it, you'll notice it's carved in the shape of her trademark serpents.

Her face is fresh and all of her dark hair has been wound into intricate braids that cascade down the curve of her spine. She's removed the bandages, bearing the deeper wounds.

Will sidles up next to me displeasure written all across his face. "You're drooling." There's blatant disgust in his tone, but it doesn't matter, I drink her in. Every agonizingly beautiful inch.

Even after torture, drugging, and no sleep - she is breathtaking. From the corner of my eye I can see Axel's effort to restrain himself from going to her. I know, because I had been exerting that same effort at the manor. She slinks over to my side, the sway of her hips jingling the metal corset. Her gold eyes darken to the color of honey when they meet mine. *I wonder if she listens in on my mind, if she can read every one of my emotions as well. If she can feel the same pull as I do, or if her hatred smothers it.* "We were gone..." I start to say, but she interrupts.

"Three days. I heard."

Will clears his throat, "we have things to talk about. Your disappearance has caused...issues. Not to mention what she said before you two ran off!" He's raising his voice.

"What no welcome home?" I taunt. I would've figured he'd be more upset something had happened to me. Will rolls his eyes, bringing a hand up to his forehead.

"You can't just usurp." Bennett says quietly. "Ror— do you really want to do that?" I sigh, scrubbing my hand down the stubble that's grown out over my jawline.

"Well, apparently, I don't have a choice. I made a deal."

"You made a deal you didn't *know* about! If you let her do whatever," Will flings his arms around wildly at her, "she has planned...then we are *past* treason at this point. I don't even know where we've landed. You're not just damning yourself Rorin - you're damning me, Bennett, and now Millie." He slumps down onto the couch his head between his knees. Millie goes to sit by him her face surprisingly neutral as she pats his shoulder.

My head hurts from the back and forth. *"You should've fucking told me this was your plan."* I snap at her through the seal.

I wanted just a moment's respite on our return, a chance to catch up on restful sleep.

"You were so desperate for help and whining about not being daddy's favorite, I didn't think you'd care." The way she says it makes me feel like I was an idiot to not see this coming.

"This is why you wanted to come to Valen. Why you were so okay to leave the military? Do I get to know why you want them dead?" The pieces sort of fall together but regardless the pit in my stomach grows.

She shrugs, picking at her clean nails. *"I'm tying up loose ends."*

"Loose ends? That's all I get?" I scream into her mind.

"They took something they shouldn't have." The words sink into my stomach.

"And after you take it back? What then?"

"What, you're not going to try and stop me?" She asks, a tone of surprise in her voice. But I ignore her question.

"Afterwards, Eveera. What then?"

"Afterwards, I go home." My heart twists at her words. *Fuck.* All of the mixed feelings over the past few days, over the past few *hours*. The brief moment after we'd killed our abductors where I thought we'd come to some sort of amicable companionship were all nothing to her.

She's going to put me on the throne…she's going to involve us all in regicide. *Oh bleeding gods… "Don't feel too badly princeling."* She purrs in my head. *"I was your leverage. Now, you're mine. Besides we're just playing a role. Remember?"* I've made a deal with the devil and signed it in my blood. I've killed for her now too, and what hurts the most isn't the subtle betrayal or manipulation, it's that when this is over she will go home and rid herself of me.

Here I'll be left, a king, forever infected with her.

EVEERA

Rorin's question plays over in my head again and again, *"and after that?"*, while I stand here with four heavy heads in a satchel and a finger tucked into one of my small pockets. The prince gives a nod to the soldiers standing guard at the door who are pretending to not notice the growing pool of oxidized blood by my feet.

The loud sound of the wooden hinges is deafening as the grand dining hall opens up. Our soldiers move in a formation in front of us so that they walk in first. Rorin, stands at my side, his brows drawn tightly together.

"Why are you making that face?"

He keeps his focus forward. *"Something is wrong."* Rorin pushes through our guards, signaling them to circle back around me quickly. Much to my shock, they listen, blocking me completely from view and unfortunately also from seeing. "Father." His voice is hard, laced with as much hatred as he can muster.

"They set us up." The words rush out of him quickly, I can feel the violence in his Wield grow as his control slips. I shove at the guard's backs

a few times, forcing them to part their barricade of bodies. Very slowly I move the few steps necessary to stand to the side of the prince.

On the left of King Eiser is a greasy, sickly pale man. There is an air of arrogance around the two of them that is stifling. The grimy male stands up, as if he were the host of the dinner, and widely opens his arms to greet us. "Well, you must be the Queen of the hour. No offense to Queen Mareese, of course. It's just that its not often our world truly gets to see the *Nightmare Queen.*" He laughs. The sound is grating, and there is a sneer in his voice as he calls me by the nickname.

"*Baelor.*" Rorin says into my mind. *So,* I think, *this is the tyrant of Hadar.*

"*We could kill them all now. It's a little lack luster in my opinion, but between the two of us...*" I tell him, my fingers curling around his and squeezing. I don't know why I do it, maybe to comfort him. Lately my hatred for the prince has been so...temperamental. But if nothing else, I can chalk it up to the game we're playing. The ruse in place that we are lovers. That explanation will have to be enough for now.

He subtly shakes his head, "*no. Not yet.*"

"*It takes care of both of our problems.*" I try my Wield coaxing his. Only a few eyes wander to the weight in my hand. When he doesn't answer I concede, "*have it your way.*"

I saunter up to my intended seat. By no coincidence I've been placed directly in front of Baelor and a young girl - she can't be older than Millie - as sickly and gaunt as the king next to her.

Thwump! I drop the sack of heads that lands centered between the two kings. The burlap opens slightly revealing their gaping mouths, glassy eyes, and the hack marks. Gasps ripple around the table and one lord retches. "I believe these belong to you." I say.

Baelor's laugh assaults my ears again. "And what made you come to that conclusion, Your Highness?"

"Hmph. If they're not yours, then they must be *his.*" My finger lazily points to King Eiser.

"That is a remarkable accusation!" The man, Birk, shrills.

Rorin's familiar scent and presence engulf me as he reaches under my chin to tilt my cheek up at him. His soft, warm lips press against it. "Excuse my beloved, she has a tendency for theatrics." He tilts his head at the table surveying the men we killed, "their heads were a bit difficult to remove with only dinner knives handy."

I've zoned out on everything else that came after the word 'beloved'.

The chairs scrape out from beneath the table as we take our seats. Rorin reaches underneath mine pulling me closer to him to then casually drape an arm across the chair back.

Mareese is stares at us in horror. "Have you nothing to say of her accusing your father for being responsible for the-these men?!"

"To that? No." He says and my gaze settles on his mouth, the blaze of that kiss burning still. "But, to the company you've invited to our table, I have a lot to say."

Eiser flags over a servant to clear the heads from the table. The poor thing gags and heaves the whole way as he does so. "Now now, son, inviting them here is all in the name of peace."

"Ha. *Peace.* Of course, how could I forget." He says the word 'peace' like it's something stuck to the bottom of his shoe.

"War has never won anyone anything, Rorin."

Disbelief crosses both of our faces. Coming from the man who refuses to witness the actual carnage his seat partner has caused to Vellaran citizens. "It seems to have won plenty for King Baelor here. The ruler of now three kingdoms, and the occupant of a fourth. War seems to agree with you."

"It will not win him Vellar. While you were off..." his hands wave around, gesturing at nothing in particular, "gallivanting and *killing*, we have been drawing up a treaty. A treaty that will serve us both without any more bloodshed." The two kings share a look that I zero in on. "But that is hardly dinner conversation. Dinner I am sure many of us are no longer hungry for."

I can feel the vibrations of Rorin impatiently tapping on my chair. My hand moves over - of it's own accord, *again* - and squeezes his leg lightly. My serpents slide down my arm to connect to him. As if they could absorb and tether his magic the same way they do mine to take the edge off.

My eyes snag on a glint of golden blonde hair. Millicent juts her chin at the girl in front of me. A pitiful thing. Hollowed cheeks and deep set eyes. The ruby curls cascading down her back are severe against the paleness of her skin. She's the shell of a girl. My magic feels for any indication of fear, but all I sense is a darkness that mirrors my own. Looking to Millie again, I can see her mouthing something. "Pru-el-la" her lips repeat the name a few times until it clicks, *Pruella...Baelor's only daughter. What a liability she must be.*

As if she senses my magic probing her, her eyes dart up and around. "Pruella, isn't it?"

"Yes, Your Highness."

"Oh now, none of that. You're a princess in your own right. Formalities are such a bore." Rorin's heavy presence weighs in my mind. I angle my face only slightly towards him. The arm behind me tenses but he doesn't send anything down the seal. "How do you feel about your father's tirade of mass genocide?"

Her back straightens a little. "I support my father's efforts to do what he deems best. He's a great King. One who has grand plans for our sister kingdoms."

Rorin and I share a look. "*Sister Kingdoms?* Is that what you're calling them?" The prince laughs in disbelief while she nods.

"Sounds like you are a devoted and obedient daughter, Princess. Your father is fortunate." Eiser praises her, the slight not going unnoticed by either of us. "Although! It would seem Queen Eveera was the most fortunate. No parents to disobey or disappoint."

Tap. Tap. Tap. "Mm. Yes. Being orphaned is so much better than pesty parental disappointment." Calloused fingers lace into my hair, moving in slowly circles on the base of my neck.

The king swirls his goblet one…two…three times before tipping the contents into his mouth. The resemblance is there between father and son but Rorin looks far more like his mother. A travesty really. "Enough of this. Peace is duly in order and what a better time with the Valen Celebration in less than three days." Applause and compliments round the table, praising the two kings for their amicable relationship. But I don't believe it, Rorin called it before we entered the room, they're setting us up. I can't help but smile to myself.

So many deceitful plots in place. So many games. It will be fun to see the fight. It will be better to be the victor.

RORIN

I opted for the comfort of my desk after the disastrous dinner with Baelor and my father. I've chosen that comfort for the past couple of nights in fact. Since coming home my sleep has been fitful. A torturous melody of Eveera's screams in that cell is on a constant loop in my mind followed by seeing my father mingling with the man I've single-handedly been trying to end for the past few years. Who's killed our people, good people of Vellar.

With each nightmare I wake up sweating and panting. Murder the first thought in my mind. The rage I felt seeing those men handling her, the things I have imagined that they might have done during our states of unconsciousness. The things they'd suggested they would do. If I hadn't cut off their heads, I would do it again for as little as a wrong look in her direction.

Tick tick tick.

The large clock's mechanisms clicking together become the metronome to my thoughts and I zone back in on the maps, payrolls, condolence letters, and missives piled on the wood. "Father, what game are you playing at..." None of these coordinates, or formations make any sense. Going back months in the paperwork, I see the same pattern. *We were pigs being led to slaughter.* But why? Why kill so many innocents, innocents of Vellaran blood and then break bread with Baelor?

The hour hand strikes forcefully. I sign the final condolence notice for tomorrow and stamp it to be sent tomorrow. I make quick work of the buttons on my shirt, stopping short in the doorway. Her small frame is spread haphazardly across the large bed. Limbs bent at awkward angles, the side of her nightgown riding up just under her curves, and her once neat braids are fraying where the curls refuse to be bound any longer.

One...two...three...four...

"She'd be pissed to find you doing that." The sudden intrusion of a voice behind me has me reaching for the dagger at my hip until I realize it's only Axel.

Snooping bastard.

"Shh. You'll wake her and then we'll all be paying for it." He scoffs quietly before walking about to the bed. He tucks a loose curl away from her face, straightening the blanket afterwards so that it covers her exposed leg. His closeness to her is irritating even if I understand it.

"You do that a lot I've noticed."

I peer up at him as I unlace my boots. "Do what? Piss her off?"

He chuckles, his voice much quieter now. "That too, but no. Watch her so closely. Someone who didn't know you might think you are ogling her chest."

"I am not ogling her chest."

"It's a nice chest." He teases looking for my reaction.

I give him a pointed glare, "*you* are not ogling her chest either."

He laughs, raising his hands in defense. "The way you watch her...well it certainly riles Ezra up." He backs away from the bed.

Prepared to end the conversation there, he's halfway out the door by the time I decide to give him an answer. "I count the rise and fall of it. Her chest that is. Reassures me she is still breathing."

A crease forms in his brow, "okay." The wheels turning in his mind are obvious as he tries to work out my reasoning past that.

I place my hand on the comforter, looking down at the sleeping queen who in this state doesn't look nearly as formidable as she does awake. My fingers, with a mind of their own, ghost over her cheek. "There have been one too many times now where I thought it would stop moving altogether. And it would be my fault."

"Wanting to avoid guilt?"

I don't dare look at him as the words tumble from my lips. "If she died? There wouldn't be a corner of this world I could hide from the guilt of that. It would be my undoing." The click of the door lets me know he's gone, with no more words needing to be spoken.

For the first time since the bathroom floor, I risk sleeping next to her before dawn. With the weight of me dipping the mattress down, I expect her to wake up. I'm more caught off guard when her arm and leg fuse around my middle. Nails digging into my bare side. A very rare moment of vulnerability from such a hardened individual. If she could see herself...a laugh bubbles in my chest. I imagine if she could see herself, I would be subjected to an onslaught of cursing and threats.

My hand wraps around her, cradling her head into me and a sigh slips. Conscious, Eveera may be able to claim she hates me, but this version of her now only feeds my hungry delusions. How perfectly her body molds to mine. The way the silk of her slip feels against my skin. I keep my hands chaste hoping to shut down waking up a different kind of beast. My free arm stretches to put out the sconces and at the movement, incoherent mumbles pour from her lips like syrup.

"Shh...we're pretending. Just sleep, beloved." The word comes out for the second time in the past two days. The first I could convince myself it was for the part only. The part we chose to play. The part we've persistently reminded the other of. But in all honesty, as I brush away a few stray curls and draw circles on her back's raised scars, I mean the word. But she wouldn't accept that, she'd stab us both in the heart before she allowed hers to feel for mine.

A cold chill spreads over me. My sleep addled hand reaches for the limbs that are no longer wrapped around my torso.

Smash! "*Fuck!*" My feet hit the floor, carrying me out of the room.

Eveera, tangled mess that she is, is bent over shattered glass. The scent of new bourbon fills my nostrils. My arms cross my chest as I watch her, flummoxed and frantic. *"Evidently sleeping with me has driven you to drink."* Her head snaps up to see me leaned against the doorway.

"Maybe I was just ridding you of your intolerable liquor."

"Ah. The spirit is intolerable but sleeping with me was okay." Her brows crease in annoyance as she goes back to fumbling with the broken pieces.

By the new look on her face she assumed I'd moved over in her direction to help clean up. It sours the moment she realizes I came only to retrieve a more aged bottle of my favorite drink. I take it with me and sit myself on the cool stone of the balcony that goes mostly unused. Why stare at and admire a city that only holds a morsel of kindness for me? The clinking of glass shards dissipates in the background. The queen takes a place by me with her knees tucked up under her chin. The short material of her dress falls, gathering at the hip.

Damned, bewitching woman.

My lips wrap around the bottle rim followed by the familiar burn as my eyes stay glued on that bunched fabric. "You're staring."

I raise my eyes to see her scowling. *Always perpetually pissed off.* "I'm admiring." I droll.

"Ad..miring..." I nod my head taking another drink. Her eyes follow the movement of the liquid trailing down my throat, making heat crawl up the back of my neck.

I smirk. "Feel it's only fair. Your limbs climbed me like a desperate animal when I got into bed. I might as well admire the owner of those limbs."

"Fuck you." She growls.

"When and where?" I suggest. Her eyes widen in alarm triggering an alcohol loosened laugh one that's deep and hearty. She shakes her head, looking at the ground as her shoulders start to shake. Her body rumbles with laughter, the sound rich and real. And that, *that* is a sound I want to hear all the way into my grave.

Eventually the laughter dies down. Heavy thoughts settling down between us. Baelor, the war at my doorstep, the war in my *home*. And maybe not for her, but for me there is a third war. One where my mind desperately doesn't want to feel for her but my heart knew I was fucked the moment we met. I swirl the bottle - now nearly empty - in my hands.

"You hate that they don't love you." Her words catch me off guard, searing me through.

"You love that they hate you." The sound of the liquor bottle dragging on the stone beneath me echoes between the two of us. I've had far too much alcohol and she has had far too little for this conversation.

From the corner of my eye I see her sad smile. "Yes." She whispers.

My finger drags along the rune on my wrist. "What if they didn't, hate you that is."

The smile on her face falls flat, replaced with mild irritation. "You don't get it. The things that others say, the fear that pours out of them when they see me. I *revel in it*. I made their fear of me tangible. The endorphins that rush through as they cower by my simple name. It makes me insatiable." She bites down on her lip. "I don't want to be anyone's hero. I *like* being their villain. It is not something that needs to be fixed about me. It is not something I am willing to change. My people know that, everyone else should too." There is confidence in that truth for herself. One that I find I envy. The citizens in this kingdom, save for my soldiers, made me to be a villain. A mistake. A scourge on their good name. I've always tried to make them feel differently. But hearing her words...

"Your people though, they love you. You may be someone's villain, but you aren't theirs. Not the way Baelor is to his."

Gold eyes pierce into mine. "They don't love me, *princeling*. They respect me, there is a difference, and that is a right Baelor has squandered by his ambition. His army has a keen ability to be calculated. But he himself lacks such a quality. He is a tyrant." Fingers slip into her braids, freeing them of their ties and pins, rich dark hair cascading down her back. "Those that raised me did not raise me to be a tyrant. But even still, I would much rather have my people's respect and fear than their love. With fear they don't risk betraying you. With love that is not a guarantee." The octave of her voice deepens with that last sentence.

She shifts uncomfortably on the stone, stretching out her legs and leaning back on her hands. The serpents inked to her skin have all coiled themselves around her neck and chest. As if they are snuggled in for sleep. Against my better judgement, I find myself changing my own position.

My head hits the silk of her slip. Nestling against her stomach so that if I stare up I will see just the underside of her chin. Eveera's whole body goes rigid at the change in our dynamic. Those golden orbs wary of the contact, I lazily smile up at her. Like our conversation is one of light instead of painful truths. Her muscles relax under the weight of my head and she returns her stare to the sky. *It's just the alcohol.* I remind myself.

"Tell me about them." It comes out unintentionally. A whisper of a thought.

"No." Her tone is harsh, but when she looks down at me her eyes are filled with defeat, and I know should she tell me about her parents she would be giving up control. Control of their memory.

"Tell me." I plead while raising my thumb to wipe away a traitorous tear of hers.

"Why?" She gasps. "Are we to start comparing battle scars? To start bonding?" The break in her voice fractures something inside of me. A renewed desire to go back in time and save her from this. Had it never happened there would be no scars for me to trace on her skin. There would be no look of contempt in her eyes.

My palm rests against her slick cheek. "She must have been otherworldly for the only way to cope with her loss was to punish yourself." I don't hide the anger in my voice as I admit *for* her that the scars littered all over her like patchwork are her therapy. I knew what I walked in on back in Bair wasn't a first time offense.

Her teeth suck that pouty bottom lip into her mouth. "She was. They both were. Loved by everyone. But most especially her. When she died we all felt the ground shift," Her eyebrows draw together in their usual fashion, "she believed in the Fates. Trusted them. They had made her softness a strength. But when my mother birthed me it was made clear to her that in this world, your softness would either make or destroy you. And that if I were to survive them, the *loss* of them, that I would have to be hardened." Rattled breaths sound under my ear. "I found her. You saw, you know. She knew too, she knew it would be me. With her clairvoyance there was no manner in which the people responsible for...*dissecting* her, had caught her off guard."

My arm winds around her waist, pressing us closer together. I can hardly look at her. There should be no reason that she allows me to touch her. But she doesn't push away. "Instead of drowning in her blood, I painted myself in it. I rose up to be exactly what she designed me to be." The pleasantness of our bodies wound together the way we had been in bed is in direct contrast with the words leaving her lips. "I survived her so that no one will survive me."

I see it so clearly. How the world will burn at her feet and I vow to myself there, that I will be the one to light the match.

I've not seen Eveera this morning. She left after her admission, leaving me to lie on the cold stone. Whatever warmth had been allowed to form between us must have been due to the alcohol.

Every moment I feel we get closer, that I have weaseled my way into that stony black heart of hers, she retreats and forces up another wall. It's maddening. And if I weren't humiliated enough, the new nightmare plaguing me has taken turns with a dream of her in that damned slip. The feel of it against my cheek, waking with an ache between my legs. Like a bloody teenager who's just learned about sex.

"Rorin." My name echoes distantly in the back of my mind. "Rorin." The voice says again. I blink the boredom from my eyes, and return to the company at present.

This morning has been the first my father has called on me since our return. As a part of my responsibilities for the Celebration, as my mother makes her final preparations, my father dragged me into this damned council meeting where I have to be subjected to listening to the insolent commentary by my father's Lords.

"Sorry?" My hands clasp in my lap. Trying to make myself look interested in what they have to say.

A collective sigh of frustration echoes throughout the room. "We were just saying, it might be prudent for you to attend this Valen Celebration...*alone*. Of course we understand your "friend", the young queen will be present but many other ladies will be too. You'll be in need of a wife here soon enough, it's time you started looking." Chancellor Finnigan states, his face twisted into disapproval.

"The Princess Pruella will also be in attendance. In the name of peace it may be prudent for you to show her some attention." Lord Birk's voice unsettles me on a good day. But at the suggestion of Pruella...well, a decent prince would have refrained from grimacing at the thought of dancing with anyone other than the queen who plagues his mind daily. But I am no decent prince.

My palms press tightly against each other. "As enticing that all sounds. I'll pass."

My father's eyes, for the first time in a long time, seem genuinely tired. A glimpse into that stony facade of his, perhaps. "A disappointment."

"Yes well, you've survived my many bouts of disappointment thus far. I'm sure you'll survive this one also." A series of disapproving glares are shot my way as my father continues droning on. My stomach sours at the thought of socializing with Baelor's offspring. There is a reason he has allowed them behind our walls. I think, while staring at his profile.

It's all too quick and cozy after what Hadar's Guards have done at the command of their king...to just be so chummy? It doesn't make sense.

A cold but welcome presence slips into my mind and I have to suppress a smile. Subtlety is certainly not her strongest suit and since she hasn't spoken, I'm curious to know what she is bouncing around in there for.

"*Your Highness...is there anything you're in need of?*" I ask.

"*From you, Princeling? There is nothing I need that you have.*" Mm. *Yes very convincing, Nightmare.* Her presence quiets, leaving me again, a slave to my own boredom.

There is a tingling numbness in both my ass and legs from sitting in this gods forsaken chair the past several hours. No words, or sense of feeling from Eveera since I spooked her earlier.

Snooping around in my mind isn't usually something she's explored doing - so, I've come up with three potential reasons why she may have opened the seal. One, she is uncomfortable and sought me out to distract herself from court. But being that her existence in Vellar is at my request and therefore I am the root source of her discomfort, that wouldn't make sense. Two, she truly did need something from me and I scared and embarrassed her. Or three, she was simply being nosy. I would place all my money on the third one.

Lord Birk scowls at me as he leans in to whisper something into my father's ear before leaving the two of us alone. My father waits until the room is fully cleared to address me. His voice thick with disdain when he does.

"You could have acted more interested in today's meeting, Rorin. You will be king of this council one day."

Not if you have anything to do about it. I think to myself.

"Ah, why start feigning devotion and obedience now, father? The council wouldn't know what to do with themselves. I'd be subjected to healers for fear the royal Prince Rorin had gone mad." I halfheartedly joke.

"They already think you're mad, son, bringing Obsids to this court."

I tilt my head at him. "And what of you? Bringing in King Baelor and his spawn? After everything he set Hadar's Guards to do. After what they are STILL DOING?! You can sneer all you want at my disobedience and for bringing in Queen Eveera, but I brought her as an aide to our kingdom. Because no matter what pathetic peace treaties you have drawn, the one thing that man does not know how to do is *peace*. Look at Peverell, Mellant, and Evendell. DO THEY LOOK PEACEFUL TO YOU?!" My hands slam down at the table, mists circling around them. I *want* to Wield. To subject my father to one of the many lessons, he subject me to but—

You can't. My conscience whispers.

"Fuck her if you want, son. Get out all your twisted fantasies if that is what it takes to rid them of my kingdom." His stark blue eyes pierce into mine.

I give him a tight, saccharine smile. "Who knows father, maybe by the end of all this you will be rid of me, too." The magic drags back into my body slowly. I have to coax it back into the that tiny mental box I usually stuff it away in.

I left the discussion at that. I didn't stick around to hear his, what I am sure was a biting, retort. The pressure of this day has already been enough and arguing with him is just wasted time.

EVEERA

"*Tell me about them.*" *Damn him for asking. Damn yourself for telling the man you should hate.*

I wish so desperately that while I tried to nose around in his mind - before he interrupted me - that I would uncover some betrayal or deceit to our deal. That he was aware of the truth of what happened to them and was baiting me, leading me into a false sense of security.

Last night was so disorienting. The personal intimacy of it, the positions we sat in. He is always finding a way to touch me. He constantly touches me.

And you let him. The voice inside pesters. I'm lingering on the little things like the weight of his head in my lap, the cadence of his voice, the circles he strokes on my skin. Heat crawls up neck, flushing my cheeks...

"OW!" The feeling of a needle pricking my side has me returning to the present. The seamstress Millicent dragged me to - at the most ungodsly hour - waves me off.

"You've gone stiff as a board. How am I supposed to work with this fabric on you? Hmm?" Millie giggles at the chastisement and I shoot her a glare.

She's being fitted for a ridiculous golden headpiece by the seamstress's apprentice. Metal juts off of her head in an effort to mimic sun rays. "The queen picked it herself!" The younger seamstress squeals while fastening it to Millie's hair.

Millie sighs, a pleasant smile pasted on her lips. "She always does, Rosette." Her tone is soft with the young girl. If that's true, I've no doubt the fabric of my dress will either be tampered with or so heinous I won't dare be seen in it.

"The queen is always so generous with her requests for the celebration. It's our biggest event of the year!" The girl looks to me her excitement overflowing as she chatters on. The seamstress dressing me nods only in agreement, her old and withered eyes looking up at me. "Except you." She says flippantly, pursing her lips.

"What do you mean?" I ask.

"Magdha." Millicent hisses cutting off whatever the old woman was poised to say next. Instead she pats my hips and stands herself up to let her eyes roam over me. She pushes and spins me around to get a full look. "This will be enough. Rosette will find you accessories and your dresses will be in your rooms by dusk."

The ladies rush us out of their modiste with a few thanks and kisses to their cheeks from Millicent. I'm mildly curious as to where or what the next godsforsaken task this day require will be.

To my surprise, when we get back to the castle, it's not another errand she drops me off at but the door to my men's rooms. "You have two hours before you're needed back in Rorin's rooms." She states, her tone of voice letting me know that this is a command not a suggestion.

I shrug her off turning right around to their door, not bothering to knock. When I walk in I find Axel, Max, and Orem strewn across the furniture sleeping.

I crouch down by Axel's ear and whisper into it. His eyes snap open at my voice, "Gods above, Evie!" He does a double take of me wiping the sleep from his eyes before reaching for a pillow to chuck Max.

Thwack! "FUCKING HELLS, brother!" Max yells rubbing his head where the pillow made contact.

"You didn't have to wake them." I mutter.

Axel side eyes me. "If I have to be woken up by your sunny disposition, so do they. GET UP ASSHOLES!" Orem and Max both grumble at him, throwing obscene hand gestures our way.

"I have two hours. Anyone want to blow off some steam?" The three of them jump up, scrambling to grab their weapons and follow after me. "Aren't you supposed to be getting all dolled up or something?" Orem asks. Axel passes him up giving him a slap upside the head. "It was just a question!" He argues. "Do you want to ask questions or go stab a few things?" Axel counters. He dips his head down in submission, the four of us walking down to the training area. The room only had a few foot soldiers and guards occupying it, stares drifting to us before quickly averting away when we enter making fast work creating space for us on the floor.

The four of us form a square; Axel facing Max and Orem facing me. The younger Abrams brother gives me a wink before fading into a black cloud and disappearing from our view.

"Oh no fair." Axel whines, "we're using Wields?"

CLANG! With an arc of Max's sword, he brings it down hard on a distracted Axel's blade. "Don't act like you don't have any, Mecham." The taunt was said in jest but it was too late.

SCRAAAPPPPEEE! He drags his sword's blade against the edge of Max's before spinning on his toe and aiming for the knees. A move Max barely blocks. "Come onnnn, Mecham. It was only a joke."

"Tuah." Spit lands at Max's feet. "A shitty one, Abrams."

The two go round and round, meeting steel every time. Toeing the line of landing a blow. Electricity crackles around the hilt and pommel of Max's sword as he goads Axel. Meanwhile why they spar, I wait like a sitting duck listening for the whistling sound of Orem's magic.

My fingers tighten on the hilt of my sword. *Swoosh. Swoosh.* The weight of it swinging like a pendulum in my palm. "Come out. Come out, little Abrams. You can't hide in the dark forever. That's my favorite place to play, dear." A blur of red crosses my peripheral. I bring my sword up, angling behind me just a little and swing. *CLANK!* The impact sends pain up my wrists reminding me why I've always preferred daggers or stars to swords. They're light and quick to make their marks in comparison.

He vanishes again and within seconds, I am yanked into Oblivion my hair wrapped tightly around Orem's hand. His blade positioned at my collarbone. "You...*ugh!* Fight dirty, little Abrams." His palms are sweaty causing his hold to give a little.

All around us, darkness clouds. Only the wink of stars to illuminate wherever it is he's brought us. Orem's magic while similar to Armond's Void magic. It's uses are much more expansive and a lot less precise. Absorbing any who cross their wrath into Oblivion. Whether you go in or out, seen or heard, is at the command of the one Wielding it.

His voice echoes all around us. "I thought you liked the dark, Majesty." With his grip loosening on my hair and the weight of his sword dragging his hand down I seize my opportunity. My hand lands smack in the center of his face. Causing him to yelp, letting go of me completely. I pull all of my magic forward. My tendrils sweeping out of me, they slither and search for their mark. I plunge into his mind, breaking through every mental wall and barrier.

Images of his parents, of Max, of Millicent - *interesting* - surface. His fears becoming palpable and malleable.

Just as I bring the first of his fears to light, taunting and twisting it to reality, he lets out a guttural scream. His shadows unravel from the inside out and we both tumble to the ground, swords clattering beside us.

I keep a few tendrils wrapped around him as I pin him to the floor. "Do you yield?" Orem sucks his lip between his teeth as he fights to switch our positions. "Does it..look..like I fucking..yield?" He bites.

I drag my finger down his jaw. "Tsk tsk tsk. Such foul language from such a young, pretty face." He squirms underneath me. "Call it, Mecham!" I shout over my shoulder.

"She wins, brother."

Orem's face screws up in contempt and he shoves me off of him. A finger jabbing into my face. "You cheat."

I stick my tongue out, "you Wielded first. Sore loser." He helps me up anyways, flicking my ear before walking away to his brother. The other soldiers in the room stare at us, too stunned to speak at the spars they witnessed. Over their heads and in the shadowed corner stands Ezra, watching and by the looks of it waiting for me. I dust myself off and pass the weapons to Axel.

When I walk over to the corner where Ezra stands, he doesn't say anything at first. We lean against the wall watching the three others go again quietly for awhile until Ezra turns on his heel, a subtle command in his departure. *Follow me.*

He holds the door open for me into their apartment and then again into his bedroom. He shucks off his armor next to the bed resting on the edge of it. The gold velvet duvet looks worn, half crumpled across the unmade bed that has no posts to frame it. The room is in complete disarray, something so contradictory to his personality. The simple walnut wardrobe in the corner has clothes pulled out and hanging off the hangers. The narrow desk that's pushed against the wall under the window has his papers and correspondence all. strewn across it.

I mover quietly over to the desk and sift through the papers,

"Any updates I should be caught up on?" If there is one thing I trust he and Armond to do, it is to correspond with Felix and the general on my behalf. But that doesn't mean I don't want to know what exactly the correspondence is about.

"Uh." He stands up coming up beside me. "Well, Vada's still missing. But they're uh they're working on cleaning up the cities that were taken over." His voice is gravelly and tight and his fingers drag on the wood, curling around the papers and wrinkling them in the process.

My hand raises to his shoulder, "Ezra..."

"I don't get it." The pain in his voice is nothing compared to the rawness in his eyes as he turns to look at me. "How can you stand to be near him. How can you stand to touch him, to sleep near him, to call him the things you do in front of everyone?"

I stand there searching for the words to say. "Because I have to. To get close to his parents—"

"OH BULLSHIT EVEERA!" He shouts grabbing my shoulders and shaking me. "This isn't about his parents?! Maybe it was once but not now. No, you're in this for yourself too."

My mouth drops, not liking the feeling that takes hold as his words settle in. "I-I'm not!"

His lips press into a firm line. "You are. Five years, E. You think I don't *see*? That I don't watch? I'm your head guard. It's my whole purpose; watching you. And the way you look at each other? It's not hate." His laughter was cruel. "But it never was for him. And now....with you..." His face turns in disgust before his eyes drop to my lips. And much to my shock in the next second his lips slam down onto mine. Hard and bruising. Nothing sweet, nothing like his usual behavior. It's frantic and rushed.

"Ezra." I say in between kisses. Both my hands coming up to push on his shoulders. "Ezra, no. No." He doesn't relent on his pressure at all. My nails are clawing at his tunic, clawing at *him,* but it only makes him squeeze me tighter his hips pushing me up against something hard.

He breaks away to trail his rough kisses down my neck then back up to my mouth. "Five." *Gasp.* "Years." He pants, his tongue spearing into my mouth is an unwelcome intrusion.

I pull my head back trying to catch my breath, "Ezra, let go of me." I try again, turning my head so that he can't kiss me again.

Let go of you, or let go of your heart? The voice in my head taunts. His hair has come undone falling around his face as his forehead meets the crook of my neck. The hard thing he pushed me up against turns out to be his desk, the two of us awkwardly leaning on it.

"I love you..." he says, voice cracking. The edge of brokenness to it twists in my gut. I thought it would be disgust but this feels more like pity. Pity and guilt.

"Let go, Ezra." It's all I can muster out and that's all it takes. To break the spell winding around his grief as he leaps off me like he's just touched hot coals. Casting his eyes away from me again.

I slip quickly out of his room swiping my lips with the back of my hand. The motion taking with it whatever residue of Ezra's kiss was left.

Armond's lounging by the hearth and shame heats my cheeks. "I really don't want to hear it."

"Are you hurt?" He asks.

"What? No. No..I'm not."

He nods. "You're needed to get ready." "Oh-kay." I mouth and rush out of the room my heart racing all the way back to The Glass Hall.

When I walk through Rorin's doors the room is buzzing with commotion. Ladies maids, servants, and footmen are all flurrying around. "There you are!" Millie shouts from the doorway to the bedroom. "I said two hours Eveera! Where were yo—" her eyes drop to my lips that are still burning from Ezra's kiss.

"I am well aware of the time restraint you put on me." The dazed look in her eye is shaken off as she drags me to the vanity. Her small hands push me down onto the velvet bench with enough force to knock me off balance. She says something to the ladies maid in the bedroom who leaves and returns with brushes, pins, and a small box. Feeling content with the spread in front of me, Millie lets her get me ready. The ladies maid doesn't make eye contact. Her hands shaking a little bit as she makes quick work of plaiting and pinning my hair. I watch as the pieces of dark hair are wound and twisted into their spots. She tentatively reaches over my shoulder and slides a small box in front of me. The leather of it is soft under my fingertips and when I lift the lid a slim gold crown comes into view with black diamonds woven around each spire, like vines.

The girl's eyes widen as she takes in the gorgeous piece. Her nimble fingers reaching for it and with a few camouflaged pins the crown is secured in place. Millie peeks into the bedroom with that ridiculous headpiece on top of her head. The gown she has on however is a beautiful pale blue, her sharp collar bone is exposed by the off-the-shoulder sleeves that billow down her arms. The bodice to it is sheer around her midsection and flows out into a long train. "Don't say it. I know I look great. But you, you look half finished."

I roll my eyes, "I *am* half finished."

"Right, well, if you hadn't been off doing gods know what for more than the two hours I gave you, we wouldn't be in such a rush." She pushes me in front of a long mirror, barking at servants to do this and that.

The dress they have me step into is a deep plum, it's gossamer material hugging the curves of my body perfectly. They fasten a gold choker around my neck; a snake to match the pins in my hair.

I feel a tap on my calf and find the girl staring up at me, a gold shoe in her hand. I lift my foot enough for her to secure the shoe and lace the ties up. As a finishing touch Millicent hands me my mask for the evening. "You people don't honestly think this will disguise anyone, do you?"

Her mouth turns down into a frown, "that's not the point. Now put it on. We're already late."

EVEERA

The ballroom is blinding. It's filled with masked patrons and decor ranging in various shades of dawn and gold.

The dark hue of my dress is a stark contrast to everything and everyone around me. I look like an ink blot on a fresh piece of paper.

At the center of all of it is the royal family. Mareese's gown is various shades of orange; layers of silk draping down her thin frame, similar to petals. Eiser's wearing an equally gaudy outfit in the colors navy and gold; the two of them stand waving and greeting their guests with tight smiles on their faces.

Meanwhile their son, Rorin, is spread out on his throne. His hair is tousled, the crown on his head the only thing taming his brown curls. The golden doublet he's wearing is undone revealing a billowy white undershirt that has the barest little bit of his chest showing.

He is the picture of disorder and chaos next to his parents.

Their stares switch over to where I am as the crowd parts for me to approach them. *"I'm not in the right color."* I whisper down the seal.

"Mm. Vellaran colors wash you out." Rorin replies while his gaze drags down my body slowly, drinking me in.

"I don't think it's really your business to pay attention to what colors wash me out." I chide.

He smirks, resting his chin in his hand. "I think it was when I was choosing the dress that's on your body." Of course he chose the dress. When I get to the bottom of the dais Rorin hops up from his seat, extending out his hand. Gingerly I slip mine into it and he brings my knuckles up to his lips brushing them against the soft skin there. He then tugs on my arm, bringing me side to side with him on the steps, leaning in his breath is warm against my ear, "play along." We walk up the rest of the stairs until I am standing level with his parents. His rough hands move up to my shoulders and he gently sits me down into the seat of his throne. Mareese releases a choked sound as she watches him do it.

Rorin winks and then sinks to a knee in front of me.

"Oh bleeding gods." Mareese snaps.

One of his hands slips underneath my skirts and wraps around my calf, his long fingers moving quickly to undo and redo the laces of my heel. "Just fixing the Queen's shoe." He announces, winking at me again. Damn my stomach if it didn't drop a little. He stands back to his full height, straightening his clothes to take up a spot next to me. A possessive hand cupping my shoulder and collarbone as we notice Baelor and his daughter approaching us.

"Thought we almost had a proposal there, prince. What a shock that would have been. Pruella would have been crestfallen." My lips thin at the disturbing image of Rorin with Pruella and I reach my hand up to lace my fingers through his. "Giving out thrones there as well, I see." Baelor's proclaims stepping up to shake Eiser's hand.

"A royal deserves a throne at a celebration." Rorin quips and Baelor's beady eyes spark.

"Well, by that notion my daughter and I would be in need of one too." His lips curling into a devious grin.

Rorin huffs out a strained laugh, "yes well, maybe if you weren't waging a war against us, I would. Now if you'll excuse us, it's getting a little crowded up here." He snaps, pulling me up, and leading us down away from the other royals. The barest amount of magic is trickling between his fingers as he reaches back for my hand.

I look up at him, *"What was all of that?"*

His face is stoic as he moves us through the fray. *"We're playing a part, remember? Have to make it convincing."*

Things returned to normal quickly enough after Rorin and I stopped making such a spectacle of ourselves. The celebration melting away into all of its expected finery and debauchery. Performers, court jesters, and enough food to probably feed both the war fronts for weeks. The look on his face is all I need to know that seeing all of this wealth being flaunted about haunts him.

I finally spot our companions huddled tightly in a booth with one another. My men opted to skip the masks it would seem and because of that Millicent looks like an absurd decoration next to them. Bennett too, with his pale green outfit and mask of vines. He and Axel are laughing about something while Millicent's placed herself on Orem's knee. Mousy, Armond, and Ezra are the only three missing from the group, but I can't say I'm surprised. My stomach dips at the thought of the latter, the taste of him still sour on my tongue threatens to turn it.

Rorin grabs two drinks from a server, passing me one of them. He smirks before tipping the glass to his lips, swallowing the shimmering orange drink. I do the same and grimace. "It looks good on you." He notes gesturing a hand up and down the length of me. "The dress."

"Did you expect me to look anything but good? Ever?"

He shakes his head laughing, "no, of course not."

I make the same gesture at his clothes that he did to mine. "You don't look...awful."

His brow raises. "Mm. It's the mask, isn't it?"

"It helps." I say. His face breaks into a wide grin and I have to hide my own behind the lip of my glass.

While watching the crowd we both notice a guard flagging down Rorin. The guard's head jerks towards where an anxious looking Mousy waits. "Great. I'm sorry, Eveera. It would appear there's Will needs help handling."

"I'll come with." I state.

His eyes are apologetic. "Stay. I'm sure it's nothing but petty noble issues. Go and sit with the rest of our group, try and have fun with Millicent, I promise I'll be back quickly." I nod, setting my drink down on passing server's tray.

"I can keep her company, prince." We both turn our heads at the intrusion of Baelor's voice which has Rorin quickly shooting an arm out to push me behind him.

"I'll handle him." I say through the seal. Rorin looks over his shoulder his mouth open to object, but the guard from the doorway has no walked over here, urging Rorin to follow him. He looks guiltily between myself and the guard.

He turns around and pulls me into his chest, letting a kiss settle on the top of my hair. *"Playing a part, remember?"* He reminds as the tenderness of the kiss spreads through me. He reluctantly lets me go, and when he does a cold hand quickly replaces his touch, wrapping around my wrist, directly over the rune.

"A dance shall we, Your Highness?"

"Sure. I'll just need to melt my skin off where you touched it later." I say off handedly to Rorin.

Baelor leads me out onto the floor, we stand uncomfortably close as he spins me into the steps of a waltz. "You certainly *were* a surprise for me to happen upon. In Vellar of all places."

I give him a strained smile, my teeth clenching tight. "You're right. I'm typically happened upon underneath beds or in closets."

His eyes light, "ahh yes. The Queen of Nightmares. How could I forget? Your magic is *legendary*." The serpents on my back slither in response to the way he references my Wield.

"I imagine all magic is quite fascinating for you. Considering you have none of your own. Though I guess you've acquired quite the variety of Wielders with your occupation of Evendell. Nature magic is a unique force, to be sure. You control nature, you control the battle fields, the crops, the water supply. Funny how that is." Baelor's fingers twitch against me in irritation, but his smile remains on his lips. It dawned on me after fighting them in Bair and after see the almost desolate farms fields. Yes, armies drain resources but the rate at which they were depleting? It wasn't adding up - not for petty skirmishes. But if nature Wielders were tainting the land...the pieces of the puzzle fell together much quicker with that explanation. "You may think you have them here, with your peace treaties, and your niceties. But you do not fool me, King Baelor. My power isn't meant to be used only on the offensive. And I am not afraid of Wielding. You don't become the boogeyman without a certain repertoire."

His lips turn down in a frown. Deep lines shadowing his already gaunt and sickly pallor. "Power is not just in the ley lines, Queen Eveera. It is in the devotion of men too. You'd do well to remember that."

"It's a good thing I have both then, isn't it?" I warn as the music dies down the two of us separating from one another with a curt bow.

After Baelor slipped back into whatever hell hole he came from I decided to take up space in a shadowed balcony and wait for Rorin to come back. The celebration has gone on in all its grandeur in the meantime and my higher vantage point has given me the ability to overlook the whole of it. Down below me I can see everything and everyone. I lean forward on the railing watching the people come and go, my men are still in the same booth minus Millicent and Bennett. She's off talking with a few other ladies and Bennett must have gone and joined with Rorin and Mousy.

In the far right corner I see the bright red hair of Pruella, she's surrounded awkwardly by her guards. As if she sensed my stare, the young princess looks up into my corner, our eyes meeting from across the room. I narrow mine at her, debating on whether it would be easy to enter her mind and figure her out. It would be stupid of me to try to Wield on her in such a public setting. Especially when the people in this room save for two or three are not favored to me and by some sick twist of fate and ideals, I have a feeling they would be much quicker to defend her than defend me.

My focus drifts away from the princess and I's staring contest when I feel the all too familiar presence of him at my back. How he got up here so quickly, or how he found me draped in shadows is a wonder to me.

I grip the edge of the balcony breaking eye contact with her and staring down at all those dancing, at the king and queen staring over the court, the all too casual behavior with Baelor amongst them. Behaving like they're old friends or comrades.

His voice is low. "You're hiding." With how often he leans in to talk to me, or how frequent I feel his warm breath on my skin, I wouldn't expect to have goosebumps rise on my flesh at it every time.

Whoooosh. My breath leaves me in one long exhale, I can feel his gaze drop to where my chest is rising and falling. I noticed awhile ago that he tends to count the motion though he hasn't deigned to give me an explanation. Not that I've asked however.

"I'm not hiding. I was bored."

"Mmm. Next time you attend, I'll petition that they add a flogging or maybe a hanging?" His chest presses up against me and the rumbling of his quiet laughter vibrates across my back. I can feel the pads of his cool fingers brush a few rogue strands from my neck. The featherlight touch has me fighting every muscle in my body that wants to lean into him.

There's no one to watch you now. No part to play. Remember. You. Hate. Him. I repeat in my mind, the walls closed tight to the seal so he doesn't hear me needing to convince myself. "It's stifling. The air of normalcy with your enemy standing in the room."

If even possible his voice seems to get deeper. More sultry. "Ah. Well see, technically I have two enemies standing in the room with me. One dangerously close at the moment." He mutters against my hair, the proximity between us is serving only to prove that with each day the hard lines of our partnership seem to blur more.

"I'll remedy that." I say, pushing off the railing and pulling myself away from his nearness. I'm hoping the distance created will give me a moment to clear him from my senses.

It doesn't, and the distance is short lived.

Rorin's hand meets my wrist and whips me around so that he has me caged me against the alcove wall. The two of us are now completely shrouded in shadows, away from anyone who might decide to look up into the balcony. "Eveera." I struggle to keep my gaze cast down and sever any further progression of the two of us but it's too late. He *knows* me.

His finger hooks under my chin. "Give me those eyes, Nightmare."

Reluctantly, I look up, a war of emotions raging inside of me. His frustration mirrors my own and I see now that I am not the only one fighting this war. That I'm not alone in fighting to not lose control, to not give in. But day by day, from the moment we met, we never stood a chance at winning that war. Our chests are pressed together, both heaving in breaths. Our position is precarious against the stone.

Those molten hazel eyes drop to my lips and then my throat and before I realize what's happening he presses his lips against my pulse and lingers there. I shift one of my hands off the cold wall and lay it on his chest. My intent *was* to push him away, to rebuild the walls between us…that was the intent at least…

The tension melts from his body the moment my hand touches him back and he melts into me. His right hand comes down from above my head to grip the nape of my neck while he dips mouth to my throat again, leaving a trail of hot kisses up the column of it. I can't help the gasp that slips out as I feel the flick of his tongue back and forth against my pulse. He groans at the noise I made, his hand flexing while latching harder onto my skin.

"*What would it take to hear that again?*" The velvet of his voice trickles down the seal into my mind. His hand abandons the grip on the back of my neck, dropping down to toy with the slit in my dress. Rough fingertips graze against my bare thigh. His lips find the place behind my ear that when he nips at it causes my knees to buckle. "You're intoxicating, Nightmare." My palm is still frozen, trapped between us. The only things leaving me are sighs that should be protests but instead are only more encouragement. My left hand at some point made its way underneath his doublet and is wrinkling the loose fabric of his shirt.

A kiss presses in at my temple and Rorin lets out a dark laugh, "oh but you hate me." The tone of his voice is solemn, desperate. "*Fuck.* You hate me."

I stay rooted in my spot, I don't breathe, I don't speak. He looks at me and I can feel my face wanting to crumple at the plea in those eyes. I'm fighting the urge, with every scrap of self-resolve I have, to not throw myself at him. To not kiss him until our lips are numb and our clothes are a wadded and torn up mess on the floor. He brings both hands away from my body to cup my face, drawing our foreheads together. "I have to hear you say it, beloved. I *need* to hear you say it." He pleads, his voice almost inaudible.

Beloved. The word rings through my mind as blood rushes into my ears. *Beloved.* It's not the first time he's used this endearment but, this time, it feels real. It doesn't feel like we are playing a part anymore. "Say what?" I choke out.

He pulls back, thumb stroking my cheek. "I need to hear you tell me you hate me. Just like all those times before, I need you to tell me now. Because if you don't, I'll assume you're feeling all the things I am right at this moment and take that as my invitation. Because if you don't, I won't be able to stop. Won't be able to stop kissing you or *needing you*. I won't be able to erase the feel of your skin underneath my fingers. Hell, I may never be able to do that last one regardless." He's breathing heavily, his words all rushing together. "Have mercy on me, Nightmare. Just this once, have mercy...tell me you hate me."

He's begging me. The taunt I made all those weeks ago, about liking the idea of him begging me for something, never did I think he would be begging for this. For the three words that I've been chanting in my head as a reminder for my stupid, feeble heart.

The palm I have resting on his chest slides up slowly to lay against his neck. "I hate you." I whisper.

And I don't mean a damn word of it.

His touch falls so quickly from my face, taking rapid steps back from me. He nods, rubbing rubbing his jaw and pressing his tongue into his cheek. *"A-hem.* Thank you." Rorin turns quickly on his heel and every step he takes further away from me feels worse than the whips I've used across my skin.

You were supposed to hate him...

The words drift into my mind. A painful reminder.

I know I was...

RORIN

"DAMMIT!" I curse. I've never walked faster in my life back to my rooms than I do while leaving her in that alcove. I came this close. This. Close. To giving into everything I've been craving for weeks.

The goal when I sought her out was simple; ask permission, get denied, go against the denial, convince the queen of horrors herself to join our cause, win our cause, send the queen home.

Nowhere in there did falling in love with her become a part of the plan.

How foolish I am. Not just for loving her, but also for loving her despite knowing she will never allow herself to reciprocate it. It's maddening, everything about her. Her voice, her laugh, her scent, her salacious smile. She's bewitching, and she knows it.

Master manipulator. My conscience reminds me.

I guess one has to be when her magic is just that - manipulation. And I played willingly right into her hand. Lapping from her palm like a starved dog.

Will had me pulled aside to deal with one of the lord's - Lord Bergery - hysterical tantrums about the pompous Lord Birk. His father had been attempting to tame the explosive, so that he wouldn't have to bother my father. My father who was too busy kissing the ass of King Baelor and his daughter instead of paying attention when his own lords get out of hand.

The worst part about it wasn't even the obnoxious, over-indulgent bastards arguing — it was the fact that I had to leave Eveera vulnerable. When I saw her hiding up in the balcony I went up there to push her on her conversation with Baelor, not get distracted by her leaning on the railing, overlooking everyone with the same scrutiny she met me with in her throne room.

And because I couldn't help myself against her, I am now in my room - hiding. But even in here, she's infected everything. My wardrobes are filled with her things next to my things. My bathroom has her things in it, my bed *smells* like her - that rich mix of spice and flowers. Even my liquor. *Gone* - because of her. And so here I am pacing and obsessing over her, wishing that while the Celebration has hours yet to go that we were tangled up in the sheets of my bed. Begs and please falling off of her lips for a change.

"I hate you." Those three words. I knew she'd say them if I asked. But bleeding fucking gods if I didn't wish she could have proved me wrong. The sound of the outer doors flinging open startles me, I step out of my bedroom and run straight into Armond his armor colliding with my bare chest. "*Oof!* Can I help you?" I bark. His face is grim. The creases in his forehead prominent with his frown.

"I need to speak with you. Or rather - Felix does."

"Can it wait?" *Felix?* "Felix isn't here."

"Actually...he is. And as much as I wish it could—"

"It cannot wait." Felix says, stepping out from the hall and into my room.

"Prince," Felix starts.

"When and how the hell did you get here?" I ask, stunned to see the man here in front of me.

"We had er-have some concerns..." The door flies open *again*, now startling the three of us as Will and Bennett burst in.

"Who's this guy?" Bennett asks who gives Felix a wary look. I wave him off, gesturing for Felix to continue. I can answer Ben's questions later.

"Well, with our men already at your post in Bair it wasn't difficult to gain permission to portal there. From there I traveled by horse. You must know we wouldn't let our queen into Vellar without a few ways to get to her." *I honestly hadn't thought of it. But, I should've figured as much.* I think to myself. "There's been talk through the rumor mill of Baelor's welcomed presence here in your court. With how urgent you seemed to be about wanting to end this war with him, wanting to end him, I was shocked. Concerned you'd gone back on the fine print of your contract and were no putting Eveera in mortal danger."

Goosebumps raise on my flesh at the utterance of her name. "*I* did not welcome him anywhere. That was my father's doing." I gripe.

"Regardless. What do you know of the peace treaty your father and Baelor have drafted?"

"We know nothing." Will speaks up. Felix sighs and dread pools in my stomach as I piece together where I think he is going with this, and I kick myself mentally for not coming to that conclusion sooner.

"You think they're scheming, don't you." I say.

His lips flatten into a thin line. "It is a concern...we need to get Eveera out of here."

Bennett pushes off the hearth, walking up to me. His hand wrapping around my shoulder, "what do you mean? If you take her what will have to stand against Hadar's Guards?"

"If King Eiser has drafted any kind of alliance with Baelor, than the presumed threat is neutralized. Even if you don't like whatever those agreements are. Either way, it will dissolve the terms of *our* agreement. She must come home."

"Hold on a second, you two are just resigned to the fact that our sovereigns are really playing two sides here? What if the deal made with Baelor isn't a dangerous one? What if it really is a peace treaty?" Will asks desperately.

"Look at what he did to Ror growing up. You really think he isn't capable of concocting a scheme against Rorin? The man may not be willing to get his hands dirty but he's damn well not afraid to make someone else do it for him. Think about it - Rorin is general of his army, but won't let him actually plan anything. Instead he's been purposefully giving us shit battle plans." Bennett steps towards our friend. "We know you have your honor, and that's great, brother. But this is war and we've been at it far too long. I wouldn't put it past Eiser to decide that it's better to join up with Baelor than to lose control completely. And that's not peace for anyone other than himself."

Will doesn't say anything. His frustration is apparent with the moral battle in his head waging strong. The guilt is there too, for not being able to stop him during my *cleansings* as they called it. But even with that war in his mind, Will is loyal not to my father, not to the crown, but to me. His charge and I see the finality in his face as he concedes to that fact. "So what do we do?" He asks.

I look up at Felix and then to my men. "She said she came here to make me the only royal Collier left standing." Felix's eyes bulge. "Eveera isn't going to leave until she kills them both. And I'm not leaving until I have Baelor's head on a pike and his men strung up outside the city for what they did."

"Did you ever find out *why* she wants them dead?" Will asks, tentatively.

"Does it matter?" I snap.

His jaw drops in anger. "Well, yes, Rorin. If I'm going to be party to regicide I'd like to fucking know why!"

I take large steps towards him, Bennett the only thing blocking my path. "Guys come on." He tries, while straining to hold us a part.

"You want to know what I'd like to know? Why the fuck my father threw us out to the wolves. Why we had to watch our men die, innocent men die. Why he invited Baelor to my damn dinner table and expected me to play nice! That's what I'd like to know."

"ENOUGH!" Felix shouts, pulling me back from my two men. "You three can work out your issues on your own time, right now I need to find my queen and get her home." He looks to Armond who nods.

I know what he means without even having to say it. Eveera isn't safe here and she never was. My time is up.

But she wants something, and if Felix truly knows her, he knows she won't leave without getting it. I scratch at the rune on my wrist. "We cannot afford to lose this war. We'll find Eveera and make a plan, but she isn't leaving until we both get what we want." The four of them stare back at me. "Whatever my father and Baelor have crafted up together, I want no part. Baelor *will* burn for what he's done and I will not lose Vellar. You signed that contract with me, not Eiser, and not with Vellar. *Me.* Meaning regardless of what *you* want Felix - it's not null and void yet."

EVEERA

Gods. My body is hot, everywhere he touched me. Everywhere he kissed me, feels like my skin is burning.

I found myself standing outside of Axel's bedroom door, hesitating to open it or to confront any of them after what happened and what didn't happen but could have. No one was in the main area of the room.

When I slip into his room I find him sprawled out on the bed with a book on his chest. "Ax." I whisper tapping his nose. His sleep-addled hand shoves my finger away. "Ax." I tap again. Two sleepy eyes crack open. Confusion first crossing his face that quickly morphs into a softens as he wakes up. I feel a few traitorous tears on the verge of falling and collapse next to him, burying my face in the comforter. "I fucked up." My voice is muffled by the fabric. His hand rubs gentle circles on my back, careful of the scars there. He's always been so reverent of them even though I know he despises what I've done to myself.

The first time he saw them was after I had freshly re-opened the splits. We were sixteen and he'd barely been a part of my guard for all but a year.

He didn't ask any questions - just cleaned me up. Ever since, if I needed someone, he was there.

"Yeah, well. You're not known for making the best of decisions." I shove his knee in protest and slide down off the bed and onto the floor while he carries on. "In fact, you're known for making a lot of terrible decisions. It's become a pattern." He teases and slides down next to me, "oh come on, E. You can't have fucked up that bad."

"No, I did. Bad." He swipes thumb across my cheek taking a tear with it.

"Okay first. Up." Axel says, standing up and motioning for me to follow. He walks over to his wardrobe and grabs out a long shirt tossing it at me.

He shrugs, "if you're going to be moping and crying all night, you're not going to want to do it in that get up." Fair enough. Making my way to the small bathroom I undo my dress and slip on the white overshirt that barely passes mid thigh on me. I find him sitting on the floor again with his head dropped back onto the mattress. I slide down next to him my own head dropping to his shoulder and a collective sigh heaves from both of us. Not one of relief or comfort but one of pure exhaustion.

"So what did you do that was so bad?" He asks.

Shame heats my cheeks. "I'm feeling things." He gives me a look that says, 'go on'. I hide my face into his shoulder and mutter, "I almost climbed Rorin like a tree."

Axel snorts, "okay? You've basically been doing that for show this whole time. What's the difference now?"

"It wasn't for show this time."

His head bobs slightly against mine; a sign of understanding. "And now you're feeling things?"

"And now I'm feeling things."

His hands fall heavy on top of mine. "Do you want to know what I think?"

I lift my head up, staring at the wall ahead of me. "Not really."

"You don't like being vulnerable, and he makes you that way. Ezra - you kept at arms length - which made things easy. But the prince? He doesn't let you do that." *No he doesn't.* "You're bending your rules for him, E. But you already know that, which is why you're in my bedroom - in my shirt. Wallowing."

Thwack! "Ow!" His hand rubs softly at his chest while I shift to pull my knees up under my chin. My hair has started falling out of its braids, curtaining around my face. I don't know how to feel these things. I don't want to feel these things. The confusion, the *fear*. Everything with Ezra was simple. At least for me it was simple. Purely carnal. No emotion needed, sure, maybe there was some at the beginning. But day after day his affection began to tire me. I don't think I could ever tire of Rorin's affection or the tenderness with which he handles me, even when he shouldn't, even when I am cruel.

But first, I'd have to accept that I, too, have affection for him. *Desire*, even.

The question Axel poses next, is quiet. Tentative. "Does he know?"

Depends on what he's referring too. About my mother? *Yes.* About my scars? *Yes.* About the conglomerate of feelings I have? *Yes.* I don't know how to really answer that, but the words that leave my mouth are, "He knows."

We stayed holed up in that room for the rest of the night. The next day, Millie brought me my clothes. She doesn't ask any questions, and we get ready for yet another day of appearances. Another day of this ridiculous celebration.

Apparently, it lasts three days.

The second night isn't a ball, like the first night, but a tournament for their best fighters. It's a spectacle. One I choose to spend very little time at. Rorin and I play our part of devoted companions well, but when people aren't looking, our words are minced and our bodies repel away from each other as it always should have been.

Tap tap. Axel comes in with food piled on two plates, setting one down in front of me. Surveying my options, I pick up a chunk of bread and break off a piece. His lanky body flopping down in front of me while he digs into his own plate. The scenario so mundane, so normal that I have flashbacks to when we first met.

—

"Queen Eveera. *You* must *have a royal guard. Armond cannot be everything you need all at one time!*"

I prop each my feet on top of the council table, crossing my ankles. Alina's shrill voice is painful. Everything about Alina is painful. "Sure he can. It's literally what his magic does. It gifts him the ability to be everywhere and everything." *The glare that remark earns me is lethal. Or at least it would be if I gave a shit.*

"You cannot always rely on magic, Your Highness."

I cock my head at her. "See, that is just what someone without magic would say." *She throws her hands up in the air, squealing in frustration.*

She looks desperately to Felix, "please talk to her. She is refusing to listen." *With that, she stomps out of the room like a petulant toddler. I lean back in my chair and stretch out the rest of my body.* Thud!

"OW! What the fu—" My eyes snap open while pain shoots through my tailbone, I look around and find I'm sprawled disgracefully on the floor. Looking down on me is Felix's tan face with a deep scowl on it.

"Language." He chastises and reaches a hand out to help me stand. I dust my pants off once I'm on my feet.

"That would have been a thoughtful gesture if you were not the reason I was laid out on the stone floor." His eyes roll back as he motions for me to follow him and leads me to the courtyard where several guards and squires are training. "I already trained today, Felix, dear. And I have been out with Vada."

"Eveera. Lady Alina is right." Oh not this again. He catches sight of my face but carries on nonetheless, "we only just announced that you have taken up the throne. The entire realm is now aware of your existence when to them - for the past fifteen years - they had all thought you dead. There could be any number of threats lining up, you need more than Armond."

I smile sweetly at him, "is that not why I have you?"

"I am your Head of Council. I am not your private guard detail."

"Fine. I have General Matthis." I counter.

Felix shakes his head, "he is the general of your military." His finger wags down at the men and women sparring. "Pick." My nose scrunches up as I look over the courtyard. That's when I notice him. Tall, dark, and scrawny. Gangly limbs and probably sweaty hands are holding loosely onto his sword. At first I thought maybe it was ill training. But with how quickly he dodges the swipe of his opponent's sword and moves in with his own slash, I realize his loose hold on it is cockiness.

"Him." Felix's eyes travel to where my finger points. He sighs, before nodding and going down to retrieve the soldier.

Once he's before me I look him up and down, he can't be any older than I am. "Axel Mecham, this is your Queen." The soldier, Axel, extends a shaky hand. I can sense the fear off of him, my serpents twitching at it, when I take his hand for him to bend a knee. The look he gives me is nervous and he glances back at Felix but my head of council is staring up at the sky probably begging the gods for patience.

I smile down at Axel my mind filling with so many ideas. "Oh we are going to have so much fun."

-

Snap! Snap!

I blink a few times to find Axel's fingers in my face his expression worried. "Sorry." I say, popping a piece of fruit into my mouth.

"Where did you just go?" The worry not leaving his face.

"Just remembering." I sigh. The door swings open and Millie and Orem stand in the opening. "What now?" I ask my words garbled by the mouthful of food.

She sighs, "he wants to see you." He - *Rorin*. Nausea churns in my gut. *Great, with feelings comes illness.* Axel looks at me apologetically and helps me to my feet, kissing the top of my head while ushering me out of the room after her.

Once we're out in the hall, I lean over to her, keeping my voice quiet. "Remember how you said I would need you?" Her lips part and she nods her head up and down. "I need you." Turning I stand on my toes and cup my hand around her ear whispering what I need done. When she pulls away her eyes have darkened and she gives me one more subtle nod before taking off in a different direction.

A weight starts to ease in my chest, *soon*. I think. *Soon two wrongs will be made right.*

My feet carry me right to the baccara rose hedges. The velvet red of my dress spills out around my feet, matching the undertones and texture of the petals. The sun is setting, the rays making prisms of light through the glass hall that glitter through the garden.

"I find you here again. Like a fly drawn to sap." I turn in the direction of her voice a small smile resting on my lips. Her eyes are glued onto the hedge, not bothering to look at me. "They really are beautiful. Not my particular choice, but then again nothing of Rorin's choices these day are of my preference."

She plucks a petal clean off. "I shouldn't be so surprised you're drawn here, your mother was too." The smile I have melts off of my face instantly. *What the hell does that mean?* "Of course she would be though. She did help me with them after all." She laughs quietly to herself. The sound sending hairs straight up on the back of my neck. "I suppose she wouldn't have shared much about me. However, I would've guessed a girl as curious and calculated as you seemed to be would've figured it out by now."

My brain feels scattered. "If you're suggesting my mother spent time here then—" The thought that my mother would have chosen to be here at some point astounds me. It unsettles me. *She's trying to gain the upper hand here, calm down.* My conscience snaps.

Mareese tilts her face at me, smiling, "oh she didn't just spend time here, Eveera. Oh no. Your mother lived here. With me." *Bleeding gods.* "Well, with me and my mother. My mother was head healer, and well, Ayla...young Ayla, well she was my mother's apprentice." She looks down, walking towards another rose. "We spent years together, Ayla and I. Joined at the hip. Practically sisters." Mareese spins around spreading out her arms in a wide motion. "She helped me create this space when my betrothal to the king was announced. Many hours did we walk or lay among these flowers. Two very young girls with very big dreams. If she wasn't slaving over my mother's teachings, she was in here with me."

My teeth grind together. "How fortunate you were then, to know her." I grit out.

She shrugs. "Mm. I thought so too once. I thought the world of her. When she went back to Obsidian, my heart simply broke. Of course I was pregnant with Rorin at that point, which helped ease her loss." Her lip pouts out, "and when she wrote me that she had lost you as a babe…it was a tragedy."

The temperature in the garden drops, turning frosty. In my peripheral I see Millie's magic webbing together above us, thankfully, Mareese doesn't notice. "She had her reasons for keeping me from you, I'm sure." We move in a slow motion around each other.

"She did have a tendency for keeping things. Even things that were not hers, like my mother. How is Marjorie by the way?"

"The Lady in Black" Murph had said. *Of course. The runes…the way she spoke with such familiarity yet distrust towards Rorin. She knew, the whole time she knew.*

Mareese sits primly down on the bench nestled in the hedges. "We all thought it odd, an Obsid wanting to learn healing. Maybe even try to harness the magic. I should've known that the woman I came to call sister, was nothing more than a rat." She smooths down the fabric of her skirt, crossing her legs. "The realization of what they were doing, what they had done, didn't come until it was too late. My mother off and running to her aid when she was in labor with you. Then never returning. My son's magic coming in *tainted, disturbed, wrong.*" Venom drips from her words, a fierce hatred in her eyes speaks to my own.

"Unbelievable." I breathe out and her head snaps up to me. "You blame them for him." It's not a question, and the ferocity in which she stands up to be toe to toe with me tells me her answer. My gods, she actually feels anger towards Marjorie and my mother. Disbelief crawls up my throat, my hold on my magic is precarious. "Don't pretend you care about him now, Mareese." Confusion flickers in her eyes. "After what you allowed to happen." I circle her a little more obviously this time. "After who you allowed to touch him, torment him. Break. Him."

"You have no idea what you're talking about." She snarls.

"Sure, I do." I say smiling. "I've seen everything. Here why don't I show you." My tendrils surge out of me, seizing her where she stands so my power can warp every sense of hers, forcing her to watch the nightmare that plagues the son she claims to love.

-

SMACK! "Stupid boy!" My lip is stinging from the cut his ring opened up again. "What a dishonor you are to this kingdom! Poisonous mist! An omen if there ever was one." My vision goes black and I can feel my eye start to swell. The bones in my nose are broken. "P-please don't lock me up here again. PLEASE." His laugh rings out through the cell. "Please don't lock me up here again." He mocks before landing a kick in between my ribs. "P-please." I sob out - no NO!

-

"Stop. It." She chokes out.

"Oh yes, your Highness it looks like you really love your son. Allowing a prince to be beaten and broken down. To be debased like that. You. Did. Nothing."

She sputters at the pressure my magic puts on her. "I am innocent of what you have shown me."

"We would not be here if you were *innocent*." I switch the images to the broken body of my mother. The images of me finding her. And while I watch her I see the bitch actually has tears slipping down her face. I pull my magic back just a little bit and she collapses to the ground. I crouch down, forcefully grabbing her chin and roughly wipe the tear falling down her cheek away. "We're going to play a little game, Mareese. You hide and I seek." She struggles to rip her chin from my hold. I *could* end it right here. But where would the fun be in that? The moment my fingers let go, she scrambles to her feet running deeper into the maze. I give her a two minute head start before I let the magic consume me. It searches for her, seeking out her pulsating fear. The tendrils puncture holes in the hedges, cutting her off and halting her in her place. Her screams ring out loudly, hoping someone will hear her but with Millie's deflection Wield up not a single sound will break through.

I can feel her panicking as she comes up on every dead end. Each time I stop her I give her a few seconds before another tendril crawls it's way to her. My steps slow and intentional, her fears echoing around my mind. Each one is pompous and material. With the biggest one being the age old fear of not wanting to experience death. *Too bad*, I think.

While in her head, my mind's eye is sucked into the day Rorin's magic came in. She woke to him thrashing in bed, he couldn't have been more than eight years old. His mist was a grayish pallor clouding around him. She couldn't reach him without it burning her eyes and choking her. Her first thought was concern, that someone had come to kill her boy and she was finding the aftermath. It was only until she tried to use her own magic and failed that she summoned the courts appointed healers before she drained herself. The king and queen quickly came to the realization that it wasn't a plot to kill their son. But that this *was* their son and the tides for Rorin's life changed that day.

My magic coats the stone path completely. Her teeth chattering loudly from where she hides. I let a tendril extend out towards her, then another. Each one wrapping her like a present up against the hedges. I pull back just a little so she can look me in my eyes, the eyes I have been told matched my mothers. "You blame the wrong people." I snarl.

She spits at me, squirming underneath my Wield. "She deserved it! Your mother knew I was coming for her. And when I did, it was my mother who had to clean up the mess. It was only fair for what they did to my boy."

I throw the memory again at her, showing her how the disgust crept in and corrupted her against her own child. She spits at my face a second time, searching for a crumb of renewed courage and vitriol. "You are a parasite that your parents let fester and grow. If only the rumors they sowed of your death had been true."

I cock my head at her, pacing slowly and closely in front of her pinned form. "And what would that have solved? Hmm? You still would have come for their throats, forced them to die at your hand. Hadar would still be wreaking havoc on kingdom upon kingdom at Baelor's command." She smiles weakly at his name, brow sweating from the mental back and forth she has sustained. "You are nothing more than a pretty queen sitting atop her pretty throne."

"Are you any different? *Queen* Eveera. Do you not hide in your shadows, on your throne, feeding into everyone's fear? It's *disgusting*."

My feet stop inches from her quivering body, "you forget though. I *made* those shadows. Lying in wait for the right moment, and right now, in this moment, you are at my mercy." A tendril snakes around her throat wrapping across the skin there. Her magic is flaring, but it won't be able to do anything against the hold I have her in, she won't be able to heal herself. "Would you be willing to make a deal with the devil just to save your own skin?" I finally close the gap between us leaning in close, the volume of my words only a whisper. "You'll come to find that there are worse things than the monsters under your bed." She flinches at the threat.

"If there is a devil; I am staring into it's eyes."

My vision bleeds black as the magic takes over. The sound of my voice distorting, "flattery will get you nowhere dear. Unfortunately for you, I am the fate holding your thread, and that thread's just been cut."

The tendrils tighten around her. "Oh gods. Please. Please." She whimpers.

"You yell for your gods. But where are they now? They won't save you." With the flick of my hand my tendrils spear into Mareese. Every one coiled around her body turns sharp as a blade. Her mouth gapes, blood dribbling from the corner as she begins to choke. "Hoc memento, Mareese. Pacem non eris scies, quam morieris in manu somnia maga. Tua sunt somnia, quae comedunt animam tuam in profundis Helys." *Remember this, Mareese. You will not know peace until you die at the hand of a dream witch. May your dreams eat your soul in the depths of Helys.*

With a pull of my hand her scream is cut short as the tendrils slice down, flaying her open, all of her organs spilling out at her feet. The blood of the former queen coats the front of me and I take a step back to admire my work. I leave her there on the cold ground for someone else to clean up while Millicent unravels her Wield from around the gardens. When I exit the labyrinth the two of us stare at each other, a silent understanding passing between us until I see someone running up behind her - Mousy. He pales the second he sees all the blood. "What did you do?" He breathes.

I dust my hands us, wiping them fruitlessly on the sticky front of my dress. "Half of my end of the deal." I snap.

He shakes his head, "no. Not here. Your men, they're attacking the city. You tell me now. What did you do? Is that why Felix is here? So you can siege the city?"

"Felix?" I ask, confused, while elbowing him out of my way.

"Eveera!" Millie calls after me, "what about—"

"Leave her. Let her king be the one to clean up the mess." I order, spinning back around on my heel to figure out what's going on outside of the castle.

Mousy catches up to me his voice brimming with anger. "He won't forgive you for this."

I take a deep breath, picking up my pace. "That isn't my problem. It's his."

"You feel so little for him?" His question is quiet - as if he is unsure of wanting to know that answer.

My feet slow, stopping me in my tracks. "I feel *everything* for him."

Those beady blue eyes search my face, looking for a fault - a lie - in my words. He comes away disappointed, letting his anger resurface to cover it up. "That doesn't make any sense." He snarls, walking the rest of the way ahead of me.

Neither does my army laying siege without my command and yet here we are.

RORIN

She's been avoiding me. Today was the first day it truly felt like it was just for sure. For both of us. And the feeling I had because of it left me sick. We both left the tournament as soon as we were able. Surprisingly enough no sign of Baelor or Pruella there, at least not before we left.

I went directly to my room and she took off with Axel. His hand placed tightly around her waist as they disappeared around the corner of the hallway. When Millie came into my room this morning she retrieved the clothing Eveera would be wearing. I wanted to ask but I didn't need to. She's been in Axel's room since last night. Millie's look towards me was apologetic as she shut the door.

Jealousy burns in my chest knowing Eveera probably slept in his bed. Maybe even in his clothes. I feel childish, like a prepubescent boy just learning about girls. Logically I know this isn't the first time they have been alone together. They're practically family. But still, the need I have for her to be with me is overwhelming.

Armond and Felix have been checking in since our discussion last night. He still hasn't met with Eveera - Millie keeping him away from her, saying that now wasn't a good time. He tried arguing with her, but Armond talked him down, convincing him to just get through the second day of the celebration before riling her up.

So he's stayed in my quarters completely without her knowledge. There have been a few odd moves around the city that have kept Felix and Armond busy, but so far nothing really of note.

Finally as the night starts to come to a close I sent Millie off to get Eveera. With the closing ceremonies of today's events we will need to make an appearance and at that point we need to make a plan.

Tick. Tick. She should have been back by now. *Surely she isn't choosing to refuse my request to see her?* I wonder. *Maybe I overestimate her fascination with me.*

I reach for the doorknob of my room when— *BOOM!*

Felix and I rush out onto the balcony where we see people fleeing into the streets, screams erupting from everywhere, while more explosions are going off near the slums - *near Murph* - and at the horizon there a banner flies.

No, not just a banner...her banner. I tilt my head to look at Felix. "What. The. Fuck." I breathe out, anger boiling over as my Wield leaks from my palms. Felix's eyes are wide as he sputters for an explanation.

I grip him by the back of his next and drag him into the Glass Hall where I find Bennett, Armond, and Will all staring out at the city. "Latimer." I growl, his focus breaking to see the hold I have on her head councilman.

He draws his sword on me, and Felix tries to raise his hands to stop him. Bennett and Will jump back from him, drawing their own swords out.

"Where is Eveera?" I snarl.

"Let go of Felix, Rorin." He warns, cracking his neck.

I cup my Wield in my hand and slap it over Felix's nostrils. "I think that I have the upper hand here, wouldn't you say? Where is Eveera." I ask again, I pull the Wield back in but keep my hand in place.

"I don't know." Armond says again.

I drop Felix's almost limp body and point outside, where her banner is being held above city walls. "Explain that." The three of their heads turn and I watch as Armond's face morphs. Horror creeping into it. Commotion sounds from the hall and I see Orem, Max, and Axel walking up to us. "Oh good! Almost the whole group of Obsidian scum is here." I snarl. "Anybody have an explanation for why in the bleeding damn Helys your troops are laying siege on my city?!" I roar. Their faces all go slack as they look at the iridescent windows. No one offering an explanation.

I look over to Will. "Find her." I command and at first he doesn't move, "find her dammit!" I shout. He sheathes his sword quickly and shoves through her men, running down the steps.

Orem looks around the hall, "where are Millie and Ezra?" He asks quietly.

Armond is crouched next to Felix helping him sit up while he regains his breath. "I haven't seen him since..." His voice trails off.

Much to my dismay the jealousy in my stomach flares up again. *Has she been truly playing me this whole time, have they been planning something the two of them?* "Since what?"

"Ah, since the queen and him spoke yesterday before the start of the Celebration." I nod, biting my lip, and pacing back and forth.

I look down at Felix and Armond, their eyes guarded against me, Armond's hand still on his hilt. "Answer me this," my hands are shaking as I try to curb the anger mixing with my magic. "Would she does this?"

Her men are quiet for a moment, but Felix's strained and gravelly voice answers me. "She wanted people to suffer," *not helping your case,* I think to myself. "but she doesn't kill innocents. She would've found the people and targeted them individually. So no. I don't think she would do this."

"Let's hope you're right." I snarl storming past them and marching my way outside.

By the time we make it outside, there is a flurry of people. Guards are ushering the nobility and guests back inside away from the horrors that are transpiring outside of our walls.

Through the tunnels arrives Will, Millicent, and of course Eveera. Her face is twisted in anger and she's covered in blood. She doesn't look at me walking straight up to Axel who's now holding a bag - *when did he have time to grab a bag?* Slipping her arms out of the thin straps on her dress, he hands her a pair of leathers. She pulls the tunic over her head smearing the blood on her face. The process repeats as she slips the rest of the dress off. My men on instinct turn quickly away, her eyes look up connecting with mine for a brief moment. No emotion gives way on her face as she slides her leather pants up. The rest of her process for putting on her armor is rather simple; weapons belt, thigh holster, gloves, and boots. Millie quickly helps throw her hair into a braid so it no longer sticks to her face.

"Are you just about done?" I snap, their heads whipping in my direction. I stomp over to her, my hand coming up around her throat. Her men draw their swords but she stays her hand. Silently commanding them to hold, while she meets my eyes. Her fierce gold eyes flaring at me.

"Do you want to have it out here? Or do you want to go find out what the hell is going on in your city?" She bites and I yank her by the throat into me, squeezing it tighter. Her pulse beats rapidly underneath me.

I lean in, my nose touching hers as I lower my voice. "If you did this. I'll kill you myself." Her eyes glint at the challenge.

"And if I didn't—" she chokes out the words against my hold, "you'll owe me one hell of an apology." With a forceful push I shove her back into Millie. She's laughing, wiping at her cheek as I take the lead out towards the gates. Before we even get out onto the streets the smoke from the blasts burns our throats and eyes.

Citizens are running and coughing through it, as they try to reach safety. I notice Eveera's eyes are trained on the skies and just before I can give any command the familiar heavy beat of wings comes from above us. Vada's enormous body lands on one of the stone buildings, crumbling it's structure, and causes us all to jump back.

"Holy shit." Bennett breathes as he eyes the dragon who crawls down the rubble her head down and maw open putting her teeth on full display. Eveera gives me a long blink before taking off running, her legs carrying quickly as Vada lowers her forearm and shoulder for her queen to climb.

"Where is she going?!" Millie shrieks.

Orem nods to his queen before telling Millicent, "she'll be the aerial view."

I shake my head staring up at the sky where they disappear. *"Don't try anything, Eveera."* I snap.

Her laugh echoes in my mind, *"wouldn't dream of it, princeling."*

"Bennett," His head turns to me, "take Millie and a horse and go see what damages they caused in the area." He nods grabbing the reigns of one of the animals we grabbed before slipping past the court's walls. The rest of us climb on our own steeds and I give commands out to teams of individuals.

Armond, Felix, and I stick closely together. A few wails echo loudly, but as we walk the streets carefully it looks to be mostly minor damage until we come up on the same street as "Goldfinch". The tavern has been turned into nothing but rubble with a hole blasted completely through it, leaving nothing but a large wake of debris before us.

"What could have cause this?" Armond murmurs, leaving me with mixed feelings. I want to scream at him, want to ask that exact question to him. But the way they all are acting...but her banners. *They were her banners flying what else would explain that?* I ask myself. We continue following the path of destruction, my city nothing but a smoking carcass.

Leathery wings beat above me but with the smoke and the added cloud coverage I can't see the large beast anywhere. The sound of hooves joins in and we all spin around to see Axel and the brothers headed for us. "Any. Word. From the—" his voice trailing off as he waves his arms around haphazardly at the sky. "Aerial view?" We shake our heads. My anxiety is growing by the second now with each moment longer Eveera takes up there.

"What the hell do you think she's doing?" I snap at her men. We moved over to the outer walls and we can hear the sound of movement through the stone.

"She's got the view; she's like to do something..." Max mutters.

"She's likely to do something self sacrificing and stupid." Axel corrects him, his arms folded across his chest.

I trot my horse over to Armond's. "Can you Void me to her?" I ask.

He looks at me as if I've lost my mind, his speech stolen from him temporarily. "You want me to *Void* you to her? While she is *flying* on Vada?"

I understand how insane of an idea it sounds, but she's likely to tune me out if I just get inside of her head. "She has explaining to do. I want to know what my *leverage* is doing up there." The irritation is boiling up and out of me. "She can't avoid or ignore me for very long if I just show up on the back of the beast."

"Yes she can. She can just throw you *off* her dragon." Will argues. *Fair point.* I ignore it and look expectantly at Armond, we don't have much time if the sounds outside of this wall are any indication of what's about to happen. He sighs before grabbing my hand and fastening my hold around his forearm.

"You have to think of where you want to be. Similar to portaling. Then lean into my magic."

Will's hand tugs on my shoulder, "you're not serious." The disbelief plain in his voice.

I keep my eyes trained on Armond. "Simple enough." My mouth quirks up when I focus my thoughts to her while his magic creeps up my arm. It's cold. Nothing like a portal, but something else entirely. It quickly envelopes me and...

THUD!

"*Fuck that hurt.*" I groan. I landed awkwardly across the base of Vada's spine. The dragon didn't seem too bothered by my intrusion, it's rider however...

"WHAT IN THE GODS?!" Eveera's head whips back to see me rather ungracefully crawl my way across Vada's back and sink down into a the ridges behind Eveera.

My arm pulls tight around her waist, nestling her up against me. Despite the thick layer of copper scented blood covering her skin and hair, the smell of her perfume still carries over. My mouth grazes against the back of her head and I have half a mind to kill her, while the other wants to slam my mouth down on hers and breathe a sigh of relief that she's okay so far.

"ARE YOU INSANE?" She shouts, her voice getting lost on the wind. Her hands push at my arms trying to loosen them.

"I'D RATHER LIKE TO NOT FALL OFF THE BLOODY THING!" I shout back at her. She's rolling her eyes. I know it, I don't need to see it to know she has. "Explain yourself." I bark, as we bank hard on a draft of wind. *"What other secrets have you kept from me. One was killing my parents, two was killing my city, is there a third snake in the grass I need to be prepared for?!"*

"Is there are reason you are shouting in my mind? You're going to give me a headache, and I didn't order this attack! It's as much a surprise to me as it is you, believe me when I find out who went against orders I'll—" Her words are cut short when we tilt down, looking at the soldiers outside the wall. They carry her banner but a handful of them are placing their hands on the wall, something webbing out from underneath them and up the stone.

"Are those vines?" I ask.

"So I was right." Her words are breathy in my mind.

"What do you me—"

"Evendell. He has recruited - drafted rather - the Wielders of Evendell." The thought sinks into my stomach, heavy like lead. *"Those aren't my men. Those are Baelor's posing as my men which means..."*

"He has magic." I finish for her. Fuck.

RORIN

"*You were telling the truth.*" I say quietly. Vada, whether at the command of Eveera or of her own volition, makes a move and flies us up higher into the cloud cover.

"*Yes, I do that often. What I can't understand is why the hell they look like my men?*" Her mind a tangled mess.

"*My father's an Illusionary. He must have been smuggling them along the border, a condition of whatever farce treaty he signed with Baelor. And I'll bet you he's been Illusioning them from the moment he caught wind your soldiers were on our territory.*"

I have been such a fool thinking I actually had the upper hand on him for once. I take in Eveera's profile, her eyes focused on the battle. I'll have dragged her into this for absolutely nothing; our real armies are miles away. Her men will die. *She will die.*

"Vada has to end them." I say with a finality.

"*No.*" She snarks. "*I thought I would risk her just for* show." The dragon tilts hard to the right, our bodies sliding with the movement. She slips a little further towards Vada's wing so I hook my thumb into the loop of her belt - fastening her to me. "*I'm not...gonna..fall.*" She struggles as she tries to right herself.

"*Not taking that chance, Nightmare.*"

"*I hate you.*" She grumbles.

I breathe her in, feeling a little bit of relief that she didn't betray me. "*So you've said.*"

As we fly around circling back around and over to where their base encampment seems to be, I catch her up to speed on what we found in the city. Looking down we can just barely make out what looks to be some apparatus loaded with a large heated stone. The circumference of it almost as wide as the dragon we are sitting on.

So that's what caused the damage. Wonderful.

I hadn't realized I said that thought down the seal until I hear her quiet hum of agreement. There is no way that the ten of us; all powerful or not will be able to make it out of this. Vada will, sure. But even dragons can be felled, and by the looks of that weapon...

With a rough landing in the decimated capitol we decide that the quickest way to get out there, to potentially apprehend them, is to have Armond Void each of us to a ridge just south of their encampment that while on Vada we were able to scout out.

Vada takes off with Eveera first.

Armond repeats the process of Voiding us there one by one until we all stand concealed by the trees. Once as comfortable as we could be, Eveera and I clued the rest of our men in on what we found while up in the sky.

"Let me get this right, your father has been Illusioning Baelor's Guards this entire time to make it look like Obsidian led the attack on Vellar?" Max asks.

Orem perks up his head, suggesting that we burn out their supplies to buy time.

Max doesn't seem convinced as he shakes his head. "It won't matter what we delay - there are fucking *thousands of them* and only ten of us. Nine and a half if you count the fact that you almost already fucking killed Felix." He yells, shoving a hand towards the councilman. "What do you suppose those odds will be, hmm?" Orem shrugs, arguing that he was just trying to help.

I'm leaned up against a tree watching Eveera pace back and forth. Millie meanwhile is tending to Felix who assures her for the tenth time that he's fine. A loud whirring noise alerts us that they are loading up another one of those heated stones.

"The city won't make it much longer." Will adds, his voice nervous. Eveera stops her pacing and huffs her way over to Vada.

"What are you..." Axel tries to ask, but she's already climbing up the bony portion of her wing, and before anyone of us can argue she takes off, disappearing out of view again. None of us having a clue as to where she's gone until a loud roar sounds above us and a wave of heat rolls through the field.

"Well. That was subtle." I remark.

"Took Orem's advice. That should set them back a little." She says casually. Through the trees we can see rushes of men heading towards the burning supplies in attempts to try and save what they can.

Meanwhile, our small group unsheathes our swords and charges out onto the field. Yells of alarm sound from their encampment, signaling to their soldiers to converge on our location. Vada swoops low, releasing another wave of fire at them. Archers loose their arrows towards her causing my heart to sink into my stomach every time one of them gets close enough that I think it'll make its mark.

My blade meets the flesh of one of the Illusioned Guards slicing clean through their torso. The Wield falling apart as his body dies.

"A soldier conscripted for the wrong cause, who dies while wearing another's face. It's wrong. All of this is wrong." I murmur through the seal to her.

We repeat the process trying to cut down as many soldiers as we can. Orem runs past me, a wound weeping from his side as he charges towards another Guard. This one happens to also be an Evendell Wielder, their nature magic rolling out at Orem. The young brother anticipates it and opens up Oblivion that swallows the Wielder whole. Winking the both of them out of existence. I watch in awe as his magic works, and I hope that he comes out of it alive. A female scream distracts me and looking to my right I see that Millie is clutched in Vada's claws. Eveera's magic wrapping around her and hoisting her onto Vada's back. The shrieks grow louder when Eveera secures her between the scales and then I watch, horrified, as she rolls from Vada's back and lands directly on top of scorched dirt. She doesn't skip a beat as she bolts off into the center of the fighting.

"Must you always be so careless and selfish with your life?!" I shout into her mind as cut down the vines an Evendell Wielder is using on me.

Her grunts of effort clamor into my head as she tries to respond, "YES! U*nfortunately."* Grunt. *"For you."* Ugh! *"I am as careless and selfish with my heart as I am my life."*

I hop over the Wielded roots and arc my sword through the air, coming down and cleaving the head of the Wielder clean off his shoulders. *"Shall I take that as an admission, Nightmare?"*

"Take it however you damn well please. NOW COULD YOU FOCUS?!" She shrieks. The seal quiets as the roar of battle replaces her voice. From this angle I can see that Max is fighting back to back with his brother while if I turn the other way there Vada is with Millie, laying waste to soldiers who are heading back our way from the wall. Her flames

leaving nothing but char behind. For a second everything calms and quiets, until we hear the steady thunder of hundreds of horse hooves.

"Shit. Of course they have reinforcements." Axel shouts as he finds me.

"Is that more of them?" Armond echoes as he appears on my left.

I shake my head, "I don't kno—"

"It's Matthis." Eveera says into my mind.

"*The real one?*" I ask hesitantly.

RORIN

General Matthis and the third of Eveera's army crest over the horizon. I breathe a sigh of relief when I can't see any fuzziness or haziness while looking at them - confirming that they aren't Illusioned. That relief doesn't last long however as we hear more hooves coming towards us, this time from the opposite direction. More of Hadar's Guards.

Her army enters the fight with ease. As I fight my way through, I see a few faces of the Illusioned Guards grow wide in shock when they notice the Oriks, Shifters, and Serpentes among her ranks.

BOOM!

Another heated stone lands and craters the ground, the people closest to the blast are scattered now across the hills. Vada matches the blast with an equally destructive stream of hot fire. Her large body tilting hard to the left, throwing Millie to the side. Her hands slip from their hold on the spines and she catches barely onto the dragon's wing. Vada lurches from the touch, shaking Millie off who lands ungracefully in a heap on the ground.

I lunge for her but Orem is closer and faster. He falls to the ground in front of her, winking them into Oblivion. *"Is she dead?"* Eveera's voice slips into my mind exhausted and breathless.

"Take the nightmare away." I tell her.

"What?"

"Take it away, I need...I need help. My mind it refuses to cooperate with the Wield. Please." She figures out quickly what I need and occupies my mind helping me to tear down my mental blocks so that I can let go of the control on my magic. Poisonous mist fills the area around me, suffocating and choking those within its radius, my heart rate rising from the adrenaline rush of the magic pulsing from me.

I walk through the gray mist hovering of the ground like a fog and kick the feet of a dead soldier next to me, his eyes are wide and bloodshot from the effects of my Wield.

Commanding it back into me is easier than normal while I run away from him, looking for Eveera. It's a little difficult to find her until the mist clears. Straight ahead of me there is black magic covering about a third of the battlefield - Illusioned Guards and Wielders falling to their knees around her. The tiny queen stands at the center of all of the bodies, surveying her work until she gives a nod of her head, presumably content with the Wield's results.

As I run to her from across the way, I see someone charging towards her. Fear spikes through me as I watch her stand with her back to the proposed assailant. I grab hold of a riderless horse nudging its side to make it gallop faster, but after a few feet it feels like I'm just moving in place. I'm not getting any closer to her or *him*. Frustrated, I look down, and see that the earth *is* keeping me from her and to my left an Illusioned Evendell Wielder is responsible.

He Wields the earth underneath my horses feet while one of his eyes is on Eveera and her assailant and the other on me and the steed I commandeered. "You've got to be kidding me!" I yell, while thrusting my Wield at him. His roots wrap around the ankles of my horse and yank the beast down. I roll away in barely enough time to not have the animal land on my leg.

Quickly I scramble up to my feet, and rush at him. I don't bother with my sword, as I clench my fists tighter. My mist grows up in a column around the Wielder, the sound of him choking fills my ears. I step into the column of my magic that he's shrouded in and press my palms against his gaping mouth and nostrils. His eyes bulge underneath my grip as he suffocates. "If she's dead because I was dealing with you. I'll find you in Helys and kill you a second time." With a push I send his body backwards, crumpling in a pile, his veins are blown underneath his skin.

When the column of magic disappears, my hearts in my throat as I expect to see her with a sword through her stomach. Instead I watch as Axel's body knocks her out of the way and the sword cleave directly through him instead.

The next few moments happen in slow motion. Eveera's magic wraps around her would-be assailant, cutting through his body like butter, the pieces of it falling to the ground.

She crumples next to Axel, their foreheads are pressed together and their mouths are moving from what I can tell. Whatever their next few words were, were just for them to hear.

I take slow steps towards her at first, watching while she puts his head in her lap both arms curling around him. A guttural scream tears from her chest just before her magic blasts across the field blanketing everything in a wild loss of control. My legs eventually listen to me and I start to run towards her. The closer I get the more I can see black webbing crisscrossing her skin like dark veins. The strength of her Wield growing with each sob and scream. The force of her magic overwhelms me as I fall to my knees behind them sweeping hers and Axel's limp body into me. I have to fight against the nightmares her magic forces onto me, so I can stay with her.

I'm shushing into her hair, rocking their conjoined bodies in an attempt to soothe her. The air grows frigid in an instant while a level of deep unnerving energy settles onto the battlefield. Motion stirs around us as her cries grow louder while her Wield wreaks havoc on her body. Cradling her head to me I see living soldiers, Guards, and Wielders on their knees trying to push against it too, their screams drowned out by the pitch of her sobs.

Unfortunately, they're not the only ones pushing and rising with her magic. Every intact body on the field that wasn't left without a head or a torso halved begins to morph and rise. Slowly they look towards us, her Wield still consuming her too much to notice, the hundreds of red eyes staring at us. Including Axel's looking up at us from where his head is still cradled in her hands and lap.

I shake her violently, pulling her from Axel's warped form as it tries to gain footing, yanking the sword from it's - *his* - torso.

"Come on, Nightmare." I shake her again. "Give me those eyes, beloved. Please. We need you. *I need you*, Nightmare." Too slowly do her eyes gain their gold back, her blinks long. She takes in her bloodied hands, her surroundings, and finally, *him*. I thought the wails before were haunting. But the sound that leaves her body when she realizes is so much worse.

The former Axel cocks his head at us, the new eyes burning into my own. I wrap my arm tightly around her waist and pull her behind me while my other grips the hilt of my sword. My stomach twists as I stare at my new friend's demonized form. I'm reluctant but prepared to do what I have to. He lurches for us, his reanimated body acting with a quickness I wasn't ready for. But thankfully, Eveera was. She rips the hilt out of my hand and slices clean through his neck, severing creature Axel's head from his body. As it thumps to the ground her eyes widen and her shoulders slump. She drops the sword and reaches for me. I clasp her hand and we sink to our knees, my arms finding their place around her again. My lips press kisses onto her sweaty brow, still reeling from the revelation that came with all of the outer land creatures rising on the field.

Across the way I see an iridescent orb, I squint my eyes and see that Max and Millie are shielded inside of it. At first I am confused as I see her holding him back, but then the body a few inches from Max's hands separated only by her shield comes into view.

No. I think. *No...Orem.* And I know immediately that Maxwell just did what Eveera had to. Black starts to bleed onto the ground again, matching the inky tears leaking from Eveera's eyes her cries picking up again. Armond Voids in next to us as I stare hollowly at Axel's head. It's red eyes still open. "You have to knock her out." His voice startles me as I look up at his grief ridden face.

"Wh-what?" The word comes out garbled and choked. He repeats himself and the words sink in. He means I have to stop her.

"Don't make them..." he chokes on the words next, "don't make them suffer this fate again." Nodding, I clasp my hand around her mouth and nose, sending a small amount of my mist to her as she inhales until her body slumps against me, cutting off her Wield.

The field goes quiet. Briefly the problem of the remaining outer land creatures goes unnoticed until we feel waves of heat against our skin as Vada begins to burn them to ash. Armond grips my shoulder while

I cling tightly to Eveera, cradling her to me while he Voids us off the battlefield.

RORIN

We Voided back into my rooms where we were shocked to find Ezra standing in the center of floor his eyes darting immediately to Eveera's limp body in my arms.

My lip curls at him, "do not even think of fucking touching her." I growl.

His frown deepens. "Where are the rest us?" Is all he manages. Our haggard group of seven stare back at him. Max's tortured voice breaking through the quiet first.

"Us?" He whispers stepping up next to me, "where in the bleeding. Fucking. Gods. WERE. YOU?!" He shoves at Ezra's chest. "Where were you HUH?! LEAVING US ALL TO FUCKING BURN OUT THERE?!" Another shove sends Ezra falling on his ass. "AND ALL YOU HAVE TO SAY IS 'WHERE ARE THE REST OF US?' There is no us, Wake. You're no Commander of mine." His Wield flares to life, his whole body turning into one large electrical current. He grabs for Ezra's throat pulling him up with preternatural strength, the voltage coursing through Ezra, frying him slowly from the inside out.

"Woah, woah, woah. Max." Millie's voice is calm, *broken,* but calm as she reaches out for Max. Her Wield is bubbled around her hand as she touches his cheek, forcing him to look at her. "Let him go." His knuckles are growing white under his force. "Max...let him go."

Ezra's body thuds to the ground, the smell of burnt flesh wafting up and into our nostrils. Max shuts down stumbling into Millie as she leads him out of the room.

I walk away from all of them and into my bedroom not giving the charred Ezra a second glance. I place Eveera onto the bed, brushing a few of the bloodied and matted strands of hair off of her forehead. My lips drop to press a kiss against it, letting my forehead rest against hers afterward. "I'm sorry, Nightmare." I whisper. She doesn't respond, only twitches and whimpers. "I'm sorry." I say again.

The door latches behind me, as I face those of us remaining. Ezra is still stunned on the floor, lightning shaped burns are across his skin, red and angry. Armond stands over him, kicking his leg, until Ezra groans.

"I need to see my father." I announce before storming out of the room. Will, Bennett, and Armond on my heels.

The doors to my father's study come into view and all I can see is red. Disregarding the sentries posted outside, I bust through the doors swinging them open with force. My father looks up, startled at the intrusion. "Ah, my son. You look unwell."

"And you look like a gods cursed idiot, father."

His face twists in feigned shock at my brashness. Undeterred, I stalk up to his desk and draw my sword; the three men at my back matching my movements.

My father raises his hands in mock surrender. "Tsk. Tsk. Tsk, now, Rorin. I actually think I've been quite clever."

"I'd choose your words very carefully, father." I warn.

He tilts his head, mirth flitting through his eyes. "Or what? You'll kill me? Can't do that, or you'll leave Vellar without it's sovereigns. Your poor mother's already dead, and if you kill me you'll make yourself an enemy of the crown. Abdicating your throne immediately."

I lower my sword but don't sheathe it. "Your attacked your own city. Why?"

The man smiles, his sharp blue stare sends a shiver of unease down my spine. "Did I?" He steps around the desk, placing himself directly in front of me. His arms fold across his chest as he sits on the lip of it. "See, the way I see it. The way *Vellar* will see it, is that you brought in an enemy of our kingdom. That you brought in Obsids, which not only resulted in your mother's death, but then the city was attacked! The very queen you claimed was here to help us leaves this court with your mother's blood coating her skin, her army waiting outside the gates, and a dragon burning our fields." Bile rises in my throat as he twists the manner of events. As his words warp the horrors we all just came from, while he stayed up here, protected. "It's a shame. Really. The way they'll see it is, the Nightmare Queen's claws dug into our poor unsuspecting and useless prince, manipulation at its best. Some may even say *you* orchestrated all of this as a way to usurp the throne before it was your time."

"But none of that is true!" Will argues.

My father's face twists in irritation, "it is true if their *King* says it is true Will," a greasy smile spreads across his face, "speaking of traitor queens, I see she isn't with you. I do hope she stays where you left her. The people will demand she pay for her crimes against our peaceful kingdom. And I am nothing, if not agreeable."

My heart stops at his suggestion. I grab him by his collar, leaning closely into his face. "If anyone will have a reckoning for the events and losses we suffered today, it will be *you*, father."

My feet can't seem to carry me fast enough as we head back towards my rooms. I tear the doors open to find a charred spot but no Ezra. Racing to my bedroom door I pull hard on the handles. The bed is empty. Only a rumpled, bloody, and dirty spot remains where her unconscious body should be.

No. No. No. No. No. NO! This cannot be happening. This cannot be fucking happening. She was just here. We left her for a second, just a second. I push at the seal. *"Come on, Nightmare."* I push again. *"Come on, come on, come on."* Will and Bennett come in behind me, swearing under their breath. "She can't just be *gone.*" I say, my voice cracking. I keep pushing at the seal but it's blocked, it feels unnatural.

Alarms begin to sound loudly through the court, and Will tugs at my arm. "They're going to come looking for us we have to go." He says, his voice rising in panic. I don't budge from my spot, just staring at the place her body should still be. "Rorin come on. We have to go."

"We can't just leave her!" I argue.

"Rorin. We don't where she is. We have to go!" With a hard tug they both manage to pry me out of the room. The three of us run through the halls, dodging any passageways that are busy with soldiers, sentries, or guards.

We snagged, Felix, Millie, and Max on the way to the portal and with a clumsy shove we all stumble into the room. "Well—" Bennett grunts moving things to blockade the door, "now what?"

Convenient, I think as I look around and see no portal attendant. Guards voices begin raising outside, their armored footsteps getting closer. "Obsidian." Felix answers and the seven of us link arms and throwing ourselves into the portal just as the doors break open. With a distorted look, I see my father's furious face before all things around me fade as the magic pulls us in.

We tumble out of it haphazardly, as their attendant rushes to close it off. Eveera's council are all already waiting in the room, their eyes wide with panic. They allow us a few minutes to gain our bearings before they motion for us to follow them.

The familiar darkness of her court gnaws at the fear I have for where she is and who she's with. A very hopeful sliver of irrational thinking, wishes that Ezra was dumb enough to bring her back here, but those hopes are dashed the moment we enter the council room to where only Marjorie stands.

Staff makes room for our group to sit, leaving most of the council without a seat.

The room stays quiet until Felix takes his place at the head of the table next to the old woman who opens her mouth to speak. "You came back, *without* her."

"Axel Mecham and Orem Abrams died in combat defending their family and their Queen." Felix states, taking some of the heat off of me for a minute as I try to figure out what to say. Gasps ripple through the room along with Max's choked sob at the mention of his brother while I shove down my emotions, "Hadar and Vellar have officially declared war on Obsidian. Claiming the attack and events of this day are at the hands of the Obsids." Arguments erupt from the council members in the room, silencing only when Felix raises his hand. "Upon our return to the Valen Court, Commander Ezra Wake - head of Queen Eveera's personal detail - who had abandoned his duties, reappeared after the battle. The prince believes that he has *stolen* the Queen." More gasps echo through the room. Felix motions me towards him. I getting up cautiously, taking a place next to the two of them. "As you all have just been made aware, with her missing, it is of utmost importance we find her in this grave time of vulnerability." He pauses waiting for any interruptions before continuing. "As you also know, this means we'll need an acting regent until she is brought back safely." He turns to look at me, a hand resting on my shoulder while Marjorie's withered fingers wrap around my left forearm, facing it out and exposing the rune there.

"A blood seal was performed between Prince Rorin and Queen Eveera before they left to fight for Vellar under Obsidian's banner. Now, the fates are clear. They are bound not only by blood but by magic. Magic gifted to us by the ley lines flowing through the earth. I have touched the strings that tie their fates, interwoven together as stated by magic and prophecy." She announces. *Prophecy? What prophecy?* I wonder looking at Felix, alarmed. "Prince Rorin will be named regent in the stead of Queen Eveera until she is found."

Resounding arguments of "you can't be serious" and "the kingdom will never accept him as regent - *we* will never accept him." fill the council room. I can't help but agree while my head feels like it's about to explode.

Marjorie silences them, "it is written both in prophecy, the precedence of ancient tradition, and now in blood. You're being informed, that is all. There will be no discussion." She waves them out of the room dismissing the whole council. Not even Alina, who likes to argue with her queen, speaks any further.

Once it's just the group of us who came back from Vellar and Marjorie, I whirl on her. "You left out two very important details, woman. The prophecy and the part where I become your king." Marjorie looks to me as if I have just said something wholly ignorant. From there she huffs in annoyance while pulling a scroll from her pocket. She clears her throat, projecting it loudly for the room:

"When the light burns out the dark,
the Queen painted in blood and shadows shall rise.
Lying in wait-
The man loyal to no Wield who answers only to peril,
lay waste to all in his path.
Deals made in blood that binds.
A battle of Kings and Queens to tip the scales,
an outcome known only through Sight.
Shadows stolen and shadows returned,
enter in the Age of the King with poison for blood."

Chills roll down my spin as she finishes that final sentence. "Extend out your wrist." I do so voluntarily, knowing she will snatch it if I don't. With a few words, magic coasts across my skin, the blood droplets raise from the rune that's been on my wrist since that fateful night in her room. Merging together the droplet falls back onto my wrist, just under the original rune. A burn sears through my skin as a different marking brands itself onto me. I look up to see everyone in the room's serious faces.

"All hail, King Rorin." They say together. I mutter the words to myself, a headache already forming from the fast progression of today's events. I have questions stampeding through my mind, starting with what the hell just happened and why it means I am now the King of Obsidian and ending with me whispering down the empty seal to her.

"Nightmare...you're going to fucking kill me."

THE BATTLE OF VELLAR

Fourteen Years Earlier
Eiser

"Your Highness, we've rounded them up where you asked."

I turn to look at the no name soldier, "and the ragroot?" I ask.

His lips thin into a flat line as he dips his head down in deference to me, "they've all received a dose." *Good.* I think.

"Thank you…" I wave my hands around for him to fill in the space with his name.

"Percy, sir."

I give him a nod, "thank you, Percy." He stands there waiting for a dismissal. I give the signal with my hand as I leave the room and disappear down the corridor. My halls are filled with boisterous servants and soldiers finishing up whatever menial tasks they have left before going off to sleep, drink, fuck, or whatever it is my peasants and lower level citizens do in their spare time.

Dust makes my nose itch as I walk up the steep stairs to my son's lessons room. *SMACK!* "Stupid boy!"

"Pl-please. I ca-can't." *OOF!* He crumples to the floor on his side as I enter into the room, the priest's foot still raised and aimed for a second kick at the boy.

"You must be cleansed! Tainted, broken, cursed brat. Unfit to be king—"

I catch the wrist of the priest in my hand, stopping the next hit from landing. "Alright, Brighton. I need a moment with my son."

His face heats as he sputters, "but, but Sire."

"Out." I command, waiting for him to slink out of the room and leave us.

Rorin looks up at me, the back of his hand wiping away the blood trickling from his mouth. I crouch down, taking his busted chin in between my fingers. He tries to yank it from my grip. "Look at me, boy."

His eyes squeeze shut, refusing me, and I jerk his chin towards me again digging my thumb into where it's split. "*AH!*" He yelps. "What do you want?" His words come out in a snarl, but the undertone to them is filled with defeat.

"I have a job for you." I tell him, I let go of his chin and he falls back onto his elbows, wincing at the impact.

Slowly he stands himself up. His skin and clothes are torn. I can't remember when I sent him up here maybe...five days ago? Who can keep track these days. "A-a job?" He stutters.

I dust my hands off, checking my skin for any evidence of his blood. "For you. For your Wield." His eyes widen at the last word. "Do you want to make me proud?"

He limped the whole way, slowing us down, and annoying me greatly. "You-you said that you had a job for my Wield?" He mumbles.

"Rorin, I can't understand you when you mumble. Speak up!" I snap.

"You said that you have a job for my Wield?" He says more clearly this time.

I look over my shoulder at him. "Yes, I need you to take care of a problem for me." His brows are drawn tightly together, confusion clear in his eyes as he waits to see what that problem is. I bring him down through the lower courtyard. The light is already gone from the day, the night only growing darker under the cover of the trees.

My soldiers are barricaded around the encampment that holds the problem I'm having Rorin take care of for me. I stop him from going any further and walk up to the group alone. The soldiers part letting me through. In the center of the camp there is a group of bound individuals.

They're line up in rows, making it a little easier for me to search for one specific individual. I catch sight of him slumped over and wave over a healer mage, commanding her to heal the ragroot out of his system. He stirs, drowsily at first, until he realizes he's bound with a gag in his mouth. His eerie brass-colored eyes widen at me in both betrayal and disbelief. I laugh, stepping back as I loose my Wield out over the group of Obsidian soldiers. It ripples over every drugged man and woman - all but one of them unaware of what's going to happen. Their bodies slowly Illusion into looking like a rebel faction, concealing their true identities.

I motion for a soldier to retrieve Rorin and bring him to me.

"Son," the word leaving a bad taste on my tongue, "I thought we had taken care of our rebel problem, with the Obsids' generous help. But as luck would have it there was a rebel faction still alive and well. Devastatingly they snuck into the Obsids' camp and killed them, all of them." I watch for his reaction, his eyes widening just a bit as he processes the words. "I only just found out." The lie rolls smoothly off of my tongue, Rorin taking it all as he stares out at the second row of Vellaran soldiers concealing our guests.

His throat bobs and he swallows nervously, "so wh-what do you need me for?"

I smile, clasping his shoulder tightly. "Vellar doesn't manifest offensive magic. It makes things to where we need men - like the Obsids - to come and assist us from time to time. But *you*—" I look down at his dirtied face, eyes filled with fear. "You have a unique Wield." I give the signal for the soldiers to part, revealing to Rorin what lies behind them.

His mouth gapes, "you found the rebel faction?" He asks quietly. I nod going along with my lie. "F-father, what are you asking me to do."

My smile grows as I meet the eyes of the Illusioned Obsidian King - Killian - making sure he hears me when I answer Rorin.

"I need you to poison them all."

ACKNOWLEDGEMENTS

BUCKLE IN EVERYBODY - this acknowledgments is about to be as long as the book. Just kidding! But truly, so many amazing individuals were apart of this process and deserve a moment to be recognized (that includes all of you, my amazing readers!)

So without further ado, THANK YOU READERS for being here! For taking a chance on my very first novel, The Nightmare Queen. So much love and support has been extended my way from the minute I announced the release of this book, and I would be NOWHERE without all of you. I cannot wait to share more of The Allora Chronicles with you here soon, and I hope that you love them as much as I do.

Secondly, my incredible team. The people who helped me maintain and achieve this goal!

To my husband, Cal. You were - and continue to be - my greatest support during this entire process. The love story you have given me in our life and relationship, the man that you are, inspired so much of Rorin. I wouldn't have been able to create such a dynamic and passionate character without you as the blueprint. Thank you for being my person, my rock, the love of all of my lifetimes, and for being interwoven into every bit of who I am. I wouldn't have it any other way.

To my sister, Taylor, for being my sounding board and the first person I talked to about Eveera and the idea I had for her. You told me to "do it! Go for it!" and now here we are, A PUBLISHED AUTHOR.

Your encouragement, love, and fierce support - not just in this book but throughout my entire life - will never go without thanks. My marketing, and my online platform to showcase this book would be nowhere without you and your help in that. Your tenacity for hardwork, for putting your creative ideas out there, inspired me so much to do the same. I love you, T.

To my Alpha and Beta Readers, my sister in law Savannah and her husband Philip, I don't even know where to begin. The countless late nights, the edits, re-edits, and cover to cover advice - thank you so much. Without the two of you, this editing process would not have happened so smoothly. The incredible encouragement you have given me throughout these crucial months helped get The Nightmare Queen to where it needed to be. From the bottom of my heart, thank you. I love you guys.

To my parents, you two. My whole life you encouraged every avenue that Taylor and I wanted to pursue. You never thought that our ideas were unattainable or irrational. The both of you nurtured our creative strengths and supported us in each and everything we tried. You've always told me that, "if anyone can figure out how to do that - it's you," and that has applied to just about anything I've set my mind to. Thank you both for being mine, for allowing me to explore all of my ambitions, for being who I needed every step of the way. That can never go with enough thanks, ever.

To both of my in laws, you two much like my own parents, hopped on board with this plan and have been supportive the whole time. The excitement you have shown over this book has not gone unnoticed and I am so appreciative of that. But most importantly, you created my Cal, so thank you.

To my Mindy. Your devoted friendship, your encouragement, the letting me ramble until all hours of the night, the constant stream of support has kept me going in so many aspects of my life. There are not enough adequate words to describe what our friendship means to me. You brighten up my life and I truly don't know what I would ever do without you. Thank you for loving and supporting all of my crazy 110% of the time.

To my grandparents - all four of you. You've loved me and encouraged from day one. Two of you are still earthside with me and have cheered me on tremendously throughout this entire process - listened to my weekly phone calls, asked questions, and gotten excited with me. And I needed that. I needed you both. And two of you are watching over me, and cheering me on from a different set of sidelines. My Evitsa - you inspired Eveera's name. I needed another Evie in my life after losing you, and thus Eveera was created. I hope I have made you both proud up there. I love all four of you so much, thank you.

And finally, to my sons. Being your mom is the greatest thing I will ever do in this life. Ever. J, I hope that your dad and I's example helps to show you that you can do whatever you want in this life. That nothing is unattainable no matter if it may seem so. M, losing you last year is the reason I began writing at all. The grief was overwhelming, to put it lightly, and for both of you - I needed to help turn that grief into something beautiful. I love you two boys so much, you are my heart and soul. You are my whole reason. Thank you for making me your mom. Reach for the stars my darlings, nothing is impossible.

About the Author

C.V. Betzold is a tried and true Midwestern wife and mom. She is an avid reader herself and has been a longtime lover of the Romantasy genre and is so excited to have contributed to that!

When she isn't writing you can find her with her husband and family, hanging out with her chickens, or picking up new books to bring home and add to her never ending TBR. And she does it all with a Diet Coke in her hand!

Printed in Great Britain
by Amazon